MW01256645

Sweet
Heat

Also by Bolu Babalola:

Love in Colour
Honey & Spice

Sweet Heat

A NOVEL

Bolu Babalola

wm

WILLIAM MORROW

An Imprint of HarperCollinsPublishers

Without limiting the exclusive rights of any author, contributor or the publisher of this publication, any unauthorized use of this publication to train generative artificial intelligence (AI) technologies is expressly prohibited. HarperCollins also exercise their rights under Article 4(3) of the Digital Single Market Directive 2019/790 and expressly reserve this publication from the text and data mining exception.

This is a work of fiction. Names, characters, places, and incidents are products of the author's imagination or are used fictitiously and are not to be construed as real. Any resemblance to actual events, locales, organizations, or persons, living or dead, is entirely coincidental.

SWEET HEAT. Copyright © 2025 by Bolu Babalola. All rights reserved. Printed in the United States of America. No part of this book may be used or reproduced in any manner whatsoever without written permission except in the case of brief quotations embodied in critical articles and reviews. For information, address HarperCollins Publishers, 195 Broadway, New York, NY 10007. For information, address HarperCollins Publishers, 195 Broadway, New York, NY 10007. In Europe, HarperCollins Publishers, Macken House, 39/40 Mayor Street Upper, Dublin 1, D01 C9W8, Ireland.

HarperCollins books may be purchased for educational, business, or sales promotional use. For information, please email the Special Markets Department at SPsales@harpercollins.com.

hc.com

Originally published in the United Kingdom in 2025 by Headline Review.

FIRST US EDITION

Library of Congress Cataloging-in-Publication Data has been applied for.

ISBN 978-0-06-330696-7
ISBN 978-0-06-330698-1 (simultaneous hardcover edition)

25 26 27 28 29 LBC 5 4 3 2 1

To my dear T,
For being right on time.

Most time when you're around
I feel like a note
Roberta Flack is going to sing

Nikki Giovanni

CHAPTER 1

Of Love & Lobster Linguini

They say there are certain dramatic life-changing (or -ending) occurrences that a person can recognise are about to happen immediately before they happen. I don't know if 'they' are a nebulous counsel of sages through the ages, psychologists or a Nigerian matriarch who swears she had a dream, but I am inclined to believe it. We are spiritual, instinctual beings – primal – and we can feel and sense and guess at an altering of a destiny in the moments before it unfurls. A car crash, for instance. A flick of the wrist, vision askew, your heart jumps into your mouth before your brain can recognise what is happening. There's a split second before the fear sets in, and it feels worse than fear itself: the anticipation, the cold tang of pre-catastrophe on the tongue, the heady notes of dread tickling the back of your throat that make you want to hurl or laugh or scream or dream of anything, *anything*, but this happening.

Like the moment your heart breaks.

You feel it in the space between you and the person holding your hope in their hand, in the softness or firmness of their voice, in how their words land within you, like pinpricks, like a firebomb. Your palms begin to sting, your breath shortens, your heart thrashes like a war drum. The screech of wheels on tarmac, the overflow of emotion, regret in a gaze before they let that hope crumble in their fist as they say, 'I can't do this any more,' the airless silence before a catastrophic fall.

This is precisely how I feel – like a car crash is about to happen, like I am about to plummet into an abyss, like all my bones are about to break, like my heart is seized – in the moments just before my sweet, flawless-credit-score boyfriend proposes to me.

Or at least I think he's about to propose to me. All evidence seems to point to the fact that the man I like enough to allow to wake me at 6 a.m. and hike whilst on holiday is about to ask me to marry him.

It's date night. A term I've always vaguely hated because it has connotations with a couple you went to high school with that refer to each other as 'the boy' and 'wifey' on Instagram. For me 'date night' conjures an idea of romance constrained to shisha spots with flowery wall decals and neon light fixtures that say 'Good vibes' in cursive and looking through a 1:1 digital dimension with eyes made sparkly with the eagerness to be #couplegoals and skin radiant with the plumping properties of Facetune.

'Date night' hints at a bleakness, a mundanity, a compartmentalisation of a fun that's supposed to be infused into a couple's connection — or maybe I'm just bitter because we need it now, the romance-by-calendar-invite, because we've both been busy recently, me with trying (maybe failing) to not descend into a quarter-life crisis and him with a new system integration of a new app with a new South Korean remote development team, something I don't actually understand beyond the fact that he is up late speaking about tech in what he says is English, but actually might as well be Korean to me (a person whose Korean is limited to phrases vaguely recognised from K-dramas). So, with my boyfriend on a rare night off from speaking about robots in Korean and me having finished the last leg of *The Heartbeat: Find Your Rhythm* live tour, we find ourselves here, on *date night*, sat at his white candelit Japandi dining table. He holds my hand, looks at me with bespectacled eyes that are honey brown and sweet and soft enough to have been the place in which I rebuilt my hope in love, and says, 'Kiki . . . this is going well, right?'

My girl Shanti is a beauty editor and make-up artist which means I'm a beneficiary of her many freebies (she dishes them out to our friendship group in rotation, like Baddie Claus). It also means I have an abundance of cosmetics to put to use even on indoor date nights, one of which is a lip oil unfortunately named D Sucker Pucker. The brand didn't last very long, something about a sexism suit, but it really does provide maximum hydration of the lips, which is extremely helpful to me right now because my mouth is bone dry.

I encourage my glossed lips to form what I pray is a smile as a rapper demurs something from the speaker about wanting to meet the love of his life, but the problem is he has too much love to just have one wife. My boyfriend seems to lack a sense of *mood* when it comes to music; he is a man that had a Future song playing in the background the first time I went back to his, after all. His reasoning was that it was a 'good song', and whilst he was technically right, and him being technically right was part of my attraction to him – straightforward, simplicity, no mess, no fuss – hearing *'I want no relations/I just want your facial'* just as you are about to have sex for the first time with a guy you enjoy enough to have your entire bottom-half attacked by hot wax for is just a little distracting. Or maybe apt? Maybe it was just funny and the fact that he had fuckboi rap and not my preference (slow R&B and neo soul) is not proof of our inherent incompatibility. Besides, Tchaikovsky and Chopin are also on his sex playlist; he has a range of taste.

Bakari works with facts and metabolises them into feelings, rather than extracting fact from feeling, and therefore he is focused on the objective quality of music production, technique, skill, level of bitrate – rather than how it all alchemises with your heart, softens you, strengthens you, reinforces your mood, stimulates your mood. He believes it's the quality that really determines the suitability of a song. This is truly a well-produced song, and is in the top ten right now. That equates to the 'best' for him. It follows, then, that this man *loves* me. Simple maths.

He's looking so intently at me and the affection in his gaze pushes so deep into my chest that I feel like it makes a dent in a heart that's whirring, that's turning in on itself, trying to make sense of the fact that despite the fact that I love him, I'm sure I do, I feel like I'm going to throw up the lobster linguini that he so thoughtfully cooked for dinner.

He made the pasta from scratch, utilising his skills from the cookery class I booked for his birthday after we binged a poetic HBO dramedy about an angsty chef and his ragtag but dedicated employees-who-are-more-like-family. He became obsessed with the 'precision of the kitchen', the exacting mathematics and science of stirring and slicing and adding things together to get a perfect result, whilst I stayed triggered by seeing a stressed-out perfectionist trying to maintain the legacy of a failing family restaurant. So close to the bone it brushed ligament, being the eldest daughter of two soon-to-be-retired restaurant owners. The gifted class doubled as a tongue-in-cheek partial apology after a misguided decision to playfully say 'Yes, Chef' in bed once. (He came just as I burst out laughing. I said it as a joke and he heard it as a response to a very specific kink he had recently developed. It was all an unfortunate misunderstanding.)

The pasta's a little chewy, but he's done pretty well, and I don't think the queasiness I'm feeling is from salmonella, but rather from the fact that *he's not supposed to ask me this tonight.* Maybe not ever. I never pictured it. I'm not ready. *We* are not ready. I think my throat might be closing up. I make some attempt to clear it.

'You OK, babe?' His naturally gorgeous bushy brows crease with concern.

5

I nod, and swirl my hand in the general vicinity of my neck, indicating that something is stuck there, like food and not the words 'this is way too soon, and I'm not entirely sure I trust you to pick out a ring on your own since the last piece of jewellery you got me was a heart-shaped pendant'. I don't like heart-shaped jewellery.

Despite the fact that I'm wearing a slinky black slip dress, and it is February, and Bakari keeps his newly built sleek bachelor-pad flat at an even 20.5 degrees, my skin is beginning to prickle with a heat that could be used to soften the slightly chewy pasta. Is it possible to develop an allergy to shellfish at twenty-eight? Is it possible to develop an allergy to shellfish twenty-four hours after you shovelled M&S prawn cocktail mix into your mouth with half a bagel for dinner whilst trying not to spiral about your career? The bagel wasn't even halved in the way you'd expect it to be – it was ferally torn vertically across the hole.

I was incredibly stressed.

I still am.

I flick a longing look at my phone, face down on the table because I wanted to focus on my date on this Date Night. I kind of want to google the possible biological phenomenon of my sudden possible allergic reaction and/or discover if I am a freak of nature, but I figure it would be rude to do so given the whole 'possibly about to be proposed to' of it all. I also want to phone Aminah to have a safe space to freak out about this and ask if she knew. In another universe, my boyfriend asking me to marry him without the blessing of my best friend would have been unthinkable, but the apocalypse happened in that universe, mountains keeled over, candyfloss clouds started to rain acid, honeyed oceans churned into lava and suns sank into the skin of the sky. So now I know that sometimes the unthinkable happens despite your inability to think it, and therefore in this universe it is perfectly plausible that my boyfriend is asking me to marry him without Aminah's blessing of 'sure, but I swear if you hurt her I will invoke a Yoruba curse that will bind you in a torture of your own making'. Besides, Aminah didn't release any hints during yesterday's Tuesday Night Tea Time, although she did finally admit that she'd started what was supposed to be our *Insecure* rewatch without me, and we spent a lot of time working through that betrayal. That might have posed a distraction.

I gulp the pinot noir that I know he's been saving for a special occasion, because when I reached to open it three weeks ago after a stressful conversation with my agent he said, 'Oh, Keeks, I got gifted this after my last app launched . . . I'm saving it for a special occasion.' Even though he always gets gifted alcohol whenever one of his apps launches. He then kissed my forehead and my nose and confirmed why I was with him by whispering softly, 'How about I open this bottle of rum my mum brought me back from Jamaica?' before giving me a shoulder massage and letting me watch *Trysts in the Tropics* without his usual commentary about how shallow and inane it is, which, actually, was what I really needed.

'Yeah,' I now respond to his question, 'I think this is good.' And then, as a reassurance for both of us, I add, 'This is great, babe.' And it doesn't feel like a lie. It has been eighteen months

7

of mutual cushy affection, and the second I saw him – or maybe the second second I saw him – at a party at which I was feeling an increasing amount of chaos within myself, I felt an immediate stabilising calm and stillness.

I was at a media networking event that was dressed up as an afterparty to an unknown beforeparty, talking to a street photographer dressed up as a medieval French street urchin, who was talking to me about how 'purpose defining' he finds it to capture Black skin on camera, and regaling me about his last trip to Senegal. I had slipped straight past offended and right into aloofly fascinated. I smiled as I flicked my gaze up from the picture on his phone of unsmiling, beautiful women in front of wares of fresh produce who'd had their working day interrupted by someone who definitely didn't pay them for their time.

Sipping my champagne, I nodded in time to a B track of a 1997 soul artist who only had one album before disappearing from the scene. I loved the song, and I anchored myself to it because it helped neutralise the surrealness of being here, at a private member's club, decorated in a baroque style of red and gold and velvet and old. When looking for the bathroom, on the wall of a narrow carpeted corridor that seemed to lead to nightmares, I encountered an Italian Renaissance painting that depicted a gorgeous pastoral feast table, with roasted ham and pheasant and fruits and cakes and a little Black boy chained under the table. I was beginning to feel a little like Jordan Peele had directed this evening. It was my first capital E Event after my little podcast had been picked up by SoundSugar, the premium streaming service that had sunk a terrifying amount of money into me and what had been a post-break-up project.

Some people take up pottery, others write Grammy Award-winning albums and I landed somewhere at the lower end of the middle, deciding to talk about love and music and its intersection of strangers who apparently found a home in the safe space I'd carved for myself in my post-apocalyptic heartbreak universe.

I found I enjoyed the company. Otis and Stevie and Luther. Mariah and Babyface. Jill Scott, Bilal, D'Angelo and Lauryn. Beyoncé and Summer and Sza and Jhene and then newer R&B and soul artists, independently signed, on Soundcloud. They were scoured from small live-music nights in bars with sticky floors, strong drinks and audiences Black enough to screw up their faces when a note reached the heavens or a bass chord hit that spot deep in the belly.

It made me feel alive.

Artists started reaching out, enjoying my analysis of songs into which they'd poured their hearts, appreciating the recognition of their soul, how their art linked to heartbreak, relationships, situationships, love that felt too heavy to hold. I started getting requests to host interviews and conversations with them, and I suddenly became a space where new artists came to cement their place on the scene, on timelines, in ears, and then Aminah, with her beautiful magic branding wizard brain suggested I include video to foster 'warmth and connection, because, not gonna lie, people are gonna go even crazier when they realise that that sexy voice is coming from a sexy face'. Biased as she was, we did see an increase in listenership with the added video.

People started writing in, seeking romantic advice for me to discuss with them, or just to share a thought, or just to feel less alone, and then I found I had an Audience and then I found myself with an Agent and then I found myself in rooms with Creatives with whom I was supposed to find kinship, even when they told me they fetishised Black people and called it art.

The podcast birthed a phoenix of an old confidence. And it turned out that the hellfire it had been through had only refined it, burned off the impurities that had snuck in during a truly horrendous break-up that felt like the first half of Lemonade without any of the artistry. I'd pulled the confidence up and out from under a rubble of harsh-edged anger and heartbreak and sadness to discover it had a new clarity, a confidence that scored high on the Mohs scale. I'd been scared that it wouldn't fit on me any more.

At this party full of influencers whose influence didn't seem tied to any sort of commodity, but rather vague concepts like 'positivity' and industry bosses who double kissed and swore you were friends because they double tapped my photo, I saw that the confidence fitted – not because I fitted in, but because I knew who I was and knew that this wasn't real. It was a virtual reality, and I would have to play this game to get paid, to get deals, build my position in this industry, because I had a career to grow and an identity to forge and more me to discover and one thing I knew is that none of it would be dependant on me talking to this man whose hollow blue eyes seemed to be magnetically drawn to my cleavage.

I replied, 'And how would you define purpose-defining?'

He squinted and scratched at his stubble, releasing a whiff of cigarettes and a Santal scent that seemed to be the staple of every offbeat creative who tried hard to walk the line between pretention and cool, and therefore defeated its purpose.

'Uh, that's a great question, um . . . I guess, I realised that I wanted to, like, capture the unseen, you know?'

'Ah.' I nodded thoughtfully. 'That's so . . . profound.'

He grinned and I stepped up closer to him in what, I guess, could have been a flirtatious manner, until I lifted an upturned, manicured middle finger. I tilted my head and narrowed my eyes in gentle curiosity. 'You see this?'

He blinked, confused, I guess, by the incongruence of the promise of intimacy and the fact that I was holding up my middle finger.

'Because I'm the same skintone as those women,' I continued, 'so I'm just wondering if I too am unseen. In fact, how did you even clock me tonight?'

French Street Urchin blinked several times before he laughed, and rubbed his chin again. 'Touché. Look, I get it, but I'm not one of them white saviours. I spent loads of summers in Africa with my dad. Works in the Congo. You been there?'

It was becoming abundantly clear that I was at risk of physically harming this man. The room, already stuffy was beginning to feel oppressive, suffocating. My mandate tonight from both Nina – my agent – and Aminah – best friend and unofficial agent – had been to schmooze, to *mingle* and to say no to offers of coke, *not* to withstand microaggressions from Prince Leopold's nepo great-grandbaby.

So in order to avoid pulling his dangly cross earring right through his ear, I decided to brush past him, do another aimless circuit of the room.

So far I'd met one person from a Black-owned publishing imprint and two music agents who'd invited me to their artists' shows, and, unrelatedly, I'd declined three coke offers. A successful night so far, considering, but I suddenly felt a gust of a cool intimate loneliness. I needed to leave. I had no real friends here, and the tenuous connections I'd made had left because their careers were developed enough to not need this. Dealing with Art Hoe Cecil Rhodes would have been much more satisfying if Aminah was here, or Shanti or Chioma.

However, Aminah's parents were in town from Lagos and she and Kofi were having dinner with them, Shanti had a date with a guy she swore she would never see again and Chi-Chi was on some yoga retreat in Bali, which was almost the most Chioma thing to happen until she told us that she had got her yoga certification and was now running a class in the yoga retreat in Bali. By default, my mind naturally went to the only other person who I could have laughed about this with and, by default, my heart prickled with frost and my senses momentarily dulled. Apocalypse PTSD. He wasn't in my life any more. I wasn't allowed to think about him. I wasn't allowed to regress. I barely allowed myself to think his name, but the thing is my mind is rebellious, and it saw the boundaries I placed on it as challenges. I forced away the thoughts and their pinpricks of pain. I definitely needed to get out of here.

I snaked my way past the plush velvet booths, waiters holding trays of mini vegan hot dogs and cocktails alarmingly mixed with something called 'diet alcohol' – the night was sponsored by a brand called No Sin Gin – and a maze of air kisses and smiles that dissipated as fast as they'd appeared. I reached the lift at the end of the room when I noticed a corner that felt unoccupied, an alcove just behind the main action that helpfully had 'The Library' inscribed in gold within the wooden frame above the entrance. Safety. Old habits die hard.

I entered the carpeted, semicircular enclave, and the scent of heavy, rich-textured paper and leather encasings instantly soothed me, running warm over tension I hadn't known I was holding. A burnished bronze chandelier hung in the middle of it, which kind of gave the air that at any moment it may come to life and tell me to be its guest. The library, in all iterations, had been a safe space for me for a lot of my life, as a kid with a sick parent, as an undergrad student with a sicko revenge-porn-obsessed quasi-ex and now as an adult, removing herself from the presence of a man with a dangly cross earring. As trite as it sounded, a library always presented itself as a haven from the chaos. I inhaled deeply and exhaled slowly. Just a few moments here would set me right. I'd instantly gravitated towards a gold-embossed, leather-bound copy of *Pride and Prejudice* when a warm male voice interrupted my pursuit to rediscover the truth universally acknowledged.

'Hi, the babysitter just called.'

I turned and frowned, perplexed and intrigued by the sentence, along with the owner of the voice and the live-wire energy that ran across his narrow face, which looked as if it had been sketched by a knife dipped in roasted terracotta. He had angular cheekbones, large slightly slanted eyes, a wide mouth and a forest-green beanie from which a few spirally dark coils spilled. He was wearing a gaping white T-shirt that slung like silk over his lithe body and several titanium rings on long fingers, which seemed like they could paint or sculpt (they couldn't, but they could code). Black adinkra symbols – Greatness, Endurance, Something Africanly Affirming – climbed lazily up muscular forearms that looked as if they got their strength from hauling djembes to various spoken-word performances rather than going to the gym. His eyes were brown and bright enough to light up a place in me I thought would be forever dimmed. I didn't recognise this then, though. Then, I just thought he was simply a hot weirdo, and so I responded how a person would to a hot weirdo.

'Um. What?'

He walked further into the enclave. He smiled, and it was bright and self-deprecating and kind of shy all at the same time and I couldn't be freaked out even if I wanted to and I really didn't want to because I wanted to enjoy this old feeling of wanting to know a newness.

'So, I'm gonna level with you,' he said. 'I overheard bits of your conversation with Lionel van der Prick and decided I would jump in and get you out of that conversation, by saying, "Hi, the babysitter just called."'

I swallowed my smile. 'Gallant . . . I guess, but also bold.'

'Yes, but that would kind of be the point. It's a lie so wild that it would humiliate him and charm you. Two birds, one stone. And then I moved closer, began to hear more, and realised two things. One, that you had it handled – amazingly, can I just say – so my knight-in-shining-armour thing was kind of fucked, and, two, it was a really, really stupid idea and you are way too smart and too cool for that to work. Actually, I thought you might find it creepy. My calculations were way off. I work in data, so I should have really made space for the possibility that you would be way too cool for me.'

This time, I allowed my grin permission to show itself. 'So you followed me in here, into a secluded room where I'm by myself, because somehow that's less creepy?'

He laughed, and nodded. 'Yeah. Yeah, exactly. Well, actually, the thing is, I was supposed to pretend I just came here casually, but when I saw you I guess all I could think to say was "Hi, the babysitter just called", because your presence eroded any braincells I have left from speaking to someone who describes their job as a Brand Vibe Regulator.'

It wasn't so much a spark, or the jolt of electricity I had been used to when it came to attraction. I just knew that I felt warm, that I liked him, that I felt the ease to be me, without defences, around him. It had been a while since I'd felt that.

I could see his nerve leap into his gaze, present and volatile, before he added, 'Also I like your fit.'

I looked down – platform brogues, black wide-legged tailored trousers, an oversized blazer and a black bandeau. I was wearing layers of thin gold chains of varying lengths that slung low on my neck. An 'A' for Aminah, a 'K' for me, a book pendant my baby sister had given me and a gold chilli-pepper pendant, gifted to me because a scotch bonnet wasn't available, from someone who I still couldn't think about without becoming both light-headed and heavy. I had no idea how to dress for these things, and I still hadn't worked my way up to buying my first designer purchase, so I'd thrown my fit together by instinct and prayer, hoping I could hold my own in a party that could have been sponsored by Net-A-Porter.

I smiled. 'Thanks.'

I was wary about flirting, so I was grateful for his effort, because, though I could vaguely feel the familiar tug of want, it felt fragile and I didn't want to test it by actively acting on it.

Baby Daddy stepped closer. 'By "I like your fit", I mean you're very beautiful, but I thought just coming out and saying that might be coming on a little too strong. But, yeah. I've wanted to talk to you since I saw you walk in and you shook your head at that white guy with the locs that tried to spud you.' He paused. He cleared his throat. 'Not to say I don't also like your fit—'

He was awkward and yet assured, nerdy but with an air of unaffected cool – like everything he did he believed in. The very reason I wanted to talk to him was the very reason I wanted to go – this could be a thing, I felt like it could be a thing and I wasn't sure I was ready for it to be a thing.

In the year and a half of my singledom – well, in the last six months of it – I'd gone on torturously boring dates (if I had to answer what my favourite colour is one more time I was gonna start saying 'fathomless black, like the void this interaction should be thrown into'), thrillingly decadent but shallow dates (there is no point just saying yes to a man because he's six foot six inches), engaged in drunken make-out sessions with no heart and too much tongue (because often they just rely on the fact that they're six foot six and don't bother to learn how to kiss) and one-and-a-half talking stages (I tapped out after 'what do you do for fun?').

They were meaningless, and I found comfort in the meaninglessness because I didn't have to try, because I didn't have to open myself up to hurt, but by doing that wasn't I just opening myself up to old patterns? Running away from emotions because I was scared of vulnerability when vulnerability was where the good stuff was, the sweet stuff; vulnerability had treated me so well until it hadn't any more. My life was full with work and my friends, and finding out more of who I was, but maybe I had some space for a new flavour of joy. I knew it couldn't be the same romance as I'd had before, but maybe that was a good thing. Before this, I was yet to find a man I could bear talking to for more than thirty seconds. If my calculations were correct, this had been at least three minutes.

I smiled. Nodded. 'So is little Solange OK?'

He frowned. 'Who's Solange?'

It had been a while since I liked a man who didn't immediately catch what I threw, and so I tamped down my confusion at his confusion, and helped him out. 'What, you don't remember the name of our kid?'

Baby Daddy blinked and then nodded and laughed. 'Ah yes. She's doing well, just a high temperature, but— I'm sorry, I'm not good at this. Fuck it, you wanna get a drink with me?'

'Depends. Will they have calories? I really can't take any more of the Ozempic water they're serving us.'

'Chock-full of them. I promise. Sugar levels gonna sky rocket.'

With Bakari, everything was *simple*, cut and dry, not so much an enchanted forest of romance, but a neatly manicured national park, clean paths, trimmed hedges, no messes. I liked that. I needed that.

It was kind of funny how I was able to joke about us having a kid together within the first ten minutes of us meeting when now, a year or so on, the idea of us getting married is sending me into a conniption.

Bakari clears his throat. He looks softly nervous and his thumb presses into the back of my hand with purpose. 'Look, you've been stressed about what you're going to do when you wind up The Heartbeat's tour. MelaninMatch has just been acquired by Cypher and, like, not to be weird about it, I'm doing really well right now because of that.'

He's talking about the huge business acquisition that saw the successful dating app he'd created when he was twenty-three blow and become international. It's odd how little Bakari and I discuss money despite the fact that he's a tech founder who was on the Forbes list by twenty-five, and I always scan Ready To Eat avocados as unripe avocados at self-check-out because they're 20p cheaper. He started with a dating app created for Black people looking to find love, then created an app called ShortCutz that would pool all the barbers in your vicinity – this led to him creating Onyx, an umbrella company that would serve underrepresented communities. It had a team of twenty that was fast-growing and whose merch was responsible for everything from the giant T-shirt I wear while spooning peanut butter directly from the jar when I'm Going Through It to my stationery, with which I journal when I'm Going Through It. Both things have been put to use recently. While my boyfriend was doing Well, I was doing Fine. Technically Fine. As fine as an overachieving eldest Nigerian daughter could be after quitting their job out of nowhere. I'm down to browsing graduate courses only once a day now rather than once every hour of every day.

I slowly nod, although I'm not sure what I'm agreeing to or with. The fact that his career's soaring whilst mine is plummeting? Bakari isn't the most romantic guy in the classic way (he once called holding hands down the street 'a bit inefficient for our purposes. What is it for? You know I care about you, and it's not great for optimised walking'), but, still, I didn't think a proposal would involve him talking about how marriage might make the most financial sense like I'm in a Regency romance, and my family are struggling gentry with a crumbling manor, having to retrench. Although, I guess a Nigerian restaurant that has gone into decline because more of a certain kind of person who's willing to pay £10 for a cakepop at the 'artisan bake shop' has moved into the area may count. (They're called Fat & Flour. Their bagels are very dry.)

'Look, all I'm saying, babe,' he says, reaching for my hand and reading the confusion on my face, 'is that life has changed for me now. And I think by extension it could change for us. We're in a transitionary space, and I feel like there is an opportunity for evolution in our relationship.'

Why is he suddenly speaking like a lifestyle guru doing a Ted talk? He's always wanted to do a TedX talk. He told me this in bed once, after sex, confiding in me, feeling vulnerable enough to admit it. He stared at the ceiling, smiling wistfully as he confessed, like he'd just told me that one day he wanted to climb Kilimanjaro. Recently, he's started wearing an everyday uniform: a sleek slate kaftan shirt and navy chinos, because apparently it says 'reliable, confident. It's the colour of a man who knows who he is. Unashamedly Black, and serious'. Those were the things I liked about him – confident, reliable, knows who he is – but now I'm wondering if all his choices are made with an eye to writing a self-help book called *The Diary of a Disrupter: 93 Laws of Power to Guide the Art of Climbing the STEM of Success*.

'We've been dating for about a year now, and I think we make sense, right?' he asks.

I let the question marinate as I sip some more of his App Launch wine. Aminah is nice enough to him, but early in our relationship she once compared him to lemon-and-herb chicken from Nando's. ('Not in a bad way! He's a tasty option. Can't go wrong. I'm just saying, Keeks, he only ever kisses your cheek in public. I'm used to seeing you with someone who acted like he would die if his hand didn't brush your waist or your other cheek every three seconds.') And Kofi is coolly polite at best due to loyalty to my ex, his best friend, and love for me, his pseudo-sister-in-law, but – the ambivalence of my friends aside – we *do* make sense. It isn't the most passionate relationship, sure, and his kisses are a pleasant and enjoyable sensation rather than a heat that turns my joints molten, but it is easy, it is safe and its lack of abundance is enough for me. I love me enough to cover any gaps: the fact that he doesn't get it when I need silence at a certain part of a song to let melody and lyric sink in to my bones, that he talks through it loudly and quietly, that he thinks I am too sentimental sometimes, that he hasn't listened to one episode of my podcast (but plugs it always), that sometimes I tuck my sarcasm in, my humour, because I know he won't totally catch it, and that if he did he might not know what to do with it.

I've known a love that had overflowed out of me and them, and it had nearly toppled me over. I'd barely been able to contain it; it was too dense and rich for a body that had just started to know itself. This adequate affection with Bakari, though, this measured warmth, I like. I could quantify it. $1+1=$ Not Too Much.

Bakari looks up a restaurant with the highest rating, and takes me there. It doesn't matter what it is and he won't consult me about what I'm in the mood for – he just books it because it's the best and he says I deserve the best. We go on trips that are the result of him googling 'top ten quiet, romantic destinations' rather than places he's dreamed of visiting. He is serious, and I am less so. I get him out of his head, and he is calm enough to allow me to stay in mine. We make sense.

'I think we do.'

Bakari grins. He looks me in the eye and I swallow nothing but doubt.

'I was hoping you'd say that,' he says, 'because—'

My wine glass ripples with the vibration of my phone. A flitter of annoyance flicks across Bakari's face.

'You said you put it on silent—'

'Vibrate is silent—'

'No, vibrate is like a regular ringtone— we're not Boomers. No one has their phone on loud any more. *Silent* is silent.'

I turn my head to look at his empty open-plan beige and grey and chrome living room, past the art that came from his assistant handpicking from the 'artists to watch' list, and beyond that at the panoramic night-time view through his window, city lights against blue-black, to theatrically check if there is someone else behind me. I return to look at him, evidencing the confusing conclusion that he could only be talking to me.

'Yo,' I say. '*Tone*. What's going on?'

Apology flicks across Bakari's eyes, and he pushes his glasses up, a tick that never fails to soften me. 'Sorry, sorry, I'm just jittery and nervous and I want to ask you something serious.'

Without flipping my phone up, I silence it, pushing the button on its edge, as the edge of my own irritation smooths out in the face of the blunt earnestness in his gaze.

Bakari nods. 'Thank you.' He inhales deeply. 'Would you be . . . Would you—'

My stomach turns with lobster linguini and doubt and App Launch wine and why didn't he know I was joking when I said 'Is little Solange OK?' the first time we met and why does he have Adrinka symbols up his arm, but eats pounded yam with a fork and knife and has not one piece of African art up in this £3,000 pcm flat, and why does he let one of his business partners, a white American guy, call him 'Barry' for short because he says he reminds him of Barack Obama, whatever that means?

'Be open to having a job at Oynx?'

'I can't marry you—' It spills out, hot like lava, crashing over the question. I thought I'd swallowed it down, but it had got stuck to the roof of my mouth, ready to leap out and fuck up my relationship.

Bakari freezes the same time I do. I blink. 'Wait, what did you mean by that?' I ask.

Bakari releases my hand. 'What did *you* mean by that?'

I swallow steel. 'You first.'

Bakari is jarringly matter of fact, despite the sharp wariness in his eyes. 'You quit your job, Kiki. With no plan, except to, what, help out at your parents' restaurant?' I tilt my head at this, and he leans forward, some faded excitement finding its way through the perturbance. 'Look, Oynx is developing a program that tracks Black music audiences, studying listening habits for gig organisers and streaming platforms, and you're perfect to head the research division. Who knows that stuff more than you? I need an expert to lead the new venture, and I don't know anyone who knows more about Black music than you.'

An uneasiness rises with the breeziness with which he says this. I can't figure out if this is better or worse than a proposal. 'I'm flattered that you would want me for that, but . . . I *have* leads—'

'What leads, Kiki? Grad-school applications?'

I smart. This stings like a premenstrual bikini wax, because I *had* actually been browsing law school applications today. I could work for the UN! Amal Clooney makes it look great. Due to the time I have on my hands, I recently binged *Suits* and came to the conclusion that I really do have the butt for Meghan Markle's wardrobe. I was quite concerned with justice, having helped organise several protests in uni and attended several marches since and I've only cried during an argument with one person, who, thankfully, is no longer in my life so I get to pretend that it's never happened.

'Or are you going to go back to *publishing*?' my boyfriend continues, the word 'publishing' sounding as if it might as well be 'plantation'. Which, though technically isn't too far off, considering what I went through there, *he* isn't saying it like that for the right reasons.

'I mean, even if you did, nothing will compare with working for Oynx. With this role, you'll have a reliable, *generous* salary. And you get to fuck the boss.' I blink and cock my head. It's hard to tell when Bakari is joking, because the light in his eyes doesn't change. It's steady. He's always so steady. You know that Bakari's joking when he says, 'I'm joking, by the way.' He tells, never shows. Now, his brow raises.

'Kiki. I'm playing, babe. Although, yeah, preferably, we'll still have sex.'

I muster something that I hope looks like a smile and try to calm myself down enough to think about it for a second. My handsome, mostly sweet, *rich* boyfriend is offering me a job at his company where they get free poke bowls and a constantly replenished snack bar. The least I can do is consider it. I can call myself a woman in STEM non-ironically, and not just because I used a VPN so Aminah and I can watch the next season of Abbott Elementary.

Bakari was technically right. I didn't have a plan, and it's because I wasn't supposed to quit the pod. It was two months ago, at a meeting discussing contract renewal with SoundSugar execs and my agent Nina in an office with yoga balls, a foosball table and a kombucha fridge. Sat in a meeting room christened the 'Thought Womb' (everything was a pastel pink) and in baffling transatlantic accents by way of Berkshire by way of Clapham, executives gushed about The Heartbeat, how they were so excited about its *diverse* power and how well the live shows went.

So far, so batshit normal.

Yet, there was this odd feeling of unease in my belly, a queasiness, and I glugged some kombucha to help before remembering that I Did Not Like It. I decided then to pivot to thinking about something soothing, so I swirled my top-five Mariah Carey keychanges around in my mind. I breathed easier and mentally ran over the facts: yes the execs had been slow to reply to my emails about potential ideas lately, but the tour had sold out, and my numbers were on an incline, and though not rapid, were steady, gradually finding more of its audience. Besides, I was *here* in their office, which was an architectural stock photo of 'corporate machine made to look like a creative hub'. I was fine. SoundSugar brought up the possibility of doing a live show in New York, praising my 'unique ability' to talk to artists on 'their level'. This was good news; they were still invested in me, and my agent Nina sidled me a small, confident look. I nodded, easier now.

'That sounds great,' I said. 'How about Lagos too?' and they smiled, teeth LA white, 2016 HBO millennial-coming-of-age-show white, and said, 'Definitely! We'll definitely try and look into that – definitely, definitely explore the possibility.'

And I, used to what the repetition of 'definitely' meant in this kind of environment (a regimented apparatus desperately masquerading as fun and chill and lax, something like a youth pastor in skinny jeans) offered, 'You guys know I'm hands on with everything with my tours. And I know the infrastructure can be difficult if you're not used to the environment, but I have loads of links and relationships on the ground. I can help with the planning. I just feel like it would be cool to branch out, talk to Nigerian artists in Nigeria, talk about craft, incorporate some stripped-back live performances – think NPR Tiny Desk . . .' and they smiled harder, a little heavier, a little stiffer, and one of the execs, Tristram – fucking *Tristram* – nodded vigorously, a thoroughly conditioned lock of hair falling over his eyes so he could push it back. He reminded me of one of those Ken-doll-handsome topless models that used to stand outside American lifestyle stores in suburban malls in the noughties, stores fashioned in an old colonial beach-house style, aggressively selling a lie, well-scented husks that sold dysmorphia and fake-college hoodies, Harvard and hunger.

'Yes, and that's exactly what we love about you, Kiki. Your ability to connect widely. We love your passion.'

I'm passionate, it's true, but I like to think I'm also smart, and, wondering whether they would put money right next to their kombucha – wondering how much their love was worth – I decided to push further since I was already here, voicing ideas that made them descend into cultural panic.

'Mhmm, so I've actually been doing some research into gaps in the market, and how I could expand on the structure that I already have. I can email you the numbers and the info, but essentially this is a show about peeling back layers, discovery in art and community, so –' and I pitched the idea that had been percolating in my mind: sourcing reclusive artists, the one-hit wonders who loved artistry more than the machinery of the music industry, the ones who retreated from the beast of fame rather than the magic of creation, of weaving something from nothing. Mostly, they would be from under-represented backgrounds, those who had been pushed out by not fitting into a mould or by refusing to do so. For the first time in a while, I was excited about it; The Heartbeat had been built from finding myself, trying to make sense of my pain, or at least soothe it, and I had done that. This, though, was new, something that could propel me forward.

The execs didn't seem to share my excitement. Their faces were smiling, but forcibly vacant, trying to figure out the best way to say no without seeming racist – and not for the first time I wondered what my place here was. The thing with cultural panic from media bosses is that there is a line. They will either appease your ideas out of guilt – one exec carefully referred to me as a 'woman of melenated global majority background' (I am automatically suspicious of people who can't just say Black) – or they will fear your ideas, want to control them, tamper with and tame them. I wondered what it would be this time.

After a short silence, another exec called Verity drawled, 'Such an ambitious idea.' She clawed her hand to punctuate her point, nude shellac tapping on the table like a deranged pianist. 'Love it, definitely, definitely.' Her French tips clinked against the glass surface and further pressed and repressed the buoyancy of my hope. 'We totally agree about expansion, but, pivoting off that, we were thinking about broadening that appeal a bit in a way that makes sense with regard to what we are doing with The Heartbeat.'

When the queen died, Verity posted a picture of the queen in her youth, captioned 'Thank you and rest in peace to the ultimate Girl Boss. You're an inspiration to all of us x'. I remembered this as I felt myself stiffen, guard up. Who was 'us' and who were 'we'? What about me pertained to her *we*? Was I compromising myself by being tied to her 'we'? Who did she think I was? I flicked a look to Nina on the left of me, who met my gaze immediately, her green eyes sharpened under long lashes made longer with an armour of pitch-black coating.

At this point, we have mastered the art of silent communication. Just a few years older than me, she signed me as her first client when she was an associate agent. As a multi-generational South Londoner who was the first person in her family to attend university, she got what it was to claw out space for yourself in places where you were told you didn't quite fit. At a creative mixer whilst listening to former home-county denizens reminisce about family summers and their best meals in southern France and coastal Italy (something about locally sourced fresh fruit accessed because of family country houses next to orchards), Nina had taken a delicate sip of her champagne, nodded and demurred, 'Yeah, I feel the same about Butlins. Their buffets were to die for.'

We were both young and scrappy and hungry, and the first thing she said to me over the flat white at the coffee shop round the corner of her office was, 'Let me know what your dreams are and I'll back you. There's not enough people who are in this thing because of love and that's enough for me to wanna be in this ride with you. And if someone's moving mad I'll get mad for you. And after that if you still wanna get mad, have at it.'

Nina could be severe or sweet depending on how she wanted to use it. Her grandma managed a pub and had once stabbed a man with a shard of broken pint glass to defend a woman from a man getting too handsy – and she had got away with it. Right now, with her painted red lips and auburn hair gelled into a slick bun, she looked like she was channelling that power. Her back straightened up in protection, she angled her head so her small gold hoops glinted in the winter sun streaming through the wide Soho windows.

'Kiki already has a sprawling fanbase, and her appeal is in her specificity,' she said.

'Definitely, definitely,' Verity purred, now tapping her fingers against her oversized pastel pink water bottle nervously. 'It's just how can we move within that power, you know? So we were thinking how about we widen that magical specificity, to include other artists who are more central to cultural attention in this moment – I was at an afterparty in Annabel's –' my lips quirked

29

slightly at the location drop – 'and I bumped into Kitty St James. You came up – she just adores you. You know, her sex and dating column at the *Journal* is really gaining traction, and she was thinking you two could join forces – wouldn't that be cute? Kind of cross-cultural dating examination. You know her, right?'

I couldn't help the choke of laughter that escaped me. Katherine 'Kitty' St James, *Tatler* It Girl, the daughter of former Minister of State Agnes St James (who increased the use of stop-and-search in her tenure) and writer of the impressively named 'Look What the Kat Dragged In'. It was a dating column described as 'edgy, irreverent and brimming with girl power', which of course meant she swore a lot in it and her author photo was of her wearing a pink crop top that read 'Big Clit Energy' to display said edginess. She recently wrote an article about how racism in 'this day and age' is a concept that can be 'dick-constructed'. 'The more people who fuck people who look different to them,' she explained profoundly to us simpletons, 'the more people will realise we're all the same.' She then concluded the piece with a triumphant: 'Let us dream of a day where people are not judged by the colour of her skin, but the content of their coitus.'

Truly incredible, parts of the article whirring around my Black-girl media group chats with various iterations of 'Is this bitch serious?', 'Excuse me, just got passed over for a job by my under-qualified white colleague – lemme go find my Pearly King and fix this rn,' and, 'Séance at 8 guys? We gotta wake MLK up!!!' plus, 'He's already awake sis, in the body of Kitty St James 🙏'.

She got dragged in the Black parishes of social media, but of course Verity must have missed that. Shortly after it was published, she hard-launched her boyfriend – a well-known Black actor – on Instagram with two ice-cream emojis, one vanilla, one chocolate.

I managed to subdue my laugh, clamping it between my jaws. 'I mean,' I said, 'I could consider her as a guest.' I absolutely would not, but I figured there was nothing wrong with pretending till the contract got signed.

Verity cleared her throat. 'It would, uh, be with the view of making her a permanent co-host, but of course we would take care of you. With the renewal of your contract with us coming up, we wanted to revisit or expand the scope of what The Heartbeat could be . . . It's actually contingent on this kind of growth. Imagine the North American tour with Kitty's audience by your side! You would be . . . maximising your joint slay!' She said the last part with a plop of pride, beaming, like she was on holiday and finally got a Duolingo phrase right.

A coldness roiled in my belly, and my palms started to prickle with dread. My breath shortened with my patience and willingness to keep it sweet. 'My show isn't a safari or a gap year to add some spice to someone's resumé, and also it is *mine*.'

Verity reddened and her eyes widened. 'No! We're here to support Kiki Banjo.'

Why did she say my name like that? Like I wasn't here, when I was, painfully, present, kombucha sloshing in me, feeling the inside of my stomach sweat, because I knew something was about to shift.

'Interesting interpretation of support.' Nina's voice was crisp as a sip of ice water in Antarctica. 'Basically holding my client at gunpoint and asking her to renew her show with someone else – changing the heart of it – or leaving.'

'We love Kiki's voice – it's so bright,' Tristram said, and I laughed again – manically, probably, judging by the look on their faces.

I nodded empathetically. 'Yeah. Bright. It just needs a little more white to be bright enough.'

Verity went the colour of Mac's Ruby Woo and I don't actually remember the rest of what she said because my blood was pounding in my head so hard that it clouded coherency. All I could feel was rage, that they had the ability to take my dream and warp it whilst having the audacity to ask me to put my name on it. All I remember is that I interrupted Verity with a bark of laughter, and a 'No.'

She blinked. 'No to . . .'

I hadn't realised I said it out loud till I saw the startled look on their faces, but when the 'no' reacted with the air it sounded better, had a bass to it. So I decided not to take it back, because, actually, fuck no, hell no, *ra ra*.

I smiled widely. 'No. Nah,' and as I said it, I felt a sort of peace come over me, the kind that comes with looking around a party and deciding that it's time to leave, that you've had enough rum punch, you've shaken enough leg and bum with your girls, you've mingled, you've gisted, you've done all there is to do. You're secure in the fact that you're not missing out on shit. I didn't need any other explanation. 'No.'

When I told Bakari the next day, despite being nervous to, his jaw dropped and then he rubbed it silently for a few moments, frown deep, staring into his coffee, before venturing out carefully with, 'Kiki . . . you sure that wasn't impulsive? It's not the worst idea to work with someone else to broaden your demographic.'

'If it's authentic, the audience will come . . .'

He sighed and nodded. 'That's the hope, but, realistically, it would have been a great opportunity for you, and you could have leveraged that to get so much money . . .' and when he realised that my own jaw was locked tight and my eyes were shiny, he rubbed my arms and kissed the top of my head. 'You know what? Maybe it's for the best. How long were you going to do a podcast for anyway?'

I try to think of what I would have done differently and I come up short. It was impulsive, sure, but my impulse is always rooted in real. I don't do impulsive unless pushed to do so by emotions that are screaming to be heard. When I kissed my ex, then a stranger, all those years ago, for the first time, in a sticky-floored student party, it was – on the surface – to escape a creep that referred to women as 'females', but also it was because I wanted to know his taste. There was real feeling there: thirst, a want to know – a *need* to know. When I said 'no' in the Thought Womb, it's because deep down I knew if I stayed in that place, watching my dream be dissected and manipulated, a part of me would die. There would be no point continuing with the podcast because its purpose would be defeated.

'Kiki, come on,' Bakari says now. 'Are you really going to talk about "the top five albums to listen to when your man's moving mad" forever? It's fun, but you're capable of so much more.'

My blood feels too hot for my body and my heart feels too

cold. All my ambitions sound small in his mouth. That hasn't ever happened before. He's always said that it was *necessary*, that people need a place to feel and I help to give them that. The tannin from what I thought was celebratory wine clings to the roof of my mouth, adding to the bitter taste.

'Yeah, I know exactly what I'm capable of, Bakari, which is why I quit. And I know I'm not saving the world, but I do think I'm saving *something*. Pockets of feeling. And, I mean, this job you're offering – *tracking Black audiences* – and selling that information to corporations sounds kind of Fed-like activity to me. I don't want to *mine* our art for—'

'Kiki, come on, man. *This* is how we serve the culture. By allowing ourselves to be understood'

'*Allowing* ourselves? What are you even saying to me right now? By who? People who say Bey for Beyoncé like "Bey" as in bay leaf? Who only know about Afrobeats through a Selena Gomez remix?'

'What's wrong with saying Bey like that?'

I feel my blood pressure spiking. 'Are you kidding me, Bakari?'

'OK. I feel like we're straying off the point—'

I personally think that him thinking there's nothing wrong with saying 'Bey' like a girl who wears yoga shirts proclaiming 'Gangsta Rap & Coffee Get Shit Done' is quite a grave issue, but I'm mature enough to let it go.

I steady my breathing. 'I just thought you understood what I'm trying to do. How would you feel if someone came to Oynx – which is supposed to aid the Black community – and said you *had* to partner with someone white for it to be legitimate?'

'I would do it, Keeks. In fact, I'm about to do it. I'm about to close a deal with a French company. They know how to broaden our scope, see our potential and my future partner, Amelie—'

Amelie?! He just made that up. There's no way her name is the first thing that would come up when you google 'French names for women'. And why has he never mentioned it before?

'. . . really gets my vision. I didn't mention it before because I knew you would be extra about it. It's a good business decision. Look, I'm just saying there's a way to look out for the culture and make bank. How are you helping the average Jamal on road—'

I really don't want to think he just used the phrase 'average Jamal' earnestly, so I wait for him to tell me he's joking.

'. . . by being broke?'

Wow.

'You have the sponsorships now, the odd writing gig, but the podcast is over. You have to be realistic.'

It occurs to me that Bakari didn't even entertain the potential of the podcast finding new life elsewhere. I own the rights. I could if I wanted to. I would lack the budget and the resources, but I *could* if I wanted to. Irritation spikes through my skin. I didn't need an MBA spat back at me. I needed someone to see my dreams, pick them up and feel the heft of possibility.

'You know what, babe? Somehow, I am able to imagine a reality where your job offer isn't the only thing standing between me and having to sell feet pics. Although to be clear, I have very elegant feet and would make money off them if I wanted to, but, the thing is, it would be my *choice*. You're not even giving me a chance to figure out my next steps—'

Bakari sighs in a way that makes me wish I'd told him that the sauce in the lobster linguini needs some more richness, maybe a knob of butter cut with some sugar, and a little more salt. More *flavour*.

'Keeks, I want to hire you because I think you would be a huge asset to Oynx. It's not like this is *Mad Men* and I'm asking you to be my secretary. Although, yeah, that would be hot.'

I, again, wait for him to tell me that he's joking. Instead, he finishes off his wine. Also, I know for a fact that he has never seen all of *Mad Men*. He just pretends to.

I nod. 'Tell me, Bakari, is it some kind of, like, kink to you to be my boss? Because we can roleplay that, no need to go to this extent. And – fuck my own personal ambitions just for a second – how do you think this will affect our relationship?'

I'm definitely on my way to an out-and-out freakout. This is an odd tenor of our relationship – we don't do this; we don't argue – and now I'm realising it's because we don't have enough to argue about, and this fact is almost making me as uncomfortable as every single thing else about this conversation. Bakari looks bewildered. I get it; he's never seen me like this. Then he recomposes himself, gently putting his cutlery down and leaning back in his chair.

'I don't know, Kiki. How do you think you rejecting my hypothetical proposal will affect our relationship?'

My high horse stumbles. My mouth snaps shut. I shift in my seat awkwardly and pull my braids across my shoulder for something to do. I clear my clear throat.

'Look, I'm—' I try to source an apology. It's hiding deep somewhere within my frustration – it must be, because I can't find it, and I don't have time to.

'. . . I just panicked—'

He nods casually. 'Yeah. I got that, but why? I mean, theoretically, we work. You care about me and I care about you – so much that I am willing to have you be part of my *company*, which in a way is kind of a bigger deal than marriage—'

Is it, though? I decide this isn't the right time to dispute this, and I have to say I'm proud of my restraint. 'Focus on the conflict at hand,' the therapist I had told me in the two sessions I did before her prices had me deciding that I'm healed.

'But, Bakari, that's just it. I mean, just now you said you *care* about me. I mean, *do* you love me?'

Six months into our relationship, Bakari started signing off his phone calls, with 'love you' and I replied with 'I love you too' and that was it. There was no build up, no falling, no flying. I was upright the whole time and I looked around that day and I was like, huh, this might as well be love, right? Being with him for half a year was kind of a miracle considering there was a time I found it difficult to envision my life with anyone else but My Ex without wanting to vomit. I liked Bakari enough to not skip ahead without him (or at least pretend not to) and watch the next episodes of a show we were watching together. I liked his mum; she always sent him back with brown stew chicken for me.

When I saw him, I felt warm and pleasant, secure inside my body, my soul locked in, not reaching to curl round his, but safe enough in its company. What else did I need? I figured that might as well add up to love. It's the only love I'm available for now. No tingles, no swooping sensation, no feelings pressing up against my veins and making the air around me sing, just . . . enough. Just enough. And enough is enough.

'Of course I do,' he replies now, almost with annoyance. 'Do *you* love *me*?'

I swallow a lingering taste, not from the linguini, not from the wine, but from a forgotten time – heady honey and spice, decadent – and I say, 'How could I not?'

My phone starts vibrating again, and for some reason this time it feels like it's an emergency. There's something I'm forgetting and the tremors of my phone reach me with fervour. I need to pick it up, but I catch the frustration and confusion running over Bakari's usually placid face.

'Kiki, why do I need to say it all the time for you to believe it? We're adults. I plug your podcasts on my socials even though my audience isn't exactly yours. I support you through all your creative meltdowns – of which there are many and, honestly, it's a little extra.'

I gasp, momentarily letting the vibrating of my phone fade within my consciousness. 'Extra? *Extra?* I'm sorry if having to re-record a new podcast episode because one of my favourite artists did a surprise drop makes me a little stressed—'

Bakari continues. 'And I go on awkward double dates with your friends even though they clearly don't like me—'

'All right, well, we went on *one* double date, and, yeah, it got a *little* frosty after you told Kofi that his product-design job is probably gonna be obsolete soon due to *AI*. Besides, I go with you to all your business socials, and schmooze with you even though your tech bro buds act like my podcast is cute fluff because it isn't about crypto or *AI*—'

'Why do you keep saying AI like that? Like it's not a thing? AI is a thing, Kiki.'

'Are *you* AI? Is that why you can't detect how annoying you're being right now?'

'Actually, AI would be able to—'

'*Guy*,' I say, my voice uncovering deep Naija iron notes that lend it a lethal warning. My eyes sharpen.

Bakari sighs, and rubs the bridge of his nose, pushing up his hexagon-shaped designer frames in the process. 'Kiki, what are we even fighting about? I'm not asking you to marry me yet, and – no – we aren't ready, but we're functional. We work. We're happy. We have movie nights and like two of the same TV shows. We make recipes that we see on Netflix shows together. And we had that fun hiking holiday where we had a pretty good time in the cabin, despite The Incident.' Bakari refers to the 'Yes, Chef' fiasco with a totally straight face.

I train my eyes on his to see if he is being sardonic, but all that's there, of course, is sincerity. When he asked me if I could try saying 'Yes, Chef' again in bed without laughing, a few months after The Incident, I had laughed again, thinking he had been joking.

He hadn't been. He then said we should maybe forget the whole kink thing entirely, since it was less 'risky'.

Bakari softens his voice. My phone is still ringing, which means the person who is calling hung up and rang again. There's only one person who would do that.

'Kiki, sometimes I feel like you . . . *romanticise* things too much. And I know this is what you do with The Heartbeat, but you know that's a job, right? It's a bit, and I love that you provide that escapism for people, but that's all it is. Escapism. For you too. I mean, isn't that how you got over your break-up? But you're not in that place any more and maybe it's time to let it go. Maybe that's why you're stuck.'

There's a beat of silence and I realise then that I've inhaled sharply. I swallow and push something hard and bitter down my throat. I feel my eyes glaze. I silently pick up my phone.

'Kiki, wait—'

'My best friend needs me.'

'What emergency is it now? Someone's coupled up with some-one's ex on *Trysts in the Tropics*?'

It is uncharacteristically sassy, but an argument is uncharac-teristic for us, so maybe the antagonistic sass is regular for him. I ignore it, not least because *Trysts in the Tropics* isn't even on right now – it's a summer reality dating show. I flip my phone over to see the name 'MinahMoney' flash on the screen. With a twinge of guilt, I answer my best friend's call. For the first five seconds all I hear is heavy sobbing and my chest seizes, my joints stiffen.

'Minah? Aminah babe, are you OK? Where are you? Talk to

me . . .' I'm already getting up, prepared to be wherever she is, to fight whoever I need to fight, to make whoever made my tougher-than-acrylic-nail best friend cry.

'Am I *OK*?' She's screeching, hysterical. 'What do you *mean* am I OK?' Aminah and I have picked up similar habits in our ten-year friendship. Her warm, Lagos-princess-British-middle-class-boarding-school-meets-East-London lilt repeats questions she doesn't care to know the answer to with a heightened emotion I can't put my finger on yet. 'Are *you* OK?' she enquires at an octave that might make Mariah Carey jealous. 'I am so MAD at you! How could you keep this from me?'

I hear Kofi's voice chuckling in the background as he says, 'Baby, do you want to give her a heart attack?'

My mind starts to calculate and equate and translate, and then my heart immediately forgets any anguish it's in, because now I know what this call is about – my blood knows it – because it begins to fizz a joy that settles my stomach and dissipate my stress, and I start to feel warm as soon as the excitement in the undertone of her voice hits.

'Keeks . . .' Her screeches have melted into the sweetest, cutest giggles, the aural version of a butterfly landing on your finger on the first day of spring. 'Where have you been? Don't even answer that! I don't care! YOUR IYAWO IS ABOUT TO BE AN IYAWO, but you already knew that, didn't you, you beautiful, gorgeous, sneaky, cutie bitch! I would put video on, but um, we're in a hotel bedroom right now.'

I laugh with unbridled joy that lifts all the heavy I've been feeling off my shoulders, and I walk over to a window and lean my forehead on the glass, smiling into the skyline. When we'd been ring shopping together, my only instructions to Kofi were:

- To not tell me exactly when he was going to do it because Aminah can read me like a self-help book called *Slay Your Way to Higher Pay: A Guide for Black Women in Business* (from cover to cover, and thoroughly) and I would have to avoid and/or ignore her, which would be impossible and disastrous as she would stalk my location and demand to know why I want her dead;
- To propose to her immediately after her fortnightly gel manicure (nail colour – Vanilla Beam; nail shape – medium-length, almond).

My laughter bubbles out of me. 'My bad sis, I just thought it was the kind of thing that Kofi might want to tell you himself.'

'Thanks, Keeks,' Kofi pipes up in the background.

'Any time, bro.'

Aminah faux-groans into the phone, but it does a shitty job of hiding her delight. 'Ew, whose best friend are you anyway? Let's be focusing. MAID OF HONOUR! WE'RE GETTING MARRIED! YOU READY?'

It isn't until a tear drips off my chin and lands on my chest that I realise I'm crying, and it isn't till I lean back and look at my reflection in the window that I notice I am beaming, a silly wide grin taking over my whole face, my eyes dancing. I notice Bakari quietly clearing the table behind me, avoiding looking at me. I swallow and focus on the singular joy of my best friend getting married to the love of her life and say, 'I'm more than ready.'

It isn't until I hear Kofi in the background, chuckling and murmuring, 'Shit, you lot think you're the only besties in the world. Let me call my best man. He's been waiting on standby,' that my whole body tenses with aftershocks of an old apocalypse in this new world of mine.

I realise that my assertion is a bold-faced, egregious lie.

CHAPTER 2

Sending You Forget-Me-Nots

'Let me get this straight,' Shanti says, pointing a fork at me like a dagger and tilting her head to the side in deceptively gentle inquisition. Her brown Indo-Jamaican curls curve like question marks, enquiring in sync and her extended lashes bat in a way that inform me that she's about to come for my neck. 'Your fine tech-billionaire boyfriend offered to fund your life, and you said "nah, I'm good"? With all due respect, sis, you've lost your fucking mind. Like, I'm actually worried about you. You've taken your social-justice warrior shit too far. You're not Angela Davis, you know. No one with a Soho House membership can *truly* be a socialist. Rest.'

I baulk at this. 'Um, actually, I got given a year's free membership because I did that talk last year!'

Shanti releases a smug smile. It's beautiful, and somehow always manages to offset the potential of meanness with the warmth of her heart. 'My point is no one is perfect and sometimes you gotta chill a little and take one for the team. And by *one* I mean a private jet.'

Aminah's doe eyes roll in sync with mine, shaking her head as she elegantly pushes a pile of smoky jollof onto her fork with her a knife. 'Ashanti abeg, chill on my babe.'

I throw a smile of gratitude at my best friend as she continues with, 'He's not that fine.' She smooths a hand over her sleek ponytail and pushes it across the shoulder of her oversized tweed blazer, an action that really serves to display the Jupiter-sized rock on her finger. 'Nor is he a billionaire. I googled him this morning to double check—'

I place my flute down on the table. 'Seriously?'

Aminah's eyes widen prettily in protest, an indignant pixie with her round, button nose and heart-shaped glossy lips. 'I'm not saying he isn't good-looking, Keeks – he is. For a skinny man. He looks like LaKeith Stanfield but cleaner. I'm *just saying* he's not good-looking enough to be doing all *this*. Like, who does he think he is, undermining your ambition like that?'

I chew on my reluctant smile. Only Aminah could do a smooth save like that.

'OK. Thank you. Regardless, can we keep our voices down when talking about this?' I furtively look across the scattered Saturday lunchtime crowd of Sákárà.

Spritely late-winter sunlight streams through the open shop-front facing the East London high street, illuminating the cosy utilitarian interior of satin-smooth black laminated metal tables and azure velveteen dining chairs – virtually all of which are empty. It's not that I fear what the patrons of my parents' restaurant would have to say. There are precisely two. One of them is an UberEats driver collecting an order and the second is my uncle Kole, sat at the table closest to the bar with a Guinness and engrossed in a spirited debate about the state of Nigerian politics with my father. Dad's leaning an elbow on the faux marble bar, calling people 'utter nincompoops' whilst gesticulating passionately with his free arm like he's conducting the merry band of Yoruba drummers in the giant acrylic painting that hangs behind him.

A flood of warmth rushes through me at the familiar sight, quickly abated by a sobering coolness licking at the edges of my reality. I hadn't told my parents about my issues with Bakari because that would necessitate telling them that it was because he offered me a job, and then they would ask *why* he'd offered their eldest child a job – practically ensnaring her to a life of servitude to a man. That is not what they came to this country for. Though my parents know I stepped back from the podcast, what they don't know is that my savings are fast dwindling and my job search is getting increasingly frantic. I'm applying for any and every job vaguely in media. Last night, I applied for something called a 'dream alchemist' at an ad agency, which I *think* has something to do with copywriting, but I can't be sure. I *do* know that they have a contract with an alternative-milk company and came up with the tagline: 'Get your nut. It's good for you.' So maybe they need me. In any case, on account of not wanting to worry my parents about the exact degree of my joblessness just as they're about to sell up the restaurant and retire, mine and Bakari's situation needs to be kept under wraps.

'Well –' Chioma's already soft sing-song voice lowers even more as she slices into her moin-moin, and she shrugs – 'why would him being a billionaire be a draw anyway, even if he was? I think your decision was admirable. As we know –' Chioma waves a relaxed hand in the air, her multiple dangling bracelets creating an extra percussion for the DeBarge song emanating from my dad's 'Eighties Groove' playlist, which is sliding out of the restaurant speakers – 'there's no ethical way to be a billionaire – and yes, Shanti, that includes your favourite make-up mogul—'

Shanti pointedly pierces her fork into a piece of fried beef, holds it up and smiles innocently at her vegan best friend. 'All right, Erykah Badon't, I don't see you complaining when I give you freebies.'

Chioma bites at her smile, recognising Shanti's playful teasing immediately. 'First of all, Erykah *Badon't* is an oldie.'

'But a goodie. A classic,' I chirp.

'And secondly,' Chioma says with some triumph, 'just for that, I'm gonna wear a nude-pink lip with no brown liner, a cheap wig from a beauty-supply shop, throw it up on Instagram and caption it #ShantiShowedMe.' Chioma concludes with the hashtag that many of Shanti's 25,000 Instagram followers (and counting) use when employing the style and beauty tips and tricks she gives in her bite-sized videos.

Chioma has had her hair in deep auburn locs for years now, but, still, Shanti gasp-cackles at the threat to her nascent influencer empire.

'You're so wrong for that because you *know* that as someone who has been on my Instagram grid multiple times you're an outward representation of the @ShantiShines brand and I can't have you out here looking like you're the Black For Hire that goes on right-wing panel shows talking about how people need to get over colonialism.'

I snort. It's been almost a decade since Aminah and I coalesced with Shanti and Chioma in uni, two friendship pairs from various sides of a sororal social spectrum, joining forces. We were peace and love and South London fire meets Naija girl acerbity – couture and thrifting, unified with the sisterly ability to roast each other and a willingness to kill for each other if necessary. We're wildly different, and it works, a symphony and rhythm unto ourselves. It fits; we click.

Aminah smirks while pouring more of the champagne my dad brought out especially for us. 'Look, I'm all for Shanti doing promo for the billionaire make-up mogul if she gets me that unreleased bronzer in time for my wedding. Anyway, we're missing the point of this.'

I readjust myself on my seat with some relief, sitting up, glad we can return to the reason for this Blackwell Baddie Brunch, which wasn't just to dissect the dire state of my romantic life, but also to plan the events for the coming months: hen do, engagement party and various miscellaneous things that are under my jurisdiction as Maid of Honour, Deputy Bride and Head of the Bridal Committee as my full and proper titles assigned to me by Aminah dictates.

I clap my hands together. 'Exactly.' I drag my tablet across the table. 'When is everyone free for bridesmaid dress fittings?'

Aminah shakes her head. 'I *meant* we're missing the point that you've broken up with your boyfriend—'

I prickle in my black square-neck bodysuit, suddenly feeling warm, despite knowing my dad keeps the thermostat at an even 20 degrees. 'We haven't broken up—'

Chioma tilts her head thoughtfully. 'Um, whilst you know how I feel about the institution of marriage – no offence, Aminah.'

Aminah nods imperiously. 'None taken. You know how I feel about the institution of thrifting and wearing clothes that could potentially carry evil spirits.'

Chioma is unmoved, and shrugs, 'Fair, but I always do a sage cleanse for them.'

'Babes, if you have to *exorcise* your clothes before you wear them, maybe you're doing something wrong.' Shanti frowns as she chews on some of the peppered fish.

Chioma picks up the pink crystal she has hung on a gold chain round her neck and holds it in Shanti's direction – I presume to ward off her bad vibes – before turning back to me. 'Anyway, you kind of said no to the *idea* of marrying him, which I totally agree with, but knowing the cis straight male ego . . .'

Shanti raises a perfect brow. 'It kind of sounds like you've broken up.'

I rub my temples and lean forward on the table. Aside from not wanting to distract from Aminah's news, this is precisely why I hadn't told the gang for a month. My friends – who I adore – simply wouldn't understand, and would make the situation seem more problematic than it actually is. Whilst sure, fine,

49

it's technically a fact that after that night Bakari and I decided we needed some space from each other to recalibrate, we both maintained that this was temporary; it was confusion with my career that meant my head wasn't straight, and he needed to understand that it wasn't a bug he could troubleshoot. We still share a Netflix account! We know the terms of engagement; we know we'll be getting back together. The argument had got heated for us, *but* in the grand scheme of passionate fights it barely hovered above two English people jostling for a place in a queue. Besides, when I went to his to pick up my favourite bra that I'd left there, we ended up making out for three minutes as he said goodbye. Proof that this is not a clean break.

It had happened like this: he'd said, 'It's weird without you around,' and I replied saying that I knew what he meant, even though, actually, though I missed him, it was kind of fine. Mine and Bakari's romantic relationship is such that we work around each other, our lives overlapping in very specific ways in which we both agree. We don't do random, sporadic sleepovers – we plan ahead. We don't 'hang out' – we have activities. Dinner, co-working, movies. Specifically, movies that he's read about and confirmed are good before we go. Movies slated to be Oscar-nominated. He wants to be sure we wouldn't be wasting our time. If any of our friends has a birthday party, the other is not obliged to come. We don't talk to each other about work unless for a specific reason – an acquisition, for example, or, say, an unceremonious quitting. We aren't entangled. I'd had that before and not only is it a bitch to extricate yourself, but, when you eventually do, you have to wait for a piece of yourself to grow back. No, this is better. I miss him in a sense that it is weird not to text someone to ask if I should pick up some Thai on the way home.

He continued: 'It's like my life algorithm is off. I'm meant to slip on a lipstick on the floor of my bathroom whilst shaving, or tune out *Trysts in the Topics* whilst sending an email and I know I don't like cuddling, but it's strange stretching out at night without finding you there. And now I might be a cuddling person.'

I thought this was sweet, even though all of this hinted at the sort of comfort a cat gives you. Humming in the background of your life, present for affection when necessary. I'd stepped closer to him to offer a hug of camaraderie, except he thought I was going in for a kiss, so he pulled me in, and I gave in, thinking, *What's the harm?*

It was nice, it was pleasant, it was warm – tongues doing what they were supposed to, but politely so (after you, no, after *you*,) – and whilst I did kind of want his hand to slip to my butt I knew he wasn't an unbridled-passion kind of person. Bakari is measured, and so in his head he calculated that this was the appropriate amount of intimacy for two people who currently need space, but who are still theoretically romantically interested in one another. He was probably right – Bakari estimates most things accurately – except, I guess, when it comes to how offering a job to his girlfriend might affect the dynamic of a relationship.

Bottom line is, as that kiss proved, 'It's not a break-up,' I say now, decisively, spearing my fork into a piece of roasted tilapia.

'What's not a break-up?' My dad's eyes twinkle with gentle

curiosity behind his neat, rimless glasses as he approaches our table with a pitcher of what looks like Chapman, sloshing orangey red with flashes of green and yellow – sliced cucumber and lemon – bobbing alongside ice.

My friends' eyes pop open in alarm as I reply smoothly, 'Um . . . the latest situation between JLo and Ben Affleck.'

My father nods with profound understanding as he sets the drink on the table, folding his arms across his blue short-sleeved, button-down shirt with authority. 'Oh yes. I strongly believe they will sort out their problems. Sometimes you just need to have space to clarify your mind in regards to what you want.'

I smile fondly at Olatunde Banjo, a curious mind who reads everything and anything – including showbiz news – and speaks like a professor. 'Exactly.' I shoot pointed looks at my best friends, who are swallowing grins. 'That's what I'm saying—'

'Sometimes you need to grow apart to come back together again stronger. It was like me and your mummy in '87—'

I arch a brow. 'Mum told me you broke up for two weeks.'

My father looks confused by my clarification, heavy brows furrowed. 'And so? Separation is separation. I thought I was going to die. I was sweating at night like I had malaria. I couldn't eat. Couldn't sleep. My whole body was just weak. I even went to the doctor. Dr Lawrie in Camberwell. He looked at me like I was mad and said malaria-carrying mosquitos were "quite rare" in London. Anyway, I had no choice but to believe that my affliction was love.'

My friends' trapped giggles burst forth at this admission as my potentially Oscar-nominated father raises a hand to his bald head, feigning distress at the memory. 'I grew up in that fortnight. Realised I couldn't live life without her. In fact, my body rejected the break-up. She was fine, though. Saw her at a friends' party the following week with a new hairdo. She asked me why I was looking skinny. I just had to beg her.'

The weight of affection bends my lips. In my mum's version of the story, she convinced her friend to have a party just so she could bump into my dad. She got her hair cut especially for the occasion, borrowed her friend's miniskirt. I, of course, would never divulge this. It could contribute in dismantling an intricate system that stush Yoruba women have built for generations, using cunning to move to men without showing their working.

Aminah sighs and rests her chin on her laced hands. 'Man, you and auntie are couple goals. I can only pray me and Kofi are like you guys some day.'

My dad chuckles. 'Kofi is a smart young man. I've seen you two together. He knows when to be quiet. You'll be fine. Just don't be afraid of the work. Love each other enough to do the work. The biggest mistake people make is thinking a relationship should be easy just because loving the right person is easy. Yes, love is sweet, but it also needs *steel*. Gumption.'

My mind snags on this and my own smile stiffens. *Love each other enough to do the work*. I tried. I'm sure I tried. Didn't I try? Why didn't *he* try? And I am sure, so sure, almost sure, I'm thinking of my relationship with Bakari, until a face emerges in my mind's eye. A strong, majestic nose, full lips, eyes that could look at me and discombobulate my vestibular system. Not Bakari.

No. Dread – panic – crawls up my nervous system. Ever since Aminah announced her engagement, it's as if the tangible prospect of seeing *him* has shaken me up, unearthing long-ignored questions that are sharp enough to pick at the plaster I've pasted over buried memories. It's absurd. I won't be seeing him for almost a year, and even then he is the *past*. Bakari is my present. Ish. As previously stated, we still share a Netflix account. My dad's voice interrupts my burgeoning emotional spiral as he surveys the near-empty dishes on the table.

'I hope you ladies enjoyed your food?' he asks, as he does every time my friends eat here, as if he doesn't personally oversee the cooking of their food, making the fish extra spicy for Shanti, the smoky jollof even smokier for Aminah and ensuring the moin-moin is totally vegan by making a special batch with vegetable stock instead of beef for Chioma. He doesn't do alterations to his menu for just anybody – 'Do people think I just cook without thinking? Am I a *fool*? Is this a drive-thru?' – but he loves to indulge my friends as if they're adopted daughters. He nods with contained satisfaction and a dollop of pride as my friends gush over his dishes, like they always do. 'Good. Well, I'm glad that my food kicks.'

I suppress my smile. 'It "bangs", Daddy.'

Dad is nonplussed as he blinks at me, confused as to why I would think he would give a shit. 'Ah, bangs, abi, punches? Ki lo kan mi? What's the difference? I'm just glad you all ate well.' He nods at me and squeezes my shoulder. 'Your mother's waiting for me to pick her up at home so we can go to Grandma Akinyele's seventieth birthday party. Thank you for covering general management for the rest of the day – I know it's a Saturday and you should be out there shaking a leg—'

I haven't worked in Sákárà since just after uni, but these days we've been short-staffed – business has been slow since the demographic of our stretch of high street has shifted. A Gail's has replaced the old phone-repair shop where Mr Abdi fixed my smashed phone screen for free when I was twenty-two. A cheese-and-wine shop has nestled into the place where Ms Eunice used to tell us, with a straight face, that she was out of jerk chicken. There's a SpiritCycle opening a couple of doors down, which is especially insulting because it's a knock-off of another brand of workout class where you ride a stationary bike as someone shouts at you. The faces that walk past the storefront now have less variety, evidently less interest in hearty Nigerian food and wear more athleisure. All of this means less customers, less income, staff cutbacks and more of me helping out where I can.

'Dad, it's fine.'

My dad frowns at me gently, tilting his head to the side. 'But are you sure? Because I can still get your uncle Kole to do it . . .'

I cast an eye at one of my dad's oldest friends, who in the past ten minutes has managed to completely pass out whilst sitting upright, nodding himself awake with his own snores every few seconds.

I slowly shake my head, my smile wry. 'Daddy, I've told you to stop giving him the pounded-yam-and-Guinness combo before 6 p.m. It's fine. I promise. I've got, um, work to do anyway. Research. For an article,' and by this I mean emailing every single media contact I have with a cursory 'Hey! Long time! Up for a coffee?' hoping the scent of desperation is light.

He bends to kiss my forehead. 'Ọ ṣé ọmọ mi. I'll see you later. Enjoy the Chapman, girls. It's my special-edition recipe, since you all are celebrating Aminah's engagement. And, Kikiola, when you talk to that small sister of yours tell her that just because she's away at university doesn't mean she can skip out on going to church.'

I assure my dad that I will make sure Kayefi is still working on her salvation, before he waves goodbye to my friends and makes his way out through the back.

'His special-edition recipe for Chapman is rum, just by the way,' I say, pouring out glasses for everyone.

Shanti cackles, 'No disrespect to your mum, because I adore her, but would your dad take me as a second wife? I'm done with the streets, and I think I'm leaning towards older men these days.'

I toss a napkin at her and roll my eyes. 'Piss off, Shanti.'

'Yeah, Shanti, please. Have some class,' Aminah says, picking up her drink. 'Theoretically, if anyone's second-wife material, it's me. Not in relation to Kiki's dad, because, gross. He's like my dad. I just mean generally. I think I have the sort of *joie de vivre* necessary for that role. And so much less pressure, you know?'

Chioma hums thoughtfully. 'It's not really a role, though – it's a *partnership*. When I was in that polycycle with the drummer in that free jazz band and that lawyer—'

I stifle a laugh. 'OK, my disgust at the fact that this conversation started in reference to my literal *dad* aside –' I have to address this quickly – 'I don't think that was a polycule, babes.'

Shanti smirks in agreement. 'Yeah, lowkey the lawyer was a link you had while you were dating the drummer—'

'But they knew about each other!' Chioma protests, indignant at the suggestion of her conventionality.

Aminah waves her hand. 'Sis, stop trying to force this thing. Your little drummer boy was in my DMs crying, asking how he can win you back.'

I laugh. 'Begging to be the only one to have access to your *pa rum pa pum pum*.'

A gust of laughter ripples Shanti's drink as she sips. 'Yeah, Chi, your free-love era was a trip. You were like pre-Kiki–Malakai in uni.'

Shanti immediately seizes, her smile dropping like lead. The air around the table seems to still at the seeming slip of tongue, as it always does when someone inadvertently mentions my ex. Aminah's eyes widen, and Chioma is inspecting her moin-moin as if searching for meat product. Into the gap slips Patrice Rushen's 'Forget Me Nots', blooming into the quiet, ridiculously.

I choke out a rigid laugh, its edges scraping my throat. 'Guys, you're allowed to say his name, you know. Stop being weird about it.'

Shanti visibly relaxes with a slight huff of relief. 'OK, cool. So that means I can ask if you've thought about whether your issues with Bakari have anything to do with the fact that Malakai's coming back from the States for Minah's engagement party—'

Aminah raises a denim leg and taps her Gucci Princetowns against Shanti's YSL slingbacks in a way that I guess she thinks I don't see.

Heat flares through my body and my stomach makes moves that make it seem like Simone Biles can only do cartwheels. I push out a laugh that manages to squeeze its way past the heart (mine, incidentally) that's currently chilling in my throat.

'Um . . .' I focus on pouring some more Chapman into my glass as my nasal cavity prickles with panic. 'He's coming back for the engagement party? That's in two months?' I sip my drink, hoping it will aid me in appearing nonchalant. I've clearly forgotten my dad's heavy-handed pours of rum because I cough heartily, and in the process add to my chalants rather than ridding myself of them.

Aminah looks nervous. 'Are you OK, babe?'

I raise a finger as an errant splutter escapes. 'I'm great. Like, *so* great. I just thought that Malakai wasn't going to be able to come because of work. You said he was going to come closer to the wedding. Which is in, like, ten . . . months.' That sounded like I was still holding on to a few chalants. 'Not that it matters, obviously.' I hope this addition brushes them away.

Aminah nods and scratches the side of her neck with the edge of a sharp nail, a habit evidencing her discomfort and her lying tell. The last time she did this we were playing Never Have I Ever and instead of backing a double tequila, she asserted that she'd never had sex in a communal space, as if Malakai and I hadn't once walked in on her and Kofi on the sofa in the villa we'd shared in

Crete. They were doing things I immediately sought to erase from my memory via ouzo.

Aminah clears her throat. 'Right. I did say that, but Kofi told me last week that Malakai has some meeting in London that's around the time of the engagement party . . .'

I raise a brow. Aminah and I don't keep things from each other, ever. We know every white lie, every secret, every kink in our truths, every hurt behind a razor-edged comment and every swear word behind a smile, and so it's bewildering to me that she would keep the fact that in a month's time my ex would be in the same city as me for the first time in two-and-a-half years.

'You know what, guys,' I say brightly after a moment of silence that Shanti and Chioma respect like kids observing their parents in a silent disagreement at the dining table, 'let's just lay this all out there. Yes, the ex I haven't spoken to in two years is the best man at my best friend's wedding. It's not a big deal! We're adults!! Who used to have sex! We can co-exist and work together! Sophia Bush did fine working with Chad Michael Murray on *One Tree Hill*!'

Shanti raises a brow. 'Is that another one of your American white-people shows?'

'Yes,' says Aminah gravely. 'Keeks, your voice just went very Mariah whistle-note high. You sure you're OK?'

I lower my voice. 'I'm fine. I'm *fine*. One thing I know for sure is that we . . .' I amend. We are not a *we* any more. 'He and I love you and Kofi lots. So there's no reason for all this tiptoeing, because it's not about. We're irrelevant in this all, actually.'

Aminah's bright eyes shine through me as if I'm glass, and it makes me hyperaware of the fact that I am feeling fragile, like I could shatter with the (in)correct amount of force right now.

'OK,' she says softly. 'Thank you. Look, I know I should have told you before. I'm sorry. I was just waiting for the right time.'

I need to push the thrashing, the crashing of my heart away. I need to beckon the bright to ward off the dark of the potential storm, so I manage to force out a wide grin. Apocalypse aftershocks have been beginning to rattle through me for the past month. I think of the wedding and I feel overfull with excitement – my body thrums with the thrill of it – and then the chaser of tremors occurs, a destabilising feeling from nowhere that makes my chest feel tight and my heartbeat pound and my stomach swirl.

I force a shrug. 'It's fine. You don't need to treat me with kid gloves. Look, I can even say his name now. Remember when I couldn't?' All of three seconds ago? 'Malakai. See? *Malakai.*' While I do immediately become slightly lightheaded, this is obviously because of the chaotic mixture of champagne and what is essentially rum with a splash of Chapman. It has nothing to do with saying the name I haven't said out loud in over six months.

My friends' smiles are rigid as they make various sounds of pacification.

'You said his name at a totally normal pitch—'

'Sis, we know you're not stressing about him—'

'You sound totally at peace . . .'

Shanti clears her throat into the lull that follows and reaches for her baby pink Telfar. 'Um, well, I've got a birthday booking for tonight, so I gotta go and prep. She's this influencer with,

60

like, a hundred thousand followers and is crucial for my brand expansion.'

Chioma quickly nods, rising with Ashanti, and reaching for her woven tote, 'Yeah, and I've got a life-drawing class tonight so I'll leave with you—'

'Oh, I didn't know you were teaching today,' I say, grateful for the change of subject.

Chi-Chi's an assistant interior designer who sometimes moonlights teaching art in community centres for extra cash.

Chioma shakes her head as she throws her faux-suede hobo bag over her shoulders. 'Oh, nah. Not today. Modelling.'

I raise my brows, impressed, 'Oh yeah? Well, bless them with your tiddies, sis.'

Chioma nods gravely, putting her hands together solemnly and dipping her head like a humble faith leader. 'You know I will. It's my humanitarian duty. I've been given a gift of stupendous rack. What kind of person would I be if I didn't share?'

Shanti shakes her head and kisses me on the cheek before she bends down next to Aminah and whispers, 'Oh shit, forgot to say – am I able to excuse myself from bridesmaid duties? Like, theoretically, what if I just want to be a regular guest? Because I love you, but I know that you're going to be a bridal terrorist and I am not Kiki or Chioma. I don't have their patience and it's not a good look to beat a bride's ass before her wedding day. I've done it *on* a wedding day before, but that was a whole thing. She came for me first.'

Aminah's expression becomes stone, her beautiful face so

devoid of emotion it sends a chill down my body. Aminah and Shanti are almost the chaotic good and chaotic evil of each other, their positions switching according to the situation.

'Ashanti Jackson, you better be *fucking* joking.' When Aminah swears, it's an occasion that makes your heart jolt and your palms prick (think, *Yes, this is the purpose of swearing, this is the emphasis for which it was created, to send chills, to straighten your back*), 'because I did not enter this friendship nearly a decade ago for you to flop on me now—'

Having read the teasing crack in Shanti's face and being re-assured a Baddie Battle isn't going to occur, I relax into my seat and she squawks, 'Shit, man, you're just so easy. Be calm. It would be an honour, bitch. I *will* slap you if you talk to me crazy, though.'

Aminah chews on her reluctant smile and rolls her eyes as Shanti kisses her cheek with a loud smack. The two have their own friendship treatise that consists of a comfortable sharpness and the veneer of a grudging affection that you can only find in sisters who are mildly competitive with each other.

'And I'll slap you right back, honey,' she says.

'Wouldn't have it any other way,' Shanti trills before she and Chioma wave their goodbyes and head out to the high street. Aminah and I look at each other in the din of Sister Sledge insisting that we are family, our silence pointed.

While I initially came to know Shanti and Chioma in second year through the very normal friendship meet-cute of their being previously romantically entangled with the man I was to fall in love with, mine and Aminah's friendship started on the first day of university. Together, we stripped an obnoxious rugby boy of his toga after some mild racial and sexual harassment on his part at the bins outside our residential building. It was love at first shared spite. Mine and Aminah's relationship is that of soulmates: my best friend, my sister, my person. It never lets up, our love for each other only growing as we do. More than a shared adoration of Beyoncé, our inability to take shit and our dislike of men who wear dangly cross earrings, is the fact that our minds exhale in sync. Our differences sharpen each other. She knows me like she knows herself; she's part of me, as much as I'm a part of herself and as much as I'm a part of myself. As if to prove the point, she lowers her chin and reaches out to hold my hand across the table, leaning forward so the 'K' in her gold pendant, previously lying in the square neck of her white bodysuit, dangles over her empty plate.

'You're mad at me.'

'Nope. I'm not mad, Meenz. Just confused. How could you not tell me that Malakai was coming for your engagement party? I was prepared for the wedding – it's a while away – but the engagement party is basically tomorrow—'

'I know, I *know*.' Aminah straightens and guilt dances across her face, immediately abating the tightness in my chest, softening my annoyance. 'I was just waiting for the right moment to tell you, but then time kept on passing by and I got swept up in wedding stuff.'

I nod and squeeze her hand, because annoyance at Aminah doesn't metabolise well with my body. My blood rejects it – it lies heavy on top of it and restricts its flow – and so I let it go, because it's hard to carry and because I understand why she did it.

She went through the break-up with me, my pain pulsing through her as she held my hand and as she lay next to me on the bed; it travelled in waves through the silence of her texts that remained unread because I was so scared to pick up my phone in case he texted and in case he didn't.

I clear my throat. 'I get that.'

Aminah nods carefully. 'And how are you about the Bakari situation? Gist me for real. How could you not tell me for a month? We speak every day! I even know your bowel-movement schedule. You're quite regular these days.'

'Yeah, I started putting chia seeds in my porridge. Anyway, I didn't tell you because it really *isn't* a big deal. Or a break-up! We'll figure it out. I just think it's weird how he thinks that he could just offer to be my boss and think I'll accept. It's like he doesn't know me. He once got me a necklace with a heart-shaped pendant.'

Aminah's face is one of delicate disgust, her nose crinkling slightly. 'Ew.'

'Yeah.'

'Gold?' she says with some generosity, throwing Bakari a bone, hoping that he at least got my favourite metal tone right.

I wince. 'Silver.'

Aminah gawps at me. 'No.'

I sigh, resting my chin on the base of my palm. 'I know.'

'How did I not know this?'

'I didn't want you to know it.'

Aminah considers offence, tilting her chin slightly and narrowing her eyes. She then nods decisively. 'You know what? I really respect you not telling me. Gifting heart-shaped jewellery is like someone proposing on Valentine's Day.'

I stretch out my hands in the air. 'Thank you! Or having a Great Gatsby-themed New Year's party.'

'Unoriginal.'

'Redundant.'

'Right? Like the theme is already glittery enough! The theme is innate in the event.'

Aminah shudders and shakes her head. 'You think he has a workplace kink? Didn't he have that "Yes, Chef" fantasy?'

I gasp and slap her hand. 'Oh my God. Thank you! He fully wants to do up *Fifty Shades of Bae*. Also, when I told him to, um . . . talk to me in bed, all he could come up with was, "You're a star", which felt kind of boss adjacent. But, like, not in a hot way.'

Aminah nods and sips her Chapman like it's an elixir of knowledge. 'See. This is what I do. Connect dots. Part of what being a communications executive means. And what *you* do is create on your own terms. You wouldn't be you if you didn't do that. You would at least want to find something else of your own to replace The Heartbeat, but I guess it was his way of being concerned. No offence, but he's kind of like an alien who is learning to be human. In a cute way!' she rushes to add. 'His silver pendant heart was in the right place. And that's the only amount of generosity I'm gonna give him.'

I smile, warmed by the fact that, as usual, I didn't have to explain. She knows me. That little hiccup before was a glitch. We're good. We're always good.

'We'll figure it out,' I say. 'Besides, this is your moment! You're getting married to your second-best friend! We spoke about this when we were *nineteen* and now you're spending your life with the guy who you loved enough to let him finger you in the photo-booth during the Afro Winter Ball just before you got crowned king and queen—'

'It wasn't fingering.' Aminah smirks and we click back into place. 'That's so crude. It was very good pressurised pleasurable rubbing.'

I choke on my glug of water. 'And this is less crude *how*?'

Aminah ignores me and looks wistfully at the ceiling in what looks way too close to a flashback for my comfort. 'So weird, though, that after ten years that moment remains memorable—'

'Well, though you were pleasurably pressure-rubbed by him before, this pleasurable pressure-rubbing did mark the formal start of your relationship.'

Aminah nods sagely. 'And also yours. The Afro Winter Ball, not the PPR, which I have now decided I want to turn into an initialism.'

'I guess it might come in handy in the future.' Aminah releases a delicate snort that sounds how a fairy might when it sneezes. In my top-five favourite sounds. 'Well done. Anyway, that was also the night you had sex for the first time. I'll never forget the look on your face over those dry-ass continental-breakfast croissants the next morning at the hotel. I just *knew*.'

'Yeah. You passed me a muffin and asked me if I wanted it buttered. With a fucking wink,' I say with a roll of my eyes, as a bizarre heat rushes through me at the memory. It resists repression, surging forward into my mind's eye, stubborn and searing. Soft hot lips pressing against my skin, sensations so decadent they felt like sin. He'd gently kissed every part of my body till I was soft enough to melt into the moment, feel safe in it. He made sure everything in me was assured of his want, which made my own want make itself known between my thighs and in sighs and in goosebumps and in nails into his back, and in IloveyouIloveyouIloveyou, a new taste on my tongue, but familiar in its feel.

I swallow. This is just sexual frustration. It's biological, not emotional. This is basically just like hunger. Or needing to go to the bathroom. It's been a while since I had sex. Not even PPR. I haven't seen Bakari in a month, but, even so, we hadn't had sex in two due to his travels. Also, my boobs feel particularly perky under my fitted black T-shirt. Clearly, I'm ovulating.

Aminah's eyes widen with a little too much glee. 'Oh *ho*. Are you joking me? See your face just blushing anyhow.'

I flick my eyes to the ceiling, partly to dramatically demonstrate exasperation and also so she can't look deep into my eyes and therefore my brain. 'Aminah, please. I can't blush.'

'We've been through this – you absolutely *can* blush. Your cheeks glow more, and, also, when you're blushing you bite your lip, and you literally just did that about sex you had eight years ago.'

I hitch a casual shoulder up and flip my braids across it, hoping it will dispel the heat crawling up my body. 'I was actually biting my lip with the effort of trying to remember the first time I'd had sex because actually I'd forgotten, so thank you for the reminder.'

'Wow, sarcasm. Prickly. See, I knew you were discombobulated by this Malakai thing—'

'Um, I'm perfectly combobulated, thanks.'

Aminah arches a brow, which I suppose she thinks is knowing, before I see her visibly let it go, pivoting carefully. 'So what's going on with the job situation?'

I sigh, rubbing the bridge of my nose, relieved as I am at the subject switch. 'Sis, I don't know. I've been looking. I have a conversation with some friends at an online music magazine about an editor position, but it's still just a *conversation*. Everyone in my network has been telling me there's no jobs going, and if there *are* they're applying to them themselves. I dunno. Maybe Bakari was right? Maybe I shouldn't have quit so recklessly.'

Aminah shakes her head with some disgust, holding a bejewelled hand up. 'Ew. Never say that in my presence again. You did the right thing. Heartbeat is about *heart* and they wanted to attack it—'

'Well done.'

Aminah twitches her shoulder in acknowledgement of her own wit. 'But, yeah, they wanted to make it soulless. You know I'm all about securing the bag, but I know you. This wouldn't have been worth it for you. I'm proud of you. It was bold, but –' her gaze flickers in concern – 'I mean . . . are you OK? Like, for money? Because, you know, it's tight with the wedding, but we could definitely help . . .'

She broaches it gingerly. Before this podcasting gig, Aminah's always been more *comfortable* than me, her parents having owned a Nigerian snack empire, and it's never been an issue – she's never made me feel a way about it — and when I worked in the restaurant during uni summers she'd come almost every day, keeping me company. One time she'd tried to help, but she almost came to blows with an uncle who clicked his fingers at her to get him more Guinness (shockingly, not Uncle Kole).

I shake my head. 'I appreciate you, but I'm good. At least for now. I still have a few Black Creative paid panels. The Heartbeat's cache can carry me for now so I'm not gonna have to sell my clothes just yet—'

'Ugh, and nineties Black romcom girlies wept, wondering where they would get their brown-leather mini and sleeveless mock-turtleneck crop tops from.' I stick my tongue out at her and Aminah smirks.

'I love it. Sultry. And you're gonna kill it like the boss babe you are.'

'Thank you, sis. Seriously, though. I'm all good.'

Aminah's long-lashed gaze searches mine for a few moments. She straightens and nods to herself, seemingly satisfied by what she's found. 'OK. Good to know. Because, um, there's one more thing I need to tell you.' She drags my tablet towards her across the tabletop, and stares at it, deliberately evading eye contact. 'Firstly, this is so well organised. You've sorted the aso ebi styles by colour! Amazing. What would be the Yoruba version of Marie Kondo? Moji Kondo? That's what you are. That's one of your middle names, right? Mojisola.'

I tilt my head. Whatever she wants to say is about to stress me out. 'Spit it out, Meenz.'

My best friend sighs and clears her throat, pressing her hand against her décolletage. 'Um, so we're changing the date of the engagement party. For three weeks' time.'

My food feels like it's going to crawl back up my throat. 'As in twenty-one days?' As if there's a chance that three weeks actually means six months, that maybe I've gone through twenty-eight years of my life not understanding time.

Aminah nods, her eyes wide. 'I'm sorry. It's just that's when my parents are going to be in the country at the same time as Kofi's. One of my big-mouthed sisters blabbed to them about us having an engagement party and they insisted on coming even though I said it's just meant to be a gathering of our friends and cousins. I know it's a lot of stress for you, and, look, I can do the bulk of the planning, obviously, and it's just meant to be a small, lowkey celebration anyway, so—'

I force a smile out and try to calm the anxiety crawling up my body. 'Aminah, you've got dress shopping, and the actual wedding venues to sort. I said I'll help you plan the engagement party, and I will.'

Somehow, through prep for job interviews and *conversations* and dealing with the fact that, actually, I'm going to be seeing my ex-boyfriend in *three weeks* for the first time in almost three years. It was one thing adjusting to the fact that I'll see him at the wedding, another to know it would be in two months and an entirely different *realm* to reckon with the fact that I'm going to see him before my new nail infills grow out.

Aminah stares at me flatly. 'You're freaking out.'

I laugh so forcibly in dismissal that I end up choking, spluttering on my denial.

Aminah's expression remains unchanged as she passes me a glass of water. 'Kikiola, I've known you since you still thought it was cool to wear ironic lace chokers.'

'You wore them too!'

'Exactly. Our relationship is such that we have been in deeply uncool trenches together. You can't hide from me.'

'I am not freaking out. The short notice just ups the pressure, is all, but it's fine! I got you. My job is to make your life easier in this process, and I know managing two sets of African parents isn't going to be easy, so let me do this for you.'

'And Malakai?'

'Oh, sounds like you got something in your throat too, sis. You're making a weird sound. Want some of this water?'

Aminah smirks and raises her hand in surrender. 'OK. I've heard. I just love you and want you to be OK.'

'I love you and I am OK.' I squeeze her hand. 'Now save all the mushy shit for your fiancé. Can we focus on what we're here to do?'

She laughs, the tension lifting from her face as she perks up and shimmies her shoulders in excitement. She's a fairy whose sole power is to be able to banish any potential annoyance by being ridiculously adorable. The inability to find her infuriating is infuriating.

'OK,' she says. 'First of all, let's refrain from using "hen do". Am I an animal? I am not livestock. I don't *cluck*. I like "bachelorette".'

That's one thing the Americans did right. It sounds elegant, sophisticated. Now, how do you feel about a renaissance theme?'

'Art history or "Alien Superstar"?'

'If we do it in a Tuscan villa, maybe both at the same time.'

I reach over for my tablet and scroll through the meticulously detailed pages on which I've been focusing all my attention instead of job enquiries.

'Art history is on page twelve, and Beyoncé is page five. I've contacted the RSPCA and PETA and apparently you can't cover an actual horse in silver bodypaint.'

My best friend gasps with faux dismay. 'What the hell?'

'I know. It could be argued that denying an animal the opportunity to be part of something so iconic is the *real* animal abuse.'

'You should be a lawyer.'

'Sis, I've been saying *since*.'

'I mean, your bum was created for a pencil skirt.'

'*Right?* How To Get Away With Slaying. Speaking of,' I say through our cackles, 'let's talk looks.'

And I proceed to pour all my energy into convincing her that she doesn't actually need eight costume changes to signify the Greek modes of love. ('Red for Mania to represent us being Crazy in Love,' my best friend said.) It takes time to whittle it down to three, and I'm grateful to redirect my energy from figuring out how to not feel emotionally disembowelled at the sight of the man who stole my heart for, it seems, the sole purpose of breaking it.

CHAPTER 3

Words of Affirmation

Three and a half years ago

'Marry me,' Malakai's gravelly voice rumbled into my ear, sleepy and molasses slow, 'All you need to do is say when and I'll drop to my knee.' It sent tremors through my sinfully spent body, prompting me to turn to him. The sight of him was like a warm knife through butter: melting me, rendering me into easy softness. It still tripped me up after five years, the firm luxuriance of his mouth, the depth in his eyes calling me to come dance with its light. My heart, as always, skipped a beat and fell into his rhythm. I smiled into the dark silk of his skin, let it turn into a kiss and tasted the salt of his sweat, or my sweat – of our sweat – and ran a hand down his chest.

'Awkward. I thought this was casual?'

His lips curved against the folds of my ear and nipped at it, the rogue flash of teeth and tongue more of a reason for the quickening of my breath than the proposal. Malakai proposed in varying iterations, periodically.

'Baby, PETA's gonna hate me for the amount of goats I'mma lay at your feet for your dowry,' his playful voice would tease, or, 'I think I need to make a visit to Mr and Mrs B. I have a question I gotta ask them. It's cognac for your dad and red wine for your mum, right?' Or, 'Tell Aminah to answer my texts on time for once in her life. I need her help on a shopping trip.' A pause. 'Don't tell Aminah that verbatim, just tell her to *please* answer my texts on time if she feels like it. I wanna go ring shopping.' Or, 'Are you sure you don't want to walk down the aisle to "Thong Song"?' Or, 'I don't ever want to stop doing this with you,' whispered into the tender stillness of our post-coital calm, to which I would reply, 'You sure you got the stamina?' and he would pull back and arch a brow and his voice would make like Christina Milian and dip dangerously low as he asked, 'Scotch, what did you just say to me?' and I let my smile be wicked and my face be serious and say, 'Oh sorry. My voice is a little hoarse—'

'You're welcome—'

'From karaoke last night—'

'You actually don't rate me.'

'Anyway, I *said*, are you sure you have the stamina to—' and he would shut me up by proving he had the stamina to, proved it with his mouth and proved it with his hands and the thick and thickening part of his body that was surely proving itself against the cushion of my behind as we spoke, which actually was my whole game anyway. Sucker. Or maybe that was me, because every time he did this, made some intimation that he was so sure one day he would be my husband, that he was so sure of me, of us, that five years on I was still it for him, that he didn't regret the utterly fucking insane thing of standing in front of our university peers at a giant ball and declaring his love for me at twenty years old, my heart forgot what it was supposed to do for a few seconds, suspended in the sweet knowledge that the love of my life wanted to spend his with me. The knowledge was theoretical for now, of course, I was twenty-four and he was twenty-five, with so much to do and to learn and to become. The reality of it was further in the future, but, still, the weight of its existence anchored me to us.

Malakai slid his hand down my stomach and then below my waist, where he sought purchase to press me closer to the firm flame of his body. Moaning at the pressure of his palm against me, I bucked as he pushed a finger into my heat. A taut arm secured me to him as he went deeper, added a finger and a maddening motion that saw a building pleasure begin to ripple restlessly through a body that suddenly was no longer tired. I was grateful Malakai had an empty flat; I could be as loud as I wanted to be.

Malakai's lips moved against my left lobe as he whispered again, with the best kind of cruelty, with the power of someone who literally has your pleasure in the palm of their hand, 'How casual does this feel, Scotch?'

I sighed. 'I hate you.'

'I know, baby.' His lips were hot and soft against my neck, in turn making me hot and wet, a tropical storm, and I pushed into him in response. 'So it's a good thing this is just a fling, innit.'

I smiled through my quivers. He was such a dick. I loved him. I wiggled around and freed myself enough to reach back round and hold him there. He hissed and tensed as I stroked slowly while he firmed further in my palm. My eyes began to blur, heady with power and pleasure as his hand signed our language into me, his motions making my thoughts a sensual smoothie, and just as I was about to guide the length of him into me, galvanised by his groans, my diminishing gaze focused on the time glowing on the laptop screensaver on his desk across from the bed. Why hadn't my alarm gone off? My eyes drifted to see my phone off the charger on Malakai's bedside table, presumably dead, somehow disconnected through last night's athletic antics. My molten body stiffened.

'*Shit*. Shit, shit, shit!' Malakai reluctantly released me as I detangled myself from his comfort, leapt out of bed and contemplated if a three-minute shower was enough to get the scent of sex off me, and whether I could get away with lotioning in the bathroom of Jupiter Press before the Monday-morning town-hall meeting.

'Shit, where's my bra?'

'I think –' Malakai's plush lips curved in an annoyingly satisfied smile that made him look obscenely sexier as he reclined, chest taut and topless, looking like some Yoruba deity – 'somewhere on the corridor floor.'

I rolled my eyes and dipped out of his room to scoop the black M&S lacy number from the floor. I'd do a whore's bath. Is that what they call it? That didn't sound right. Sexually Empowered Woman's Quick Cleanse. Unless, it was a reclamation of 'whore'?

Either way. Pits and pussy. And teeth. I needed to brush my teeth. I'd shower properly at the office gym at lunch. I came back to the room as I clasped my bra on and Malakai groaned in an entirely different tone to a minute before. 'Take the day off.'

I yanked the pillow out from under him to bash him on the head with it. 'I can't *take the day off*, Kai. Some of us aren't shadowing a BAFTA-winning director who keeps the hours of 4 p.m. to 4 a.m. three days a week!'

Since graduation, Malakai had rolled through short-term contract stints at various production companies and post-production houses as a runner, whilst filming weddings and christenings and motives and fiftieth-birthday parties for fifty-five-year-old aunties as a side hustle. He was just at the brink, wondering if he should use the economics minor of his degree and apply to a sleek shiny firm for a nebulous job that involved numbers – or, at his more desperate moments, work for his dad in Lagos – when he met a script editor step-cousin-twice-removed at a traditional wedding he was working at. Over a screeching mic and an MC who made a joking innuendo about the bride and pounded yam that made only the groom's uncles chuckle, he told Malakai that his company was holding a networking mixer for young Black creatives. It was here, in the basement of a Soho cocktail bar called Smoke & Mirrors, that Malakai had met and subsequently charmed Matthew Knight, British indie darling turned Hollywood juggernaut, the first Black man to win an Academy Award for Best Director (a visually gorgeous and excruciating film called *Primative*, a loose retelling of *Things Fall Apart* by Chinua Achebe). 'The fight for freedom goes on, and art is the spear,' he'd said in his viral rousing acceptance speech for a film produced by Black Viking, the production company he co-founded with his Swedish partner. Malakai hadn't wanted to ask if he could send him a link to his short films, *Cutz* (about the music of the Black barbershop) and *Untitled* (a meditation of love and youth and, incidentally, me) out of fear of looking like a 'beg'.

What he was really afraid of, I knew, was rejection. It was so close to what he wanted he could taste it, and losing the opportunity would leave him hungrier, emptier. Just before graduation, he had submitted *Untitled* to a film competition, and, whilst it was the only film that had received a 'special commendation', it hadn't won – it lost out to a short film called *Siren* about a white policeman who falls in love with a 'gang-affiliated' Black woman from a council estate. He'd tried to hide his heartbreak from me, but I felt it. Malakai's swagger had stumbled, and he hadn't really made anything since, with his ideas restricted to scrappy notes and liquor-loosened rhapsodies to me while we were on dates. But Malakai was brilliant, like, objectively *brilliant*, and I didn't just think this because of how he kissed and how he touched and how he fucked and how he loved me – in an elemental way, like I was air, water and fire and he were a palaeolithic man looking for something to worship. I thought it because it was true.

He had an eye for the most visceral of feelings and a heart for the most evocative of visuals, and he was created for this, for capturing moments, helping to tell stories, for helping people feel less alone. It was part of him; on a walk, he'd stop, and nudge me, gesturing for me to clock the big brother helping to tie his little brother's shoelaces, or the elderly Nigerian couple holding hands on the tube, or the group of boys at the back of the bus roasting each other, or sometimes he'd nudge me to look at me. I would be sitting on the other end of the sofa, my legs outstretched over his whilst I read a book, and he'd stop watching his movie and watch me.

'What?'

'What you mean, what? *You* what, Scotch.'

I would see me in his eyes, and my breath would turn round on itself, disorientated by the fact that I was the sparkling thing that made his eyes glitter like that. I would sink into his softness.

So I knew that my job, then, was to make him look at himself.

'*Ah*, cool, yeah, I get it.' I'd nodded, soothingly rubbing his back. 'So you'd rather beg your dad to work at his property firm in Ikoyi, yeah? You wanna go back to him and tell him that he's right, and your filmmaking career is the dream of a fool? That's great. I've always dreamt of being a Lekki housewife, as you know.'

Malakai slowly turned to look at me. I tilted my head and looked right back at him.

He sent the links to his films the following day, and, as I predicted, Knight had asked him to come see him the following week. And now, a year on, my boyfriend was the protégé of one of the most acclaimed directors in the world, frequenting afterparties with entertainment's elite and asking me if I could skive off my assistant job at the publishing house in which my role was to order lunch and warm a boardroom seat whenever a white editor (they were all white) needed A Black to wheel out so they could poach a *timely, powerful* book about race.

Malakai picked up my hand and kissed it. 'Seriously, I'm sorry. My bad – you're right.' The heat of his mouth awakened a tart hunger between my legs, like it wasn't relatively chaste compared to the other places he'd been kissing last night. I was still so fascinated by how my body reacted to him after five years, reduced to chemical reactions and sensations so rich that they made me leave the confines of my skin, burning me into vapour, but somehow also making me fuller, more *inside* my own body.

'Sit with me for a second. Just a second, baby.' His gaze was honey and drenched want, and any protestation I had got stuck in it, drowned in it.

His hours had been more erratic lately, which meant we hadn't been able to spend as much time together. Karaoke with our friends last night had been the first time in two weeks. He pulled me back down so I was sat on the edge of the bed, enabling him to wrap his arms round me, pulling my back to his chest so he could rest his chin on my shoulder. I momentarily forgot where I was supposed to be. It seemed kind of fucked up that I was to be anywhere else but there, sat with the heat of his heartbeat against my shoulder blade, his arms securing me to me. I inhaled deeply, let the steadiness of his affection settle in my bones.

He murmured against my skin. 'I just hate that you get so stressed about a job that treats you like shit.'

I sighed and coughed out a humourless laugh. 'Yeah. Me too.'

My journey after graduation was a little bumpier than Kai's.

Whilst he had a clear direction – he wanted to make films – for the first time in my life, it occurred to me that I had no idea what I wanted to do with it. Throughout uni, I'd been decisive, ambitious: get high grades in my Media and Politics degree, then ensure our university ACS, Blackwell, didn't crumble under my presidency, then it was to get into my master's programme, then it was to get a distinction in my Global Politics and Popular Culture degree, and it wasn't till I'd completed all that, that I realised I had no idea what to do with my life. My skills – understanding people, talking about pop culture, music and feelings – didn't exactly have a career pipeline. My parents were pretty chill for Nigerians Of A Generation, but even then I was beginning to feel like a second-gen cautionary tale, the kind that aunties would tell their kids about. 'You know your radical cousin, Kikiola? With her nose-piercing? Look at where that her useless degree got her. You better sit down and face your law books.'

I enjoyed politics, but wasn't sure I could enter the public sector without losing my mind. I wrote all the time, but didn't know if I was good enough to attempt journalism, finding the intersection of my interests tough to write about in a field where it was music *or* politics *or* relationships. I considered America – I'd had a summer fellowship at NYU where I'd done well – and I knew Malakai and I would be fine. In my mind, we were an inevitability, a certainty. We were the sun and nothing could sink us, but when I left uni all the media and broadcast connections I'd made told me they couldn't afford to sponsor a visa. So I signed up to a media temp agency in London, and just as I was wondering whether I should just work at my parents' restaurant full time I found myself temping as an office manager for a six-month mat cover at Jupiter Press publishing.

I smiled when I made the teas. I went to pub birthday drinks where I learned to fake-drink gin and tonics forced on to me so they could feel like they could trust me, like maybe I was one of them. I complimented their shoes or their new fringe and asked questions about the charity race they did with their running group and their weekends at Soho Farmhouse and listened to them whisper about how they were cheating on their boyfriend with someone from their running group, because smiling and nodding and saying 'wow' and 'totally' and 'so true' every few seconds seemed to ensure trust. I listened to how, actually, plot twist, he was who they spent the weekend with at Soho Farmhouse. Nothing was required of me but to be a sentient ear.

When slowly I started asking them questions about books they were working on, they asked *me* questions, for some reason shocked that I read everything that passed across my desk. When I had listened to enough sloppily shared secrets in the basement of a Monument pub, an editor (who'd tearfully confessed to me that she'd been sleeping with her best friend's ex who just so happened to work in marketing) asked for my CV and told me to apply for an editorial assistant role.

'We need someone like you,' she said with an oddly deployed wink, and I wasn't sure if she meant it because of my intelligence or race or my presumed ability to keep secrets, but frankly I didn't give a shit. It was a job with *potential* and it had editorial in the title so my parents could tell everyone I was an editor if they wanted to, which they did. I wasn't sure it was exactly right for me, but who had a job that was exactly right? Not everyone had a direct calling like Malakai. I loved books and reading, so maybe it was right enough.

The maybe, however, was a little disconcerting. I'd always felt certain of so many things in life – of *myself* – and now I felt like I was in a place where I was losing my individuality a little, my voice. I'd been working there for a year, and a girl who happened to be the niece of the Head of Marketing had been hired to be assistant editor, despite the fact that I'd unofficially been doing the tasks required for six months.

Then when I'd come across a breathtaking short story by a young Senegalese girl about Mami Wata, an editor had sucked some air between her lips and said that though she 'enjoyed' my 'initiative', and that I should 'keep it up' (with a tight-lipped smile that one might give to a small child holding up a picture of a wonky triangle they'd drawn), she said she found fairy tales too archaic and, plus, 'Race-bent Little Mermaid is kind of overdone. Don't you think?'

And instead of asking her how it is possible to 'race-bend' a humanoid mythical creature with gills and telling her that the blunt-bob-chunky-fringe-sack-dress-dirty-white-trainer look was overdone and, in fact, basic in its attempt to be chic, and how it was impressive that she surmised this all from a story she clearly hadn't even deigned to read, I said, 'Sure, Pippa, I get it,' which made me quite grossed out at myself.

I didn't get it, but I couldn't say I didn't get it, because the one time I vocally disagreed with an editor (that we maybe shouldn't make an offer on *Bars*, a book by a white guy with a buzzcut who took it upon himself to write about the link between prison and grime), I was told to 'take emotion out of it' and open up my mind more and 'if we don't do it, someone else will' and essentially that I was naïve and underexposed, despite apparently being aware and exposed enough to be the Black representation when a Black author whose subject fit their rigid remit (race) came their way.

I told myself it was temporary. I was paying my dues. And I was doing what I could: though I couldn't get an editor to read the girl's work, I was able to introduce to her a kind agent I'd once met at work. Baby steps.

I shrugged. 'But it's fine. It's not terrible.' I nodded to myself, attempting to coax hope. 'It will get better.'

Malakai kissed my shoulder. 'You're going to make it better, because you're the best. Sharp, sweet, kind, fierce. Let no one fuck with you, sugar blade.' He nipped at my neck, his accent mutating to Yoruba sweet boy. 'Sweet assassin.' His nose and lips nuzzled into my cheek. 'Iyawo mi.'

My stomach fluttered despite knowing that he was only calling me his wife as an endearment. I tamped it down, grounded myself. 'Not yet. Gotta be on my way first. Like you are. Right now I'm just . . . lost.'

Malakai shifted so he could look at me properly, and tugged my chin between his fingers. His brow creased gently, disconcerted, framing a twilight of a gaze that stirred something hot and sure in my belly. His thumb gently swept across my lips as if to wipe the self-doubt from them, wanting me to taste his own confidence in me.

'Scotch, I'm at wherever you're at. You're Polaris itself to me. If I can see you? I know where I'm at. I know I'm good. Because you can never be lost. It's impossible for you. There's something in your core that always knows what you want. You just gotta . . . stay still for a bit. Let it come to you, you know? Look, you worked hard for your place there, and one thing I know about you is that you will *always* carve out a path. One of the things I'm most sure about in life. Like it's a religion or something.'

And love, blazing and blooming, pushed out a smile, pushed out a kiss. 'What that make you, a monk?'

His hand glided down my stomach teasingly. 'Let me at that holy water. See me bow my head in prayer.'

I snorted. 'Blasphemous bars.'

'Would you stay with me if I tried it to do it for real?'

'Be a monk? I don't think your boss would like the things I want to do to you.'

His eyes flashed hungrily. 'Let's revisit that, but nah. Music.' He cleared his throat and let his croaky morning off-key, somehow-still-sexy voice reverberate through my neck, releasing more want, 'How does it *feeeeeeeeeeeeel.*'

I wanted to know how it felt, right that second, but I released a play grimace at his D'Angelo imitation. 'Pitchy.'

I heard his lazy, yawning smile echo through the pores of my skin. 'Rah. So what I'm hearing is that you don't want to support a young Black man's dreams.'

'Not indiscriminately, no, but go to sleep and try again. Let's see what we can make work.'

He bit my shoulder, his laugh muffled. 'You're too rude. You think you're the only one with a wicked tongue, Scotch?'

A delicious threat. I stubbornly held on to my train of thought despite increased difficulty. It was almost an endurance test I liked to do for myself sometimes: how long can I think clearly while Malakai's mouth is on me?

'Besides,' I said, 'musicians don't try to be musicians. You don't suddenly one day discover you're a musician. You *are* it. Can't live without it. You just *do*. You just be.'

'Oh, is it? Got it. 'Skinda like loving Kiki Banjo. Ain't no trying. It just is. You just do.' His lips brushed a shiver through my ear. 'You just be.'

I failed the endurance test.

'Kai, do I feel hot to you?'

'That a trick question?'

'I'm being serious. I feel like I have a temperature.' I picked up his hand and pressed it to my right breast. 'You feel that, right? I think I'm coming down with something.'

Malakai's smile of realisation was slow and slanted, his dark eyes dancing as he gently squeezed. 'Yeah, actually. You're on fire. Probably need bed rest.'

'That's what I thought. Damn. I was so looking forward to sensitivity-reading a fictionalised memoir of a slave owner.' I picked up my phone and switched it on, ready to type out an email to my boss.

Malakai nodded as he pulled me into bed. 'Do you know the best way to break a fever?'

'Don't say sw—'

'Sweat it out.'

'That's a myth.'

'It's not. I'm a man in STEM – I know what I'm talking about.'

'Sure. OK. Did you get your doctorate from the same school as Pepper and Sebi?'

'I'm gonna ignore your sass for the sake of our relationship. For real, Scotch, I'm a medical science expert. For instance, I can induce amnesia. Watch how I'm gonna make you forget your own name in a few minutes. Just say the word.'

I grinned. 'Word.'

He tapped his ear. 'What?'

'Word.'

He shifted down the bed, slowly kissing down my stomach. 'Say it again.'

'*Word*.' I lifted up my hand and clicked like I was at a spoken-word recital. 'Word,' through a giggle. 'Word,' through a sigh. '*Wor*—'

Became lost.

CHAPTER 4

Case of the Ex

Bakari ❤️

*Kiki, babe. I know I said I was gonna come with you to Aminah's,
but I thought about it, and I'm not sure it's a good idea. I
don't want to put up a front while we're working through our
shit, you know? It's too hard. I do love you. You're everything
I could want. I think we just need a little space to re-learn
ourselves and know how to direct our energies to this relationship for the optimal outcome. There's a thing we do at
work called a 'unit test'. It's when the tiniest parts of an app
are scrutinised to see if they operate to their best capacity. It's
how we create the best product we can. This is just a version
of that. Love you deep and strong Keeks.*

*P.S. I sent some wine to the venue. Congrats to Kofi & Aminah
again.*

I squint at my phone screen as I hover at the threshold of the event space, holding it above the case of champagne I'm lugging and hoping the words magically rearrange themselves to 'so sorry, running 10 mins late babe, see you in a bit' because I *know* this man didn't bail on me just before my best friend's engagement party whilst talking about our relationship like it's a fucking app? Why was his love *deep* and *strong* enough to engage in mild PPR with me last week when I went to pick up some shoes I left at his (it was fun and fine and scratched an itch), but not enough to haul his very well-defined (he runs) butt here? My stomach swoops in disappointment, too fast for me to catch it, as I place my phone on top of the crate whilst elegantly balancing it on one knee. I need him here. To help me carry the inexplicable case of champagne Aminah ordered to my house, sure, because it would be lovely to celebrate my best friend's engagement with him, of course, but also because I can't help but think that meeting my ex for the first time in two-and-a-half years might be a little easier with my fine, rich 30 Under 30 boyfriend – *adjacent* person – here by my side. I don't think it's such a terrible thing to admit. I need – no, would *prefer* – for my ex to know that I wasn't languishing in heartbreak while he (undoubtedly) was fucking his way through LA with beautiful women called something like Clover. They probably did yoga regularly and not just after rewatching *Homecoming* and deciding that they needed to better their life by booking a discounted beginner's class for the fifteenth time. Unrelatedly, I did, once, through a burner Instagram account, watch his story and see a girl called Clover tagged. They were having a smoothie.

Since when did he drink *smoothies*? Her bio said 'Plant mama'. She was very beautiful and had a very bouncy-looking twist out, and bouncy-looking breasts, and she seemed primarily to live in cycling shorts and crop tops. She had videos teaching women how to open up their sacral chakras. Did Malakai open up her sacral chakra? I tried one of her tutorials and got a cramp.

Anyway, my point is, what's wrong with wanting to peppeh Malakai small? I try to steady my staggered breathing and calm my fury while I hoist the crate on my hip as it slips against the satin of my bronze cowl-neck dress. It's fine. *I* am fine. In at least two ways. I can do this. I'm a modern, independent woman who doesn't need a man to vex an ex. The gown clings to the steep and soft inclines of my curves and the bronzy hue calls out the warm tones of my skin; it's classy enough to be worn in front of aunties, but sexy enough to scatter a man's mind. More importantly, I know that it makes my bum look magnificent. Like the random case of champagne, I got this.

I gather myself, and make a note to send a picture of what I'm wearing to Bakari.

I step into the room that's clattering and thudding with movement as servers ready champagne flutes. Table legs scrape the terracotta tiling, adding depth to the throwback uptempo R&B playing through the speakers, welcoming the party in with the proclamation that roses are red, violets are blue.

It's gorgeous already. I'd scored the rooftop and terrace of a trendy East London hotel that I'd been to for an album listening party. It melds Aminah's elegance and Kofi's breezy cool.

Panoramic views of the city glow through airy atelier windows and lush chains of hearts cascade from a ledge below the arched ceiling, providing an enchanted feel enhanced by lamps of burnished gold. The luxurious woody in-house scent mingles with toasted-almond notes of champagne and the spicy welcoming warmth of Sákárà's food. I arranged mini versions of Kofi and Aminah's favourite foods: dollops of iyán in little pots with ẹ̀gúsí soup dropped on top, wagyu suya meatballs, plantain fritters and fresh puff puff/bofrot (both names used on the menu to prevent intra-West African war) dusted with cinnamon.

All the food arrived at the kitchen thirty minutes before me. I feel a tiny spike of triumph. This isn't bad considering that I had three (two and a half) weeks to organise and was dealing with a romantic estrangement and endless 'coffee and a catch-up' meetings every day with media acquaintances that led to nothing. What they really wanted, of course, was tea and what I want is a job. Of course, I never shared the real reason The Heartbeat is currently no more. I'm Yoruba, and we don't give people ammunition against us. My PR line, as vetted by Aminah, is this: 'It was an amicable split with SoundSugar, and I'm just looking for a new challenge now. Yes, I have seen the ad to Kitty St James's new podcast, *The Relationship Rhythm*, and, yes, I have seen that her first guest is Taylor Swift! Incredible for her! There's an audience for everyone,' finished with a sweet, impassive smile.

SoundSugar really wasted no time in trying to replace me. I wished them all the luck in hell with their bland, dry-as-a-roasted-yam-sandwich pastiche of my show. I would manage to keep this to myself.

Then, after my artful dodge, as the matchas arrive, I would expertly divert the thirst for dirt elsewhere – have you heard that this well-known girlboss memoirist used to have an affair with that internet manosphere hero who wears his trousers so tight it clearly cuts off circulation to his brain, leading him to make takes like 'drinking from a straw was invented to feminise men'?

They would leave satiated, and I would come across as personable enough for them to keep me in mind for potential job vacancies – but it would still just be *potential* and unfortunately potential is still not accepted tender for rent or mortgage.

I feel a coldness licking at the edge of my consciousness, making the warmth flicker. When Malakai and I broke up, I was determined to overhaul my life in every way I could with a fresh start. The first was a sunrise tattoo on the inside of my forearm, created with dashes, reminding me that the sun was constant, light was constant – I just needed to wait for it. Cliché probably, but every time I looked at it I felt proud that I'd found myself again, that I conjured my own light and, more importantly, that I'd made the ultimate act of eldest Nigerian daughter rebellion by getting a tattoo. I even enjoyed the pain of it: a sort of letting of the heartbreak that had seeped into my blood.

The second way was moving into the one bedroom flat above my parents' restaurant, the repurposed high-street terrace they'd scraped their savings to buy in the early nineties. We used to live there when I was a baby and moved out when my sister Kayefi was born eight years later – then it was reserved for relatives from Nigeria who said they were going to stay for two weeks and ended up staying for two years. When a great aunt had finally left a month after my split, I saw it as a perfect space for me to nestle into, in which to put my heart back together. I recruited the girls to help me paint my room a jade-white that Chioma assured me represented harmony, Aminah proclaimed as chic and Shanti admired from the sofa, where she sat as we painted, pouring us £6 rosé into mismatched mugs. I transformed the little alcove in my bedroom into a makeshift office, and it was here that I recorded the first Heartbeat episode.

My parents plan on selling the restaurant and keeping the flat, but, still, I need to find a way to continue to pay the remaining mortgage to make it worth it for them. Besides this, I can barely stand the idea of our restaurant potentially being taken over by a start-up eatery called White Men Can't Jollof, crowdfunded by two men from Devon in beards and flannel, let alone someone else living in the place in which my parents forged a life. The idea of leaving it makes me feel hollow. I've made it mine; it's where I cried myself to sleep and where I healed, opened myself up to love again by having sex for the first time with someone who wasn't *him*, tried new Instagram recipes for different variations of 'smashed potatoes and chicken', where my best friends piled into and got drunk during my first birthday without Malakai, falling asleep on top of each other on every available surface, and singing loudly to R&B girl-group classics. (Our cover of En Vogue's 'Don't Let Go' got a heckled, 'Go off, sisters!' from an open window.) For the first time in a while I feel a prick of panic at the back of my nose, the heavy threat of a loss of control. If I think too long about the fact that, on paper, I have no job right now, I'll pass out. This isn't me. I always have a plan – a path. I grab a hold of myself. In a way, focusing my energy on Aminah's wedding preparation is a great diversion from a quarter-life-crisis. This past week I didn't even have time to be captured by Eldest Second-gen Immigrant Daughter syndrome and scroll law-school webpages. I *did* look at some designer slingbacks I could potentially wear in an office before realising that I actually needed a job to pay for them.

'You're late.' The brisk chime of my best friend's voice cuts into my thoughts, and she appears, seemingly out of nowhere like the preternatural being she is, rushing towards me on a breeze of jasmine, peonies and the argan oil she used on her silk-press.

My breath catches for a reason other than the fact that I am still carrying six bottles of champagne in my arms. I put it down where I'm stood to properly take her in; and, when I do, the sight releases the strain on my heart, and it swells. Her hair falls and frames her doll-like face in loose, bouncy curls, and she looks like a 1940s Hollywood starlet in her cream silk slip and her delicate make-up of deep bronzy warmth, and brown-lined mink lip.

'You're *late*,' those lips repeat, and I can tell by the way they immediately press together that she's stressed so I ignore the fact that this is her greeting and say, with considerable calm:

'I'm literally right on time.'

'Which is late! You're co-bride, remember! We arrive together! Plus, you were late to the venue viewing earlier this week! And you left early too!'

I steady my breathing and keep my smile fixed. She's dealing with two African matriarchs – she cannot be in her right mind. I defang with an ease cultivated over ten years of friendship. 'Well, I've been working on this for two weeks and made sure everything was set up so I didn't think I was needed. I was fifteen minutes late to the viewing because I had a coffee with an editor. You know. For my job hunt. I left early because I had to cover another shift at the restaurant. Remember?'

She blinks, as if being startled out of a trance induced by an alien Bridezilla virus using her body as a host. 'Oh my gosh. Yeah! How did I forget that? I'm so sorry. I'm just a little . . . frazzled. What happened with the editor? Did she get back to you?'

I shrug. 'She said she'll get back to me if they have any openings, but she thinks my "vibe is great", which is code for she has absolutely nothing to offer me. But anyway.' I release my slight pique and brush it off with a smile. 'Can we focus on important things? Like . . . Meenz, do you still have a groom? Because my bro must have dropped dead the second he saw you. Turn round for me real quick.'

As predicted, the disturbance melts off Aminah's face and she preens and toddles in a circle on her stilettos that just about make her average height.

'Girl, *stahp*. Really? I can't even pretend. Who am I forming for? I do look good, don't I.'

As if summoned by the call of his girl feeling herself, Kofi approaches us, wrapping his arm round her waist from behind and dropping a kiss on her cheek. 'Enough to eat, actually. Shall we call this whole ting off?'

Aminah's smile seems to emit spindles of joy across her face now, lighting her up as she playfully swats him. They look amazing together: Kofi looking as sharp as his line-up, with gleaming deep skin and high cheekbones, decked in a sleek deep-navy suit paired with a crisp white button-down, and Aminah is grace and mischief, an angel on a rumspringa from heaven, making earthly men collapse to their knees. Aside from my parents, they have been my personal fairy tale, giving me hope. It's why, as a surprise, I've started making a scrapbook, writing their love story – the plan is to give it to them at their wedding, with the blank pages open, ready for guests to sign and stick Polaroids in.

Once upon a time, there was a beautiful Yoruba princess named Aminah Bakare with excellent taste in couture and a lack of patience for nonsense . . . Then she met the Fresh Prince of the South, Kofi, with excellent taste in women (he only had eyes for her) and wasn't about nonsense (she was the only thing that made sense to him).

The beautiful thing is that none of it was a lie. I'd been there from the beginning, and they'd adored each other from the moment they set eyes on each other at a stuffy student party in Whitewell University with sticky floors, thumping bass and dozens of other options. Their spirits flowed into the gaps within each other as other spirits flowed into mouths. Aminah had tried to fight it because she was scared of being so open, because she was scared of how easy it was – and at one point it had seemed as if Kofi was tired of waiting for her to fully accept what he had embraced immediately – but in the end, after a little push and pull, their spirits won out, rushing towards each other, over the risk of pain, over Aminah's stushness and Kofi's pride, because nothing could be more painful than being without each other. I love their love and I love my friend and I love how Kofi loves my friend and I love how that love wraps around her essence.

Right now, she preens, leaning into his arms before gently shoving him with her elbow. 'We can't cancel. Kiki worked way too hard on this.'

I'm a permanent fixture in their relationship, so much so that the two are almost *too* comfortable around me, making me audience to extreme acts of PDA – so I'm not surprised or offended that Kofi doesn't realise I'm standing right here until now.

When he does, though, he directs his wide beam to me, brotherly and welcoming. 'The Killa Keeks!' he hails, before unwinding his arms from his fiancée to wrap me in a bear hug. 'You smashed it, my sis. Thank you. This is incredible.' He drops his voice, muttering quickly, 'Also, warning, our queen is sensitive tonight – mum and sisters under one roof. You know how it gets. We might have to tag team it.'

I press my lips together in a knowing smile as he releases me, nodding infinitesimally, conspiratorial in our pursuit of protecting the woman we love from herself.

'It's no problem,' I say out loud in double response.

His smile broadens as he stumbles a little on the champagne on the floor. 'Wait – this from you?'

I frown in slight confusion as Aminah jumps in front of me. 'Um, yeah! Isn't that kind of her?'

'Real kind! Our Chief of Enjoyment. Let me help you with that.

Then we're getting you a glass. I'll give this to the kitchen.' Kofi picks up the crate and heads off as I shoot Aminah a quizzical look.

My best friend links an arm through mine and draws me further into the unfilled room. I only see her mum, sisters and a few of Kofi's cousins – and notably no ex-boyfriends – so we migrate to the corner with ease to stand near the sliding doors to the wrap-around balcony.

'Is there a reason you just lied to your fiancé now? You said you ordered that to my house because it would be complicated to do it to the hotel . . . though now I'm saying it out loud that sounds ridiculous—'

Aminah lowers her voice, eyes wide. 'It's not *lying* just . . . a delay of the truth. I ordered extra champagne in case. Using some of the money my parents gave us towards the wedding. And I know Kofi would moan about how we should save it or whatever, and how this engagement party was just supposed to be a "small drink up at the house", but what's next? I get married in a barn and we make our wedding toast with mason jars?' She shudders daintily with deep disgust and waves a hand, as if the thought is too atrocious to even entertain. 'Like, let's be serious. My sister's engagement party was on a yacht off the Amalfi coast. The same one Jay and Bey rented that time! I had to!'

I don't mention that her sister is also married to a hedge-fund manager. I don't exactly know what the job entails, but I do know it probably means easy access to Jay and Bey's love boat.

'And I could have told you this if we had got dressed together, like we were supposed to. You know that Kofi wasn't supposed to

98

see me in this outfit before the event – it's bad luck. The plan was to take two separate cabs from mine, but because you bailed he had to zip me up and we went in the same car, like we were going on a common date!'

Oh, whoa. Kofi was not exaggerating. My girl is *on* one tonight. She only gets like this when her older sisters have been pirouetting all over her nerves.

She takes a deep breath and continues: 'Not that I believe in bad luck. I believe in God and no weapon formed against me shall prosper.' Her manicured hand does a little twirl around her chest that's in the vague shape of a cross: a flash of pearly white piousness. The same girl who reminded me that there was to be no pork on the menu tonight, 'obviously'. She's my favourite Chrislim.

I clear my throat carefully, gingerly venturing into the patented MinahMeltdown.

'OK, well, first of all, I think that superstition is for the wedding, not the engagement party, anyway, and, second of all, we couldn't get ready together for the same reason I'm late. I was at the restaurant overseeing your order and making sure they got it perfect. Remember, the notice was shortened and we already had another order today . . .'

Aminah's eyes soften from mild annoyance to sincere affection, her shoulders sagging from the release of irritation as she pulls me into a tight hug, enveloping me with sweetness and the scent of the Hermes body butter I know she saves for special occasions.

'Don't mind me, sis. I'm sorry. I appreciate you – this place is amazing and I'm just hot because my mum has invited, like, a dozen aunties I don't know even though I very clearly told her the engagement party was really for *us* and our friends and we only invited our parents because we had to. They have *both* weddings! Traditional and white! I couldn't invite my nail tech because of capacity, but my ma can bring the lady she's sat next to *once* at a party? Like, if I knew aunties and uncles were gonna be there, your parents could have come!'

I shake my head and put my hands on her shoulders to calm her down, gently brushing a wayward curl from her face. 'Well, I wasn't going to say, but my parents *were* invited by yours. They just couldn't come tonight because they're visiting Kayefi in Nottingham. Secondly, I never mind you, but I am going to need you to calm down and get it together. Count to ten. Regular ten, not Beyoncé countdown ten – we're short on time. More guests will be arriving soon.'

Aminah slows her breath and closes her eyes as I grab her tiny hands and breathe with her. 'Now, we're going to enjoy tonight, yeah? You're marrying the love of your life – second to me, of course – and this is the launch party. It's stage one of this process and we can't lose our shit now. Gotta save our stamina. Let's at least wait till Kofi's mum insists on serving Ghanaian jollof at the wedding.'

Her eyes flutter open and she bites at her smile. 'Not funny!' Exhaling heavily, she nods to herself. 'OK. I'm better now. Thank you.' She assesses, then appraises me, a smile growing into a glitter on her face. She smacks my butt and squeals, 'Oh my gosh. How did I miss this? You look *fine* – you're about to send me into another panic attack! Did Bakari glitch when he saw you? Did he short circuit? Did he say you looked like an ancient Queen of Nubia as steam left his ears?' She frowns and stops, as if something just occurred to her. 'Wait. Where is he? I thought he was still coming despite your R&R.'

I stare at her for a few seconds, putting that sentence through my Minah Translator. R&R . . . Ross & Rachel . . . *On A Break*. I attempt to manufacture some breeze into my voice, pray that Aminah is too wrapped up in her night to detect the counterfeit nonchalance. 'Um. He couldn't make it – work, you know? No big deal. He sends an apology. And apparently he also sent some wine ahead here.'

'Oh!' She holds still for a fraction of a second before she nods and pushes out a smile. On the surface, she buys it – or she's biding time. Either way, I'm grateful. 'I was wondering where that case came from. Expensive shit. Tell him I said thanks. I've had some already. Tastes like what I imagine Roman emperors used to drink. Tech money is sweet.' She clears her throat, catching herself, and eyeing me warily. 'You OK, though? Because if you're not I'mma *finish* that low-rent Mark Zuckerberg.'

Unthinkingly, I reply, 'Mark Suckerberg.' Aminah grins. 'Oh good, a pun. That's my Killa Keeks. So you really are all right.'

'I am. We will be fine. I'm sure of it.' Kind of. 'And I was just riffing on the pun opportunity. He doesn't actually suck, OK? I don't want you to fuck him up, but, out of curiosity, how would you fuck him up, babes?'

Aminah shrugs. 'Sabotage, obviously. I'm gonna get a Rachel

Dolezal-type to infiltrate MelaninMatch or something. Then get someone to expose it. Gonna say that he, like, recruited counterfeit Black people to fill out the numbers of his app.'

I tilt my head to the side and stare at my five-foot-two best friend. For someone so physically compact, she truly harbours a lot of righteously bellicose energy. Like a Bichon Frisé raised by tigers. I've never stopped being in awe of it.

'You know, sometimes I feel like you could be the don of an organised crime group.'

'Duh. That's why the streets call me Minah Mafia.' There's an oblique beat, and then Aminah's eyes widen so much her lashes almost touch the edge of her immaculately threaded brows in panic. Minah Mafia was the nickname Malakai dubbed Aminah after we started going out, primarily because he was terrified of her, but really because with charm she could get anyone on campus to do what she wanted, like cajoling extra donations in her capacity as communications officer of Blackwell society and convincing the acapella group to move their rehearsal so we could have an extra hour to prep for an ACS social.

The name is also a reminder that our lives were folded together once, that my best friend was his friend and his best friend mine, and soon I'm going to have to confront that fact. My heart starts pounding like an 808 and I'm choosing to believe that it's because of the three matchas I've had today, not the impending Return of the Kai, because I'm cool, so cool about it, so past it, and yes, sure, recently, more memories of Malakai and I have crawled out to curl around my consciousness from the crevices in which I buried them, but that's nothing, merely evidence of an idle mind – maybe I *should* do a masters. Or take up sudoku.

Aminah steps closer to me, still holding my hands. 'Um, he's not here yet, but he will be soon.'

I push out a broad smile, and let go of her hand to link my arm through hers as I draw her back to the midst of the gathering party, pointedly away from her mother, who is attempting to get her attention so she can introduce her to an auntie. 'Good. I'm sure Kofi's missed him. Someone here should.'

Two hours into this party, he's still not here, and I still don't care. I couldn't even if I was inclined to do so. I have my hands full ensuring that Aminah's make-up stays the perfect grade between matte and dewy with the mini setting-spray I'm keeping in my clutch and interrupting any conversation she has with her sisters after seven minutes. This is the precise amount of time it will take for them to say something that will make her want to fight them. (The last thing that made Aminah want to scream was her sister saying she looked 'nice'. 'Nice? *Nice?* Would you call the Sistine Chapel *nice?*')

Besides this, there's too much to enjoy and focus on, for instance, Shanti, in her gorgeous, form-fitting, deep-navy strapless mermaid dress is flirting with Kofi's suited-up finance-bro cousin by the bar and they are the kind of pairing that is perfect for around ten minutes until he starts talking about how he loves and respects women, but they can't 'pick and choose' when they want to be feminist and he doesn't mind paying for everything if she also understands her 'divine feminine duty'. I have no doubt that he will try to diminish her entrepreneurship. He cornered me once at one of Kofi's birthday parties and told me that he was impressed by my ability to make a career out of 'nothing', which from someone else might sound like a compliment, but from him – a man whose perma-WhatsApp status is 'the grind neva stops' – sounded like he was congratulating a five-year-old on their lemonade stand. He will, of course, end up doused in alcohol at some point in the night, but the question is which one?

Right now, Shanti is still on the champagne. Long-term friendship equips you with intimate clairvoyance and so I know that in about thirty minutes she is likely to move on to rum and ginger beer from the bar downstairs.. Her university ex, our mate Ty Baptiste (a rugby jock turned sweet sports writer and Internet Golden Retriever Boyfriend ever since a clip of him being in unabashed professional awe of a female athlete went viral), is also set to arrive any minute now and I hear he's newly single so that could potentially make things even more interesting, given that he melts to broad-shouldered goo in Shanti's palm.

And then there's Chioma, decked in a silver lamé gown, sat on a low pink velvet cushy couch by a window with Aminah's twice-divorced fashion-designer Cool Auntie in a regal purple kaftan, grey twists to her waist and a gold stud in her nose. Chi Chi is nodding intensely, eyes narrowed and giggling, totally charmed and tucking away life lessons. Just a few minutes before now, she'd rushed to me and Shanti and gushed, 'Guys. I really think that she's my spiritual soulmate. Or my future self. I see so much of myself in her. Did you know that Fela was her lover? And she partly radicalised him?'

I fought the urge to say that in the seventies it wasn't too difficult to have Fela as a 'lover', and that though I adore Auntie Wura and wouldn't dare doubt her mind or her pussy power, I do kind of think that it is more likely that it was Fela's activist mother that radicalised him. Relevant information is that Auntie Wura also makes the assertion that David Bowie only married Iman because *she* rejected him. I didn't say all this, on account of Chioma seeming so gassed that she'd found herself a new muse and role model.

Instead, I said, 'Wow, that's amazing.'

Shanti stoically sipped her drink and enquired whether Chioma was high. She is, in fact, quite high. I can tell by the fact that I saw her sneak-eat a piece of suya, which means in about forty minutes I'm going to have to dissuade her from reading people's auras – something to which I don't think a room full of African elders would take kindly. Chioma once off-handedly said to Aminah's mother that she's 'such a Virgo', which led to Auntie Rafiat looking at her as if she might genuinely be a witch.

I'm sipping champagne with Aminah's mother now, by the tall, wide windows, the city lights forming a twinkling tapestry behind us. She's a formidable former executive at a Nigerian bank, who retired early to join her husband in running a snack empire, and her clan of three strong-willed girls are born of her spirit. I am simultaneously frightened of and obsessed with Auntie Rafiat, who is kind and warm in a regimented way, like a queen who has allowed you into her court. Her attention is graciously bestowed, not merely given. She blesses me with that focus now, graceful in her tailored blush-pink, long-sleeved and square-necked lace gown. She has a fuscia gele, and her ears and neck are bedecked in shimmering crystalline jewellery that I try not to believe are diamonds or my eyes will water. Her lips are painted in a glossy matching pink lipstick and they spread in a smile as she asks me how my family are doing ('well, thank you, ma – we thank God'), how work is doing ('working on an exciting creative project – we thank God', and she nods kindly as if any of those words mean anything to her. I didn't lie to her. Creating a job from thin air is somewhat exciting in an existential doom sort of sense).

'And how,' she enquires finally, 'is that young man of yours doing? In fact, where is he? He should be here.'

I don't feel like I can quite explain why he isn't to Auntie Rafiat, who is looking at me with an expectation that is somehow both calm and impatient, so I reply with:

'Bakari? Oh, he had a meeting.' I swallow the last of my champagne. 'In Tokyo.' An egregious lie, but I figure that placing the fictional meeting out of the country would make the idea of my boyfriend(ish?) missing my best friend's engagement party because of work less embarrassing. I soon discover that this is not the case because Mrs Bakare blinks at me with confusion that manages to be on Aminah's prescribed theme of *elegant*. Her blinks are shimmery and pink, faster than normal, but not so fast as to be *uncouth*.

'My dear,' she utters with genuine befuddlement, 'who is Bakari?'

She laughs a little, like I'm an eccentric kook just saying names at her, and the question is immediately dismissed – she doesn't give a fuck who Bakari is, actually, and I am not to waste any time explaining. 'I am talking,' she continues, 'about Malakai.'

'Oh.' I put my empty glass on a passing tray and swap it out for a full one. It is an action I immediately regret, because almost imperceptibly to those not well versed in the body language of Judgemental Auntie, Mrs Bakare's gaze follows my movements, fast as a hummingbird wing, labelling me a drunken lout. There are a couple of things that might be happening here.

- I am an idiot for thinking that Auntie Rafiat has retained any information about my love life, the fact that I have had the grand total of two boyfriends my entire life not-withstanding. She met Malakai at Aminah's second-oldest sister Damola's wedding, and therefore that is who my boyfriend is. Why should I expect her to keep up with my revolving door of men? She's a busy woman with Nigerian Women in Business conferences to attend and facilitate in Houston, Atlanta and Lagos.
- She remembers and does not approve. I showed her a picture of Bakari the last time I told her about him (three months ago) and all she replied was, 'Hmm. OK. God is with you as you make your decisions, my daughter.'

One thing I know for certain, however, is that neither option demands me correcting her. In fact, she might actually find correction offensive.

So I decide upon, 'I am not sure, ma.'

She nods with a little disappointment. 'Ah. That's a shame. Nice boy. A handsome boy. I liked the way you smiled around him. With your whole body. Light and free. I wanted to ask him when it will be your turn.' She says this with a broad, warm smile as my blood makes a mockery of biology and physics and cools and heats up simultaneously. I feel a little light-headed suddenly, and there's a time warp, years and events contracting into a tight shock at the fact that a future that was once so certain slipped beneath my feet, made me fall and flail into the unknown.

There was a time where we could have sworn we were going to get married. Where he would have been by my side and would have replied to Auntie Rafiat with, 'As soon as she allows me, ma. I've been waiting,' his smile sloping, his gaze glinting at me with a light I knew, I swore I knew, a light that I had said 'let there be to.'

I'm dizzy, confused, disorientated for a split second, wondering how I got here, to Kofi and Aminah's engagement party, without him, without us. It feels as if it's a dream that I'm supposed to wake up from, like these past few years were a hyper-realistic hallucination during a fever, and I'm going to open my eyes in his bed, his arm slung over my stomach, a single eye of his flickering open and beaming light, his lips smiling at the sight of me, rolling out a syrupy, 'Mornin', Scotch. How you feeling, baby?'

Shit, how did I get here? Too much champagne. I've definitely had far too much champagne.

As if my best friend can sense my mood shifts in her own blood,

Aminah appears next to me in a second, arriving in a cloud of gourmand and floral scents, like Tinker-Bellanaija, her arm linking through my own and squeezing me to her side in protection.

'Hey, babe! It's time for your speech!' Her eyes widen pointedly, and she nods just enough for me to catch it.

I dip my chin too. 'Oh . . . yeah! Of course. So sorry.' I curtsey before Auntie Rafiat. 'Excuse me, ma.'

At her mother's angled and sceptical brow, much like her own, Aminah drags me through the light smattering of people to the front corner of the room, before turning to me with soft concern, both hands reaching for my elbows as she looks me in the eye kindly but firmly, a paramedic checking for bruises on a cyclist knocked over by a Bentley.

'Oh God, what did she say to you, Keeks? Ask you when you're going to get married? If you've considered law school? Say that you're a little thicker round the waist? Ask you to like her post on LinkedIn?'

I smile grimly. 'The first. Except she was talking about me marrying Malakai.'

Aminah groans and rolls eyes identical to her mother's. 'Ugh! I'm sorry. She's so annoying. I've told her time and time again you're with Bakari! You'd think she would approve because he's in Forbes! I showed her the piece! I think the tattoos and the wide-neck shirt he wore in the headshot let him down in her eyes. Remember when she asked me how long I had been "living the life of a wayward child" when she noticed my daith piercing for my migraines? She's just extra.'

109

I snort at this, my momentary mania abating with a dose of Minah Magic, my breathing slowing. 'Nah. It's fine, but why does she like Malakai so much? He's a director!'

Aminah shrugs. 'I mean, sure, Malakai is a director, which she does not consider a real job, but he was polite and made her laugh and took great pictures of my sister's wedding and prostrated when he met her and fixed a plate for my great-aunt, so I guess his home training went a long way. You know she's a sucker for home training.'

I make some sort of congenial sound, because my mind has now ricocheted firmly back to Malakai, who I am *relieved* is not here – where the hell is he, though? Does he think he's too Hollywood to show up to his best friend's engagement party? The Malakai I knew wouldn't have. Well, the Malakai I thought I knew. I clear my throat and my head of him. 'You enjoying your night, though?'

Aminah beams. 'Yes, thank you, boo. It's going great and I haven't slapped a single sister thanks to your excellent interruption system.'

'It was a close call, though, when I heard Laide ask if you had a second dress option.' Aminah throws an irritated look at her second eldest sister, looking like her but stretched, more hollow to her cheeks, nose a little less button, as she fires strict orders to a waiter to get her a cosmopolitan despite Aminah being firm in only wanting to serve wine here.

'Whilst wearing my shoes, no less. Witch. Can you imagine, she's unironically ordering a cosmopolitan in *my* shoes. So tacky.

110

Who orders a cosmopolitan? Are we in *Sex and the City*? She's so *old*.'

I refrain from double-checking whether it's still true that Laide is only two years older than Aminah.

I smile instead, translating the Aminah Speak. When there's a major shift in the Bakare sisters' lives, there is some tension, for unobvious reasons. It's not necessarily because of envy or competitiveness, or because of stolen dream wedding venues (although that has been an issue) – it's because they're terrified of it affecting their relationship to each other. The sisters are close in a non-cutesy manner, having each other's backs but fighting all the way.

'*Please*. There's no way she'd be able to even access those shoes if you didn't lowkey want her to.'

'Because I am the Saint in Yves Saint Laurent.' Aminah sighs like the martyr she is, and lets her gaze drift to Kofi, who is quietly nodding and chatting within a cluster of miscellaneous bros. He's smiling, but he is a little more subdued than he usually is when he's with his boys.

'I feel kind of bad for Kofi,' Aminah says as she turns back to me. 'He's having a good time, but he's a little . . . muted today. I thought it was because he's just a bit shy in front of my family, but I just clocked it whilst being with you. It's because his best mate isn't here. He's trying to hide it, but he's disappointed.' Her eyes narrow as she shakes her head, sleek, silk press and wavy extensions swishing like water. 'Man, I could *kill* Malakai Korede. When I catch that boy, ehn! So is it because he's a bigshot director he now thinks he can miss his boy's engagement party?'

111

Aminah is evidently *very* annoyed, because her accent has slipped from neutral posh to Lagosian posh. 'I went on Instagram and I saw him on that actor's stories – what's his name, Monae Noble? That overacting *goat* from that Motown show? They were at some party. If I find out that he missed his flight because he was *hungover* and doing body shots off some model's navel, he's going to have to square up to me! Doesn't he know that Ty is waiting in the wings to take his place? I—' Aminah's fully loaded now, about to unleash her clip of insults, but something must have flitted across my face, because her eyes flicker in apology. 'Oh—'

I push a smile out at her, hoping the force would repress the imagery of Malakai licking body shots out of the grooved abs of a woman who probably makes videos like 'Day in the Life of a Plant Whisperer and Choreographer' in a sultry whispering cadence. 'I think it's time for my speech.'

'Now, my girl has never been an outdoorsy type. In fact, I would say that Aminah's idea of camping would be staying in a hotel that hasn't got a pool.'

There's a warm smattering of laughter that ripples across the fifty-odd people in front of whom I'm standing as Aminah leans further into Kofi's arms and nods with a cute little unrepentant tick of her shoulder.

'That being said, I always knew there would come a day when my brother Kofi would gift her with a very . . . *very* large rock, and that she would accept.'

Whoops swirl around the room and wrap themselves around the couple as Aminah lifts her hand up, flexing it in the royal wave.

Kofi props her arm up with a triumphant, 'Yeah, you didn't know that man's a geologist?'

I laugh and nod. 'Yeah, also a great DJ and producer. I don't like complimenting men, but I will give my brother that. And the thing is Kofi has always been good at blending. He used to help out on my radio show, help create mixes, and he would always know what songs would feed into each other, which would amplify one another, bring out the harmony, the feeling . . . which would *speak* with each other. And I truly believe that when he saw my beautiful, darling sister that first time at a uni party, doing her cute little two step and shimmy – you know the one – probably wiping down a seat before sitting down, sipping on her amaretto and pineapple, he knew they would make the right blend. Feed into each other. Make each other better.'

Aminah and Kofi moon at each other, and the tenderness drapes heavy on my throat, making my voice harder to haul out. I push through it.

'. . . unlike amaretto and pineapple,' I add.

Aminah releases an indignant 'Hey!' that I gleefully ignore.

'Kofi is breezy, and Aminah . . . well, she ain't, as we well know.'

Mirth ripples across the room as I zero in on my best friend's face, as dazzling as the ring on her finger, as her soul, as the love she gives to those who she deems worthy. 'But she's a wildflower. Beautiful, defiant, blooming wherever she finds herself, knowing who she is. Her place is wherever she is, and she owns it. Man, does she own it.' Aminah's eyes shimmer and she releases Kofi's hand to make a heart shape with her fingers in my direction. I reply with two taps on the left side of my chest with two fingers. 'And, the thing is, the breeze, it needs the wildflower to help give it direction, something to flow through, and the wildflower . . . well, the breeze reminds it to bend, to twirl. They're perfect together.' Kofi drops a kiss on Aminah's temple, squeezes her to him, and she rubs his arm. An internal pressure amps up and I feel my eyes begin to mist. 'Now, uh, I'm gonna save my good stuff for the wedding toast, but—'

'I'm sorry – that wasn't your good stuff? You already have us on the ropes. Mercy, please.' Shanti heckles me from where she's stood on the other side of the crowd, to a rumble of chuckling, dabbing the corner of her eyes with the edge of a curved index as Chioma teasingly pinches her waist and throws an arm round her.

'. . . but they have something special,' I continue. 'And—' I look back into the crowd and the words I'm about to say fizzle on my tongue, the heat of his presence evaporating them into nothing. My eyes automatically snapped in his direction, not even knowing what they were being drawn to, but knowing, still.

I will always know. The air seems to shift, make way for repressed feelings that are agitated to the surface, and it seems to have shifted *away* from me because I can barely breathe. I swear I can even smell him – wood and amber and resentment. I know, because, for better or for worse, my body reacts to his presence, acetone on a papercut. My heart hisses. There are footsteps as he comes further into the room, firm, swift steps that judder against my heartbeat. Heads turn to look and a good number of the female heads stay a little while, because that's what Malakai does, he turns your eyes sticky and your heart tacky, clinging on to him, so that you get stuck, *tangled*—

Fuck, why *now*? He picks up a champagne flute from a nearby tray and that's when he looks at me and pins the remaining straggles of air I have to my ribs. I feel as if I'm being lanced with a honey-dipped blade. I almost buckle. It isn't lost on me that the last time I was standing in front of my peers giving a speech it was to declare my undying love for him. My hand slips a little on the flute and I grip it tighter.

His face, the face I haven't seen in the flesh in two-and-a-half years, is inscrutable. Time hasn't etched it, but instead brought out things it was supposed to. His cheekbones are still steep, but his jaw is wider now, covered with a beard as plush as a night sky, glistening, and his skin is an undisturbed pool of dark elixir that looks like something you can lap at for refreshment; in fact, I used to. His deep eyes carry no love, no hate, but something strong and intense, wrapped in clingfilm to preserve it or maybe to keep out . . . Keep me out. I thought I was ready, but, as it turns out, I Am Not Ready. I need to somehow expel my spirit from my body right now, and unfortunately the only way to do that is to die. I contemplate it for a few seconds (by holding my breath for a long, long time), but I decide against it for many reasons including, but not limited to:

- I cannot die because of *man*. Embarrassing.
- I cannot die in front of Aminah's mum. Even more embarrassing.
- I cannot die because of man in front of Aminah's mum. Disgrace to my family.
- I cannot die at Aminah's engagement party, because she would break her No JuJu stance to conduct a séance so she can bring me back to life just to kill me again.

Aminah has now noticed Malakai and immediately glances back at me, eyes huge with slight alarm and hefty concern and I am reminded that I need to speak – fucking *speak*, Kiki! I use my anger to melt down the blade in me, pour it over my voice so it sounds firm and I focus on anyone but the Someone.

'Um, as I was saying, it takes some bravery to hold on to something as big as what Aminah and Kofi have. To not let it go. Not everyone has what it takes.'

I flick a look across the room now. Malakai's face is a placid lake, but the corners of his lips twitch, perceptible only to those with the knowledge of what that mouth can do.

'So let's make a toast.' I raise a wobbly hand, but keep my voice steady because my heartbeat ain't and my knees ain't and my brain definitely ain't, so something has to be. 'To Aminah and Kofi. And to not letting go.' Unfortunately, my gaze, rebelling against my restraint, snaps to Malakai's as his lips mouth, 'To not letting go.'

He drains his flute and shoots me a look that's just as empty.

CHAPTER 5

Sprezzatura

'Man like King Korede!' – a bellow from Ty, deep, booming and resonant, taking me back to humid-sultry-hectic house parties at his country house and me on Malakai's lap. Now, the hail is deployed at the sighting of the Long Lost Brother done good, returning from the land of almond milk and money, from Brixton to LA and back to hometown glory. Ty bops towards Malakai through the clearing throng, tall and broad meeting tall and newly broad from abroad, two of Blackwell's former eligible bachelors reuniting. South London and Egbaland's son smiles the smile that tips his face from handsome to dangerous. It's bright, disarming, sloping, looking for companionship, inviting you to join. He does not shine it my way. Maybe it's because he knows I know it's bullshit, maybe it's because I know what it looks like when it's not trying. I stand a little away from the cluster of hugs and spuds, at a safe distance, talking to the very few people who have resisted his draw.

I murmur, 'Ah. Thanks so much. I mean, their love inspired it, really,' to everyone who says a nice thing about my speech – at least I think that's what they're saying, and I think that's how I reply. I can't be sure, on account of my heartbeat thumping amapiano in my ear. Yebo, there seems to be something hard and thin and sharp lying in the middle of my chest, and any wrong move would have it sinking into my flesh.

I'm supposed to be OK.

He shakes hands and hugs our old friends like a politician on a campaign tour and I try to focus on the people before me, but they seem to be a blur of colourful features, try as I might. And so, to check if my eyes are working properly, in an effort to be health conscious, I allow my gaze to sneak in his direction, test them out. This is not a hallucination. There he stands, in 20/20, 4K, the crew's Golden Boy, glinting handsomely, rudely sexy, obnoxiously comfortable, taking up space outside my head, far outside my heart.

Kofi approaches him casually, his excitement consciously measured as he greets him with, 'Oga,' and a playful dọbalẹ, to which Malakai lobbies a 'Chief!' punctuated with a salute. The groom-to-be, not to be outdone with the hailing, returns with a 'General,' before Malakai opts for an exotic, jovially deployed 'El Jefe!' It's this that breaks the fourth wall, and they tumble through, it, laughing, bringing forth a coda of daps and hand claps and finally a hug, with forceful thumps to the back.

'Hello? Earth to Kiki!' I jump, my best friend's voice penetrating the inner din of what I am mature enough to recognise is an emotional freakout. Aminah's waving a hand in front of my face, as she holds out a flute of champagne to me with a slight frown.

I take it with some gratitude. 'Um, hey, you good?'

Aminah's brows hoist as she watches me empty the flute in approximately two seconds flat. 'Um, hey yourself. Are *you* good, sis?'

I push out a smile. 'Yeah. Yeah, I am. I mean it's *weird*, but I'm good. In a way I'm glad he's here. Look how wide Kofi's grinning.'

Aminah darts an eye over to the boys. 'Yeah, I guess I'm glad Kofi's got his husband back. Takes some pressure off me.' I choke out a laugh and Aminah shakes her head as she surveys the scene. 'Man. Malakai's got ugly as hell. Very clapped. That Equinox membership and those green juices have not been kind to him. You made a lucky escape. What's the new skincare craze in LA right now? Octopus snot?'

'Shark semen.'

'It's eating him alive.'

I pause, note the telling quirk in her lips, the glint in her eye. A blessed friend is one who knows the time to tell a blatant lie to make you feel better.

I pantomime a shudder. 'An ogre. You sure you want him in your wedding pictures?'

'Hmm. Will photoshop him out.'

Our eyes snag and our giggles erupt and melt over my tension and then I'm OK. I swear, I'm OK.

'MinaaaahMafia!' As if Malakai's ears were burning, his eyes roam over to Aminah – and pointedly only Aminah – hand curved

119

round his mouth in a makeshift megaphone, his smile as broad and welcoming to her as it is hostile to me. It's the first time in almost three years I've really heard his voice, and the low caramel sound, smooth and decadent, flows into grooves in my psyche, knowing its way around, disturbing peace. He looks as if he's about to approach, but Aminah squeezes my elbow surreptitiously, immediately going to him, I know, to evade the awkwardness of him having to come up to us (me). She allows for a ginger side-hug and a peck on the cheek before stepping back from him, managing to tower over Malakai despite being almost a foot shorter than him. Her arms fold across her chest as she looks up at him, brow arched.

'Well, look who it is. The prodigal ashewo.'

Malakai is easy, he is always so *easy* – how dare he be so easy – my blood is spiked and heated as his smile warms with genuine affection for the girl I know he loves like a sister and who he also slightly fears.

'Our bride! Lovely to see you too, Lady Aminah. Why am I an ashewo again?'

'Without Kiki's protection, you revert to how I saw you before. A wanton slag.'

Malakai's face only twitches slightly at the mention of my name, but his expression remains perfectly placid. For some reason, I'm rooted to the spot. His brow rises with bemusement in a way that used to send flutters to my belly. I have flutters in my belly now, but that's just due to the inner battle between homicidal feelings and too much champagne. 'Wanton?'

'I've been reading Kiki's historical romances.' Aminah has now

120

mentioned me twice. She's testing him, and the unspoken, '*speaking of historical romance*,' chimes loudly.

Malakai doesn't bite into the bait, doesn't trip, doesn't stutter, his demeanour as chill as ever, as he says, 'I've really missed you, Meenz.'

'And it's so kind of you to finally grace us with your presence, Newbie.'

He scratches the back of his head, having the grace to look sheepish. 'I am so, so sorry—'

'As you should be,' she clips, before releasing a sweet smile, capping the edge of her words.

If Malakai catches the shot, he doesn't show it. He doesn't seem to have missed a beat, sliding into the gap left in the group by his absence, so comfortable, so unbruised. Then, with the smile of a residual laugh on his face, his eyes drift, catch mine, dark gaze inscrutable. My chest jerks. His smile holds rigid, but reduces by the smallest fraction. Then it raises again, hooking my breath to it. It's not amiable – it's a challenge. Who is going to be the bigger person?

The elephant in the room trumpets, garnering the attention of my friends, who, without realising it, start to bounce surreptitious glances between Malakai and I, trying to see which one of us will smash the ice. I suddenly really need to pee. And look in the mirror. Check my lips, check my tits, but I can't – I have to win this – and I push out an unbothered smile on my face, powered by the fact that I am very fucking bothered. I step forward, the heels of my slingbacks working as an ice pick, smashing the ice between us, but Malakai moves too, smooth with it, long strides, sure footed. We meet in the middle of the floor.

I'm not too big to admit that I'm momentarily disorientated by his proximity when I stop in front of him. Of course, Malakai has managed to be approximately 2.75 times more attractive than the last time I saw him, when he was already insanely attractive. Right now, I can't help but feel that this is to spite me. Breaking my heart wasn't enough – he had to go ahead and get finer too. It's not like I wanted him to look like he'd felt a gaping gap where my love once resided that shows in the hollows of his eyes, but does he necessarily have to *glow* like this? We get it, bro. Your skincare routine is ascorbic acid, Jaws's jizz and freedom from my clutches. His crisp white button-down shirt is slightly creased – he obviously dressed quickly – but he makes it look deliberate, snug in his aura of careless sauce. It fits him perfectly, confidently, not too tight, but fitted enough to let me know that he's more filled out now. Thicker, more muscular. It suits him. He's grown. Well-tailored black tapered trousers brush his leather brogues, and he smells warm, a woodsy scent of black pepper and cognac and the fire in my veins. His beard frames his mouth, full and healthy, a masterpiece you want to trace. It now curves like a scythe.

'Kiki Banjo. The one and only.'

The low grit of my name on his tongue pricks into my pores like hot prongs. I call on my cool, and tilt my head casually, like I'm not trying to drain the effect of his voice from me.

'Aw. Did you search for others in your travels?'

He releases a low chuckle. 'Nah. I figured that one was more than enough for a lifetime.'

It's a tilted comment. What he means is that he's had his fill. I won't rise to his bait. I glance at the inexplicable glass of whisky he has in his hand. *So* pretentious, with his preference for 'black coffee' and 'neat' drinks. I know people think it's a sign of dependability and confidence, but have we ever considered that the eschewing of flavour is a sign of very mild sociopathy? Maybe I should actually do a masters in psychology and make that my thesis question.

'How did you bribe the bartender? We're only serving wine here. You know, because of what happens when Auntie Wura gets a hold of brown liquor.'

'Oh, I remember from Aminah's sister's wedding. She pinched my ass.'

'You loved it.' It slips out without permission, my words falling in step with an ancient rhythm, despite the storm brewing in my thorax.

Malakai nods, face straight. 'I mean I really came here for her. She's the one who got away.'

The second that follows is silent except for the screeching Unsaid, starved of attention. Malakai clears his throat, and scratches his nose, his gaze darting behind my head before meeting mine again. 'I slipped to the bar downstairs. Asked for the second finest scotch in this place.'

A smile licks on the inside of my mouth. I keep it trapped. 'You proud of that?'

'Extremely. Brainstormed it on my way here.'

'I hope you know that you're a fool.'

'I mean you haven't been around to remind me. How was I supposed to remember?'

Malakai's doing his patented charm evasion. Thankfully, I've built immunity. We're not good. This is a pastiche of good. It's inevitable that, even in the dark, even in the apocalypse, even with the sun vanished, our rhythm would feel its way back to each other. We are capable of falling into step without our arms brushing, without our hearts touching. It means nothing. This is just the way we're wired. I pull back, just in case.

'Why were you late?'

His eyes cloud briefly, but it quickly clears. 'Flight delayed.' He raises his glass to his lips, looking at something behind me as he asks, 'Your man not here? Was looking forward to meeting him.'

Bullshit. He just wanted to state that he knows I have a man and he doesn't give a fuck. Well, I don't give a fuck that he doesn't give a fuck.

'Delayed.' The lie slips out easily. The truth of my complicated relationship status is the last thing I want to discuss with my ex in front of whom I am determined to project a post-break-up self that is well adjusted and self-actualised. As far as he needs to know, I'm thriving. Can't keep a baddie down, etc. Malakai's eyes flash and run across my form, disorientating my heartbeat. Only a couple of seconds have passed, but it's enough for heat to surge through me, for every hair on my body to stand to attention and my blood to rise like a high tide to his moon. How long does ovulation last again?

'The guy who called me "Scotch",' I say, changing topic, 'was actually thinking of the pepper.'

Kai's eyes glimmer a little, the light restrained, but present. 'Small but mighty. Adds flavour. Brings a grown man to his knees. Yeah, it makes sense.' His eyes quickly flick across me like a match, leaving a trail of fire in its wake. 'But the drink works too. Potent, can make a man feel dizzy, disorientated. Gives him a headache.' His brow arches and I nod and release a caustic smile. We're here already. Skipping right past civility. Cool.

I meet his gaze. 'Can also make a man forget his own name.'

Malakai stills and something shutters over the intensity in his eyes. It occurs to me that Malakai and I haven't been together, but *untogether* in five years. He left right after we broke up, and I realise that my body is recalibrating to the new energy between us, new tensions that jut against a comfort, fighting to be released. His gaze is a kaleidoscope of emotion, and nothing stays still long enough for me to identify it, but I can feel the heat, the pressure of whatever the feelings are, burning into me.

My lips twist. 'It's been a while.'

'Too long.'

'I wouldn't say that.' It's razored, quick, and I pause, as I remember our surroundings, the audience of our friends, adding, 'It's good to see you.'

His smile is sharp enough to almost pull me out of myself. 'Is it?'

'I'm being polite.'

'I prefer you rude.'

'It's *great* to see you.'

125

His lips allow for a gentle flick at the right corner, hooking into the left side of my chest. There's a hole already there, a battle wound. His smile stretches, but it isn't friendly. None of this is friendly. This is us fighting without fighting. We're both angry, I know, but we're letting our latent language do the work. We can do that – we've always been good at that. Our sentences will always curl around each other. That was always the easy part.

Nearby, our friends surreptitiously watch this duel, sipping their drinks, rapt by the reunion they thought they'd never see.

We drifted apart.

Without knowing it, Malakai and I had a PR line. The last scraps of our connection worked to bond us in the lie. It didn't really make any sense. Malakai and I didn't have a love that was capable of becoming brittle and thin enough to snap. Our love was many things, but flimsy wasn't one of them. We were stubborn in our own ways, we bickered, he clammed up and I lashed out, but the material of which our bond was made wouldn't allow us to drift. It needed a severance, a brutal tectonic cleaving. Our love was obtrusive and decadent. It coated us, soaked us and maybe that was the issue. It overwhelmed us, bent our bones till we broke.

Aminah knows a little more, but at the time it was too raw for me to intricately unpack without bleeding out more – so I told her the Cliff Notes, and as time went on and I healed further I was terrified of regression, terrified of reinfection, so I kept details to myself.

We drifted apart.

Besides, *I* barely know what happened. All I really know, all that matters, is that one day we were, and the next we were not.

One day my heart was intact, the other it was scattered into so many pieces I still don't know if I've got all of them back. I need to protect what I've got left. We're standing with a notable gap between us and Unsaids fill the space. Malakai's eyes scan me with idle curiosity, a quick lick of my face, my form, that jarringly leaves flaming trails that makes my nipples pucker in alertness. I sway into the still. Oh. Absolutely not. This is just my body recalibrating to the shock of being around him. Which means I need to not be around him.

I step back. 'Well. I'm sure you have people that would love to catch up with you. I'll leave you to it.'

'Look, Kiki. This doesn't have to be weird.'

I release a little huff of humour. 'We were doing so well pretending it wasn't till you said that.'

Malakai pushes a hand in his pocket, in what is a vexingly sexy move and tilts his head. 'Were we?'

I clear my throat. 'Fine, yes. Clearly, it's a little awkward, and obviously we can't be like . . . *friends.*' The word feels sharp. It grazes my heart in my throat on its way out. 'But –' I force a breeze into my words, which is a true miracle, because I feel kind of airless inside – 'we just need to doula our best friends down the aisle and help throw them a Big Fat West African Wedding. That's our only job. To love them through this and keep the peace. This isn't about us. We communicate to facilitate activities.'

Malakai nods in agreement. 'We're colleagues.'

'Acquaintances,' I affirm.

Malakai's mouth lopes in a dangerous slope that's as playful as a knife suspended in the dark. 'Just try not to be distracted by the fact that you've seen me naked. It's unprofessional.'

I squint into the air in thought, tilting my head.

Bemusement colours his face. 'What are you doing?'

'Trying to pick you out in my mental line-up of torsos and dicks.'

Malakai's laugh is satisfyingly low and deep and I resent the flutter it elicits in my core. 'Wow. You know, Kiki, acting like I'm not memorable isn't a lie I would go with. Go for something believable at least.'

I maintain my perplexed look. 'Remind me real quick, were you the one with the –' I curve my hand slightly – 'Oh, wait, that was . . .' I release a slow smile in feigned recollection. 'Well, never mind.'

Malakai shakes his head slowly, eyes twinkling in challenge. 'Nah, I get it. Telling yourself you don't remember is how you console yourself over the loss.'

I laugh loudly, as if what he's saying is ridiculous, and that I am not, in fact, lying through my teeth, because of course I remember. In fact, I probably remember too much, if I'm going to be honest. Which I won't be doing. 'Thank you for your concern, but I'm good. Well taken care of.'

'What a relief, because, you know, that *was* a primary concern of mine. I would lie awake at night, thinking, *Man, you know what? I hope Kiki's getting her back broke tonight.*'

I match the dryness in his voice. 'Oh, so you're saying I have you to thank for my orgasms?'

'Well, it wouldn't be the first time.'

Unfortunately, I flew into that, a silly little bird into

floor-to-ceiling windows in the form of a tall, handsome, broad headache of a man. I repress the primal leap to open my mouth and respond to this, but the embers in his gaze make the words turn to ash. I briefly flick my eyes to the bauble lights above us in an eye-roll and conjure new words.

'You must not remember who I am, Malakai. I *know* you. And you can't do your smooth pretty fuckboi shit on me—'

'So you still think I'm pretty—'

I ignore the shit-eating curve of his lips. 'I'm not one of your LA septum-piercing plant mum girls who hear your accent and get weak at the knees, because they think you're Damson Idris.'

'Kiki, this is the second time you've called me peng in five seconds. And I'm hencher than Damson Idris. Also, that's very specific. You been stalking the girls I've been seeing?'

Please. So arrogant. It was once, and it was over a year ago. I ignore him.

'They're not seeing your face. They're just hearing your accent. They hear one "innit" and start shaking. Anyway, I've seen what you're like around cats. You can't be on your gyalis shit around someone who has seen you freak out when one brushes up against your leg.'

Malakai actually shudders, his eyes shadowed by a faraway haunted look. 'Fur demons.'

I shake my head, and a surge in my chest pushes out a smile. This shouldn't be happening. I reduce my smile drastically, and clear my throat, hoping it will push down the disturbing hot shock in my chest.

'Anyway. We communicate when we have to. There isn't much crossover between our duties until the day so it should be fine.'

'I bet you have a whole folder dedicated to the wedding. Google docs. Shared drives. All specifically labelled. Maybe even colour coordinated.'

I blink. 'How else would I do it? Like, genuinely asking.'

'That's my girl.' Malakai's eyes flicker before he clears his throat. 'I mean—'

'I know what you mean.'

'*That's the girl who used to be my girl, but blew up our relationship* is a mouthful.'

My awkwardness calcifies into something brittle. 'Oh yeah? Is this really what we're gonna do right now, Malakai? Because if you want to go let's go.'

Malakai's face is irritatingly tight. 'I was joking, Kiki.'

'Yeah. You should have a stand-up special. Think Eddie Murphy's *Delirious* except it's called *Delusional* because I wasn't the one who walked out.'

I know I should drop it, know it isn't worth it, that it's better for us to float on either side of the abyss and not brawl till one or both of us falls, but I can't help the indignation that licks at my tongue and makes it leap.

Malakai pauses and I see a thought darken his face before he releases a chuckle broken jaggedly in half, its edges sharp and serrated, scraping across my skin.

'Nah. You were just the one who pushed me out.'

It smarts and I'm stricken. I'm careening back to the apocalypse.

130

My skin is burning and the hurt sours into anger, because anger I can hold without it eroding my strength, anger I can control and lobby back to him. My voice is a thin hiss.

'You know, Malakai, I have a lot of strength because I've done one and a half reformer Pilates classes –' and almost died – 'but even *I* can't push out somebody who don't already wanna leave—'

'You have no idea what I want to do, Kiki.' Malakai's gaze flits across me and I supress an errant, insolent shudder that grates across the fact that I want to throw my drink in his face. 'Then, or now,' he continues, 'because if you did you would know that I don't have to be out here tryna make peace with someone I don't really want to be around.'

I roll my eyes, ire pushing me closer to him, the silk of my dress brushing against his chest. I use the heat that rushes through me at the contact to power my words, harnessing renewable energy, a regular Greta Thirstberg.

'Oh my God, spare me. Thank you so much for your philanthrophic efforts. I'm sure you'll be awarded a Noble Peace Prize, Dumb-Dumb Tutu. It wasn't by force to come talk to me so why are you here? I don't control you.'

Our faces are inches apart, and Malakai's eyes dance across my features, soft mouth set firmly, the severity warring the illicit play of his gaze. It makes me want to step back, because it makes me want to step closer.

His eyes return to rest firmly on mine, opaque, heavy. 'You're right. This was a mistake. I thought we could be civil.'

'Nah, Malakai, you *thought* we could *pretend*, because that's what *you* do so well. Funny that you're a director, because I reckon you would body it as an actor.'

'Well done.'

'I don't need your praise.'

'That's not how I remember it.'

I inhale sharply, bringing in his scent, night-time drives and neck kisses, base notes of my moans, and my mind skips between fury and something that simmers hotter, that makes my skin prickle, that elicits a dark, primal beat between my legs; goosebumps raise like they're dancing.

A spark zips across Malakai's eyes and he clears his throat and takes a swig of his drink, as if catching himself. 'Sorry. That was—'

My smile is arid. 'I don't need you to be sorry, Malakai. I need you to grow up. Look, tonight is about our best friends. And, if we do this correctly, the only time we'll be around each other will be because of them. So let's just never speak about us again, focus on what we need to focus on and stay in our respective lanes.'

The indentations in Malaki's jaw undulate, and he steps back. 'Sounds perfect.'

I release some breath I didn't know I was holding. 'Good.'

'Great.'

'*Fantastic.*'

Malakai looks like he's about to add a 'stupendous' when a drunken 'Keeks!' shatters through the tensile atmosphere. We turn to see my inebriated best friend marching in heels with a balance that could see her successfully audition for Cirque du Soleil. 'I've been looking for you!' She must really be waved, because I have not moved for a while. 'Chioma says she wants to perform a spoken word poem for us and I am *not* letting you escape this. You must suffer with me! No bitch left behind! I saw the first line. It's "Aminah and Kofi . . . love that brings to life like the first sip of coffee . . ."' She shudders, and then her eyes drift to Malakai, realisation shadowing them before they snap back to me, sharp with alarm. 'Uh uh. Not this. I'm getting déjà vu. Please tell me this isn't what I think it is—'

I shrug easily. 'Malakai and I were just working out our shit. We're cool now. One big happy family for your wedding season.'

Aminah raises a sceptical brow, and folds her arms across her chest, eyes bouncing between us. 'Just like that.'

A pleasant, saccharine, popstar smile appears on Malakai's face. 'Just like that. We realised we needed to . . . talk things out. Past completely scrubbed. We brand new. Ain't that right, Kiki?'

I nod, stepping back from his increased proximity. 'Right.'

Past completely scrubbed. What does that even mean when your concept of love was shaped by how someone looked at you, saw you, knew you, touched you, like you were the essence of life itself? It means that they didn't see what you had like you did. Which means you never really had it at all. My chest hollows out a little, which is confusing, because there is nothing lost, no hope, no love. *We* are nothing. I push out a smile that's hospital-fluorescent-light bright.

'Absolutely,' I say. 'It's like we never even happened.'

CHAPTER 6

Carnation Contentment

Somehow, through a gross miscalculation on my part, Malakai and I are the only two people left waiting for our taxis after a flurry of hugs and kisses – 'You sure your taxi's on the way?' – mild threats of violence deployed in the case that one of us doesn't text when we arrive home safely and Aminah squeezing my elbow, shooting a sharp look at Malakai and whispering for me to 'be good'.

We are standing apart, facing the quietening East London high street. There's a yawning revelry mingling in the cool night air as we watch buses wheeze past along with taxis carrying picante buzzed Shoreditch House stragglers, sleeping, kissing, watching their own night back on their phones lest the good time slips through their fingers, vigilantly watching to see if their crush has seen the carefree selfie, chosen from sixty-seven identical pictures.

Like a hazy, drunk apparition, a man with a handlebar moustache and a bucket hat arrives to claim a haphazardly docked Lime bike. I bite my lip to keep my smile in, but it trips out and without realising what I am looking for I turn to my left and catch Malakai's gaze, and fuck, no, there it is. His eyes, waiting for mine, the light in them leaping out at me.

'You see that too, right? Like, I'm not imagining that.'

I shrug. 'I have no idea what you're talking about – Oh, wait, you mean the Victorian ghost bike rider? Mr Ramsbottom? You don't know about him? You've been in the States too long, man. Came here from 1863 a few months back. Just one of those regular London things, you know. Like how you're never really too far away from someone who used to be in *Skins*.'

'Is that true?'

'I feel like it should be.'

It's a nonsense conversation and it feels easier to float into this to avoid the emotional intensity that's wedged itself in the air between us. I clear my throat and check my phone – only four more minutes.

Malakai looks at me rigidly from where he's stood, half a metre away, as if the jasmine-and-pink-pepper fragrance I'm wearing is a pathogen. 'Where's your man? I thought you said he was delayed.'

I swallow, and focus on my phone, ready to lie, but I find that my tongue can't make its way around the words, too used to telling him the truth, even with the abyss between us, the Unsaid and TooMuchSaids swirling stickily in the air.

'He wasn't delayed.' I swallow and look up, meeting Malakai's gently curious gaze as he turns half a step to me, a hand in his pocket. 'He wasn't going to come in the first place. We . . . we're sort of . . . on a break.'

Malakai turns to me fully now with an interest that's stark naked, his brow slightly creased. 'Why did you—'

I snap, chin up, 'I wasn't really in the mood to divulge the specificities of my relationship status to you.'

Malakai holds my gaze before nodding slowly. 'Understandable.' He pauses, and his eyes dance across my features. His face is inscrutable, but I can almost taste the flavour of the light in his gaze, sharp and sweet. 'I'm sorry to hear that. I hope you guys work it out.'

I huff a corrosive chuckle. 'Yeah, OK.'

Malakai turns to me fully, vague annoyance flitting over his features in a way that pronounces the strength of his brows, the malleable sensuality of his lips. 'You know, believe it or not, Kiki, I'm not badmind. Your misery doesn't make me happy.'

I baulk and turn to him sharply. 'Excuse the fuck out of you. Who said I'm miserable? Do I look miserable to you?'

Malakai runs his eyes across my form, and he makes me acutely aware of the fact that I forwent a bra, of how the evening breeze has hardened small softness, how the satin of my dress kisses my hips. I feel like I'm standing on honeyed quicksand. His eyes flick back up to meet mine, face betraying nothing, but his jaw is tense. 'No.'

He sniffs and scratches the bridge of his nose, looking back out into the street. His voice is casual, like he's just speaking to pass time. 'So, what does that mean? You're happy about the break?'

I'm cornered. Heat crawls up my body as it dawns on me that I wouldn't know how to answer that question even if I wanted to. While I miss Bakari on some level, it's been . . . tolerable to have a little space to figure my shit out. I meet Malakai's gaze to let him know I am deliberately ignoring him, before cutting my eyes away to look at my phone, tapping it alive to see that – *Shit*, my Uber's cancelled.

Malakai clears his throat, accepting the subject change. 'How long till your Uber's here?'

I look at my phone, on two per cent and trying to reconnect. 'Uh. Like, six minutes.' I'll deal with the lie in six minutes. For some reason, the cancelled Uber feels like a little failure, and I need to show him that I have control over every aspect of my life, that I'm good, so good. 'How long's yours?' His finger scrapes the back of his head – his awkward tell – and he looks at something beyond me. 'I didn't call one.'

'What? Why not?'

'I booked a room at this hotel for a couple of nights. More convenient. My short-term rental's ready in two days.'

'So why are you . . .' I pause as clarity clicks. 'Malakai, you don't have to wait with me. I'm cool by myself. I'll just wait in the hotel foyer—'

Malakai runs a hand across his face tiredly, apparently finding this whole conversation tedious. 'Kiki, please don't tell me what I don't have to do. I'm gonna give a shit about whether you're safe or not. Don't make it weirder than it needs to be. Besides, this is for me. I won't feel good leaving you here by yourself.' His voice is unsentimental and he barely meets my eyes, his gaze darting to a poster for a Dua Lipa fragrance at a bus stop as if he's extremely fascinated by the resurgence of the popstar-branded fragrance phenomenon. I feel a shift and softening that I immediately brace against. All right, he doesn't want me dead. So? I don't want him dead either. I know Malakai and he would do this for anyone. It means nothing. Nothing, like my phone battery right now. One per cent. I swear under my breath, but apparently not low enough because Malakai catches it, eyes alert. 'You good?'

'Um.' The pride I'm forced to swallow lodges itself in my throat and my voice comes out quieter. 'My phone is literally about to die. I gave my portable to Shanti and she's taken it home. Do you mind calling me a car? I'll obviously pay you back—'

The smug quip I half expect doesn't appear, and Malakai cuts in. 'Don't do that. You know I got you, but I think it's safer for you to be in a car with some charge.'

I sigh and nod. 'Yeah, you're right. I'll just charge it at the hotel reception—'

Malakai looks exasperated as he moves closer to me. 'Kiki, it's, like, 1 a.m. Just charge it in my room.' He pauses, discomfit shadowing his face. 'Unless you don't feel comfortable, which obviously is cool—'

I can't imagine a world where I would ever feel unsafe with Malakai. At least not in that way. Romantically, though, he might be a death trap. The problem is how at ease my body feels around him. I'm unsafe around the version of me that appears in his prox-imity, but he can't know that. He doesn't get to have that power. And maybe the only way to rid myself of the risk is to confront it.

I shake my head quickly. 'No, of course not. I mean of course

I do. I mean yeah. Cool. I'll, um, come up.' I try my best to be casual, but apparently my voice wears the aural version of an evening gown.

Malakai frowns, bending slightly to make sure I'm looking at the sincerity in his eye. 'You sure? I mean I could wait with you in the foyer if—'

'No, you're right. It's not a big deal. I'll be out of your way in fifteen minutes. Thanks.'

Malakai's nod is clipped and he steps back for me to move forward. 'After you.'

I walk ahead of him, and maybe, *maybe*, I add a little swing to my hips as I do, because, while I don't want him dead, I can at least torture him.

'Since when do you celebrate Valentine's Day?' Malakai calls from the kitchenette as he plugs my phone into the socket. Apparently, LA money is doing him nicely, because his 'room' is around the same square-metre area of my entire flat, a plush seventeenth-floor suite split into an open-plan living room and bedroom. The floor-to-ceiling windows face a stunning cityscape, the London lights forming their own constellation against the navy of the winter sky. I've stationed myself at the window, staring at the twinkling glass and steel vista so I don't have to look at him. I'm trying to limit intakes of his fineness in my weakened state, but now I turn to him, curious.

'Pardon?' It was never my thing. I'm one of those arseholes

who finds it performative, who thinks if love is celebrated all year round it doesn't need to be proven on a capitalistic day with heart-shaped chocolates and overbooked restaurants and pressure, so much pressure, to prove affection. People who weren't partnered being told that being in a relationship is the default. Situationships engaging in pretence for One Night Only, before reverting to the emotional hopscotch the next day. A single day shouldn't call for romance, but romance, when real, calls on itself on all our days, in all the nooks of a relationship, sinking into the contours of your connection; Malakai taught me that. And every thirteenth of February, Malakai, with his tongue in his cheek got me a bouquet of carnations with 'Happy Unvalentines Day, Scotch' as the note, and a slice of Tottenham cake, my favourite. He chose carnations because of a line in my favourite poem, 'The Way I Feel' by Nikki Giovanni. Nikki meant like the evaporated-milk brand, but I don't think Malakai knew that and it never mattered to me. He mattered to me. So much so that my heart twisted up with it, every year on our Unvalentine's Day, which defeated the purpose, but really proved ours, because it was just for us. Unique to our world. But that was the Before times, pre-apocalypse, pre-calcified resentment and hurt that makes the space between us frigid.

Last year, Bakari had got me a shiny designer bracelet popular among the luxury influencer set; it was objectively beautiful, and I, uncharacteristically, posted it, satisfied with concrete proof that I was capable of a love that wasn't with Malakai Korede. Now, Malakai stands some paces away from me, like he can barely stand to be around me.

'Don't ask how I know, but last year I saw a picture of you. Posted up, wrist glistenin'.'

'You Insta-stalked me?'

'Why are you smiling at that? Don't smile at that. Someone badmind sent it to me.'

A thrill runs through me at the idea of Malakai perusing my photos. 'Sure. Is "Badmind" what you named your subconscious?' I tease. Did he do it topless? In bed at night? Did he accidentally double tap once, praying I didn't see the notification? I'm not naïve enough to not know that the curiosity is normal, nothing necessarily to do with wanting, just . . . access to a memory. Still, I savour the thought.

Six months after our split, I went on a glo-up thirst trap spree, my twenty-something second puberty (and break-up) weight gain spreading my hips, filling my ass, and I felt good, sweet in my skin, replenished, *new*. Shanti was the creative director on a girls' trip to Mykonos as she contorted me into *Sports Illustrated* poses that would have made Tyra inform me that I'm still in the running to becoming an easy, breezy cover girl. I like that Malakai saw that, that I didn't wilt without him. What did Destiny's Child say? You thought that I'd be weak without you, but I'm thicker, thought that I'd be stressed without you, but I'm penger. Something like that. Aside from that one moment of weakness on his stories, I didn't get much from my Insta-stalking of him. His new social-media presence is all urbane austere aesthete: beautiful photographs of *scenes* of Black Life and gleaming side profiles and abstract photos of, like, a gold chain on a white shirt, but barely anything of himself.

Before we broke up, it was very much that, but with pictures of him and his friends sandwiched between a grainy film, pictures of the Blackwell crew on a night out – laughing, chilling, dancing – he would find the light in any dingy bar we were in, brown skin glowing, falling over each other, obsessed with each other's company. Scattered sporadically would be lowkey encapsulations of me – maybe one of me laid out on a couch on a Sunday, jersey shorts and crop top, face nestled in a book. Caption: 'I hope everyone is thanking God for their blessings today. I am. To God be the glory, look at this glory.'

Now, Malakai looks unapologetic, eyes defiant. 'Fine. I was checking to see if the quality of your photos had gone down without me taking them.'

I quirk a brow. 'Right. And what was your professional conclusion?'

He pauses, and says, voice flat and matter-of-fact, like he's teaching a class, 'If the subject is good, there's a limit to how bad a photo can be.'

I tilt my head to disrupt the sharp thrill that shoots through me. 'Oh?'

Malakai's expression doesn't change. 'Kiki. Come on . . .' His eyes flicker momentarily down my form and I repress the flare in my core before he meets my gaze again, lazily. 'You know you're gorgeous.'

There's no sentiment in this. He says it like it's a bland observation, like he's bored, annoyed at having to say something so banal. I think this makes it worse. My body responds to this statement as if he's offered to strip me of my clothes with his teeth. My breath turns in on itself; my core constricts. I can feel all my reason melting and so I hang on to the hook of his initial query to haul myself back up.

'Um, to answer your question, I'm still not into Valentine's Day like that. I guess I was trying to prove something to myself maybe? By going all in. By embracing it fully. Like extra credit.'

Something acetic flits over his features, but he bites at it, nods, his voice blandly enquiring, 'And you didn't want to do the extra credit with me.'

'I didn't need to do it with you.'

'Because our relationship wasn't enough—'

'Because we were more than enough.'

He stills and I swallow, panicked, trying to subdue the Too Much that leapt out, but it's too late – so I qualify it with a truth, 'Or I thought we were.'

I turn back to the deep early morning sky, mainly to marvel that despite talking to Malakai about relationships it hasn't clattered down with the constellations, but also to avoid looking at his face. The plume in my belly has dipped steeply, dangerously. The air between us vibrates with an energy I recognise. It's not a neutral thing, an energy generated with anyone you could theoretically kiss; it's *ours*, calibrated to us, by us – it cannot be replicated. It's dawning on me that this may be catastrophic.

I feel Malakai step closer behind me, and every hair on my body stands to attention at the static.

'What were you trying to prove?'

The question draws my attention from the lights in the dark outside and back to the lights in the dark of his eyes to see the curiosity in them searing.

'That I was over you.' My gaze meanders to his mouth, because I can't help it. It's dusky and velvet and full; if I bite it, want will drip all over me like juice from a ripe mango. 'Which I am.' Truth licks at my lips the same time his tongue darts out to wet his. 'Emotionally.'

I can feel myself turning against sense, rebellion bounding against my brain. There's a primal, prowling flavour of boldness that only awakens around him, and while I've tried to tame it, it rattles against my ribcage. It's zooming within it, making itself known. I see Malakai's throat depress slightly and I am acutely aware of every molecule in the room, every atom of air between us.

He nods, fighting his own petty war, his eyes running between my eyes, my lips and now they fall to my gown where my nipples, rock under satin, preen under his focus, pushing up against the fabric, petulant, having had to suffer the absence of his attention for so long.

'And physically?'

'Physically . . .'

I know exactly what Malakai looks like when desire is colonising his senses. He blinks slow, like he's doing now, his mechanisms of reason becoming sticky with lust, and it's a loop, a contagion, because the intensity of his focus makes it hard for me to think, to breathe, to remember that this is a Bad Idea.

'. . . it's hard to be in the same room as you.' I draw half a step nearer, despite my brain's direct orders to grab my phone and leave. 'My body's . . . angry at you.'

Malakai's lids are heavy now, his eyes hazy, stormy cirrus clouds. 'Yeah? My body's fuming. It's hard . . .' Malakai tilts his head and the scan over my body sends a hot shiver through my form . . . 'to even look at you.'

His scent wafts over me, hits me like a drug, and I realise why I recognise the notes. 'You smell good. Is that the same cologne I got you four years ago?'

'I bought another bottle after it ran out. Shit ain't cheap. You must have really been down bad.'

'I was trying to run up my Amex points.' The corner of Malakai's mouth flicks up, and he looks at me in the way only he can – with knowledge. His eyes read my face, dancing between mine, my lips, my nose, and over and over again. I know this refrain well. It used to be my favourite part of my favourite song, and warmth in my gut moves, silky and molten. It's a mirage, I know, a ghost feeling, but I'll take it for now. This is just for now.

'You look good, Kiki.' Malakai lifts his hand to gently hold my chin with his thumb and forefinger, and my breath hitches. 'Is that the same face you had when I met you eight years ago?'

'More or less.'

'More.'

He allows his thumb to budge just shy of a couple of centimetres, a fraction of a stroke, but I feel it in my joints, in my toes. Electricity thrums through from the base of my belly downwards.

I swallow the new lump in my throat as he continues, 'Which is unreasonable, but I've never known you to play fair.'

The heat in his proximity erases a patina from a dormant want in me, making it new again. I'm in grave danger, because, though my brain recognises that there is nothing here, my body doesn't seem to be acknowledging time nor space, just this feeling I get when his body is millimetres from mine, a hot need, the instinct to slip into his skin. The light in the suite is dim, amber, with the lamp, and still, in the dull, his skin has a lustre that lures my lust, and my body's trust stretches out, yawning, missing the sweet mellow of his energy. Man, he's so beautiful to me still. I can't deny that. I also can't allow my heart to follow where my body clearly wants to go. It's barely recovered from its last contact with Malakai Korede. I just have to be vigilant, strict, in not letting my desire delude my feelings.

The energy between us pulls tauter, denser and I know he feels it too, because the hollows beneath his cheekbones twitch with tension. His lids become heavy, weighed down with want, his gaze compressed sharp gems, cutting through my reason. The need seethes in my body and I retreat to breathe a little, steady myself, causing his hand to fall from my face so I can look to the gleaming electric stars of London for relief – one last attempt to slow the train of terrible decision-making. 'I don't know how you didn't miss this view while you were in the States.'

Malakai doesn't say anything. I turn round and there's been a shift in his face, a shadow of doubt warring with his want. He swallows and steps back, scratches at his jaw, running his hand across his head, clearly stressed. 'Kiki, I think you better go. I don't want us to do anything you're going to regret.'

My thumb itches to sweep against his lips. I could close my eyes and read them. 'Don't you mean something *we're* going to regret?'

Malakai's look caresses my body, the silk on my skin, the dipping gape of my dress, the peaks of my chest, the soft spread of my thigh, before they reach mine again. The corner of his mouth curls slightly, dryly. 'No.'

It's irresistible trouble. I'm drowning in it, savouring the taste before it gets to my lungs. My knees are weakening. I choose to bait, reclaim some power – it's addictive knowing I've got his focus, toying with it.

'*I'll* regret it, though? You lost your touch? I'm impressed by the self-awareness.' I tilt my head up at him. Malakai smiles at this shameless challenge, a grin that's so genuine it's startling. It's decadent, delicious. The latent stress on his face has fled. He closes the gap between us in a single stride. He cocks his head, doesn't touch me. 'You'll regret it because you'll want to do it again. Then you can tell me if I've lost my touch.' His words wrap round my throat and dive between my legs. I almost whimper. I call on the last scraps of sense and strength, managing an eye-roll. need to be able to pretend to myself that I tried to put up a fight. 'And what makes you think that I'll even let anything happen? Who do you think you are?'

Malakai shoots me a gently bemused look and leans forward so his lips hover against my ear, almost brushing my skin.

'Kikiola, I'm the guy who knows exactly what you look like

when you want to fuck.' He gently brushes my braids from my shoulder, his breath now gliding over my collarbone, the heat sending me feverish, sweating, shivering. 'And I know how you're in the mood to be fucked too.'

A dam bursts, desire rushes through and something else too, and even without the immediate slickness I feel in my thong, I know that it's over. No crying, maybe some begging. I need him inside me as soon as humanly possible. Denial is a river between my thighs.

I need one last confirmation that I'm not alone in this natural disaster.

'All right. I got an idea,' I say.

'I'm all ears.'

'We clearly have . . . unfinished physical business.'

'Is that what we're calling it?'

'Well, what do you wanna call it?'

'Fuck frisson,' he declares.

'No. As I was saying, how about we do a thirst amnesty? Get all this . . . inconvenient sexual tension out of the way once and for all. How do you feel about that?'

Malakai doesn't move, and a spark of amusement lights up in his face. My eyes follow the quick flit of his gaze and drop below his waist to see his erection pressing against the material of his dress trousers, proud, present, transfixing. My mouth almost waters; my pussy pulses at the view. I want to feel how he feels about it. Multiple London landmarks on sight tonight: the Shard, the Gherkin, Malakai Korede's hard-on for me.

'I *feel*,' he replies, 'like downstairs the second you turned round and swayed your ass I knew I was fucked.' Kai's eyes lick along my form brazenly. 'And I know you did that shit on purpose too.'

I smile wickedly, turn back towards the window and press myself against him in reply. I'm *awake*, an old thing in me, alive. This is a me unique to this space, this taste, under Malakai's gaze. His hands automatically slide round my waist, silk against satin, and pull me flush against his increasingly hardening dick. A moan escapes my mouth at the impact. His hands glide from my hips up until they skim my breasts, a whisper of touch that causes me to buck against him, grinding in a tight circle that makes him gasp against my neck, frustration tightening his voice.

'*Shit*, Scotch.'

His voice, strained under my power, is a high – one to which I worked hard to lose my addiction, and the heights it takes me to now, on first contact, are dizzying, startling.

Careful, Keeks. The familiarity is thrillingly foreign; I never thought I would feel this again, and I don't want to stop, which means I probably should. Probably is brushed away with Malakai's hands as he smooths up my dress to cup my breasts, squeezing them firmly in retaliation, and I whimper as his thumbs encircle my nipples, sending impulses to my core to slicken for him, get me ready for him – man, I am so ready for him.

'You know how hard it was for me tonight? Trying to focus on conversation with other people when all I could think about is how sexy you look in this dress? How much I wanted your tits in my hands?' His lips burn against my neck, his words branding me to his need. 'How bad I wanted you in my mouth?'

He pinches the pebbles hard between his thumb and forefinger and I release a hiss of pleasure and a rush of lust wets my panties further. It's anguished bliss; fuck, I missed this. I manage to push my voice out with the last of my reason, because I am now acutely aware of how dangerous this could be. 'Rules. We . . . we need rules.'

Malakai's face is against my neck, his nose and lips brushing my throat. 'Whatever you want.'

The strength it takes not to melt is Olympian. 'And I know you know this, and casual hook-ups are what you do . . .'

I feel Malakai pause, falter for a fraction of a second as I continue: '. . . but I just wanna confirm. This can only be a one-time thing.'

His chin grazes my shoulder with a nod. 'Agreed.' I reach behind me to stroke the bulge in his trousers, and his hand rises to my throat and squeezes in a way that makes my hips roll shamelessly, sluttily. 'Just to . . . get it out of our system. So we can focus on our lives. No emotion involved.' His teeth nip at my throat, fingers firm around it, feeling the vibrations of my moan. My eyes blur from pleasure, the city becoming nebulous dots of light under the heat of his hand. 'This ain't about getting back together.' His mouth moves against my neck, the softness creating a sweet friction with the sharp pinch of his hungry little bites.

I sigh. 'Mhmm. And we don't talk about us.'

'Good rule. And no pet names or nicknames. No "Kai".'

I smart, but he's right. Too dangerous, too familiar, too confusing to call each other what we did when we were in love.

'No "Scotch".' His hand slips to the high slit of the dress on my thigh, feathering up and down, conjuring greedy goosebumps, and I stand apart, wanting him to slide up, needing him to, pressing harder against him, relishing the feel of his firmness against the softness of my ass. 'We never talk about it after this moment. It never happened.'

I bite my lip, repress a groan of desperation before managing to let out, 'Yep. Because I don't want to get back together with you.' Even if I were still in love with him it would be too costly, too dangerous. I might not get all of me back this time.

'Believe me. That's the last thing I want to do.' Somehow through my horny haze, I feel a ridiculous sting, as if I didn't already know this, as if that isn't the point, as if I don't feel the same. Malakai made it clear; he doesn't want long-term. I was a trial. I was an error.

I turn round and look up into the burn of his eyes. I want this. This version of *this*. Simple. No fuss, no mess.

'Good. So we're settled.' I step back and gently flick the straps of my gown so they fall off my shoulders, revealing the heft of my breasts. I slant my head, letting every filthy thought I've ever had rush into my eyes. 'Now, tell me more about you knowing how I'm in the mood to be fucked. Because I'm having trouble believing y—'

It's a new Big Bang, a new world after the apocalypse, same but different, our desire made fiercer with familiarity. We're ravenous,

151

ferocious, lips sucking, tongues laving, deep strokes stoking the fire in me further; it's blazing now. Malakai's smile is wicked as a hand wraps round my neck in precious possession while the other one slides down my back to squeeze the plump of my ass cheek. When he moans into my mouth with relief, I feel a new sun explode into being within me. I decide to ignore it, to not interrogate it – I'm going to let it be.

'Is this what you wanted, Kiki? When you were walking in front of me, is this what you imagined me doing?' His hand slips under my dress now to grip into the flesh, and he whispers against my face, 'Because all you needed to do was ask nicely.'

I smile as I reach down to slowly stroke the prominent swell in his trousers, and watch his eyes cloud, feel his grip on my right cheek tighten. 'You have a lot of chat for someone who's about to be moaning my name.'

Malakai's hand maddeningly migrates from butt to in between my thighs, swirling his hand in slow circles on the flesh there. The anticipatory pleasure pushes my head back – Malakai braces it with his hand, bunching my braids in a tight fist as his other hand floats up, and up, and up, just shy of the thrumming juncture of need. He lightly traces the V of my panties, his finger edging the lace.

'You first.'

I release a frustrated feline sound and cover his hand, try to coax it to touch me there, but he doesn't budge. He's so *strict*.

'Nah, Kiki. Use your words. You're grown.' His voice is a rough grunt that brushes against the tenderness of his kisses on my neck, the sucks sending sharp darts of desire to my core. 'Tell me how bad you want me to stroke you.'

And I hate it because the answer is *so* bad, I-Should-Not-Want-It-This-Bad *bad*, so bad that just his words have me soaked. I look into his eyes, and his intense, singular focus on me, his face etched with undistilled want for me, throws me back to a million versions of us. In the lust-filled clouds in my brain, I can't separate those versions from this version. *No.* Panic spikes through me, and I turn round, facing the balcony doors to rest a hand on the glass.

'Touch me from behind,' I say. 'I want to feel you against me as you stroke.' It was a truth couched in fear. I can't emotionally afford eye contact right now. The risk is too deep.

If Malakai senses that anything is off, he doesn't mention it – he acquiesces, quickly, his hand slipping under the thin lace of my knickers to trail a finger against the slick slit, and he speaks low in my ear.

'Look at you, Kiki. Pussy drenched for me. Does my touch feel lost to you? Come let my touch be lost in you.'

It's unfair, really, how I almost come, just from that. Unfair how he knows how much I like it when he talks to me like that. I mew his name as I roll my hips to encourage movement, and Malakai's finger slips in, thick and elegant, coaxing, teasing, playing me like I'm an instrument finely tuned to his melody. My vision blurs as I swirl my waist, encouraging him to go deeper as another finger follows.

'Kiki, you feel perfect. I love how you move on me. Keep working me in just like that,' and it drives me crazy. I am now fully humping his fingers something feral, my hand sliding down the glass as I grind against his erection, giving the City of London a show. I'm not a natural exhibitionist, but in this particular biome

153

of mine and Malakai's attraction to each other, something wild in me always blooms. Or maybe this is a natural state, dormant until stimulated by his touch. This is why we couldn't last. It's too much, the energy too unruly. He reaches for my left breast and rubs a nipple, raining hot, sexy, sloppy kisses on my neck as his fingers do their labour of lust. He slides in impossibly deeper, stroking gently but precisely, with the confidence of someone who knows where they're going, knows where to press, how to cajole my ecstasy. He switches the pressure suddenly, his fingers gliding firmly, racketing up the pleasure till he finally slips his finger up till he finds my clit, rubbing mercifully, intently, a universe of nerve endings going hectic at the heat, at the blessed reunion with his touch, while his other finger shuttles back and forth mercilessly inside me. It's too much, not enough. I press against the coolness of the glass for relief, pushing further into his touch, writhing in sync with his motion, barely able to contain the blooming bliss.

I rasp, '*Malakai.*'

'Come for me, Keeks. You're doing so fucking good—'

We said no nicknames, he's cheated, but I don't have time to be pissed because the pleasure ricochets through me with no warning, so quick it takes my breath away, the orgasm rushing in so fast I gasp, thrashing against him, coating his hand with all the want pent up from the first time I set eyes on him tonight. He drops kisses on my neck, my collarbone, my cheek, so treacherously tender that I'm glad I had the wisdom to not look into his eyes. I remind myself again: this is temporary, one night only, a purge of passion. When I turn round the fire in Malakai's face is burning blue, ravenous.

His hunger has reached its peak. He brings his fingers to his mouth and licks. It's so fucking nasty and I'm rapt; it's a wrap.

'Sit down on the sofa,' I say through a pant, entranced.

The corner of Malakai's mouth flicks up wolfishly before he does as told. 'Yes, ma'am.'

He situates himself on the couch in the small living space of the suite, sitting back, legs set apart, deliciously waiting, as I slip my dress completely off my hips, slide my knickers off, kick my heels off. Malakai watches me, mesmerised, eyes following my movements till I am completely naked in front of him. He utters, one word, '*How?*' – a jagged, awed breath that tangles up in my chest in a way I decide to package up, not think about. This is merely physical.

My curves are a little softer, wider now, and Malakai is a man that likes to knead, squeeze, press. I approach him slowly, relishing his brazen, ravenous attention before straddling him, roughly grabbing his face and kissing him filthily, my tongue licking into his mouth, sucking his lip. It's lust, but frustration leaks into it, contaminates the unqualified thirst. It's emotional frustration, a tang of anger, and something softer, sweeter that I ignore. I focus on the top notes: the taste of Malakai's kisses. Decadent dark chocolate, unrefined desire for me, my own boldness, his confidence, honey, spice. His hips buck automatically in candied violence, a sweet, addicting force that pushes his firmness into me in such a way that I wet the fabric of his trousers anew.

I grin, place a finger across his lips and let it drag down. 'Patience . . .'

His eyes are glazed with mischief, thirst. 'You're evil.'

'So you better do as told, innit.' I make quick work of unbuttoning his shirt. Malakai rips it off his body as if it's on fire, and then I drop kisses on his chest, swirling my tongue across his nipple. Malakai hisses and when I raise my head he leans his against mine as he releases a heavy, ragged breath.

'There she is. Sweet assassin. I see you're still out here tryna kill me?'

'I thought one of your superhuman powers was immunity against my assassination attempts?'

'It's been a while. Defences have weakened.'

'Sometimes a little more poison's the antidote. You know. "What doesn't kill you makes you stronger".'

'Not sure that's true, but I'm ready to die finding out.' Malakai's smile melts off his face as I unbuckle his trousers, lifting up slightly so he can push them down, along with his boxers. His dick springs out, proud, as impressive as ever, and I wonder briefly if it's weird to say I've missed his dick – I decide that it probably is, but the truth is I have. I want to lick it, reacquaint myself with the essence of his taste, so sweet to me, but I control myself. I need to limit my dose of Malakai – just enough will grant me immunity, too much may kill me. I give him a firm pump over the hot velvet steel. Malakai groans and his hand wraps round the back of my neck.

'Shit. Be careful. I don't think you know what kind of power you have.'

I lick my palm and Malakai's eyes become black blades at the sight. He's lost the last of his mind. I smile and kiss his neck as I stroke along the firm length, a thrill running through me.

'No, I know. I just wanna make sure you don't forget.'

'That was never a possibility.'

Something in my chest flickers again at the rough whisper, but I ignore it, palming his sensitive tip so he hisses.

'Kiki, you gotta go slower – you're gonna make me—' His voice is a strained rasp, his hands gripping into my thigh, making indents.

I grin as I nibble his neck, enjoying my revenge. 'If you wanna be inside me, Malakai, you gotta say please.'

Malakai's eyes flash dangerously in a way that lets me know I'm going to pay for this next time. A sharp thrum of anticipation runs through me before screeching to a halt. There will be no next time. This is the only time. The *last* time.

'*Please*, Kiki.' His hand glides up my belly, gently rests on my breast as he brushes his thumb across my nipple, before squeezing. 'Let me make you feel good inside. Let me do that for you. I know you can take it.' He flips it, transforming the begging into him doing us both a favour – I marvel at the Malakai-Alchemy. It works immediately, I'm now near aching for him.

'Where are your condoms?'

'Front compartment of my carry-on.'

I arch a brow. 'Your carry-on. *Really*, bro?'

Malakai shrugs, his smile faint. 'Always be prepared. Easily accessible. And look how it came in handy?'

I roll my eyes and scramble off him, grab them and rip a packet open, kissing him as I work it over his thick length.

Malakai holds my face, his eyes hazy. 'Kiki. You sure, yeah?'

I baulk at the gentleness with which he holds my chin. This

isn't about *gentle*. This isn't about soft. This is biological. I'm sure I want to have wild sex with Malakai Korede right now. I am *not* sure that it's a wise decision. I'm *very* sure that I couldn't give a solitary fuck. In reply, I hoist myself above him, guiding his tip into me as I slowly lower myself back down. We both hiss, gasp at the exquisite sting of him stretching me, as I gently work myself down his length, reacquainting myself with the sharp, tight, indulgent feeling.

Any semblance of composure Malakai has is completely lost. '*Kiki*, you feel so good – it don't make sense . . . *fuck*,' and he's right, it doesn't make sense, because it feels like all the sense in the universe. It shouldn't feel so good after all this time. It shouldn't feel like we're picking up where we left off. The newness shouldn't feel so warm, so right, but instead of thinking about that I stop thinking altogether as Malakai rasps, 'Ride me, Kiki.'

I do as told, feeling the sweet ache, lifting myself up and down the length, with Malakai's assist, his hands spreading across my ass, pushing me up and hauling me back on him with a satisfying slap of skin as we rediscover our rhythm. He angles his hips and I release a sharp cry as he hits me in the spot that he knows drives me crazy and drips become a deluge, wet sounds mingling with my cries, his sighs, to form a sonata I thought I'd never hear again.

'Right there, Malakai. Hold it right there—'

I look down at his face and regret it. It's exquisite. He's lost in this moment, maybe found in this moment, focused on me, in this. It's tacky with a quicksand made from the grains of my desire. It's also the face that broke my heart. It's also the face that walked out on me. A world I knew crumbled around that face. And it's a face that wants *this*, but not necessarily me. So I look back up, straight ahead, to the bed that I deliberately avoided, and the pleasure rackets up my body, making me bounce harder as he fucks me back harder. It feels deliriously wonderful, but I'm too aware to come this way, right now, with my guards creaking their way up in self-defence. It feels dangerously safe, my body sinking so easily into the delight. I bend forward, and bite and suckle on Malakai's throat. I know I'm cheating, knowing that's his spot, knowing it's what makes him unravel quickly while he's inside me. I need this over. The risk has got too steep, and I miscalculated.

Like I knew it would, Malakai's thrusting increases in pace, frantic, his fingers digging into my thighs as he calls my name. My heart seizes because I like it, because I need it like air. My heart starts pumping again. Then my heart seizes because I like it, because I need it like air. When he comes, we collapse against each other, slick with sweat, breath spurting out in ragged gusts.

He drops a kiss on my shoulder. 'Damn. That was . . .'

I still can't look at him. It's too expensive, and all my emotional energy is spent. My head rests on his shoulder as I catch escaped breath. 'Yeah. It was.'

Malakai gently pushes me up so I have to meet his gaze. He brushes the braids away, holds my face while scanning it. 'Hey. You good?' His eyes are gentle with genuine care, soft enough to sink into.

This close up, I notice the slight bags under his eyes. Without thinking, I stroke the thin skin there with my thumb. Surprise flickers across Malakai's face, but he doesn't move as I sweep across his cheek gingerly. It could just be travel – with the flight and the time difference he must be exhausted – but concern pricks at my gut. *Is* he good? I know his work schedule is crazy, and he'd lost so much before he went to the States – more than just us. His family are mostly in London and I know he has a cousin in upstate New York, but his world was here. Was he loved on there? Did he have somewhere he could feel safe there? Why does that matter so much to me? Is he happy?

'I am,' I reply. 'Are you?'

Malakai smiles, somehow both filthily and sweetly. He stops the circuit of my thumb by grabbing my wrist, kissing my palm. 'How could I not be, Scotch?'

My head feels light. My heart throbs something manic, growing three sizes. It's a shitty, terrible, sickening thing. For a split second, the last two-and-a-half years vanish. I forget. I forget the heartbreak, the tears, the world crashing down. I remember us like this, always like this, easy, tender. I remember the feeling of it being safe there, of wanting to stay here. It is *not* safe here. This is an illusion, playacting. I cannot stay here. I scramble off him quickly, reaching for my knickers, slipping my dress on.

Malakai's face falls with realisation, his hand flying to the back of his head. 'Shit, sorry, I forgot—'

'No, it's fine. It's fine.' Like repetition might will it so, an incantation to manifest this into something that isn't a huge fucking mistake.

Malakai watches me, momentarily dazed, before he rights

himself, tearing his gaze from me like his quota for pretending to care has been hit, and then going over to the bathroom to throw the condom away. We sit back next to each other, our skin shiny from the exertion from getting closure. I read somewhere (well, a TikTok therapist said) that closure is a lie we tell ourselves to hold on to something. I don't know why I remember this at this particular moment. Malakai and I are *closed*. Sealed. I feel the synergy we achieved when we were skin to skin calcify. We turn to each other, say, 'So,' at the same time. He chuckles, I laugh. Nothing is funny. It's strange, awkward, because we have never been awkward after sex with each other. We've never had to be.

'We got it out of our systems,' he says finally, and something in me cools.

I nod. 'Right. We addressed it. Got rid of it.'

Malakai's face dims a little. Maybe the appeal has worn off quickly. 'In many ways this was the mature thing to do.'

'Look at us. Slaying the ex thing.'

'We should do a TED Talk on it.'

'How to Eliminate Ex Stress: Sex.' It's not my best.

Malakai shoots me a short, courteous smile before he clears his throat. 'Uh. Do you want a glass of water?' like he's asking a colleague if they want a cup of tea while they pop into the office rec area. I guess that's virtually what this is. Two people, who worked alongside each other to reach the same goal of achieving orgasms.

'Yeah. Thanks. And, um, could you please get my phone while you're there? I should probably call an Uber—'

It isn't my preference to get into a taxi with the scent of sex clinging on to me, but getting into a shower here just seems too intimate, too risky. Malakai's face shadows briefly – probably realising we have made a colossal error – before nodding. 'Yeah. Course. No problem.'

He goes to the kitchenette whilst my mind races. I am not entirely sure this was the best decision. Actually, I am definitely sure it was the worst decision I could have possibly made at this time. This was supposed to kill all Malakai Korede-related thirst, but I'm feeling like something has been stoked. Sex with Malakai was always good, blessedly so, considering he was my first time. I always wondered if maybe that's part of why it was so good – not just our connection, but the fact that my desire evolved with him. I learned the power of my own lust with him. I don't know how gassed I am to confirm that this isn't true. Our sex was good because it was us. Yet *us* didn't work. We crashed, burned. Ultimately, right now we are two near-strangers. So why couldn't I look into his eyes while he made me come undone?

When Malakai passes me the glass of water and my phone, his whole demeanour has shifted, drifted. We weren't exactly cosy before, but now he's barely looking at me. He doesn't even sit back down next to me, instead busying himself with putting his shirt back on, moving his fancy Japanese luggage around – that luggage does not need to be moved around. He's doing *anything* but engaging with me. It stings, and I'm angry at myself for letting it; if he wants to be a dick about it, it's fine with me. My phone has come alive with power, and as I open it to call an Uber I see a text has come in:

Bakari 🖤
Kiki . . . you look stunning. I'm an idiot for missing out on
  tonight. I should have been there for you even with everything
  going on. Hope you're keeping well. Love.

It's in reply to a picture I'd sent him earlier in the evening,
before Malakai had arrived – what I dubbed a Freakum Selfie,
one taken in the flattering light of the hotel bathroom, tits pushed
out, hips jutted to the side, gaze seductive, mouth slightly parted.
It was designed to fuck with him. Clearly it did the job, but the
satisfaction I expected to feel is muted for some reason. I notice
the time stamp – it was sent a few minutes ago. My eyes jump
over to where Malakai is folding his shirts away. Why is he *folding*
his clothes away when he's leaving this hotel in two days? What
a freak. My palms prick with nameless anxiety. I have no doubt
in my mind that he saw the text. Technically, I don't owe him an
explanation, and technically this has nothing to do with him. Still,
I feel uncomfortable, icky and, bizarrely, a feeling of betrayal. The
question of who I'm betraying swirls in my psyche unanswered.
It might be myself.

After I book my Uber, I clear my throat. 'Malakai.'

Malakai looks up at me and smiles a customer-service smile. It
cuts me. 'Kiki.'

'I know you saw the text.'

'So?'

He's right. *So?* He doesn't give a shit because why should he?
He doesn't want me like that. *I* don't want him like that.

BOLU BABALOLA

I clear my throat again. 'I just . . . don't want there to be any confusion. Any messiness. I just want to be clear that this . . . this is all above board.' I struggle to find the right words to navigate this. Above board? What is this – a business negotiation? *Is* this a business negotiation? How do people even talk about having sex with their ex while on a break with their boyfriend? 'Um, I'm unattached.' Maybe not like this.

Malakai looks at me with a wryness cut with dark incredulity. 'Yeah? Man's texting you at 2 a.m. Seems pretty fucking attached to me.'

It clips at me, and I slip my head to the side, my defences coming through like barbed wire. 'Yeah, well, you know what, Malakai? Not everyone goes no contact when they break up with someone. Some people still give a shit.'

Malakai's brow twitches, irritation clouding his features before it clears, his face immediately placid. He shrugs. 'The great thing about this arrangement is that I don't have to get into it with you. It's cool. What's there to be confused about? We both have our own shit going on. Like we said, this is a one-time thing. This was a little thrill from your regular life, and this was . . . this was a nice way for me to be welcomed back to London.'

Nice. *Nice.* Like I took him to dinner at Nando's and not to Nirvana with how I rode him fifteen minutes ago. It's like I could have been anyone. Maybe I could have been anyone. Maybe I *am* anyone to him. My stomach drops and I release a humourless laugh before shaking my head, gathering my things.

'Real mature,' I mutter under my breath.

Malakai stops moving around the room, turns to me. 'How am I immature, Kiki? We both got what we wanted out of this.' He pauses. 'Unless you're feeling guilty?'

I roll my eyes. 'Please, Malakai, I'm not you. *I* respect the boundaries of my relationship. Maybe it's your own conscience that's pricking you and you're projecting, because you're the kind of guy who lies to his girlfriend about—'

Malakai's eyes become stony. 'I never lied to you, Kiki.'

Old hurt stirs, ancient history groaning. 'You might as well have.'

'You should have trusted me.'

My nose stings. 'Yeah, and you should have given me something to trust.'

Malakai stills for a few moments. His jaw holds rigid, and his emotions are packed tight under clingfilm again, muted, compressed. He then nods ruefully, steps back and scratches at his beard.

'You know, Kiki, maybe we just didn't know each other well. For example, I didn't think you were a cutesy heart-emoji person, but you are.'

I blink at the sharp turn. 'What the hell are you even talking ab—'

'Your man's name.' He says 'man' like it's something fetid. 'The emoji next to his name. You must really love him.'

I almost laugh at the ridiculousness. It never occurred to me to put a heart emoji next to Kai's name. We *were* the heart emoji. He was my whole fucking heart. Kai was enough. The mention of

Bakari sits uneasy on me. I do love him. I'm sure I do. Although now, when I think this, there seems to be nothing real for the idea to grip on to, this idea of me loving Bakari. Before, I was able to reach for tangible proof for it to sit on, but now it slips, falls. I find nothing. The idea of my love for him slides on the sleek new memory of Malakai making me come in full view of London. After Malakai and I broke up, it was about eight months before I even considered another man to be a sexual entity.

My phone buzzes, saving me from the answer I was never going to give, alerting me to the arrival of my Uber.

I look up at his face, inscrutable, tense. 'I have to go.'

He nods, moving aside so I can walk to the door. 'I'd appreciate it if you let me know when you get home.'

'Sure. Thanks for the charge.' I immediately internally curse myself. Why did I have to say it like that? Like he just energised me with his superpowered dick? When I reach the door, I cough. 'I guess I'll see you when I see you.'

Malakai's walked me to the door, but he barely meets my eye as he nods tightly. 'Yep. It was fun, Kiki.'

And I don't know why it's this statement that haunts me on the ride home. It sits on my spirit obtrusively, making my heart itch. I don't know why it's this that makes my eyes sting, and the tears fall and for me to sob so hard that my driver, a concerned uncle, hands me a pocket tissue and says, 'It will be all right, sister. It will pass.' I hope it does. I don't know why it hurts. It's not supposed to hurt any more.

CHAPTER 7

Sisterhood and Non-disclosures

CONFIDENTIAL:

Dear Kiki Banjo,
You are one of the very few selected guests invited to an exclusive, intimate audience with a critically acclaimed R&B artist.
Please sign and return the attached for more details.

'So beautiful, Meenz.'

'Stunning, Smallie.' Damola, Aminah's heavily pregnant eldest sister sighs in agreement with me, fresh from her babymoon in Turks and Caicos, beaming over the steam of a specially requested cup of herbal tea. Elegant in a camel knit dress, she pulls a tissue from her Kelly, dabbing at the corners of her eyes. 'These bloody hormones.'

'Iyawo, Kofi! Looking like an ohemaa for real!' Laide calls out from where she's sat next to me on a pink velvet couch, flute of champagne in the air, chunky gold bangles jangling. 'Turn round for me, sis, pop it small.'

Aminah preens and totters round in a circle on the plinth. She strikes a pose, hand on her hip, the other poised in the air.

'Yes.' Laide grins and leans forward to smack her sister's bum, her leather skirt and oversized jacket squeaking with the movement. 'It even makes your puff-puff bum look bigger.'

Aminah smirks and does a little twerk and sticks her tongue out, and Laide squawks, 'Small bum-bum dey shake oooooooo!'

We all burst out laughing, hopped up on free champagne, and the glee of the moment. When they're not bickering, it's a joy being an honorary member of the elite Bakare sorority, folded into the way they play, love, tease.

My best friend turns to her mum expectantly. 'What do you think, Mummy?'

Auntie Rafiat is sat on the opposite corner of the boutique's padded ivory dressing room in a flowing purple kaftan, perched on a boucle armchair. She tilts her head as she runs her gaze across her daughter's frame, expression neutral.

Aminah's smile wavers. Laide clears her throat and sits back down next to me, crossing one thigh-high patent-leather booted leg across the other. The designer's assistants facilitating the bridal fitting seem to sense a shift in the air, because they wisely announce that they're going to get another bottle of champagne.

Finally, Mrs Bakare's shoulder twitches in reply. 'Well, my dear, if you like it, it's fine.'

Oh, *shit*.

'Oh, shit,' Laide whispers under her breath.

Damola begins to rub her temple. Several expressions ring across my best friend's face, but hurt chimes the loudest. Her eyes glimmer.

'So you hate it?' My heart tugs. Her voice is softer, younger.

Auntie Rafiat scoffs and purses her lips, painted wine today. 'Oreoluwa, you're always so dramatic.' She's using Aminah's middle name? I buckle up. A long day's about to become longer. We've been here for two and a half hours trying on dresses and this is the first that my extremely particular friend has unequivocally loved, her eyes glittering the moment she set eyes on her reflection. My skin begins to prickle with stress. I sip more of my champagne.

Laide mutters to me, 'Yo, where's the lady with the other bottle?' as she turns to peek through the curtain next to us.

Auntie Rafiat continues: 'Where did "hate" come from now? I said if you like it, it's fine.'

I can see the effort of Aminah restraining her eyes from flicking up to the chandelier in the dressing room. Her respect for her mother battles against her intolerance at being tested. 'Mummy, just say what you want to say—'

Auntie Rafiat is impatient. She repositions herself on her seat, and folds her hands across her lap. 'Wòó, Oreoluwa, ma stress me. Fi mí sí 'lẹ. I've said all I've wanted to say. You look nice, ah!'

'*Nice*.' Aminah's voice is deceptively gentle. I see the frustration simmering under her surface of placidity. 'I see. When Damola tried on her wedding dress you cried!'

Auntie Rafiat swirls her wrists with open palms in a gesture of innocent bafflement. 'I don't understand. Must I cry every time?'

'Yes!' Aminah literally stamps her foot. 'If Laide ever gets married, I bet you'll cry when she tries on her wedding dress!'

'My dear, I will cry because it means that Allah has performed a miracle.'

Damola snorts in sync with Laide's gasp.

'Um, why am I in it?' Laide rises in protest, gestures to the room. 'Can we please focus on Mummy not liking Smallie's dress because she thinks it's slutty?'

Aminah's eyes widen. '*Excuse* me?'

Damola groans. 'Laide, what's your actual problem? Aminah, don't mind her. Can you guys chill? You're stressing the baby—'

'Who is the "you guys"?' Auntie Rafiat's sharply drawn brows rise to the edge of her coifed hair.

Damola sighs. 'Sorry, Mummy.'

With an eye roll, Laide sits back on the couch. 'Anyway, isn't it better that the baby knows what it's getting into? It probably loves the excitement since all you let it listen to is dry-ass Beethoven.'

The normally – *relatively*, for a Bakare – impassive Damola kisses her teeth. 'Um, "them" not *it* and there was a *New York Times* study that shows classical music stimulates intellectual growth in embry—'

Laide shrugs and waves a hand in the air. 'Whatever it is. If you don't play that baby some Victoria Monét or something. Besides, why doesn't *The New York Times* have a study saying that playing Fela for babies stimulates intellectual growth, huh? He's a classic to *us*.'

'Hello!' Aminah damn near screeches. 'Can we go back to the matter at hand, please? Mummy, what do you *really* think?'

There's silence. I stay very still in the hopes that maybe I might disappear. Eventually, Mrs Bakare lifts an imperious shoulder. 'I just think that you should have gone to the boutique I suggested. This one is too . . .' She makes a facial expression that is somewhere between a pout and a scowl. The sentence is complete. Aminah squints at her mother, and I see the quiet seething. She glances at me and I discretely move my hands down in a placating motion, mouthing, 'Beyoncé Countdown.' She swallows, nods and I see her recite the lyrics in her head, eyes closed, breathing meditatively. Eventually, her eyes flicker open calmly, and she smiles serenely at me before turning to her mother, speaking evenly.

'Mother. The other boutique is two times the price of this already very expensive one, and, besides, this is a Black-owned boutique that I took time to research. You only want me to choose your boutique because your friend's daughter also got a dress from this boutique and you don't want it to look like you're doing "follow follow", but I like this dress.'

Aminah's mother pauses for few moments before she blinks slowly. 'I don't know why you're making all this noise. I said it's fine.'

Aminah's nostrils flare, and I immediately rise up, stand in front of the plinth, taking her hands in mine, and looking at her in eyes that are already tearing up. 'Meenz, you look beautiful. Seriously.

The dress is everything on you. Your dream dress for when you marry your dream man.'

Risking the wrath of Mrs Bakare is made worth it by the grin Aminah gifts me. She squeezes my hands, raising her shoulder to her chin. 'Thank you, Keeks.'

The assistant returns with a bottle, suspiciously on time, and enquires brightly, 'So what do we say, ladies? Is it a yes to the dress?'

'No,' Aminah says, staring at her Caesar salad, after coming back from the restaurant bathroom, 'this is all wrong. I asked for the dressing to be on the side.' Her eyes flick up at me. 'Why didn't you tell them when they put it down? You know I like to control the pour.'

I sip my Provence rosé and keep my face as delicate as its finish because I know that this is not about me. I tilt my head to the side. 'Why didn't you go with the dress, Meenz? You loved it.'

She stabs at her salad, apparently forgetting all about my negligence. 'I mean yeah, I definitely did, but maybe my mum is right. I don't want it to look like I'm buying the dress just because her friend's daughter got hers from the same vendor. I set trends! I don't follow them! Remember when I started doing slick-back ponies in uni and then everyone started doing slick-back ponies? Besides, Sekemi Lawal – said friend's daughter – deliberately splashed me when we were at a beach house in Lagos once when we were fourteen, because I was talking to a guy that I didn't know was her crush. OK, maybe I did know a bit, but she was kind of a bitch before that. She would love it way too much if she thought I was copying her!'

I reach out to hold her hand, biting at my smile. 'Hey. Nothing can ever stop Aminah Bakare from being original. That dress was stunning and *you*. This wedding should be about what *you* want. It isn't about copying. You wanted a dress from that designer for years, babe. You're gonna let some frenemy stop you from doing that?'

Aminah relaxes, and squeezes my hand, some of the stress and irritability eking out of eyes that were glimmering a little when she returned from the bistro bathroom. 'You're right. They said I can decide in a week anyway.' She delicately tugs the skin by her eyes upwards with her forefingers. '*Ugh*, sorry, it's just . . . having to hear all of these opinions all the time is driving me crazy! And not just my mum, but, God love her, Kofi's mum too, who I adore, but, you know, she has no daughters and she wants me to wear the lace gloves her mother wore at her wedding. No offence, but I don't want to look like a Victorian ghost bride! Plus, the other day at work, my manager Charlotte said she would be letting me take the lead with the Tolami Benson athleisure-line campaign, which is an amazing opportunity for me to flex, because I know she sees me as her little grasshopper and is grooming me for her job for when she becomes account director and then Ollie – you know, my work nemesis, goes –' she adopts a light, Chelsealite drawl – '"That's super exciting! A lot to take on with wedding stuff, though. Charlotte, let me know if you need me to share the load with Aminah," with this bullshit smile to me. You know the one where the eyes look dead and their lips go flat?'

'What a bitch.'

Aminah's eyes widen. 'O ṣé o! Exactly. Obviously trying to muscle in on my path to being the Comms and Branding Queen I was born to be!' Aminah flutters her eyes closed and inhales deeply. She shimmies her shoulders, shaking the stress off. Then she puts her hands together in prayer and smiles serenely, gaze open and warm. 'And I am back. Bad energy, stay far away. Please, distract me. Tell me about you. What have you been up to?'

I spear a cocktail of chicken, lettuce and crouton onto my fork and slide it into my mouth, crunching slowly. I haven't told her about what happened with Malakai a month ago. I've barely told myself. I don't see him for nearly three years and the *second* I lay eyes on him I'm in his bed? Well, on the couch of his suite? Extremely disappointing. Malakai had texted me when I got home that night.

Just making sure you're home safe. Take care.

Take *care*? Basically a 'fuck you'. I thumbs-upped the message in reply. What was I supposed to say? *Yeah, I'm home safe technically, but, the thing is, am I safe from you? Because my skin is still tingling where you touched me and when you called me Scotch a part of me I thought was dead twitched just like my pussy does whenever I think of you stroking me in front of the London skyline, which is bad because you clearly resent me, a notion proven by the fact that you just told me to 'take care' like I'm a casual hook-up from a party and not someone you dated for five years. Shit. I am a casual hook-up from a party. Never mind. Ignore all of this. Also, fuck you too!*

I just didn't think I could say that. It would compromise the cool, evolved, aloof stance I've decided to assume. I'm a grown-up. Exes have sex all the time and go on to live perfectly healthy lives afterwards. We haven't spoken since because there's nothing to say. We had emotionless sex because we wanted to. That's it. Still, I need to unpack this to someone. This is partly the reason I suggested a lunch after the fitting at a cute little bistro in Greenwich round the corner from the boutique. Yes, to give Aminah space to decompress after what I knew would be a high-stress situation, but also to detangle what's been on my mind for the past month. I venture into it carefully. I don't think she'll judge, but somehow I don't think her directive to 'be good' included sex with Malakai. Some might say it expressly meant *not* doing that.

'Um,' I say, garnering all the strength I can from salad and rosé, 'I've been up to quite a bit actually,' just as Aminah pulls her glass from her mouth and splays a hand across her chest like a truth is bursting forth.

'Wait, oh my gosh, quickly, by the way, I have to say I'm very impressed that you and Malakai are managing to be grown about your break-up. Kofi says he's barely mentioned you. With you looking the way you look? I mean I can't lie, I really thought Malakai was gonna try and spin the block at the engagement party. And you're, like, all vulnerable after the Bakari thing . . . I just figured, I dunno, you might have done something silly. I mean can you imagine?' Her face is a picture of perfect horror at the idea. I force a laugh out of my tightened throat, my words suddenly becoming too tough and bulky to cough out.

'No . . .'

'I mean the HBO drama! And God knows the last things I need right now are more liabilities and contingencies, and I don't know what my maid of honour and best man getting into a *situation* would be if not a liability and contingency. I just need good, peaceful vibes. Please promise me that you'll continue to, like . . . *not*. Letting Malakai Korede put you inside trouble is not what you need right now. It would be a regression too, you know? You've come so far.'

I have been gently frowning and nodding in bland agreement whilst she's speaking, my thoughts spinning, palms prickling, and it's only when she tilts her head at me in enquiry that I realise that I am still nodding and smiling like someone who has been lobotomised. So, instead, I smile widely, brightly, manically, like someone who is on opioids, before chocking out a laugh that comes out far, far more high pitched than I intended.

'Exactly. Imagine the mess? No, nothing is happening between Malakai and I –' the truth – 'and nothing ever will' – an ardent belief.

'I'm proud of you, Keeks,' Aminah says so sweetly that I feel sour. She shakes her head. 'Sorry, my bad, I interrupted – you were telling me what you've been up to?'

Somehow, from within the spin of my mind, I'm able to pluck out something coherent and true. 'Oh! Um! So. Don't freak out.'

'I will not.'

'Thank you—'

'. . . promise such a thing.'

'Must you do that every time?'

Aminah beams. 'Of course. It's fun. You fall for it every time.'

'OK, well, seriously. I had to sign an NDA for this, so please, please, don't tell anyone.'

Aminah gasps. 'Oh my gosh. Which rapper did you sleep with? How could you not tell me? Is it gonna embarrass me? Tell me if I need to fix my face to remain neutral *now*.'

I reach out and grab her wrists. 'Aminah, I have not slept with a rapper.'

Aminah relaxes, relief sagging through her body. 'Oh, thank God. I just think we are too grown for our voice notes to be used in interludes. Although I would approve if it was, like, an exceptionally sexy one. Like Skepta. So what's up?'

Despite the uneasiness of the prior few minutes, I allow myself to feel some positivity, some light after a tumultuous month. It's fine that I didn't tell Aminah what happened between Malakai and I. All it would do is give her something to stress about, and it's not anything to stress about at all – in fact, I really doubt we'll see each other until the wedding. I'm actually very unbothered about it. It was just good sex with people who know each other's bodies. The crying thing was just an aftershock from seeing my ex for the first time in a couple of years. Emotionally healthy, and normal. A cleansing, actually, and now I'm purified from the noxiousness of love and lust for Malakai Korede. Telling her would be pointless and *selfish*, if anything. In fact, this is one of the few moments in life that one can tangibly pinpoint as a moment of radical selflessness. I'm comfortable with this reasoning, and relax back into the moment.

I inhale deeply. 'So Taré Souza's invited me to what I *think* is a secret gig?'

Aminah's eyes widen in glee and she squeals, before looking around the restaurant and hiss-whispering, 'Oh my gosh, yes! That's amazing! I mean *duh*, of course, why wouldn't you be on her radar? You're her number-one ride-or-die stan.'

Taré Souza, an R&B and soul artist, came onto the scene when I was in my second year of uni, and I immediately found kin in her music. She had a six-track soul R&B EP called *Sun in Me* released through Soundcloud. It seared through my skin and wrapped itself around a heart that was learning love. It was Lauryn Hill nodding at Sade and hugging Lala Hathaway and spudding Jazmine Sullivan with something new and crisp on the way, a softness that was razor-edged, love expressed like it was a knife that could cut through pain or simply cut you. It was a melancholia that was whimsical, joy that was visceral.

And as I muddled my way through life, falling stupidly in love and getting heartbroken and falling cautiously in love trying not to get heartbroken, so did she, getting signed, touring around the globe for it, her star rising as I grew into myself and she grew as an artist. Critics called her a wunderkind. Then her artistry shifted slightly, leaning into the athleticism she learned as a child gymnast and becoming a fully fledged popstar with choreo, the music getting lighter in theme and heavier in production, her audience widening. She was on the cover of *Rolling Stone* that year, her most recent album, *Glow in the Dark*, was rumoured to have been a shoo-in for Best Pop Album at the Grammys, when abruptly, just when she seemed to be on the precipice of superstardom, Taré Souza disappeared.

All her socials went dark. She withdrew her album from award submission despite the inevitable consternation of her label and new, hungry vampiric fans who fed off her eccentric personality, people who looked nothing like her, who would insist that they had a 'Taré Souza' living inside them when they did something they thought was quirky.

People wondered about her safety, her sanity, wondered if she was pregnant with her manager's child, and then her Instagram account popped back up with a single message, white against a black background, with her trademark tongue-in-cheek frankness: *Seeking Freedom. BRB. Keep my spot warm, or don't. I'll burn my way back in anyway.*

And from then – though she might be seen in LA clasping hands with a chiselled Magic Mike-franchise cast member, or reading *All About Love* with a blunt propped in her pout on a beach in Barbados, or in the background of a Met Gala afterparty having a drink poured in her mouth by Megan Thee Stallion – she was never, pointedly in the spotlight. Then last year she dropped a free poetry ebook out of nowhere, no promo, no interview. *Notes from Exile.* She posted the cover on Instagram and linked it in her bio. It was illuminating, stripped bare – and moved me so much that I covered it on The Heartbeat. I was happy for her – though the latest music she'd released had been fun, it seemed kind of incongruous to who she started out as, a musician whose melodies gave me some sort of sacred guidance for everything I felt.

Now it seems like she's finding herself again.

When my agent had got the email, I had no idea what to expect, but a thrill ran through me. Maybe the selectively reclusive artist was planning a full comeback, and she wanted me to cover it somehow? I could use it to leverage myself into editorial, pitch it to a few publications. That was the practical side of it, the 'I need a fucking job' side, but I was also an unabashed stan, curious to know what she's been up to for the past few years, what she would perform, what her presence could mean for the landscape of music.

I'm as nervous as I am excited, and getting to share it with Aminah stabilises me a little. She isn't as big a fan as I am, but she enjoys her music enough, a balance of 'moody girl R&B' (me) and 'shake bum-bum bops' (her). Technically, though, I wasn't even allowed to share the fact that it existed to her, the invitation contingent on signing an NDA. I figured that best friend privilege would override an NDA. I pray that it holds up in court.

'Man, this would be so good. See how God is blessing my girl. When Allah says yes, nobody can say no!' I smile at her remix as she continues: 'Taré hasn't had a public appearance in years and she invites you? This will definitely open up opportunities for you. I'm so gassed, sis!'

I'm cautious still, pushing a crouton across my near-empty bowl thoughtfully. 'Let's see. I mean what if she still thinks The Heartbeat is a thing?'

Aminah is unmoved, and she raises her brows, hoists her shoulders up in an unspoken command that I should gather myself. 'OK. And so? The Heartbeat is *you*. You make it pump. You finesse it.

You Killa Keeks it. Don't waste this opportunity.' She waves a butter knife in my face. 'Or I'll make you wear . . .' She pauses, drops the knife with frustration. 'Damn it, I was going say I'm gonna make you wear an ugly colour as your bridesmaid dress, but you look good in everything.'

I snort. 'My bad.'

'Like, I would have got away with it too if it wasn't for your meddling beauty. OK, I'll make you walk down the aisle with Kofi's shiny-suit cousin at the wedding. Remember when he told you he puts the *fine* in finance? And have I told you he's started a podcast? Called Money Talks. I'm sure he'll want to tell you all about it.'

I cackle and throw up my hands in surrender. 'Shit, yes, OK! Opportunity won't be wasted. You are *wicked*.'

Aminah beams in triumph. 'I think you mean the wickedest. Now, you sure you can't smuggle me in? Tell them I'm your emotional-support bad bitch—'

'Well, that's kind of exactly what you are.'

'And that should really be enough.'

'Right? But, nah, they were very clear that if you bring a plus one you won't be allowed entry. Apparently, it's a "specially curated guest list by Taré herself".'

Aminah sighs. 'Fine, if I can't come, you *have* to tell me all about it. Obviously, I won't tell anyone, but if you don't gist me I might die and that would be terrible for Kofi.'

'I solemnly swear to let you know if Skepta is there.'

'Thank you. That's all I ask. Oh, and because you're single now, if he is actually there, you have to take one for the team—'

'And by one you mean . . .'

Aminah's face is grave, void of a stitch of humour. 'You know what I mean, Kiki.'

I smile widely. 'I'll do my best. For us. For you.'

Aminah pretends to choke up before raising her glass. 'To sisterhood. And non-disclosures.'

I clink my drink with hers, settled, warm, as I giggle, full of fermented grape and love. Whatever happens, no matter what happens, I will always have this. 'To sisterhood. And non-disclosures.'

CHAPTER 8

High Esteem

'Mhmm, yeah, no, I understand.' The bell of Sákárà's door chimes as I rush out, one hand holding my phone to my ear, the other pulling my braids from under my maroon trench. I hoist my suede sack bag over my shoulder – from the eighties, stolen from my mum's wardrobe – holding on tightly, like it's some kind of talisman to stop me losing my shit. My mum is a serene queen, but, as I attempt to channel her, the righteous temper I've inherited from my father roars. Supressing the urge to call the person on the other side of the line an utter nincompoop, I lift my phone slightly from my ear to check my ETA. I do not need this shit right now. The invite said 'starts promptly at 8', and it's currently 8.05. Thankfully – and bizarrely – the location is only a twelve-minute walk, and I'm moving like Dina Asher-Smith if Dina Asher-Smith was really good at strolling. I adjust the dress I've hastily changed into after another last-minute shift.

I thought hard about what to wear to Taré's gig, knowing there would be people to impress (Skepta), but not wanting to lose myself. I opted for a black, backless, boat-neck, flare-sleeved minidress, sexy enough (Skepta), but casual when necessary. I paired it with seventies-style knee-high tan leather boots with a flared heel, accenting the fit with dainty gold rings peeking out of my sleeves, and my armour – gold hoops.

I look more put together than I feel, power-walking towards the De Beauvoir Town location whilst trying to convince a magazine editor acquaintance that 'Really, it's fine that you can't make the coffee tomorrow. And thanks for letting me know that the music-editor role's gone to someone in-house . . . But if any roles come up – great . . . OK . . . Thank you . . . The podcast? Oh, I'm not sure if it's coming back . . .' since the big streaming company that paid for everything pulled out and I can't afford to do it all myself sustainably. 'Yeah, um, a shame. OK. Well, thanks again!' I add 'for *fucking nothing*' into the crisp evening, shaking my head as I hike past the storefronts I used to know by heart.

I inhale the blue-black late-winter air, upon which, mercifully, the scent of fried chicken floats faintly, holding on for dear life. I try to calm myself down, and the streetlights blink on as if in encouragement. If a local fried-chicken chain is surviving, so can I. I need to cling on to this belief. The editor is the third contact who's flaked and I can't help but feel that SoundSugar has put a career hit out on me. I could go back to publishing again, but it would mean almost starting again from the beginning, and now that I've had a taste of doing work that isn't hampered by outside voices, it would be even harder to tuck myself in, make space for playing the game.

But I also don't have the luxury of fucking around. Now that my parents have potential buyers for the restaurant, they could sell up as quickly as three months and I need to figure out if I'm going to be able to keep this flat as soon as possible, which, right now, is unlikely considering all I'm doing is writing the odd music review on a viral TikTok sensation whose lyrics seem to be AI generated every other week. With my refusal to accept wages from my parents and my sinking savings, there's a lot riding on tonight aside from watching an artist I admire and potentially pulling a grime legend. The exclusivity of the guestlist could lead to crucial contacts and I'm in desperate need of a lifeboat. My phone chirps, and I look down, feeling anxiety abate slightly at the name.

MinahMoney
Killa Keeks 🔪 🔪 🔪. *You can do it! Love you! MWAH*
  (that was for Skepta x)

I remember I can swim.

*   *   *

> *I saw your river by the road,*
> *As red as your tongue, flowing.*
> *I cupped, lapped, coughed and Vega*
> *Came out, giggling.*
> *I have*

You and a verse within,
The galaxy in my bones,
Created from not a thing,
And every
Night I pray,
Let there be light,
Let us be light.
I lust,
Only for the sweet heat,
Under my skin.
Taré Souza – 'Notes in Exile'

Something is wrong. Upon arrival at the imposing Victorian townhouse, an assistant wearing Carhartt and a bad attitude leads me down a flight of steep wooden stairs and into a plush room that's suffused with incense. It looks like the powder room of a goddess. The atmosphere is so intoxicating that it dissipates my immediate anxiety surrounding fire hazards. Jewel-toned rugs and handmade artisanal leather poufs that seem to be from northern Nigeria dot around a room that glows amber, with walls painted a rich burgundy.

I put down the lack of crowd outside the house to the fact that I'm late, and attributed the lack of chatter as I walked down the stairs to a reverence for an artist at work. Taré Souza is at the centre of the room, perched on a stool that sits on a small round podium, cradling a classical guitar and accompanied by a man with locs playing djembes. She looks ethereal. A halo comprising a deep wine Afro-puff frames a seraphic face with umber skin that glows in the dim light and a button nose glinting with a ring. She's in a cream silk bralet, a matching kimono, expertly ripped jeans and a pair of dainty heels. It's an outfit that says she floats from building into car and back again with her feet barely touching pavement, a graceful R&B fairy.

The only thing that moves is Taré's mouth, which stretches a fraction, in welcome for me. It's magical, and it would make me feel like I was the only person in attendance here, even if I wasn't literally the only person in the audience. I look around to see if there could be more people hiding somewhere in the open space. There are not. Not even a whiff of Skeppy. In front of the stage holding Taré is an empty embroidered pink armchair. I blink at it as my heart drops. The gig is over. I've completely fucked it. Maybe it was, like, some kind of experimental performance where she plays one song and everyone dips? Did I miss an email? Did information get lost in Nina's inbox?

'I'm so sorry for being late.' My palms dampen in complete mortification. I put them on my thighs to surreptitiously dry them, but I'm met with a slither of skin and some leather. Hardly moisture wicking. 'I, um, had to cover a shift managing my family restaurant and we couldn't afford to shut early . . .'

Why am I babbling to this lady whose voice has made me *weep*? Why would she care, after I've completely disrespected the honour of seeing her perform for the first time in five years? *And why am I talking to her directly?*

Taré tilts her head and gestures to the seat in front of her. 'Girl, chill. The show can't start without you. You're right on time. Take that sexy trench off and sit. Get comfortable.'

I do not know what is happening, but I also know that this is a direct order. So I do just that. My coat is whisked away by her moody assistant as I sit myself down and try to calm my twitching heart. Cool. This is just an inexplicable private concert in front of one of the most elusive talents in the world. Maybe tomorrow I'll do brunch with Sade, since God is just doing anything. I don't have time to wonder if this is an extremely vivid dream, because as soon as my butt makes contact with the cushion of the seats Taré's fingers start dancing on the strings of her guitar, humming into the mic, capturing my attention. My bare legs prick up with goosebumps.

Her eyes wise and alive with emotion, Taré sings my heart out and makes it her dominion. In the flesh, she's smaller, slighter, like all that's tethering her to this earth is the heft of her voice; it's husky, multi-tonal, an instrument in and of itself. Soon I forget the surreality of this situation, and the only thing that feels strange is how familiar her energy is despite never having met her, despite this oeuvre being new. Her voice has soundtracked so many moments of my life that this soothes like a hug from an old friend.

Now, her voice and her guitar conjure memory from melody and mood. I see Malakai and I listening to her music in his tiny uni room, me wanting to slip under his skin, him already in mine – so deep in mine, me wanting to stay there, in that moment, if it was the last thing I ever did. There's something about how a good love song can swing low into your gut and hit at a spot between pleasure and pain and yearning and bliss, this feeling that this, *this* is what music was created for – this transcendence that somehow makes you leave your body and become more aware of it at the same time. Something like a first kiss with the right one. That first kiss that tells you everything outside of it is wrong because nothing could be as good as this.

Good songs like this melt over your skin and make your heart beat faster and you come into the understanding that feelings can be real despite being intangible. TikToks from therapists barrelling through their Hippocratic oaths to tell us about their clients repeat mantras of Feelings. Aren't. Facts. Sometimes true. Sometimes insecurities dictate our feelings – we project thoughts onto other people and let them trap us – but a good song stirs emotion with knowledge. What you feel is heightened, affirmed by melody, by lyrics that paint you true. It makes feelings come alive, make themselves known. They come clear like cool water down your throat on a summer's day. What you feel is real.

And sitting here, in this basement, I'm clear on one thing: Bakari has never made me feel like this song. Fact. The sultry blues of these songs make me think of hot kisses that make your bones crumble to brown sugar that melts in a mouth that makes you moan, makes me think of believing in a love that could weather whatever, because it is the weather, it is everything. I told myself that a love like that could only be temporary for me because it had to be. It has to be. Because, yes, a love like that sets your heart on fire, makes you feel understood, known, but that's the danger. When you give your whole self, your whole self is at risk, but when you enter a love that holds the increments you give yourself permission to give it's safer – yet at what cost? I'd felt safe – content – with Bakari, but did I ever feel happy? And what's the value of 'safer' anyway, if nothing precious is at stake? The last song ends, my own applause cleaving my questions open as Taré stands up, beams and bows to the audience of one as her drummer leaves silently.

'Thank you, beloved,' her voice coos, deep and smooth. 'I really appreciate you being here. You know, I've been travelling around the world for such a long time, and I really wanted my first show back in London to be special. A conversation between me and the people who get me.' I wonder who counts as 'people', considering it's only me here. I frown with some confusion just as Taré's hipster sprite passes me a cocktail that has seemingly been procured from thin air. I sip it, the best Tommy's margarita I have ever tasted in my life. This is how I know I probably fell on the way here and this is some sort of concussion dream.

'*Damn.*' It slips out, with no acquiescence with my brain, sharp citrus tap-dancing on my tongue. 'You know, it's weird, this is my favourite cocktail—'

'I know all, babes. I'm basically omnipresent.' The aroma of peonies, success and a crystalline melisma flows into my immediate atmosphere and Taré Souza sits in front of me, after her assistant pulls up a purple velvet scalloped chair and places a murky green cocktail in her hand. Taré is even more dazzling up close. She has poreless skin decorated with a glittering burst of sunset hues framing eyes fanned with fluttering lash extensions. There's a slight empyreal shimmer on her cheeks, and a congenial grin on her face. She looks like an Afrocentric pixie. It's only when she gives my arm a light pinch that I reckon with the notion that this may be real life.

She squeals, 'Kidding! I got my people to ask your agent. You OK, babe? You looked like you went somewhere while I was singing. It happens, but I'm always curious about where people go. I'm just a pilot. I know roughly where I'm taking you, but I don't know where exactly you're going to go in that destination, you know? I don't know your inner world. Like, I'm a beach bum, but maybe you're someone who likes to hike at 5 a.m.?'

'Yeah. Definitely not.' I laugh, and the action forces me to immediately ease up, relaxing. The bizarreness unlocks a freedom; how could I *possibly* mess this up? Besides, I've interviewed plenty of artists in my time. I can do this. So what if I've had sex to her voice?

I shift in my seat, leaning forward. 'So, you ever went on a really bad date and you feel the need to escape your reality so you, like, go to a happy place in your brain? For survival? This experience was the opposite of that. I felt so *present*, and it opened me up. I wasn't escaping inside my body I was like . . . discovering and rediscovering things that I knew and didn't know at the same time. Memories. Questions I have. Emotions. It was . . . it's the most beautiful thing I've ever been part of. Really. I mean I've been to amazing live shows and I'm still not entirely sure what's going on here, but this was . . . *is* out of this world. Your new songs are beautiful. I still think this is some kind of fever dream, and I don't know if, like, this is some kind of art-immersion experiment where everyone gets to be an individual audience, but . . . thank you. It felt sacred.'

Taré's eyes glimmer, and she smiles. 'Where did you go mentally? I mean when you were on a bad date and you felt like you had to escape?'

'Oh!' I shrug. 'A two-week baecation with Skepta.'

Taré roars with laughter then takes a sip of her strange cocktail, batting a bejewelled hand. 'A two-week baecation with Skepta is overrated.'

I snort with surprise at her candour and press my glossed lips together. I suspected she might be like this — fun and smart, a woman after my own heart — because of the way she used to run loops around thirsty, graceless press who tried to force her into her box or pit her against other artists. She'd swipe the mic from them and ask them who *they're* fucking since we're all being nosey here. Celebrities are wont to disappoint, their sheen smudging with proximity and their authenticity crumbling under pressure, but Taré seems fun for real, real for real.

'You're lying,' I say boldly. 'I don't believe that.'

Taré pauses for a moment and crosses her legs and for a second I think I've crossed a line, played a little too close to overfamiliarity. Maybe Taré's one of those stars who only enjoys banter on her terms, relatable as long as you play by her rules, but her face breaks into a bright smirk, eyes twinkling with mirth. Her cocktail, I'm noticing, smells really strong — what *is* that?

'Yeah, girl, I'm lying. It was heavenly. That man could be a yogi the way he opened me up in ways I could never have imagined. Made me as flexible as Britney in 2000.'

My laugh wrestles free. '"Oops I Did It Again"?'

Taré squeals. 'And again and again. I just wanted to tell someone that I had a two-week baecation with Skepta, honestly.'

I nod with grave understanding. 'A constitutional right, actually. Written in the Sneaky Link bylaws. Loose lips sink ships, except when the ship involves a man that God created when she was feeling in a generous spirit. Had her iced coffee, got all her errands done on time and then decided to create a little something for the girls. A treat.'

Taré squawks with glee, a delightfully raspy sound, considering her angelic singing voice. It's loud and filthy and completely charming. 'Whew. Knew I would like you. I mean I listen to The Heartbeat all the time so I guessed I would, but you can't assume people will be cool just because they *seem* cool, you know? But you're cool.' She breezily echoes my own apprehension like it's nothing, before sipping her snot-hued drink again.

Emboldened by curiosity, I say, 'Thank you so much. Can I ask what you're drinking in the spirit of me being cool?'

She smiles. 'Oh, it's an elevated matcha margarita. Antioxidants with a kick! Try some!' She shoves it in my face, and I see no choice but to take a sip. I immediately want to gag. It's powdery and bitter and a little gets stuck in my throat. Alcohol shouldn't have *bits* in it. It prolongs the consumption process and you don't want time to really think too deeply about what you're swallowing otherwise you wouldn't really do it. A philosophy that could apply to a few things.

Eyes watering, I cough, swallow some spit and pass her back

the glass. 'Mmmm!' An errant cough escapes and I sip my own drink to soothe my throat. 'A kick!'

She looks pleased, and both her shoulders rise in delight. 'Amazing. I'm partnering with this tequila company as their brand ambassador so I'm trying out new recipes for this little tie-in video series.'

My smile remains fixed on my face and I nod slowly at this terrible idea. 'Oh. In that case, why don't you go for something accessible? Matcha margarita may be a little . . . of an acquired taste and you may want something that hits instantly. Like your music! Something sweet, sultry, dark and indulgent like your voice. What's your favourite fruit?'

Taré tilts her head at me with gentle interest. 'Cherry.'

'Perfect. Make a cherry margarita and call it the Taré Twist. Or La Souza Vita!'

A small grin begins to spread across Taré's face as she nods, her eyes switching from something bright and open, to something sharper. 'That's so interesting,' she says slowly. 'You fucking hated that drink.'

I open my mouth to deny this, but nothing comes out, and I find I don't really want to lie. I don't think she's trying to catch me out, but I also don't see the benefit of not telling the truth. I pull a face. 'Yeah. I found it kind of revolting. The taste to me . . . it's giving Hackney Marshes. Or Hollywood anti-vaxxer bathwater. Sorry.' If Aminah were here she would admonish me for not being able to 'pretend small', but, honestly, telling Taré the truth was for the greater good. Allowing people to drink that might fuck up her brand and their guts. I'm being a humanitarian.

Taré twitches a shoulder. 'Don't be. Like you said, it's an acquired taste and, plus, there really is no campaign. It's my own personal drink. I like the kick. I just think it's fascinating that you didn't lie to me. I mean you said *something*, but you never said you liked it. And when you realised that your opinion on it might count for something, you suggested something you thought was better, smoothly as fuck might I add, without me wanting to hit you.'

What is happening? I can't tell if I'm messing this up or bossing this. What is *this* anyway? She'd invited me to this event out of nowhere, and I'm the only person here. I idly wonder if I'm being recruited into the Illuminati. Although, I do think being successful – or at the very least employed – is a prerequisite for being recruited. Also why can I recognise the taste of the frog-piss drink sticking to the back of my throat?

'Sorry – what was the name of the drink again?'

'Elevated Matcha Margarita,' she says it breezily, like I asked her the colour of the sky.

I nod as a faded memory begins to bring that weirdly botanic taste to the forefront. 'Sure. And what makes it elevated? There's this um, tang to it—'

Taré turns to her assistant, who has been scrolling listlessly on their phone, sat by the door, 'Yo, Celestial. What gives it the tang?' She turns to me in explanation. 'Celestial's done mixologist training. I give her a mood, and she comes up with a drink. This is one of her creations, actually. She's the only person I allow to make my drinks for me. My experience in this industry means I don't trust a lot of people. Plus, I'm half Nigerian, half Brazilian, so I'm very superstitious. So many people in this life are badmind.' She looks back up to her personal bartender as she replies, in a chill tone, 'The tang's from THC.'

I nod with forced composure. 'Cool, cool. Um. And by THC did you mean to say CBD?' I scratch at my neck. 'Just to clarify?'

'No, no. THC. I like to unwind after performances. Tap into another plane.'

'Cool. *Cool*.' Am I still nodding? I think I am. I tell my mind to stop nodding, and I think I've achieved it because my hoops have stopped moving.

Taré is genuinely horrified, a hand flying to her mouth. 'Fuck! It's the teeniest, tiniest dose, though. Like a pinch. That's something I should have told you about, isn't it?'

I hitch a casual shoulder up. 'Preferably, I think.'

'Of course – oh man, this looks terrible. I am so sorry. I'm just so used to the drink I forgot—'

'You know what! It's OK! I needed something to take the edge off anyway. So, um, back to—' I veer her back on course, realising that soon enough we're both likely to lose track of where this conversation is supposed to go.

Taré claps her hands. 'Right!'

I'm realising that Taré is like an eccentric little fairy, her shrewd, brilliant mind flitting and fluttering at lightning speed, her magic not evil nor angelic – it just *is*, at the whims of her desires.

'You probably want to know what's going on. Like I said, I've

196

been a fan of your work for a while. How you connect music and vision and human emotion – how you understand it, how you're curious. You clearly listen with your whole body. Music isn't just a moment for you, it's an experience. It's personal history. You dive deep. Make roadmaps to emotions, to artist evolution. You're like . . . some fucking music archaeologist wizard bad bitch.' Her hands dance as she's speaking, conducting an orchestra of the sections that form my self-esteem.

'Um, thank you . . .' I warm, a tension I didn't know I had releasing, parts of me stretching out. Though this might be the effects of the cursed cocktail, it also just feels good to be seen, to know that what I did with The Heartbeat wasn't all for nothing. It got me here, talking with someone whose artistry inspires me.

Taré shakes her head, and sips her nasty drink, 'Mmm-mm – thank *you*. You know, you've seen things in my work that I wasn't able to articulate myself?' She sits back and shakes her head, stretching an arm on the back of her chair and crossing her legs. 'And I'm kind of narcissistic so I'm very preoccupied with my work. When I heard that you weren't doing the podcast any more, I did some digging. Asked about you at SoundSugar. Told my people to tell their people that I wanted to work with you. Go on your show, maybe. You know what those fuckers said?'

Apprehension makes my tongue heavy, so I shake my head.

Taré grins widely. 'They said you were "difficult to work with".'

My stomach sinks with the confirmation that my hunch was correct. SoundSugar were blacklisting me. This is why all my meetings were falling through, why I was struggling to get my foot up anywhere. They were pre-empting my talking about what they did by trying to snuff me out. And now they were compromising my opportunity to work with one of my dream artists.

'And in the same breath,' Taré continues, her face lightly strewn with some merciful disgust, 'they offered me a chance to come on their new podcast with Kitty St James. "Similar vibes," they said. I looked it up. Similar vibes like how fast fashion churns out a dupe for a runway show overnight, but it don't fit right. Don't look right. Strings running. Colour fading. Destined for the landfill of nepo-baby mediocrity.'

I swallow my anger, and it sits tight in my throat. 'I see.'

Taré tilts her head, eyes earnest. 'Hey. It was exactly what I wanted to hear, Kiki. When the wrong people call you difficult, you're on to something. Trust me. It's all I needed to know to know exactly what happened. They tried to pull you apart and sell you in pieces, right? Tried to extract your essence without the *you* of it?'

Humiliatingly, tears spring into my eyes, tears I'd been holding back, because I've never had time to sit and really *think* about what happened. I just kept moving, working through applying to jobs, doing shifts at the restaurant, fucking exes – *fucking* exes – and helping Aminah with her wedding. I haven't had a moment to catch my breath. I now feel it all in my chest, the pain, the fury, the possessiveness.

I shake my head. 'I'm sorry. I don't know why I'm—'

Taré reaches out for my hand, squeezes. 'That's OK. I know why. Look, they're threatened by you. They tried to do the same to me just because I was sick of being silenced. I tried to play the game for a while, told myself I just need to get to a certain stage and then I can take back my power, but it doesn't work like that. Because that "certain stage" kept looking further and further away. I woke up one morning and barely recognised myself or the music I was making. I was sick of feeling like I was compromising my soul, you know? That's why I took a hiatus.'

I nod, confusion and gratitude and potential highness battling it out in my mind. 'I really appreciate this. It makes me feel less . . . scrambled, I guess? Understood. And, honestly, this is all so amazing, but . . .'

'What's this all for? We're getting there.' Taré sits back and beams impishly. 'Tell me what you thought of the new music, Kiki. They're beta versions, so be honest.'

I swallow, my mind still whirring, attempting to catch up. The bizarreness of the situation is so heightened that ironically it makes it easier for my mind to answer questions on autopilot. 'Well, the first few songs were beautiful, and I could see the influences, but I think that's the issue. They're so close to something transcendent, but I can *see* the influences. They'll do well for what you want to do, but there's something embedded in the songs that's fighting to get out. I guess it depends how far you wanna go, how experimental you want to go. The last song, though? Is perfect. Otherworldly. But together, all of them, they're this epic tapestry. A story. I don't know if you've thought about visuals, but I'm thinking not quite Afrofuturism, but a . . . Taréfuturism. It fuses everywhere you've been with everywhere you've been wanting to go, everything you will be—' I stop for a second, realising that I have essentially told

Taré how to do her job. 'I mean those are just general thoughts. I'm no exp—'

'Stop that.' Taré has been looking at me with eyes narrowed in focused assessment, and now she nods to herself, her smile broadening. 'Don't doubt yourself. I think *you* have something fighting to get out. I see it. Look, I'm in a new phase of my life, Kiki. I've split with my record label and I'm almost done with building a new team. I've written this new album, but I'm still honing it, figuring out its story.' She waves her hands like she's conjuring the reality from air, and her eyes dance around like she sees it. 'A visual album. A documentary with the album, alongside music videos. I want the documentary to be the definitive script on my work. I'm not doing any interviews or explainers. This will be it. Not a reinvention, but a reintroduction. In four months, I want to do an intimate pop-up gig that will double as the music video for the lead single. It will be a mix of professionals and just lovers of music. I want it to feel real, authentic. The whole project will be released behind a paywall on my website.'

I try and fail to subdue the burgeoning thrill running through me. 'Taré, this sounds . . . amazing. The intentionality behind all of it disrupts what the industry is becoming right now . . . It's incredible.'

Taré's lips curl in bemusement. 'Yeah, well, I'm glad you think so. Because I want you to be my creative producer for the documentary, and that gig.'

It's entirely the wrong time to take another sip of my drink because I splutter so hard I have to thump my chest. 'Sorry, I'm . . . what?'

Taré shifts in her seat, her eyes glittering with resolution. 'I have a gut feeling about you, and I'm trying to listen to that more these days. I think I need your eye and your ear and your heart. I want you to helm the documentary, interview me as I embark on the creative process leading up to the release and help explore my . . . musical resurrection journey. This is going to be the definitive media for the album. I'm not going to do any interviews. I won't be on any podcast. This will be it, and I feel like you're the perfect person for it. You also, I think, have what it takes to help create a magical show. Plus, you're a truth-teller. I need that around me. It will be a gamble – I won't lie to you. I don't know what the reception will be and it's almost entirely self-funded. This shit is all independent. It's gonna be intense – this is a tiny space of time, but I know it has to be now. I'll pay you as much as I am able to, but I'll be honest and say that it won't be what you would get if you were being paid through a major label. It's a labour of love and faith. Plus, you can't take on any other jobs while you're working on it. This has to be it. I need complete discretion. Obviously, we will discuss further and get lawyers and managers and agents involved, but for now – how does it sound to you?' In her eyes, I see not quite desperation, but something heavy lining the effervescence and passion.

She swallows and her smile wavers a little. 'This album helped me find my way back to me. I just know that you *get* it. That's what matters to me. I can't make promises, but I know this is special. It won't change the world, but it can change *someone's*. Make them feel less alone. I think that's what The Heartbeat did too.'

Her words are heavy enough to land within me with a thud, agitating a hunger. I haven't felt like this since I came up with The Heartbeat, and, yes, the woman sat before me is a little high and kind of quirky, but some of my best friends stay a little high and kind of quirky, and something about the glint in her eye is reassuring to me. I see someone like me. Anchored by a vision and fuelled by passion. I remember the last time I collaborated with someone to create something special; it was in university, and, yes, I sort of fell in love with my co-collaborator, but I also fell in love with the *process*. The alchemy of visions, and adjusting and perfecting and tweaking and moulding to make something beautiful. It was a uniquely satisfying feeling, making me feel full up within my skin, like I was pouring into all the parts of me that were created for creation. A million questions turn in and around themselves on my mind, and I don't know if it is the Elevated Matcha Margarita, but I'm OK with keeping them at bay right now. My palms prickle and I feel butterfly wings in the pit of my belly, the kind you feel when you're on the edge of something that you feel will impact your life. This is a *job*. A dream one. I flick my eyes from my glass to Taré's expectant shimmering face.

'That last song you played? It's perfect, but you didn't give it a name. What's it called?'

Taré shrugs. 'I have no idea. It's more like . . . *conceptual* than literal. Love lost then found again. Not just a person, but in yourself. A rebirth of something. It's yearning, but triumphant too. The yearning is in the process. It's hard to pin down.'

I pause, and let the memory of the lyrics and the song and its atmosphere wash over me, humming a little.

Taré releases a sly smile. 'Oh. She's a singer. Collab?'

'I have a residency in my shower. I have an idea for a title. How do you feel about "Phoenix"?'

Taré tilts her head in thought, eyes narrowed before they gleam and her face brightens and, just like that, I think we've formed some sort of team. 'Please tell me you're about to say yes.'

I smile, the thrill of possibility thrumming with THC in my veins, about to reply, when Celestial appears — literally appears — next to her and whispers in Taré's ear. She grins and claps her hands. 'Amazing. Tell him to come down.'

Taré turns to me, conspiratorial. 'Full disclosure, the person you're about to see is an old link of mine. Well, we had one month of bliss before we went our separate ways. Decided to keep in contact, because, shockingly, I actually liked him as a person. I don't keep in contact with straight men unless absolutely necessary and he's cool enough. Do you know how hard it is to find a guy that's sweet and funny?'

I release a sardonic chuckle. 'Yeah and I'm still recovering. Look, um, I can get out of your hair — I can just email your people tomorrow morning—'

Taré waves a bejewelled hand in dismissal. 'No, no, so here's the thing — I invited him here specifically because I wanted you to meet. He's heard the new stuff, has an eye, and I'm thinking of adding him to the team, but I wanna check the vibes first. If you don't like him, we can explore other options. My judgement could be compromised by his charm. And other things.'

I raise a knowing brow. 'Oh yeah? That good?'

She smirks. 'Sis. And he's nineties fine. Look, I'm not stingy, and I'm all about professional boundaries.' I assume that this is despite accidentally allowing me to ingest THC. 'So nothing can happen again, and I don't want it to. Necessarily. We're better off as pals, but if you wanna have a go—'

I compose myself, containing an incredulous bark, because a few minutes ago I was jobless and now I'm in the absolutely insane position of creative-producing a project by an artist I admire whilst balancing an offer of one of her ex-lovers on my lap. I should tell my mum, so she can give it as a testimony in church this Sunday. I'm guessing Taré doesn't have an HR department.

I adjust myself on my seat, managing to sound level. 'Uh, I trust your taste, but I'm currently on a man sabbatical. Nothing can shake me. Not even hoop earring Denzel.'

Taré husks out a raucous laugh. 'Good to know. Because this man is that dangerous.'

Her gaze snags on something behind my head, and her smile turns minxish. 'Ay. Speaking of the devil.'

Pointing at the gold cross pendant on my neck, I say, 'Don't worry, I got you.' I rise with Taré and turn round, ready to potentially perform an exorcism, when she chimes, 'Kiki, the director I wanted you to meet.'

Director. She never said he was going to be a director. I know before I know. Horror curdles my blood, thickening it so it seems to stop in its flow through my body as my eyes crash land on the very last person I want to see right now.

'. . . Malakai Korede.'

CHAPTER 9

Phoenix

Film: Untitled
Director: Malakai Korede
Producer: Kiki Banjo

Untitled is commendable in its tender exploration of young love through the lens of an ambitious and meticulous filmmaker. Korede, with an inquisitive eye, treats its subject with gentleness, a curiosity that could veer into scepticism, if not balanced by the questions posed by producer Kiki Banjo. Stunning interstitials depict romance on campus: the first crush, blush, kiss, date and Banjo's radio show. The producer and director make an exquisite team, pushing and pulling, challenging and learning as they go along. It feels as if we are falling in love with them; and in the end there is a precious reveal that makes the sojourn all the more satisfying. Though this film did not win the final prize, we want

*to specially commend it; unpolished, raw, it displays a truth,
and we are excited to see what Korede – and indeed Banjo – do
next, whether it be separately or as a team.*

My hand, weakened by the phenomenon of abruptly halted blood
flow, slips round the glass I'm holding, the liquid splashing my
burning skin as I release an incredulous, *'Kai?'* He blinks at me,
equally stunned, his smile drooping off his face like cheese off a
sloppy pizza. Lovely to know the new superpower I've acquired:
the ability to disappear all joy from Malakai Korede. Oh God – a
horrific thought hops into my mind – did he come here thinking
he was going to *hook up* with Taré? I feel light-headed, need to sit
down, but sitting down would be weird right now, just a bizarre
cherry on top of a towering sundae of fuckedupness and so I stay
very still, hoping not to agitate my heartbeat further.

'Oh, he actually prefers "Malakai",' Taré chides sweetly with
intimate confidence. My nostrils immediately flare. 'I tried to call
him "Kai" once and he got all twitchy, says he hates being called
that. Male artistes are *the* most sensitive.' She walks up to him, loops
her arms round his neck, brushing her lips on his cheek before
booping him on the nose. 'Right, babe? You're kind of a diva.'

Malakai's arms move slackly around her in greeting, his gaze
still on me.

I wonder what would happen if I vomit on this Moroccan rug
right now? It looks very expensive. Would she take the cleaning
fee out of my rate? Will I even have a rate to dock, because am I
really about to take on a job to work with my ex-boyfriend who

apparently has had vigorous sex (I am imagining it as vigorous – judging by her arms, Taré clearly does some kind of strength training) with my would-be boss? My stomach churns dangerously and I feel like I'm sweating beneath my skin.

'Oh, sorry. I'm so embarrassed.' I turn to Malakai who looks just as nauseous as I do as he drops his arms from round Taré. I don't know if this is gratifying or infuriating. '*Malakai.*' My blood, now apparently flowing, seems to be making up for lost time by pumping so hard through me that I can hear it pulsing in my ears. I feel like the pressure could expel my soul from my body. I wish it would hurry up and get it over with. There's a very real possibility that my nose might bleed.

Malakai is still staring at me, visibly stricken. 'Kiki. I didn't know you'd be here.' I clamp my eager 'well, no shit' in between my jaws. We were supposed to ignore each other till the weddings, five months from now, enough time for all residual tension to fade into nothing, for me to book several therapy sessions and for my butt to get even bigger to enlarge his own regret. What I say now can make or break the situation, I know, and it is imperative that I maintain a semblance of cool maturity, obtain the upper hand.

I clear my throat. 'My bad. I'm sure you were expecting to see Taré alone.'

Malakai's gaze flattens into a blade that slices through my double-meaning with ease and then he looks so deliciously scrambled, so unwell, that for a moment, triumph breaks through my own acute distress. Then I remember that he's had sex with a woman who was once on the cover of *Vogue* Arabia.

208

'Wait.' Taré's eyes jump between us, her brow furrowing gently. 'You two know each other?'

'From uni.' It leaps out of me. 'We know each other from uni.' I am not about to jeopardise a potential career definer by making things even more unnecessarily messy. Malakai swallows tightly before affable charm suffuses his face and he shoots Taré an easy grin, quickly recovered, gathering his senses. One thing Malakai hates is looking rattled in public. 'Right. Uni. Friends of friends. We're acquaintances, really.'

I bite the inside of my cheek to stop my eyes from rolling. 'I mean basically strangers.' When he goes low, I'll go scuba-diving in petty.

Malakai laughs, eyes brightly screaming 'ain't shit funny'. An admittedly sadistic sharp shock of satisfaction runs through me. I've slipped under his skin.

He speaks through teeth that are a shade away from being gritted. 'Although I do remember my people saying you had a crush on me. Thought it was kinda sweet.' Dick. He's gone drilling into the earth's core. My cheeks rage and my hand itches around my glass of watery cocktail. I want to splash it in his insuffer- ably smug face. He knows all the paths to my irritation and he's enjoying the journey. His eyes glint, knowing, playing, pulling on a grasp of civility.

Taré gasps in delight. 'You're lying!'

'He is, actually.' I shake my head, smiling with a geniality that I hope gleams like a knife's edge. 'You must be thinking of someone else.' I run my eyes across him. A huge mistake really, because what I see reinforces the fallacy of my next sentence. 'You're not my type.'

Malakai pauses, and his gaze briefly flashes a private screening of a filthy featurette depicting him holding my orgasm in a single hand. His brow twitches and he chuckles softly, self-effacingly, pressing a palm to his chest in phony, pantomimed apology. 'My mistake. Must have got you confused with someone else. There were a few.' I think this man may have a death-wish.

I sip my drink and bite into the smooth pebble of ice that slides into my mouth, crunching into the cool to calm my boiling blood and to stop myself from saying something that would get us both into trouble. Malakai's smile widens, reading the action accurately.

Taré, somehow, is oblivious to the fact that she stands in the midst of a battleground and claps her hands, 'Oh, I love this! A reunion! Perfect. Let's sit down.'

Malakai pulls a teal velvet chair over to us with the same enthusiasm as he would to watch a Tyler Perry movie and we sit stiffly in the world's most awkward triangle. The effort that Malakai puts into not looking at me thickens the air. Taré twirls into it.

'So, Kiki, I'm sure you're familiar with his work, but Malakai's an incredible director, just a *gorgeous* visual eye and world-building skill, and, Malakai, Kiki's voice and ear and emotional knowledge and intelligence and imagination . . . *shit*, I get tingles thinking about the stories you guys can help me tell, which is why I needed you both to meet, get to know each other. See if we can get a creative throuple going on, you know?'

I briefly wonder for which sin I'm being punished. Like, what possible reason could there be for the cosmic joke being played on me now? Is this because I told my dad I found a new church to go to in lieu of going to my old family one when actually I've been listening to a Gospel playlist every Sunday whilst cleaning my make-up brushes? I know for a fact that Taré couldn't have seen mine and Malakai's film, *Untitled*, because it's on the seventh page of a Google search and password protected on YouTube, so this really has to be some sort of divine inter-tension.

I rub my neck and nod. 'Sure. Sure. Cool. Cool.' Celestial appears again to place an old-fashioned in Malakai's hand and he immediately gulps it, his grunt of agreement warbling into the glass. I watch as the liquid glides down his throat. I idly imagine licking it. Clearly the shock of this entire situation has rattled my senses to such an extreme that all my impulses are scattered, so 'lick' is placed where 'throttle' should be. It is an inconvenient fact that he looks typically fine though, with his white shirt, brushed forest-green flannel overshirt and tan tapered chinos. Trim, but no longer as slim as he was when we were younger, his muscled broadness fills out the dinky chair in which he's nestled. I'm staring, something I only realise I'm doing when Taré's raspy laugh interrupts me.

'I gotta say, Malakai, you're the loose link here. Kiki's the one I really want and if she doesn't like you, you're out, so play nice, yeah?'

Malakai pulls the glass from his face and leans back in his seat. 'Come on, Taré. You ever known me not to play nice?' Taré's brow hitches, and her mouth twitches in flirtation. 'You sure you want me to answer that in front of company?'

It strikes me that I don't really have any valuable possessions to leave to anyone, and Aminah will be so pissed to have to make one of her sisters her maid-of-honour. These thoughts occur to me because I am now certain that I've died after doing something so fucked up in my earthly life that I am currently in my own specially designed pocket of hell. There is no other conceivable reason why I'm being forced to witness my ex-boyfriend flirt with a stunning, talented, fun woman, who could be responsible for me being able to pay a mortgage.

Theoretically, of course, I don't care. Malakai can do what he wants. We are a non-factor, and this is none of my business. Realistically, though, I'm feeling kind of violent. My eyes drift to his shoes. Very nice. Special edition Nike Dunks in a nineties block-colourway: pink, green, yellow. They suit him. I want to microwave them.

Taré's smile tilts and she raises a brow at this and turns to me. 'Didn't I tell you, sis? He's problem.'

I release a brittle laugh. 'Thankfully, not mine.'

Taré grins. 'I like you. He needs someone around to humble him.' She turns to Malakai, asking, 'She's a vibe, right?'

He barely looks at me, voice brusque. 'A delight.'

Celestial appears again to whisper into Taré's ear. Taré nods in response, and turns to Malakai and I.

'OK, I have a twenty-minute Zoom call that I gotta take right now – the joys of being independent is that nobody can do this shit for me—'

'Wait – is this building your office?' I ask as she floats up, kimono flowing behind her.

Taré shrugs. 'Well. Potentially. I rented it for the week because I wanted it to be accessible to you. I asked your agent the easiest place for you to travel to. It's handy too, because there's a studio in the loft. A musician used to live here. If you say yes to my offer, I can rent it for three months and can make it our base.' She smiles at me as I process this information. 'No pressure, though! I'll be back in about twenty. Think it over. And feel each other out! Chemistry is important!' she calls over her shoulder.

I wait to speak till I hear the click of the door that follows Taré and Celestial leaving.

'So, obviously, this situation is untenable. You have to turn it down.'

Malakai blinks at me before breaking into rolling laughter.

'What's funny?'

'You, Kiki. Your entitlement is hilarious. I rate it, actually. If you don't back yourself, who will? But, in any case, I'm not turning shit down. Why don't you?'

I fly forward in my seat, incensed by the inanity of the question. 'Um, because I *need* this. I don't have my podcast, I just found out that SoundSugar have *blacklisted* me and my parents are selling Sákárà so, even if I wanted to quit it all and just continue the family business like this is some cute made-for-TV movie, I can't! And plus, what the hell do I look like quitting my dream job because of a man?'

Malakai stills, humour fleeing from his face. 'Your parents are selling Sákárà? Shit. I'm . . . man, I'm sorry to hear that.'

Too many feelings simmered to the surface and now too many

213

truths have spilled out without permission. I play with the idea of shutting the line of conversation down, but Malakai's face is intent, earnest, free of cockiness, and I can tell it's despite himself. I lean back in my seat, and swallow, pushing a braid from my face, lowering my eyes so I can get it all out fast without the words touching my heart.

'It's not a big deal. Business has been slowing down for a couple of years now, and it's getting too expensive to run. They want to move to Lagos. They deserve to rest and I'm happy for them—'

'But it's still hard.'

My gaze snaps to his, and his eyes are confident in their read. Malakai has cut through my script – the one I tell myself and others – with a truth I've run away from. I've tried to strip sentiment from fact, because what good is it? Even if I wanted to keep Sákárà, how would I pay for it? Run it? Intellectually, I also get why they want to sell. They've made the money they needed to and there are endless opportunities for catering businesses in Lagos, a city where no one needs an excuse to party – birthdays, funerals, christenings, a Friday. Everything is a reason to jaiye – chop life or life will chop you and, while we're at it, chop food, because what is life if not good food and eating it with people you can laugh with, dance with? It would be a practical business decision at their age, regardless of slowing business.

I get it, they see me and Kayefi as their true legacy, and after Mum's health scare years back, they want to take life easy. They don't need to revive a struggling business, so why should they? But for me the restaurant was more than a business, a conduit for our

214

survival; it's a testament to my parents' ability to spin gold from grit, the way the restaurant would fill on Sundays after church, on Eid, the home away from home for international students, a way for people to connect with their roots over a soup, swallow and Supermalt special. Many a raucous AFCON viewing took place there, and in the nineties there was *dancing*. A real old-fashioned dance floor whilst dining, a live band that played Palm Wine high-life, Jùjú music, throwback Motown covers, some African gospel depending on the occasion.

At seven years old, I would sit on the counter and watch the romance unfurl: the flirting, the easy glamour of the women with their fresh press and curls. Red lips smirking, smiling, kissing their teeth in prelude to a potential kiss, heavily perfumed, waists curving in a way that was both sexy and royal, aware of their sensuality, but being careful not to be lewd, because, after all, they were praying women, God-fearing women. And the men would lean on the bar and spit game by saying they were being murdered by beauty, in fact their smiles were slitting their throats as they spoke. And there would be fights too, when, for instance, the man who claimed he was being killed by fineness turned out to have a wife at home. If we were lucky, she would rock up to the restaurant to show him what it would mean to really be killed. Sákárà was a place to commune, and even though our people are scattered now, they still exist. I know they do. The people who want to laugh and dance and eat at the same time. However, I had no idea how to present that to my parents without sounding like a child who doesn't want to move house.

To Malakai's statement, I shrug. 'It is what it is.'

Malakai's brow quirks in scepticism of my nonchalance, but he says nothing before nodding carefully. 'And, uh, I heard about The Heartbeat, but I had no idea about the blacklisting thing. That's fucked. It was great work.'

I pause, unable to resist asking, 'You listened to it?'

'Only on nights where I couldn't sleep without listening to the dulcet tones of your voice.'

'Dick.'

A dry smile curves Kai's lips. 'Believe it or not, Kiki, I didn't want to listen to a podcast loosely referencing our break-up, but I read stuff around it. I know it was incredible. It's you. That's what you do.'

Malakai's face is largely without effect, muted emotion saying the words free of sentiment, but his eyes are trained on me, and I see a light fighting to get out. I'm trying to remember that I was mad about something, but I can't grasp it. It never occurred to me that Malakai would find the break-up difficult. I mean he got to go to America and live his dreams, unencumbered. I've latched on to Malakai's gaze, and just as I see a shift, a softening, there's a shuttering over.

He looks away and sips his drink before saying, 'OK, cool. So you need this job. I do too.' I catch myself, try to reclaim all the shrunken parts of anger I had moments ago and shoot back, 'Why? Aren't you the Hollywood wunderkind? Matthew Knight's protégé? You've gone clear.'

Malakai pauses, runs his eyes over me as if trying to assess the safety of this interaction, and I see his gaze, seemingly unknowingly, snag briefly on the bare skin exposed. Unfortunately, my body reacts with no heed to the precarity of the situation, my pulse skidding, the slither of thigh between the hem of my dress and my boots skittered with goosebumps. I cross my legs, as Malakai, having apparently concluded that it's safe to proceed, leans forward, legs spread and elbows on his thighs, and looks into his drink. The movement brings him closer to me, wafts his scent to me, his heat. I raise my chin as if in defiance to the residual (disappointing) lust I still feel towards him.

'You know, his show *Motown* was my idea? I pitched it to him. Developed it with him.'

I sit back up, a shock of indignation spiking through me. 'What? I had no idea—'

Malakai nods with a rueful smile. 'Yeah, and that was deliberate on Matthew's part. He "let" me direct a couple episodes, though.'

Episodes that I have, in fact, watched. When I saw his name on the *Variety* announcement, my pulse skipped, and a stupid, wide smile spilled on my face. Then it turned hard, frigid, split me in two. It was a year after we broke up, and I was over it, swore I was over it, and yet the announcement sent me bawling. I tried to disengage, but it's hard to ignore someone you used to love achieving a dream you wanted just as badly for them. Hard not to feel some kind of caged joy for them, a happiness that burns because you were supposed to be there next to them as they did it. You were never supposed to be experiencing it from afar, muted, unable to scream 'You did it!' to anybody, but your own memories.

Still, at night, in bed, under my covers I watched it on my laptop, illicit, like it was the freakiest porn search, as if I was keeping it a secret from myself. His episodes had all the hallmarks of the Kai touch. The direction was soulful, sensitive, evoking emotion from the smallest thing – a sip of coffee, a sigh with focus on the lips. It was beautiful. The general concept of the show is good too, straightforward, a deep dive into Motown artists, each season focusing on an era, exposing the glitz and the grit with a slight romantic sheen. It's clever, but the concept outweighs the content – it often veers into kumbaya bubblegum. While I did see Malakai's directorial credit, I saw no developmental credits, or even exec credits.

Malakai releases an empty chuckle. 'Matthew said he would help me mould it. Guide it. He obviously just took over. Wiped my name from everything. Took over my story ideas, made them . . . just *floppy*, you know? Saccharine, respectability shit. He told me I didn't have the experience to make it into the great thing it could be. And I could have gone legal, but I would have lost and it would have followed me around. Nobody would wanna work with me. My agent told me that was the way. That I take this loss for big gains later. And, I can't lie, I'm still waiting for the gains. And, you know me, Kiki . . .'

He's put his drink on the floor and laces his hands together. I know he says it flippantly, with no gravity, but looking at him, speaking with a flinty resolution in his eyes, I know that on some level it's true. There's a part of me that will always know a part of him.

'. . . I'm not one to run away from paying my dues. I'd do anything if I get to make my shit. And I kind of think that was the problem? Matthew knew how hungry I was. Working for his production company was meant to be this huge thing in my life. And in so many ways it was. Opened up worlds. Got me into rooms I never thought I'd be in. But I feel like he's trapping me. He's put me in a couple of his writers' rooms, and brings me along to all these dickhead LA parties, introduces me as his mentee, but . . . it feels like smoke and mirrors. Some weird thing he does to make himself feel like he isn't a solipsistic prick. I haven't had time to work on my own ideas in a year and a half. And I'm grateful and I know I'm lucky. I'm not complaining, but I can't say that not being able to work on my shit isn't killing me.'

He sits back up with a sigh, extending his leg so it almost brushes mine. An odd rush of something that has the flavour of protectiveness courses through me, hot and insolent. Malakai's ideas are so alive, so considered, weighty, multi-dimensional and I hate the idea of someone not only stealing them, but watering them down, robbing them of their magic – his magic. I may not like him right now, and things may always be tense between us, but I'll always be able to recognise his love for his craft. That never wavered even if his love for me did.

Malakai coughs, gathers himself and shrugs himself up. 'So nah, Kiki, I can't turn this down. I haven't told anyone that, not fully, but you need to know that this isn't just some sort of plaything for me. This project is a lifeline. A way for me to really be creative. To get back to me. Get my name really out there. Matthew was a good stepping stone, and I don't regret it, but this . . . this feels special. Taré is special.'

My skin flares at the last sentence, a deep, spiky burn snaking through my veins. It's an objective fact that Taré is special, but I'm wondering if he's saying it with objectivity or because she's special *to* him. And if they share something special, and we shared something special, then how special could my special be? And is my tolerance to THC that low, or is this a legitimate question?

I swallow. 'What is it about?'

Malakai blinks. 'What?'

'Your feature idea.'

Malakai looks at me for a beat. I've always been able to tell when an idea is percolating in his brain, waiting to be unlocked. I can see the agitation in his eyes. 'Fatherhood.' He doesn't ask me how I know. I nod and clear my throat.

'OK. So. We both need this.'

'Looks like it.'

He pauses, tilts his head. 'Out of the new tunes what's your favourite?'

'It doesn't have a name yet. But it's the one with the lyrics about fire.' I close my eyes and hum for two seconds. When I open them again, Malakai is gazing directly into me, electrifying me with knowledge.

'That's mine too.'

'There's a smokiness to it.'

'It's mad,' Malakai affirms, 'Like, both filthy and purifying.'

'And the bit where it gets a little funky?'

220

'Ooh *wee*,' Malakai releases a low whistle. '*Nasty.*'

'Yet still takes you somewhere sweet.'

We stare at each other for a few moments. I nod to myself. 'OK. *OK.*' I rub my hands on my thighs as I contemplate the reality of our situation. 'So it's only about three or four months. We keep it professional. We don't talk about anything personal. We work together up until the release – and, I guess, the wedding and that's it.'

'And you're cool with that?'

'Why wouldn't I be?' Malakai raises his brows and I force out a laugh. 'Oh. You mean because you've had sex with our potential boss?' I roll my eyes. 'Get over yourself. I'm a grown woman, Malakai. I'm not gonna let your dick get in between me and my bag.' I pause. 'Unless *you* can't handle me working on this. For whatever reason. In which case you can still walk away.'

'I can handle you, Kiki. You know that.' His dark, coruscating gaze makes my breath syrupy. I must remain detached from Malakai's panty-melting sensibilities or this is never going to work.

I clear my throat. 'We also obviously can't tell Taré about us.'

'Well, no, not now. We'd look unserious, but why did you do that in the first place? Taré's cool. She wouldn't give a shit.'

I roll my eyes. Men are so slow. 'Because this job is too important to me to risk having her project whatever we were onto my work, for better or worse. I want her to take my work at face value, not in the context of me being the ex of a guy she once had a thing with. I mean it's not even relevant. I just want to be able to maintain professionalism and I don't want our connection to affect that. I mean not our connection, our—'

'History.' Never to be repeated.

'Right. History. Prehistoric history. Like, mammoth-and-sabre-tooth-tiger history.'

Malakai tilts his head. 'Are you high? You blink a lot when you're high. I've only seen it once before, but that time you blinked a lot.'

I tip my chin up. 'If you must know, I accidentally had a sip of Taré's weed tea.'

Malakai is trying and failing to trap a smile. His eyes glint. 'You have the tolerance of an ant. When we were in Amsterdam, I had to convince you that a demon wasn't crawling up your throat – you just wanted to cough. You typed "pray for me" in your notes app and held it up to my face.'

'Well, that was the Kiki you knew. This Kiki's handling it great. Do you have a snack on you? Like a packet of pickled-onion Monster Munch?' Somewhere in the recesses of my brain, I am aware that asking Malakai for a snack I last had when I was nine probably undermines my detached stance.

Malakai's mouth twitches. 'Nah. Sorry.' He reaches into his sleek laptop backpack and pulls out a bottle of water. 'Have some of this, Bad Gyal Kiki. It's new. You won't get lurgies.'

He watches me, eyes glittering, as I swig from the bottle with large gulps that immediately settle me, balancing my mind. 'Feeling better?'

'I didn't need anything to feel better from, but thanks.' I pass him back the bottle, but his pinky and ring finger overlap my hand and a shock of heat flings my eyes up to his, already burning.

I snatch my hand back, but it's too late. He feels it, I feel it, and it's undeniable that the energy between us will forever be undead, immune to anger, heartbreak, sparking obnoxiously. One touch and I'm reminded of my pleasure in being at his mercy. Of his being at mine. It means I just have to work harder to fight it, because clearly Malakai does not want all of me. He may not even be capable of it any more. I know this. I'm so sure I know this. What was I meant to know again? Malakai untwists the cap of the bottle and sips from it. His mouth where my mouth has been feels nakedly intimate. It feels obscene.

'So how we doing, gang?' Malakai and I jerk in our seats as Taré swishes in, blunt in hand, and settles back into the seat between us. 'What do we think? It will be intense. It will be long hours. It's one thing for me to want to collaborate, it's another thing for you to want to. I require commitment, all hands on deck. I'm trying to keep this team intimate.'

Malakai's gaze drifts to mine and snags so firmly that it tugs at my core. I wonder how the ventilation works in this basement because suddenly it's a feat to breathe. Taré continues with her rallying speech.

'. . . So while – if you both say yes – you'll meet the rest of the crew soon, you two will be working closest together. I want the film to be stripped back. Naked. Raw.'

She looks at both of us with all the seriousness of a head of state talking to her cabinet. 'Are you both prepared to do that?'

Malakai and I look at each other, and the glister in his eyes is made sharper against the one I know is in mine. It's a challenge. This is twisted, profoundly complicated and risky, but it could also, potentially, be pivotal. I'm not going to let some pesky tension – sexual or murderous – get in the way of me and my bag. We're going to have to somehow make this work for the sake of our careers, and we have to manage to separate the personal and professional for the smoothness of our best friends' wedding.

Malakai shrugs. 'I'm ready.' He tilts his head to the side and I see its shadow – the Jodeci smile, the Ginuwine grin, that D'Angelo 'How Does It Feel'. 'You ready?' The flame in his eye is like a flicker of a lighter. I won't burn this time, can't burn this time.

To prove my point, I gesture at Taré to pass the blunt. Malakai's brows tick up and the corners of his mouth flick down as he does a tiny nod, like he's saying, 'Oh, yeah? That how you're feeling?'

I inhale from the burning, narrow tube even though I (in)famously do not smoke due to aforementioned incident in Amsterdam where I thought I needed an exorcism.

'Been ready.' I level his gaze with watery eyes and fail to swallow a violent cough.

CHAPTER 10

You Only Live Once or Twice

'*Cut* – Taré, you're doing great – hey, Kiki, can I have a word with you quickly—' Malakai is frowning at the monitor, his hands hitched on his waist, headset on. Irritation at the interruption surges alongside – perhaps, God help me, because of – the acknowledgement that he looks distractingly attractive. He's grumpy, focused and exhausted after several hours of shooting Taré's recording sessions and interviews with me. There's something quite sick about someone looking that good whilst overworked. After two weeks of balancing *Phoenix*, Aminah's increasingly frenetic energy and the sporadic restaurant shifts, it's taken a skincare overhaul guided by the strict and expensive counsel of Shanti to push the baggage carousel from under my eyes. But, on the other hand, Malakai gets to look alluringly dishevelled, like he's the hero of a new Ryan Coogler action movie, sweating slightly in the warmth of the studio, navy T-shirt slightly creased and displaying a hefty bicep that I kind of feel the urge to bite. Arsehole. I hold on tighter to the irritation. It's useful, regardless of reasoning. It helps maintain professional boundaries, keeping rabid thirst at bay, while reminding me that there can never be a future here – that I don't *want* a future here.

'Why?' I sit back on the low maroon leather couch of the attic studio and glare at him. 'I was in the zone. *We* –' I gesture to Taré, sat next to me while genteelly sipping a cup of hot water and lemon – 'were in the zone. You can't just disrupt the flow of two people in conversation like that—'

Malakai's mouth slants humourlessly at this. 'Yeah, thing is, Kiki, I can, actually. It's my job—'

'Well, it's *my* job to make sure the overall vision is achieved and I don't think that—'

'Guys, is everything OK?' Taré enquires absent-mindedly – in three seconds she's found time to slightly detach herself, pick up her phone and start scrolling.

Malakai maintains my stare for a few seconds, eyes like granite. Unfortunately, since we've started working together, I've discovered that some residual telepathy has remained from our relationship. Turns out even when you consciously uncouple, some of you remains unconsciously coupled. Right now, in the flash of his eyes and the twitch of his sharp jaw, he's asking me if I really want to get into it with him in front of Taré. Since the 'decent rate' that Taré is paying me is twice what I got whilst working on The Heartbeat, I decide to suck up my ire, and indulge Malakai's tyrannical directorial whims.

I throw a smile at Taré. 'Totally. Everything's cool.'

Smoothing down the suede of my mini skirt, I rise to cross the chevron hardwood of the studio to meet Malakai by the monitor. He shifts slightly to make space for me, and my arm brushes his, the static of his skin and light smattering of hair sending spindles of flames up my skin. Thankfully, he's too busy being Spike Up His Ass Lee to notice.

'See that?' We're out of Taré's earshot, but, still, he lowers his voice as he points to my face playing back on the screen. I swallow and focus on my image. There's a deep crease in between my freshly threaded brows, and my glossed lips are pressed together tightly, eyes narrowed. I look pissed.

I shrug and straighten up. 'I don't know what you're talking about. All I see is my new skincare regimen working. I look radiant.'

'Yeah, Kiki, you're a beautiful woman – that isn't the point,' Malakai says brusquely, and there's a wing flap in my belly that jerks my attention. It's a feeling that has hibernated for so long I thought it was dead. That's concerning. The only thing to do with resurrected warmth is to bury it. 'I know your face. You look *annoyed*, Kiki,' he whispers. 'We can't have the warm, empathetic conduit between Taré and our audience look irritated—'

'Are you trying to police my expression of emotion?' It's a complete reach, of course, but he's right and I hate that. It's worth a try.

Malakai's unmoved, blinking at me flatly. 'Say that again like you don't believe it's bullshit.'

I tip my chin up and entertain trying it again, but don't have the energy and I don't really remember why or what I'm arguing for. I grudgingly concede with a roll of my eyes. 'Fine. *Fine*. I hear you.' I fold my arms across my black baby tee.

Malakai's brow pops up and he places the back of his hand against my head, his face assuming a look of feigned concern. 'You got a fever? Because there ain't no way Kiki Banjo's conceding defeat to me so easy.'

We haven't touched – on purpose – since the night we slept together, and the sensation jolts through my form. We'd been working relatively well together in the planning stages since the *us* of it all was easy to avoid. We were just two co-workers focused on schedule, logistics and direction with very little time for angst or awkwardness. We both meant it when we said we weren't playing about this job. Now, though, our bodies are forced to confront each other's presence holistically, with Malakai having to literally look at my face on a screen and judge whether I'm doing a good job or not. I was mentally prepared for the reality of this intimacy, but, physically, my body is on high alert, my cells disorientated, confused by the bordered proximity with a man that used to raise goosebumps from my skin with a single look. Can you use 'used to' if the last time that happened was a mere two months ago? Or two hours ago? Or two seconds ago? Or right now, right fucking now.

I tilt my head away from his touch with a light swat. 'If I have a fever, it's because I'm having a bad reaction to your micro-management.'

'Look.' Malakai puts his hands together in gentle pleading. 'All

I'm asking is for you to listen to the answer of the question without looking like you want to throttle someone.'

I peer at my face again. It's unmistakable. I look like I'm fuming. 'That doesn't even make sense. Why would Taré's answer to my question make me angry?'

'You tell me.' The way he looks at me is sharp enough to slice through my sinews, creating tracks of hot liquid gold like I'm a kintsugi piece. *No really. Tell me.* I brace against the exposure and rub my forehead as if I can force my cracks to close and push his searing gaze out. 'You know what? I just have a lot on my mind today, and we've been doing this for hours.'

Malakai's gaze flicks across me, and I see his director-mode glitch again as he articulates the question I already read in him. 'What's on your mind?'

'It's personal. We don't do personal.' I'm too emotionally disarmed to knit my nonchalance together tightly, and I see Malakai latch on to something that slips through, too fast for me to catch. He steps closer, his heat licking at my goosebumps before they hatch.

'Scotch—' He coughs, like the nickname was a tickle in his throat. 'Kiki. I'm asking you as a colleague.' He darts a look at Taré, who is still engrossed in her phone. 'Whatever's bothering you bothers me. I know what you're like normally. You're good at what you do – you're usually locked in – but you went back to the restaurant for the managerial shift earlier today and ever since you've been back you've been off.' The easy, silken incisiveness makes me shiver.

'It's fine. I'm fine. I just . . . You're right. I'm off my game. I'll snap out of it.' I roll my shoulders as if shaking my previous grouchiness off, and leave for the sofa, because Malakai's eyes were softening, the sheen of professionalism dulling, and I can't afford to sink into quicksand right now or ever.

'Hey, sorry about that,' I say to Taré, whose eyes raise lazily from her phone screen.

She waves a hand. 'Oh, it's fine. You guys got it. Sorry. I'm just texting my producer about Track 2 – there's some shit missing, right? What is it? Strings? It's supposed to be sparse, not hollow . . .' she mutters, before saying out loud, into the speaker of her phone, leaving a voice note, 'SPARSE, NOT HOLLOW? VIOLA? NOT DAVIS. INSTRUMENT, BUT ACTUALLY WITH HER EMOTIONAL GAMBIT, YOU KNOW?'

I very quickly learned that Taré was meticulous in ensuring Malakai and I care about the project as much as she does, because she needs people to trust whilst she loses herself in the music-making process. She doesn't want to have to micromanage or think about what we're doing. She's heavily involved in the doc to a point, but in the name of energy preservation she has hard boundaries, knowing when to step back and let us do our thing with our own creative process. A heavy sense of awe pushes at my trepidation. I'm *here*. Part of this moment. I get to help make it into what it is supposed to be. I allow myself to vanish into that reality. Taré's designed the studio to be almost an exact replica of the room in which I saw her performance, and I realise that it's her default custom personalisation – colour, warmth, peace, insularity between the connectedness. Candles are dotted around on every available surface and the air is hued amber and fused with tuberose and jasmine. We sit in front of the vocal booth and control deck, sites from which I've witnessed Taré conjure magic in the past fortnight. I breathe the space in, shut the noise in my mind out and home in on Taré. She's devoid of make-up – having done a six-hour recording session – but her skin is glowing, even more beautiful, in what I realise is her recording uniform of silk pyjamas.

I've figured out that they're kind of like a mood ring, reflecting her temperament of the day. Today they're a baby pink, so she's relatively calm, but feeling playful, which means I can go a little deeper, probe more.

Malakai's read my ease, I know, because I hear him say, 'Action.'

I lean back into the sofa, tucking my legs beneath me. 'So you say you want this song – "Lost Boys" – to feel more sparse than hollow, but to me I already get this sense. It feels like a hazy dream. It's sensual, hedonistic, and listening to it feels like you're high. It somehow separates psyche from body. What was your headspace when coming up with the feel?'

A mischievous smile sneaks out from Taré. 'Man, my headspace was *high*. That's how I felt. Disembodied from who I was and who I wanted to be and who people thought I was.' She almost speaks in a spoken-word cadence, words running into each other and suddenly pulling back. *DisembodiedfromwhoIWASand . . . who I wanted to BE . . . andwhopeoplethought I was.*

It's hypnotic, and she lulls me into her space as she adjusts herself so she's facing me, sitting cross-legged, like we're at a sleepover.

'When I made my first album, I was working primarily from a place of *hunger*, you know? I wanted to get my voice out there. I had shit to say. I wanted to show the world all my soul because I didn't know if I would get another chance to. I was fearless because I had nothing to lose. And then when it was successful . . . there's, like, a funny thing that happens when you achieve your dreams. All the fears you didn't have come rushing through. You're, like, stuck in anxiety. You second guess your instincts. Music is what I do, who I am, but you now have all these voices, this audience who is, like, screaming at you through their screens to do this or not do that. It's out of love, mostly, but at some point it doesn't matter what it's from. It's just noise. And you have all these other people to now answer to other than yourself because so many more people are invested in your success, which at some point has become nothing to do with you and everything to do with them. Their *stake* in you. A return of their investment. And you don't want to be ungrateful, because so many people would kill for this position, so you tell yourself to appreciate the noise, to . . . to acknowledge it. And then you're just *terrified* about disappointing people and then you end up incapacitated—'

Taré's gaze blurs as she goes back to where she was, at the time, no longer looking at me, but looking at herself. I nod, not wanting to break her out of where she is, but wanting to unravel the threads a little more. I venture in gently. 'So it sounds like you felt as if you were losing yourself. And you have all these different identities

232

warring – which you can hear in the music . . . There are places where you modulate voice – you're whispering and then you're belting and in the end it sounds like you're almost taking control of the chaos. Sexy, sultry. You're seducing it. It feels triumphant, but also incomplete in a deliberate way. Like this situation is good for now. The answer for now. You're subduing it, not stopping it.'

Taré smiles and props an elbow on the back of the sofa, resting her chin on her palm. 'That's exactly it. And so the song is reflect-ive of a period where I decided to take control of the lack of control. Lean into the inhibition. Sex. Drugs. Drinking. I did whatever till those expectations felt obliterated. Everything was about id. I won't lie – it felt really good for a while. I wasn't *me*; I was just my senses. And one day I just started humming this tune, while I was in a fog, and it became "Lost Boys". So I was in LA around two years ago, spent a couple of weeks locked in a hotel room with a cute boy who felt just as lost as me. An artist like me finding his way. It was nice having company without having to talk. It wasn't romantic in the traditional sense, but it was . . . special. This, like . . . unspoken mutual understanding. We were connected in this way of . . .' Taré pauses and looks into the high vaulted ceiling, looking for an explanation . . . 'needing to be anywhere else but where we were – and I don't want anyone to get *gassed*, like he wasn't my muse or nothing like that, but that moment just pinpointed a feeling I'd *been* having.'

I can't look at the camera – the interviews are supposed to feel organic, real – and so I can't see Malakai's expression, but I feel it. It sinks into my belly like something leaden. Taré hums the melody to herself, eyes closed, swaying with some contentment, before she looks at me, eyes glimmering. 'So, yeah, this song is about disembodied bodies finding each other, being lost together. It can't feel hollow. It would defeat the purpose. There was no salvation in it, no, but there was some solace— *Fuck.*'

Taré's phone buzzes with a message. 'Sorry, my girl is on my dick about going to this party that I really am not on. I'm so tired, man – HEY, BABE, WHAT'S THE VIBE? I'M NOT DOING NO PRIVATE MEMBERS SHIT TONIGHT,' she shouts into the speaker of her phone, presumably sending a voice note to her friend.

Malakai cuts and I look at him to see his eyes slightly glazed, stunned, like he's being pulled elsewhere from inside himself. Something is askew, and I begin to care too much before I can stop it. When he notices me looking in his direction, he seems to be yanked back out, his face breaking open in a smile so genuine it sends a rush of hot honey through me as he mouths, 'That was perfect,' and it shouldn't feel so good, so satisfying, but it does, and I decide to keep it a secret from myself. I can relish this feeling and not acknowledge the source.

'Hey, so this is random –' Taré's voice yanks me out of my questions, breathy with what I now recognise as delight at her own – 'but do you guys want to go out tonight? I just discovered this party is in a location that has a garden where I *think* I want to shoot part of a video – it's on the list, Malakai – and this is a great opportunity to check it out. Team social?'

Mine and Malakai's gazes snap to each other's immediately,

and his hand flies to the back of his head as my excuse trips off my tongue with ease. 'Um, I would love to, but I have to wake up early because my best friend – Aminah – wants me to check out this wedding venue with her and her fiancé tomorrow morning – her mum's insisted on tagging along and I need to be there as a mum-whisperer. And to stop Aminah saying anything she'll regret since her parents are paying for the venue.'

Taré frowns lightly in confusion. 'But aren't you also covering the restaurant tomorrow night? Isn't that kind of a lot? To mama-sit all morning? I mean I know how hard I'm working you. When are you gonna chill?'

My skin pricks uncomfortably at the articulation of a latent question that's been burgeoning. I've been trying to starve it – it feels illicit, wrong – but the truth is Aminah's been more stressed lately, which has led to an increase of late-night phone calls, which poses a problem when it's before a morning where Taré has decided that she wants to start recording at 6 a.m. to 'capture the essence before it's diffused'. I'm also trying to cover for my mum and dad when I can; they're almost sixty, and there's no reason for them to be at the restaurant when it's home for me and I can get some work done on my laptop whilst managing three employees and the six customers that come in every day.

I shrug, and push out a smile. 'It's fine. I'm fine.'

Malakai's eyes are flickering with curiosity again, and it slips under my skin, presses on my pulse.

Taré's brow quirks as she turns her to attention Malakai, tilting her head coquettishly. 'And what's your excuse? Hot date?'

There's a beat of silence in which I feel a sudden burn in my chest, and Malakai's eyes widen slightly before he releases a stilted chuckle, dipping his head and scratching his ear.

'Not tonight. Uh, I just need to go through some rushes and I'm hanging with a friend tomorrow morning.'

Or maybe he does have a hot date tonight and the 'hanging with a friend' thing is a cover for morning sex and a lazy brunch with his lover – God, does he have a lover? Why am I saying *lover*? – and isn't in the mood to divulge it to two women he has had sex with. This thought does kick-ups with the prosciutto-and-rocket sandwich I had for lunch. I glance at the time on my phone – 9 p.m. A date at this time is likely a precursor to sex. It's, of course, none of my business. This is just a casual observation by someone who takes note of the nuances of intimacy. This is all part of my job. Taré unfolds herself from the sofa, and stands in between Malakai and I, hands flying as she attempts to proselytise to a weary congregation.

'Ugh! What the hell is this? Come on. I need my teammates energised and relaxed. I know I've thrown you both in the deep-end. It's Friday night and you're both like, what? *Five* years younger than me? We've worked hard this week. Live a little. We're not dead.'

I see Malakai stiffen a little at the last sentence, a shadow falling across his face and slipping into a line between his eyes. It's the same as it was a few moments before, like he's fighting a memory. A cold dampness scrabbles at me from the inside, and I wonder what he's thinking about and then I recognise what he's thinking about. The recognition weighs my veins down. I can see him receding into somewhere I've seen him go before, somewhere dark, and the last time it happened I couldn't reach him. The last time he was there we broke up. A piercing protectiveness surges through me, and I'm ready tell Taré that we'll be sure to go out next Friday, that Malakai's right – we have a tight turnaround and a strict schedule – when Malakai shrugs. The shadow lifts in tandem with the corner of his mouth.

'You know what? You're right. We're not dead. I'm down.' The idiotic intense spike of protectiveness retreats. So he wants alone time with Taré. They seem to have maintained a professional distance this past fortnight, but maybe that's what they want me to think? What if Taré extending the invite to me was a ruse because she knew I would say no? For all I know, they're sexting outside of our text chain, hooking up whilst I've slipped out to the restaurant, staying behind to have some hot recording-studio sex—

Shit, what if they've had sex on this sofa? I shift on my seat slightly, untucking my feet from beneath me. Oh my God, I am sitting on a sofa that's potentially carried the imprint of one – or both, depending on positions – of their bare asses whilst they orchestrate a prelude to a *dick* appointment—

'Kiki? What you sayin'?' Malakai's voice breaks into what was probably a rapid loosening of my hinges, and I jump a little to see him looking at me with surprisingly gentle enquiry. 'We out tonight?'

I twitch my shoulder with a synthetic breeziness that I reckon I should probably win a Noble Peace Prize for constructing and say, 'You know what? Why not,' and it's all going so well, except I overshoot the chillness in the breeziness recipe, knock the residual madness I had from my spiral a few seconds ago into it and over-compensate completely. The result of this is me uttering something that will definitely haunt me for the rest of my days. '*YOLO!*'

'Kiki, can I say something?' Malakai and I have been sitting in the back of the sleek private-car service for about five minutes, both of us scrolling on our phones, waiting for Taré to surface from the house. His voice is gravelly and serious enough to let me know that he's about to be on some bullshit. I sigh, and stop scrolling social media looking for something, anything to distract me from the fact that I'm about to have a night out with my ex and his ex-fling. And from the fact that I was so rattled by the very idea of them having sex that I glitched and said something a middle-aged white male TV exec would say in an attempt to sound 'urban'.

'No.'

'Well, I'm just gonna speak anyway. I don't say this enough, but I just want to thank you . . .'

My jaw tightens, and I cross my legs, turning to see his eyes glittering with mirth. Unfortunately, the sight of it immediately sets off a tickle on the inside of my mouth, but I refuse to succumb to his bait. He blinks slow, in insincere sincerity.

'. . . for, honestly, for making my evening. No, my day. No, my fucking life. Kiki Banjo, you have provided me the joy of my life by saying the word "YOLO" in the year of our Lord 2025.'

I roll my eyes. 'Doesn't say much about your life, then.'

'Oh, my life is very blessed, but I just could not have foreseen a gift this big—'

'*Foreseen?* OK.'

'This is how I know God is real. Ey, boss.' He raps the plastic safety screen between us and the driver with his knuckle. 'Do you mind putting the gospel station on? I got worship on my heart.'

A tiny, disgusting little snort slips out of me. In all honesty, I'm impressed at Malakai's restraint. It's been an hour since that godforsaken moment and all he did at the time was blink at me in complete and utter shock and confusion before twisting his mouth in what I could recognise was a Herculean attempt to keep a smile in. I knew he would make me pay for it eventually. I'm just glad he had the decency to do it when we're alone. He had to wait the entire time it took me to go home, get ready and come back to Taré's to unleash my punishment, which means it's had time to marinate. He's ready to have fun with it and make my life a misery. Malakai has let his smile out now, and it is dazzling, wicked, having the time of its life at my slip into cringe. My stomach flips at the sight like some masochist, the kinky freak.

'Nah, seriously, Keeks,' he drawls, relaxing back into his seat, after assuring our driver that it's fine to remain on CapitalFM because Michael Gray will help us get in the mood for the weekend to begin. 'Are you like . . . OK? You coming down with something? Or was it that tiny, *minuscule* bit of diluted THC you ingested weeks ago that altered your brain chemistry?'

'All right.' I slip my phone in my orange mini Telfar. 'I'm in a generous mood. You get one more.'

'Cool, because I have one more question. Did you get any travel sickness when coming to work today? Because you did trek a long way.'

I bite a lip that's crying out to curve before nodding slowly, anticipating his thread, because I know his rhythm. 'Oh, you mean my journey from 2011? It wasn't too bad. I got to stop by Soho House in 2016 and tell Meghan Markle while her first date was in the bathroom that he's cute, but it isn't worth the stress. That she should go for someone like Trevor Noah. Smart. Funny. Hot. Not connected to an outdated form of rulership predicated on imperialism.'

Malakai cracks, laughter breaking free and setting me alight, and it's been a long day so I don't have the energy to fight it. The sound washes over me, and hibernating flavours of joy take flight.

'Wouldn't you have to know Trevor Noah for that to work?' he asks.

'Well, I do. We became mates after he invited me on *The Daily Show* in 2015 to talk about my new invention, TikTok. Which I created in 2014.'

Malakai nods in solemn understanding, light hop-scotching in the dark of his eyes. My body responds. Tiny, pretty-winged creatures from parts of my soul flap unsheathed in dusty, abandoned crevices. 'OK, so were you on there as, like, a child prodigy or did you maintain your current age while you were travelling dimensions?'

My fingers thrum with a familiar buzz I've missed the feel of. 'Current age. I did visit myself, though. Told her it was all gonna be OK and my boobs were gonna come in great, eventually.'

Malakai's smile is tiny, so polite it's dirty, eyes glinting with trapped play, but saying nothing, respecting the foundational tenets of our working contract. We fade into a silence that for the first time since we reunited feels comfortable. I bite my bottom lip to tuck away the persistent curve and look outside the tinted window to the dark street yellowed by streetlamps. It's started raining and the light patter massages my bones. That's it — I feel *relaxed* for the first time in so long that I can't remember when the last time was. We've been waiting in the car for eighteen minutes despite Taré saying that 'she'd be right out'. Thirteen minutes ago, I was itching to be on the move. Now, for whatever reason, I don't feel in a rush to go, like moving might disturb the delicate peace I'm feeling.

'Would you ever do a do-over?' Malakai's voice rolls into the quiet static of the car. I turn from the blurry window and scan his face, the warmth still there, but with a trepidatious curiosity edging it.

'What do you mean?'

He hitches his shoulder. 'Like, if you could go back in time for real. Do things differently. Would you?' The air crackles with more than just the sound of the radio, the energy spitting and fizzing and making my palms prick. His question is swollen, and I'm scared of what will happen if it splits open.

I think about it for a second and answer cautiously. 'I don't think so. Everything led me here. I'm not too mad at where I'm at now.'

Malakai turns and looks straight ahead, at nothing, eyes narrowed in thought for a few moments before he nods. 'Yeah. Me neither.' In a beat, the rain outside pummels a little heavier, and he adds, 'But I still think I would do some things differently. Better.'

Something twists violently, painfully inside me, making it harder to breathe suddenly, and a sharp sensation appears within my left temple. *Why would he say that? Why did he say that? Why did he have to go and say that? What does he mean by that?*

And I know it's my ego, because Malakai's life is expansive, and in the grand scheme of things I'm a blip, a glitch in the trajectory of his life, and it stings, but it's true, and, still, I can't help it, arrogantly, selfishly, I want to know where I fit into that thought. Does he mean not kissing me at that uni party eight years ago? Does he mean not walking out of a hotel room three years ago? Does he mean not having sex with me three months ago? Does he mean none of that, because, remember, I'm a blip, a glitch in the trajectory of his life and it doesn't matter either way?

A thawing has happened between us, I feel that, and I'm allowing myself to let it feel good – it's easier than wrestling it – but the Unsaid still makes it hard for me to breathe easy. It gets stuck in my throat every single time I try. I ask the question that's been clinging to the roof of my mouth.

'That guy Taré was talking about. The non-muse muse for "Lost Boys". In the . . . in the hotel room. That was you, wasn't it?'

Malakai turns his head to look at me. There's a middle seat between us that I didn't realise had disappeared until now, when it appears again to remind me that there's still a gap here, one that was once a chasm and that perhaps, with some grace, is now a crevice, but, still, it's here. The shadow has fallen over Malakai's eyes again and now I know why it feels so familiar, why I recognise its contours. I've seen it in my reflection before, and maybe that's why I didn't want to see it at first. It's hard to look your own pain in the eye. It's heartbreak. My lips part, but I can't speak because the Unsaid is still turgid. I really want to cry and I don't know why. Malakai opens his mouth, but it seems like the same thing is happening to him. My phone buzzes – a voice note from Taré.

'HI, MY BABESSS, OK, LISTEN. I'M SORRY. I AM A MESS. I WAS CHANGING AND I JUST GOT THIS IDEA FOR A SONG AND I STARTED DITHERING AND PLAYING AROUND WITH THE GUITAR AND I THINK I GOT SOMETHING – LOOK, LISTEN TO THIS . . . HANG ON . . . IT'S GOOD, RIGHT? DON'T WORRY. TELL MALAKAI I GOT MY HAND-HELD – I'M FILMING IT ALL. HE CAN WORK HIS MAGIC WITH IT. HE'S SUCH A DIVA. OK, SO YOU GUYS GO AHEAD AND HAVE FUN. JUST SAY THE PASSWORD AT THE DOOR. I'LL MEET YOU THERE IN AN HOUR OR SO. OK, LOVE YA. BYEEEEE. DON'T DO ANYTHING I WOULD HAVE DONE THREE YEARS AGO! . . . OH, SHIT, SORRY. THE PASSWORD IS "DESERT RAIN".'

I play the voice note out loud and the shadow in his eyes is swallowed by a light that reappears as he laughs and runs a hand across his face. 'Wow. We've really been out here for nothing.'

Like a coward, I greedily take the out offered instead of dwelling on what just happened. 'The song does sound sick, though.'

'It does.' He clears his throat. 'So should we still go to this ting? That cool with you?'

I shrug. 'We're here and we're here. Let's go.'

Malakai smiles. 'I like that. We're here and we're here. Let's go.'

CHAPTER 11

Desert Rain, in the Here and *Here*

Malakai lowers the car window and says the password into the crackle of an intercom. Ornate black gates swing open to reveal a behemoth of glass and brick. Honeyed light flows through its panes as amapiano drums thump so loudly the sound permeates the thick tinted glass of the sedan. Through six-metre glass panes, I see high ceilings and geometrically irregular glass shapes hanging from them, creating a glowing halo around the house. Those chandeliers definitely cost the same as the GDP of a small island. I make a note to snap them and send to Chioma, tap into her interior-design intel to see if I can get details of just exactly how unethical this place is that we're about to enter, just for bants.

The tyres smooth over the sprawling driveway, lined by inground spotlights, creating a path of moonlight for us. The plaque on the pillar at the gate named the mansion 'House of Alkebulan', which I find an intriguing name for a home in Hampstead Heath that looks like it's owned by a tech billionaire in a murder-mystery caper.

'Mango.' Malakai's voice dips into the silence, warming me. We had fallen into a conversation so easy in the twenty-minute car ride that I had begun to feel uneasy. My bones were starting to slip into the satin of our words, smoothing around each other even when they were jabbing. I tell myself that this was a good thing, not a reopening of what we were, but the maintenance of a new healthy working environment. We're congenial colleagues, that's all, professionals who are bonded by a zany boss. We can be out together, alone, without it getting weird, because we're grown-ups. Except, I guess, when Malakai starts saying random words as if the potential awkwardness of the situation is making him malfunction.

'What? You hungry?'

We're pulling up to what looks like a line of mostly G-Wagons forming a V, at the apex of which sits the house. Preternaturally sexy people step out of every other vehicle, dripped out in select-ively styled designer, and I already know when I get out the car the air's gonna smell like Francis Kurkdjian's burp. 'Well, yeah, I'm hungry, but, nah, mango's our code. If either of us want to cut, we say the word.' Malakai turns to me as the car slows to a stop, his eyes nebulas, and I can feel them birthing stars in my eyes; he's calling me in to conspiracy. His gaze is dark and bright and carrying every colour, limitless possibilities, and I can see it, he's in this, he's sold, we're here and we're *here*, and all of a sudden I know that this night is going to be a unit unto itself. Whatever is born here dies here. You only live once – that's the motto, baby, mango.

I smile. 'OK.'

We stand at the threshold of the tall, wide double doors, the limewashed walls and fine wood floors thrumming with the sound of a sublime DJ mix that marries Kaytranada with afrobeats. The bassline agitates something loose in me. I shrug my shoulders free of my trench in rhythm. That glad gleam in Malakai's eyes moves in time to it as he offers his hand to take it from me. The coat falls off my body like peel from an overripe plantain and Malakai's eyes fall with it, down the curving cling of my orange mesh maxi dress, sheer enough to whisper the shadow of a black thong and black bra. I feel full up to the top of my skin, like if you scratch me I'd drip gold. I'm feeling good, feeling like I look good and Malakai is looking at me like I'm what God was thinking of when He proclaimed that all He made was good.

He releases a small smile, shakes his head, murmurs, 'You're a danger to the streets.'

And I say, cheeks aflame, 'Remind the mandem to look both ways.'

And this is OK. It's OK to confront all that is animal here, look it in the eye and tame it. We're grown. We've already had sex. It went well and ended badly. We won't do it again. *Professionals.* Nothing personal.

Malakai rolls out a laugh that unfurls like a red carpet on which my sense glides – God, what is happening? I'm not even drunk – as he takes my coat, steps to the 'cloakroom' to the left of the door, a room that is approximately the size of my flat. Two young people in black stand in front of several rails of hangers, handing out tickets. Malakai approaches them and someone with a tray offers me something they say is 'rum and sumn'. I take two and then I look at Malakai, who has now shrugged off his bomber and I drink. Intoxication twice over. Double cooked.

Something shifted in that car. Something happened when we laughed together.

He didn't need to change because life is so easy for a man, especially a man with arms as distractingly substantial as his. He's in all black, and it works on him – black tee, black slim-fit Dickies chinos. Only thing with colour on him is his cross pendant – gold and heavy – and his eyes – brighter and lighter now. I realise that Malakai has been carrying something heavy, because now he's looking like he's lost some emotional weight, some weariness from his face. What has he been running from?

I've hung back, and Malakai has to look through a wall of moving people to find me, and when he does his eyes spark. I see him actively restrain it as he walks towards me. It's inexplicable, and the Unsaids still hang, the unargued threatens to choke, but our words have been tripping and falling over and around each other since Taré's, finding home in the nooks of each other's sentences. It's almost, kind of, sort of, like we might be becoming friends again. I can't figure out if it would be bad. I just need to be vigilant. Colleagues. Professional. Maintaining a healthy environment for my best friend's wedding.

'So, whose yard do you think this is?' he enquires as I pass him his drink. We cast our attention across the wide 'hallway' (throughway) lined with a glittering Black diaspora of celebrities ranging from A to B list. An Afrobeat giant, an Afropop starlet, a grime star that Aminah would be very happy to see, a Ryan Coogler muse and a dancehall queen are but a few out of a constellation that is scattered across this bougie shoobz. They are dotted up the broad curved stairway that's lit up with hidden LED lights, like the steps are leading to heaven or a party within the party. Fame denizens continue to pour through to the open space of one of at least three living areas. They roll out into a garden with an intricate courtyard that from my vantage point looks to be split into two levels.

'Young Nigerian tycoon. International school accent, somewhere between Valley girl and landed gentry,' I say as we walk through the throng. We pass a lively kitchen, gleaming white marble with an island that could double as a stage, filled with hors d'oeuvres. I spy a cooking range that my chef's-daughter eye tells me is worth a smooth £16K and has never really been used domestically.

'Nah. If they were a Nigerian, we would have seen them by now somehow. They would have made themselves known.'

I laugh as we walk through a large 'living/entertainment space' – I know this from years of bingeing reality shows about luxury properties. It could also, effectively, be the inside of a luxury club. There's a booth behind which one of the hottest Afrobeat DJs stands, conducting the vibes, a fully operational bar and plush cream sofas that really, for me, are the biggest indicator of net worth this evening. This is the kind of environment that in the past has made me want to crawl inside myself, not knowing where I fit in, how I got here and, right now, I begin to feel the telling itch.

I look at Malakai and he's holding himself a little more rigidly now, but when he looks at me, he relaxes a little.

'How you feel about a Litlympic competition?' he asks.

The Litlympics was devised at Ty Baptiste's country-house parties: a series of nonsensical dares and races with no incentive but bragging rights – the punishment was always a shot. A thrill runs through me, hot enough to make my tense nerves recline as I survey the crowd.

'We race to find out who owns this place through . . . gentle conversation with our fellow guests,' I suggest. 'I mean *technically* it counts as work as *technically* this is a recce. We'll check out the garden later.'

Malakai grins. 'Loser has to say YOLO out loud in conversation to the nearest person with a Grammy.'

My laugh comes out in a sharp burst. 'You're fucking evil. OK. Cool. You better not find yourself near Rihanna. That'll be embarrassing. For you I mean. I'll thoroughly enjoy it.'

'Why, because she'll fall in love with me and my very presence would threaten the peace of a happy home? I dunno, I think I'd make a great stepdad. I've always wanted kids – you know that—'

I freeze, and a millisecond after, when his words have calcified in his mind, he stiffens and our precarious peace tilts, the Unsaid unsticking beneath it. Yes, I do know he always wanted kids, because at one point we took it as a categorical fact that we were going to have them together. We discussed names (Sisqo was vetoed by me, Knowles by him). We spoke about *when* we got married, not 'if'. Malakai said he wanted to walk down the aisle to 'Int'l Players Anthem' and when I pointed out that men don't actually 'walk down the aisle' he replied that he didn't have me down as someone who conformed to traditional gender norms.

'What next? You're gonna cook for me every night? Pack my lunch? Welcome to the twenty-first century, Kiki,' he'd said with a sassy roll of his eyes.

Fuck.

Now, my stomach threatens to feel funny, or it does, actually, if I'm honest, a pang that has notes deeper than nostalgia, which would be bad enough, but, no, this has a tenor of yearning. We were good once. So good. Malakai and I have perhaps friendlied too close to the sun, but I decide to catch a tan instead of let it burn the understanding we have cultivated.

I skip past it with a breezy smile. 'So we have ten minutes to do the challenge.' Relief flits over Malakai's face as I continue: 'We're not allowed to directly ask – it has to come up in casual conversation.'

Malakai nods. 'We meet by the bar.' He slides his phone out of his pocket. 'And we start our timers—'

'Hey – sorry – are you Kiki Banjo?'

I turn round at a light touch of my shoulder to see a gorgeous woman, slightly older than me, with closely cropped hair and angular cheekbones.

'Um.' I dart a look at Malakai, who for some reason looks delighted. 'Yes.'

The woman smiles and puts her hand out for me to shake. 'I'm Soraya Sackey – an exec at Akassa Productions. Been wanting to meet you for a while, actually. I've missed your podcast! I saw your sweet farewell post to your listeners on socials. Have to say I was surprised to see you weren't coming back for another season, but I'm sure it's for good reason. What are you up to now?'

'Lovely to meet you! I know Akassa! Huge fan of your work. Really beautiful cultural archiving and art. Um. I've actually been producing a project that I can't talk about in detail. It's for a musician. I'm kind of facilitating the creative direction. So. That's what I'm doing right now.'

Why can't I talk like somebody who has interacted with humans before? Soraya Sackey squints her eyes in confusion, understandably, because I barely know what I'm saying, flustered by no longer having The Heartbeat to hide behind as my identity, not having a shorthand for success, legitimacy.

She nods slowly. 'Oh, OK . . . so is that what you're doing long-term? Producing? What's your scope?'

My *scope*? That's a great question. What is my scope? Why can't I scope my scope? I can't believe I'm embarrassing myself like this in front of a woman with geometrically flawless winged-liner. I want to die. I'm also fairly aware that a production I can't talk about sounds distinctly made up. My pits prick, and I'm probably about to say something that will make things decidedly worse when Malakai's cognac voice slides in smoothly, surprising me.

252

'So you know how some people have a drink and start brag-ging? Kiki's issue is the opposite.' He gently touches my elbow and it steadies me, lances me of nerves – I'm here and I'm *here*. 'She has a drink and forgets she's a big steppa.' He glances at me with such a blaze of affection that I feel convictions singed. New credos I set for myself such as One Must Not Get Too Close, and You Are Allowed To Vaguely Fantasise About That Tongue Thing He Used to Do, but These Fantasies Cannot Be Propped Up By Any Warm Feelings About His Person fray around the edges. Malakai continues, effusively: 'She's actually a cultural producer, working on art that centres truth and craft – it's kind of mad watching her work, actually. She's almost like an artist whisperer and a surgeon at the same time. The way she connects the person with the art and gets them to pull out these . . . intricacies about music and culture . . . I don't know anyone who does what she does like her. I mean, have you heard her retrospective linking artists like Summer Walker and Jazmin Sullivan to 1930s southern blues artists? Mad.' I watch him speak, waiting for the joke, the catch, because though I know Malakai was never anything but my biggest fan in our relationship – memory or maybe hurt mitigated that truth because it made our break-up easier to comprehend. I needed to forget that in order to move on, needed to believe that though he wasn't an innately bad person, he wasn't *right* for me. Yet here I am, reminded that Malakai became a Brandy-esque vocal Bible when it came to singing my praises. He means it too, his words weighty enough to leave comforting, toasty indents on any doubts that I might have.

Soraya's bemusement melts and she laughs genially. 'Oh, I haven't, but I need to check it out, sounds intriguing.'

I find parts of myself returning to me, and I quip, 'Well, I think it's sort of grounding for us to know that wastemen are not generationally exclusive, you know? That still, we will rise.'

Soraya grins. 'You're doing important scholarly work. So you guys . . . work together?' She glances at Malakai with mild curiosity, clearly trying to ascertain our connection. Same, sis.

'Yeah, sometimes. I just point the camera and shoot, though. Kiki kinda adds a gravity to my direction—'

'Well, that's true – I'm ready to talk my shit now.' Soraya laughs as I continue: 'But Malakai's direction is seriously beautiful, and it's really fun for me to play in and find something to carve out of – it's a great prism to work within as a storyteller, and so much of what I do is broken open by his direction. Really insightful, soulful stuff, finding magic in the mundane, the sacred in our culture. The project we're working on actually comes out later this year – we're under a nondisclosure, but it's the kind of cultural deepdive we do. It's storytelling and documentation at the same time. We'd love to send it to you when it's out – if you're interested at all?'

'I would love that.' Soraya sips at her flute of champagne, eyes bright. 'You know, it's weird. I always meet someone I wanted to run into whenever M throws one of these.'

Malakai and I share a look, before he turns to her and says, 'Hmm,' with such profundity that an obnoxious cackle gets wedged in my throat.

I nod. 'Yeah, I feel like that's what M, does, you know – *connects* people.'

It's brave, but it works, because Soraya's eyes light up. 'Right! I dunno how she does it, but she just *impacts* art.'

'That's so crazy – I was just telling Kiki that. That I think of M as an Impactor of the Arts. Wasn't I just saying that, Keeks?' He turns to me, eyes bright and playful, and it takes everything in me to subdue a godforsaken giggle.

'Mhmm. You were just saying that.'

Malakai turns back to Soraya, asking with a sip of his drink, 'How long have you known her? M, I mean—'

Soraya squints into the air. 'Oh, let's see, there was Edward Enninful's birthday party . . . and then Diana's Ross's dental-care initiative launch party – Ross's Floss . . .'

'Oh wow. She's such a Titan of . . . the industry,' I say, desperate for the revelation of which industry exactly, because there is no way the word 'YOLO' is going to be uttered when a very famous rapper I have had sex dreams about is a metre away from me. He'd been my hall pass when Malakai and I were together.

'All industries, really,' Soraya says unhelpfully, and Malakai smiles triumphantly at my flopped investigation attempt. 'Did you know, she was having a conversation with Kendrick at one of these things, and she says something to him like, "There's an intrinsic knowledge in our community. It's ineffable. You know when someone is like us and you know when they're not like us," and years later . . . Look, I'm not saying she deserves a credit. I'm

255

just *saying* I have a good feeling about the space this conversation is taking place in. She inspires art.'

Malakai and I both hold so still that I can feel the tremors of the hyperactive molecules within him bouncing rapidly, hopped up on the revelation that whoever is throwing this party has influenced *rap beef*. I don't know how he's going to metabolise this information. He might swoon like a Victorian maiden in a romance novel. I look at him and see the effort it's taking for him to pretend that the sentence that was just uttered has not completely decimated his chill.

'Anyway,' Soraya says warmly, unaware of the scattering that she's just unleashed onto us, 'it was such a pleasure meeting you both. Let me know your details and we'll stay in contact.'

We do just that, and Malakai manages to wait till she's out of earshot before he bursts forth with, 'She definitely meant Lamar, innit? As in, Kendrick Lamar? Fuck it, this might have to be a joint mission. We need to find out who this party belongs to together, Scotch. I'm serious.'

A tray full of suya sticks passes us by and I grab two and pass him one. We find ourselves walking through the heady throng of enough shiny, successful people to theoretically make me feel nervous, but I don't care any more. I'm here and I'm *here*.

'We need sustenance, because I feel like tonight could change our lives. When we find out who M is I mean,' I say as we walk out onto the terrace. Plumes of cigarette smoke mingle with weed and a melange of scents thick enough to choke, but I'm breathing easy in what feels like the first time in a while. The cool evening air nips at the thin mesh of my dress, but it feels refreshing, because

I feel warm from the inside, fizzing like all my cells are hopping up trying to taste as much of the night as possible.

Malakai nods. 'I reckon M probably knows where D'Angelo is and could get him to make another album.'

'I think M knows what happened in the elevator between Solange, Jay-Z and Beyoncé.'

'She for sure knows the name of the woman wearing the thong that inspired Sisqo's genius.'

'You know what? Maybe M is the friends we make along the way.'

Malakai laughs and it fills me up in such a way that I really don't need a snack any more, and so maybe that's why when I take a bite I find myself unmoved. Malakai, however, also looks unimpressed.

'These are dead, man. Nothing on Popsi Banjo's.'

I snort as I perch on a concrete bench that I imagine has been designed by a highly acclaimed architect, but is highly uncomfortable. 'Remember when my dad put extra-hot yaji on the suya the first time you came to the restaurant? Wanted to test how well you could handle the heat. He said any man who wants to "court" his daughter must be able to handle intense pressure without sweating. "If he can't handle a little peppeh, what else can't he handle?"'

'Listen. I thought I was gonna die. He was asking me my intentions whilst my entire face was on fire'

'There was a vein poppin' on your temple.'

'I just had to become one with the pain. You know how Simba saw Mufasa in the sky? Yeah, I saw my grandad.'

I howl, my eyes beginning to water, and Malakai nods with gravity, eyes twinkling, as he sits next to me.

'The one who died before I was born. His spirit told me to carry on, in the midst of the pepper choking me. My grandad told me that this was all for my future wife and this was just a trial of manhood I had to get through. Man just had to firm it. I was there to impress my girl's pops – nothing was gonna mess with that.'

My laughter quiets, but the awkwardness I expect to feel doesn't come. It feels good to acknowledge that what we had was *good*. My phone vibrates and I see two things: a text from Taré informing us she can't make it and a missed call from Aminah. She calls me again and I stare at her name flashing on my phone. I know enough by now to know it might be because she's decided on different flowers or a different sort of fish for the entrée or she wants to switch up the style for her bridal hair, and I brace against it. I can't be on call right now.

Malakai wraps the suya stick in a serviette and puts it to the side. 'You need to get that?'

'No. Taré isn't coming any more by the way. So, um, we don't have to stay if you don't—'

'Why would I want to go?' his tongue nips out to lick some residual spice left on his thumb, 'I like to finish what I started.'

I can see shimmering, feverish waves in the air between us.

'The Quest To Find M, I mean,' Malakai says, glancing away from me with a quick clearing of his throat. 'If I can consume suya spice that would break the Scoville scale in front of your dad without dying, discovering the identity of a mysterious cultural benefactor is a piece of piss.'

I release a stilted laugh and try to will a grip to come into my possession and fast. 'Well, you definitely earned his respect. And he thought you were hilarious. You know, afterwards, he laughed so much there were tears in his eyes? Thought it was the funniest thing in the world that you refused to drink any water as if you were legit trying to prove something.'

Malakai's brow props up and his face sobers. 'What do you mean? I *was*. I was trying to prove I was good enough for you. That was serious business for me,' he rubs his chin with a brusque laugh, 'Man, I wanted your dad to like me so bad you have no idea. It meant a lot that he did. Shout out to Grandad for carrying me through.'

I smile in bemusement. 'I know you're playing, but . . . just so you know, my dad didn't like you because you managed to handle a lethal amount of spice, Malakai. It's because he saw how you were with me.'

Malakai is quiet for a while. He stretches out a leg, then leans forward, resting his elbows on his knees. He turns to me, head bowed, releasing a rueful smile that immediately fails in its purpose of keeping things light. 'Your pops must hate me now.'

'My dad would only hate you if I hated you.'

I pause and look out, seeing an Oscar winner making out with a Tony nominee. It's nice when people find each other. I turn back to him, and the only thing left is truth. 'I'm angry at you. I'm confused by your actions, but I don't hate you. I could never fucking hate you. Trust me – I tried.'

Malakai's eyes glimmer and he swallows, turning away from

me before nodding quickly, as if to shoo away any soft feeling. Eventually, he says, voice gravelly, with a light choke of a laugh, 'I'm angry at you too. Confused by you too.'

'I think I'm pretty straightforward—'

'Nah, Kiki, you're anything but.'

'Really? Because I don't think it's complicated to want someone who tells you the truth.'

'I think it's complicated to say you love someone and not trust that they would never do anything to hurt you.'

'And yet you did, so where does that leave us?'

Malakai's eyes glint into mine, reassuming the stand-off into which we're perpetually finding ourselves, melting into a rhythm and then tripping over our past.

I release a stilted gust of a laugh. 'Why does it even make a difference to you? Whether I hated you or not?'

'It kept me up at night.'

'You don't have to be a dick about it.'

'I'm not, Kiki.' Malakai swallows and looks ahead, as if trying to conceal emotion. He cracks his knuckles, and his breathing feels considered. 'It was the weirdest fucking thing. The idea of you hating me . . . Man, it made me feel like shit, but, also, I couldn't deal with you *not* hating me. Like I needed to believe you hated me so I could, like, un*stick* myself from us.'

There's a somatic discordance within me, something in between the delicious relief of knowing that Malakai could have never hated me if he hadn't wanted me to hate him, with the petty belief that he might as well have, since he walked out on me the way he did.

The most damning thing of all is that I know exactly how he feels. I know what it feels like to desperately want to unstick yourself from a relationship that seems to be tacked on to you on a psychic level, so tight, so strongly, that the more you struggle the worse it gets. You beg for anything to help you rip it off, desperate enough to manufacture a belief that the other person hates you. I try to examine what it all means in my mind, but the material is so soft that it falls apart when I try to hold it, look at it closely, see what it is, what it means. Maybe it's for the best.

So all I say in reply is, 'Sorry I disappointed the spirit of your grandad. I mean you stomached all that pepper only for me to end up not being your future wife.'

Malakai guffaws and shakes his head. 'I wouldn't stress. You were as close as it's ever gonna get so I think he'd be cool with it. I don't think I'm ever gonna get married. I don't think I'm built for it. Just one of them things. I don't think it's for me.'

A knowledge tilts within me, and I can't figure out if it's comforting or discomforting. Was I forcing him to be who he wasn't? What was real with us? In a way, it should be liberating to know that maybe we were never supposed to be together. In another, it kills me, twists the memory of us into something you'd see in a trick mirror, a joke, a nonsense.

I clear my throat of a stupid little hurt. 'I thought you said you didn't really listen to the podcast? Because . . . I dunno . . . you kind of gave Soraya a comprehensive breakdown.'

Malakai chuckles, leaning over his knees. 'You have to drive a lot in LA. Traffic. I had a lot of time on my hands and I'd already finished listening to my Bible audiobook.'

'Ah, the one narrated by Katt Williams?'

Malakai roars with laughter, and again I'm lit up, places I forgot existed re-energised, ghost towns coming alive, machinery churning into movement. It's a headfuck, how our connection tilts us like a seesaw.

'Yeah, exactly. Joseph finding out the baby wasn't his hit different.' He straightens and turns to me, eyes glittering. 'Seriously, Kiki. Do you know how gassed I was back there? I'm sorry if I went a little crazy or overstepped. It's just . . . that big boss lady recognised *you*. Do you know how sick that is? Your work is real and it speaks. It always has. I saw you get spooked a little. I don't know what's going on, but I need you to remember who you are. If you don't, I got you. During this process, I mean.'

Malakai holds my gaze so tightly it draws me closer to him. It must do, which is why I find my thighs pressed up against his, his bare arms kissing up on the thin mesh covering mine, his heat unsettling truths such as This Is A Bad Idea, and We Could Never Get Back Together and I Can Live Without The Tongue Thing He Does. Those truths toss and turn so violently with his proximity that they break in half, and those halves break into halves and so on until the truths turn to dust, and I am suddenly not sure if they were truths to begin with or copes I constructed to look like them.

'We're on a mission,' he volunteers into our quiet, as if reminding himself.

I nod and look around for the first time, noticing the intricacies of the garden, with two terraces, and a set of backlit stairs that seems to be the only place free of people. An idea takes hold of me, moving my mouth before my brain has time to resist, to call it Bad.

'Follow my lead.'

Malakai's mouth ticks up in intrigue as I flick my head to gesture at him to rise. I get up, slip my phone out of my clutch, pressing my index to my tragus on one ear and my phone to the other.

'Hey, my darling.' My voice has become a slightly transatlantic drawl with a posh Lagosian curve nipped from the Bakare sisters. 'OK, so where did you say you were?' I ask my phantom friend loudly as I stride towards the stairs where one bouncer seems to be loitering. 'Oh, OK, sure – yeah, I'll be there in a second—' I walk with purpose, heels clicking against the patio, speaking loudly, and walk straight down the stairs, Malakai right behind me, just as the young-looking bouncer interjects with, 'Sorry, ma'am—'

I turn round, faux distractedly. 'Sorry, one second, sweetie,' I say into the phone as I shoot the bouncer a dazzling smile. 'I'm sorry, sir, is there a problem?' I twitch as if someone is arguing with me on the other side of the line. 'Oh, honey, no, no, one of your bouncers is stopping me . . . No, I'm on my way, M – No, no, you don't need to come down. I don't want any trouble. He's just doing his job.' I turn my gaze to him and mouth 'Sorry!'

He shakes his head and says, 'No, I'm sorry, ma'am. Please go right through.' I shoot him a candied grin of gratitude. 'Oh, thanks so much – you're a doll. Can my assistant come through too? What was your name, by the way?'

'Of course. And my name's Zane.'

I touch the bouncer's elbow, look him in the eye and watch him blush. 'Thank you, Zane. You're such a sweetheart.'

I continue my sashay down the steps, and Malakai whispers into my ear, so close that I shiver, 'That was impressively genius, batshit insane and slutty. I'm kind of scared of you.' I nod in gracious acceptance of the compliment, ignoring a tiny dancing plume of desire pirouetting between my legs. 'Very kind of you to say. It was nothing.'

'Yeah, that's what scares me.'

Malakai steps in front of me to haul open the heavy cedar door at the base of the steps, as I say, 'OK, so I reckon that conversation is too long to figure out who M is. We need to go out in the field. *Explore.* Go off the beaten track. Going upstairs is too passé, but *downstairs?* I bet that's where all the secrets lie— Oh my God—'

Malakai and I walk into a semi-open enclosure that boasts a *sub* garden – a garden within a garden, looking like an enchanted glade, shrubs illuminated in the dark, large looming trees forming a loose fence around a glass construction in the middle, within which I see a blue, glittering pool. A patio path is set within the shrubs leading up to it, and Malakai turns to me, face split open in a grin.

'Midnight swim.'

'Are you serious?'

Malakai hitches a shoulder in a shrug, that lustre in his eyes calling me to cavort, we're *here* and we're here. 'We're at a ridiculous party thrown by a mysterious culture-shifter. We're virtually anonymous. Give me one reason why we shouldn't?'

I try to form one, just one, but there's a growing heat within me, and it desiccates all the ingredients I need for reason, such as sense and emotional self-preservation, because, let's face it, I am toasting my hands on a friendly fire that threatens to blaze into an inferno. Malakai Korede is going to put me in trouble. Malakai Korede is currently putting me inside trouble. I want to put Malakai Korede inside my trouble.

He turns to look at me, smile slanting in a way that makes my heartbeat tumble, and says, 'You good?' and the answer is no. No, I am not 'good', I am fucking great, actually, like after you've taken a post-operative opioid and you don't feel any of the searing pain you've been through, but instead a strange, euphoric joy, as if you're floating above reality. This is fine.

'Yeah. I'm good,' I say, terrified, because I mean it.

Malakai, ever the gentleman, turns round as I peel my dress off, revealing my lacy black bra, my thong, folding my discarded clothing carefully and placing it on the purple-and-white terry-cloth lounge chair by the indoor pool. The light is low, the four corners of the glass structure glowing a muted gold that approximates the light of a sleeping sun, and through the glass ceiling, stars blink, saying – it seems – *Sis, what the hell do you think you're doing?*

The truth is I'm not thinking at all, just feeling.

The air in the natatorium is temperate so there's no reason why there should be goosebumps on my skin, but there is no reason why I should be here either and here I am, so here the goosebumps are.

We've been meticulous about our spontaneity; surveying the space earlier, we saw a door at the far end that led into a luxe shower-room, in which we found neatly folded (presumably) clean towels and a hairdryer, alleviating fears that we would have to tread damply back to the party while dripping evidence of our delinquency.

Malakai walks to the corner of the room where there's a system speaker. He fiddles with it, says, 'This room is soundproof,' and for the first time, I notice it, how there's not a sound to be heard but us, our footsteps, our breathing, our decisions. While his back is to me, I use the steps to descend into the pool, to submerge myself slowly, readying myself for the smart of cold water, but nothing comes. It feels warm, just right, light on my skin. I jump in just as Lucky Daye's crooning fills the space from Malakai's phone to the speakers, licking at my senses just as the water laps gently against me, welcoming me. Malakai walks back towards the pool, and I try to extend him the same courtesy as he did me, focusing on swimming and treading water as he strips himself of his clothes, but I snag on his snug boxer briefs, and air becomes iron in my throat. My gaze drops to his thighs, sturdy, muscular and thick, and how did I miss that when we had sex two months ago? Maybe it was for the best that I did. I might have lost more of my senses, because the wide plains of his chest was enough to blow the wind out of mine. Malakai has always worked out as a way to work through things, clear himself of thoughts, and it seems he's had a lot to work through in the past couple of years. It's more than that though. It's how his body fills the space he moves through, as if making the air bow for him. An ownership of his physicality that makes my pulse skitter. He jumps in and laughs at my squeal at the splash, hands protecting my made-up face, and then we find ourselves in a corner, me with elbows leaning against a step as my feet float, Malakai stood in front of me, water just above his waist.

We look at each other like this for a few moments, soaking in the absurdity, the air between us fraught and smoky, and I don't know if it's because of the heat between us or the destruction from our world-end.

'I have something to tell you.' Malakai's eyes flick from my face to the curves of my chest hovering against the line of the water. The thrill of his obvious desire is a drug, sending electricity and bad ideas through my veins, and I try to metabolise the energy into the strength necessary to survive the moment.

'Yeah? What's that?'

'I'm M.'

I snort at Malakai's blank face, at the telling twinkle of his eye, and it's a beat before he laughs with me, gaze sobering.

'Nah, you were right. About the song. Me and Taré's song.'

I cool, swirling my arms through the water for a while, trying to configure my thoughts. 'We don't have to talk about it. You don't owe me anything.'

Malakai's voice is low, gentle. 'I know, but I'm willing to be open about it. If you want me to be. At the end of the day this *is* fucking weird. I dunno how I would feel if my boss was someone you'd . . . been with.'

A rigid laugh ekes out of me, with a little relief. 'I mean, you wouldn't take the job. Such is the male ego.'

Malakai chuckles, dips his head, scratches his jaw, looks at the water. 'Yeah, I guess you're right.'

My smile fades. 'Go ahead.'

Malakai looks at the gently rippling azure of the water. 'Uh, OK. So we met, like, two months into me being in LA. At a party.'

My stomach dives in the deep end. Two months? That was like three months after we broke up. That's *it*? That's the amount of time it took him to jump into bed with someone else? I was still holed up in my room wailing to Summer Walker and huffing peanut butter, jar to jowl. I stay still, because I don't want any hurt or misplaced anger to slosh out of my eyes now that we're doing relatively OK. I keep my face clean of feeling.

'Oh,' I say. Well *done*, Keeks. Maturation. Void of chalants.

Malakai looks up, eyes, not apologetic, but empathetic – as if he understands how the revelation could wound. 'I was . . . a fucking mess, Kiki. I was in this new city where I knew no one but my boss. I'd just lost so much that I felt lost myself. I felt like I was an imposter, living someone else's life. Felt like I was sleepwalking half the time, honestly. And I was at one of them Hollywood parties where everybody pretends to be best friends whilst secretly hating each other. Some fuck-off house in the Hills. Kinda like this, actually. I'm tripping out. And I'm drinking too much, and just getting frustrated – people are talking to me, right, but it's like they're talking to me because they like the *idea* of talking to Matthew's latest protégé, and I'm exotic you know, Black, but British.' He laughs lightly. 'So they're treating me like some sort of specimen. Which makes no sense because so is Matthew—'

'Yeah, but Matthew speaks like he's out of an Agatha Christie novel. And he doesn't have your face.' I don't say it as a compliment, but as a fact.

Malakai gives me a slip of a smile. 'Anyway, someone offers me some stuff, some young white director dude. I say something like, "Nah, not really about it," and then *they* say something very, very fucking racist about what he "knows" I get up to. Said I can be "myself", that I don't need to pretend around him. Then . . . well, I kinda lose it. Get up in his face. It's like . . . it's like I've been dying for a reason to lose my shit and then this Quentin Tarantino-wanna-be motherfucker has given me the reason.'

His eyes flash with old anger and he's straightened his right hand like a blade, jabbing his left hand with it to punctuate his words. 'I been waiting for one. And Taré's been watching all this from where she's been standing in the corner – had no idea she was there. She interrupts the fight, whispers to me, "I'm gonna give you two choices. You can either stay and fuck up your career, or you can come with me and have a great rest of your evening."' He pauses, clears his throat of nothing. 'So. I follow her up to one of the rooms.'

I swallow and fight the tightening feeling in my stomach. I'm reeling from the revelation of Malakai's loneliness, of his anger, at what might have happened if Taré wasn't there.

Malakai misunderstands my silence and says, 'I can stop.'

I shake my head because I have a feeling that Malakai needs to get it out, and I am here in the tacit capacity of 'friend'.

'We're in it now.'

Malakai rolls out a hollow chuckle and nods, running a hand across the back of his head. 'Anyway, we start talking. She said she heard my accent and immediately knew what I was going through. Said she's been going through it too. Said she was lost too. This was just before she quit everything. We smoked a lot. Drank a lot.' The unspoken *fucked a lot* punches me in my gut and I swallow the blunt pain. 'And, yeah, it became this . . . casual situation. We were both trying to forget. Both coming from bad break-ups, emotional shit, and we both didn't want to talk about it. We didn't really wanna feel anything. We spoke about work a bit and we felt like we got each other in that sense, but, if I'm being honest, that was the main connection. Chasing numbness. Not wanting to feel anything real. It wasn't necessarily emotional, but . . . we had an understanding. We got what each other wanted at that time.'

It twists in my stomach, but I surprise myself by understanding, clarity cutting through the petty jealousy. They were two single hurting people wanting to stop the hurt in a city where no one really knew them.

'I mean on a regular day it would be wild that I was hooking up with Taré Souza, but in the mental state I was in everything felt like a hallucination anyway. And also . . . I kind of didn't see her like that? You know, Taré Souza, the artist we listened to? I guess because I met her in a different context. And Taré's great close up, but I also realised she's just human. Normal. And going through what I was going through. So it was kinda like . . . why wouldn't this happen? It lasted about a month. It was a haze. It sort of . . . fizzled out. We both knew that it was gonna end. We checked in with each other once in a while, but we knew it wasn't like . . . a *thing*. We stayed friends. Just friends.'

I nod slowly, managing to keep my feelings in check, ignoring the acuteness of my relief.

Malakai moves to stand next to me in the water, leaning against the wall. He pauses, splashes lightly, face tight from balancing emotion. 'That was a dark time for me, Scotch. I wasn't myself. I didn't want to feel like myself. And when Taré was talking about it I was reminded of it. I'd blocked it out. And I feel like I haven't been able to look at it – or, like, I dunno, *allowed* myself to look at it like a dark time for a long time. I think I need to say it out loud to avoid going back there.'

The warm light kisses the planes of his face and adds a fluorescence to the sheen of moisture on his skin. I look straight ahead because I know Malakai doesn't want to feel like he's being examined right now.

'I'm . . . Kai, I'm sorry for what you went through out there.'

I'd imagined Malakai living it up, enjoying the freedom from my shackles, but knowing he was in pain lacerates me in a way that I didn't expect, and I stop myself from saying, 'I'm sorry I wasn't there,' because it's nonsense and yet it's the only thing that makes sense for me to say in this moment. I *am* sorry he was hurting. I *am* sorry I wasn't there for him. Instead, I reach my hand out underwater for his. His hand clasps around mine immediately. It feels like a secret. In this underground indoor pool in this secret garden, underwater, we can hold hands and no one will know. We barely know.

271

Malakai looks down at me, eyes glistening with gratitude, before saying, 'Tell me why you were upset today, Scotch. Please.'

I want to tell him that he's forgotten the rules, but the pleasure at my nickname is so concentrated, so sweet, that I can't bring myself to, and, besides, what are rules here? This place is like an airport: time doesn't exist so the past doesn't exist. You can have a beer at 6 a.m., bare your soul to your ex in your underwear. I inhale deeply, and exhale something that's been wrapped tightly around my chest.

'We had viewings today. For the restaurant. One of them was a couple from Berkshire. They wanna make it into a cheese-and-wine bar. Sam and Cherry. Walked into Sákárà and said it "smelled exciting". I don't know how it came up, but they started talking about how much they loved Afrobeats – said their kid can't get enough of Rema and Selena's "Calm Down".'

'Oh. Right. I see.' Malakai's thumb strokes the inside of my palm absently and it's making me slightly dizzy, the deliberate, small movements comforting me and sending chills through my form at the same time. He valiantly tucks in the multiple comments I know he has loading, giving me space for me to pull out my words.

'It just made it real. I think I've sort of been . . . burying the truth of how it feels, you know? But it sucks. It really sucks to know that the place that was full of such love and family is going to be sucked of its soul. And I *love* port.' Malakai shrugs.

'Overrated. Port is just gentrified Magnum. You can get that from any bossman. You don't need Sam and Strawberry for that—' I laugh and I feel a knot unwind within me as I shake my head.

'It just . . . scares me a little, if I'm honest. So much is changing. Aminah's getting married, which is amazing, but it's *change*. What if our relationship changes too? I feel it starting to happen and I can't . . . I can't afford to lose her. I'm already losing a home I've had for my entire life. My parents are moving to Lagos. I'm building a new career, which is exciting, but terrifying. I don't have any real financial literacy so I'm bingeing *Industry*. It's not really helping. Also, I'm trespassing in a millionaire's pool. What is happening? Who am I?'

'Whoa.' Malakai tugs at my hand, pulls me forward. I wade in front of him. He frowns gently at me. 'What's this? Look at that crease in between your eyes. Massive brain just *whirring*. You're Kiki Banjo. That ain't just any name.' He ducks his head and his hand tilts my chin up to ensure I'm looking him in the eye. It's a move that would be bold in literally any other context, but in this one it doesn't make sense that he would do anything else. It presses me more firmly into me, like I wasn't sitting snug before. 'It's going to be OK. Change is good. This is just an evolution. It's scary, but all good things are a little scary in the beginning. Shit, you know what I did when I found LA scary, but you're way braver than me. Always have been, Scotch. You'll find your feet, just give yourself a little grace. You're always so hard on yourself, man. Why? Bottling things up. I need you to do unto yourself as you do to others.' His smile slopes. 'And, look, you and Aminah love each other and it will be fine. You will always be fine. Sákárà is a representation of something in you, you're allowed to acknowledge what it means to you, and you're gonna pour it into everything you do so it's going to live forever. No matter what. And this isn't just any millionaire's pool – it's my pool. I told you that already.'

My heart could double as a floaty it's so full up, and maybe that's why it leaks over to my eyes that instantly feel heavy. I manage to choke out a quiet, 'Thank you K—Malakai.' Malakai shakes his head in gentle dismissal of my gratitude, like what he's just done was nothing, when it's far from nothing. The ease by which he did it only cements how Not Nothing it was. No one has ever made me feel this way: secure in my skin and also transcending anything that could confine me. That's depressing because no one has ever broken my heart like him either. Malakai's face is so open, and earnest I want to run to it, but something makes my movements tacky, I keep getting stuck.

'Why do you hate being called Kai now? Is that new? Or were you just humouring me for the entire duration of our relationship? Something you said I could say because it sounded cute?'

Malakai's eyes fasten on to me tightly, and I see a tiny battle in him as he decides how much he wants to say. Maybe he's trying to decide how extensively facts will implode this fragile truce we have going on.

He swallows. 'I told Taré that because it was easier for me to say than the truth.' His jaw tightens as he looks at something beyond my head, before meeting my gaze again, the heat in them curling the air in my throat. 'I hate being called Kai by anyone who isn't you.' His voice is naked of affect, which overwhelms me because he's saying it like it's fact, and I really wish he wouldn't do this, because it's getting hard to remember things I should.

He lifts my chin with his thumb so I can look him in the eye. 'That name belongs to you, Scotch. It's yours. No matter what's happened between us.'

It's yours. It lands in me and wreaks havoc on my reasoning. I am tilting my neck to allow his hand to slip to my throat, and it does, because it knows what to do. His eyes dip to the tangle of gold necklaces lying against my clavicle, and he picks up a charm between his thumb and forefinger. 'You're still wearing it.' It's a chilli pepper pendant he gave me on our third anniversary. 'Couldn't find a scotch bonnet. You believe that? Hold that for now,' he'd said then, 'when I get my money up I'll get one commissioned for my baby.' I forgot I'm still wearing it. It's part of my daily rotation of jewellery, part of me. I've never stopped wearing it. I don't think I even noticed that I've never stopped wearing it until now.

'It's yours,' I say.

Our noses graze, and his breath is fragrant, delicious. I want to keep it for myself and wear it on my wrists, taste it in my mouth. His other hand has wrapped round my waist, pressing me closer to him, and I feel his firm length against my softness. I let out a moan that I should technically be embarrassed by, but isn't this whole thing technically embarrassing? Yet, I am not, I feel bold with it, secure with it. Malakai's eyes flare at the sound of my pleasure, his breathing staggered as I slowly swirl on the hard evidence of our chaos, curving a leg around his hip so he can mould into me. His hand lowers to my butt cheek and he grips and groans, as I trace his lips, as I move to nip at his neck in possession, tongue branding him as I slide my hand down his chest, relishing the firm feel. *It's yours.* Then I snag on the other part of his sentence. *No matter what happened between us.* Like our break-up was a mild disagreement, not a shattering of my world. Maybe it really is something he can brush under a carpet. Something light enough to flick away. I feel the sting of cool air waking me up from what was clearly a haze of nostalgia-fuelled delusion blurring my vision.

Shit, what am I doing? Why am I here, listening to R&B, wet-dry humping my ex?

I shake my head as I hop off of him and back away, 'Nope. I can't do this. You may be able to do this casual one-foot-in, one-foot-out shit, but I can't. OK? I can't do this.'

'Scotch—'

'You LEFT.' My voice echoes across the room, my eyes hot and wet. 'You left, Kai, and I was a *wreck*.' My hand slaps hard and wet against my chest, my voice rasping. 'It was humiliating. And you may be healed enough to do . . . whatever the fuck this is, but I'm not. I'm not built this way. I respect whatever we had enough not to do *this*. Because this is a dead end. Shallow. And you know it, and maybe that's why you want it, because there's no future here. You said it yourself: you're not *built* for long-term relationships. Sorry, but I can't use my energy this way. I've worked way too hard on myself to be distracted by something that is never going to work.'

Malakai looks like he's about to speak, eyes coruscating with conflicting emotions, the edge of his jaw pulled sharply, before he sniffs and nods. 'You know what, Kiki, you're right.'

Right. I am right. I'm so right. It's not like I wanted him to fight back. Tell me I'm wrong, that actually he wants me, all of me. It's not like I want him, all of him. This is good.

'But don't demonise me for something you were cool with three months ago,' Malakai continues, steel falling over his eyes like a shield or an axe. 'It's better you tell the truth, which is you don't like who I am, and it worked for you for a time, and now it doesn't. Now I sully this idea you have of yourself. And that's cool, Kiki. Really, it is. I just want you to be honest, since you're the one who talks about truth so much. You never wanted this to work because you never really believed I was more than the fuckboi you first met in uni. Deep down. You know what I think? I think it gave you thrills to think you'd changed me. And it hurt your ego that I was the one who left, not you.'

My breathing becomes shallow with fury, hurt, exposure. My skin smarts. 'You know what? Thank you for this, Malakai. You really clarified some things for me.'

'Yeah, likewise, Kiki.'

My eyes narrow, and I'm so hot I feel like the water is steaming around me. I've never wished I could hate someone more. I realise in order to storm off I'm going to have to walk up the pool steps virtually naked, which really defangs how serious I am. Nevertheless, I cough and do just that, blood pumping hard in my ears, heart caught just as it was about to fall again, grateful, so grateful, that I stopped myself from being fooled twice.

CHAPTER 12

The Definition of Insanity

Four years ago

I woke up at 1.07 a.m. to pee. And still, now, if I see 1.07 a.m. on a clock I say a prayer. I happened to look at my silenced phone and saw six missed calls from Malakai. Alarm immediately surged through my body. I called him back and what I heard turned my blood into frigid sludge. He was hyperventilating, voice wavering, barely breathing, barely getting words out. Each ragged breath wrapped round my heart and squeezed. All I could make out was, '*He's gone.*'

Through a constricted throat and what felt like an eternity, I asked who, though somehow I knew.

His voice splintered into tiny fractures as he wheezed terribly, as if all his strength was going into breathing. 'Dad . . . heart attack . . . sleep.'

I do not remember going to the hospital. All I remember is being there, my dad's coat – the first one I grabbed – over my pyjamas, seeing him and his mum and his little brother, Muyiwa, all huddled together, a compact bundle of wails. Malakai's arms were round them both, though his knees were barely holding him up, and by the time I got there Malakai had already packed his emotion tightly away. He talked to the doctors, his eyes bloodshot, his face numb, as his mum wailed her denial. She cried, soul-rattling repeated protestations of 'no', willing it not to be so, rejecting reality, calling truth to battle, because there is *no* way her larger-than-life husband had succumbed to death; *no*, they were supposed to go to Lagos next weekend; *no*, what did they mean?; *no*, what will her sons do without their father?; *no*, *no*, they should take her to see her husband immediately because somebody somewhere was lying, maybe even him . . . even though she'd been right next to him when it had happened; he was asleep . . . he was asleep. Muyiwa was racked with sobs, convulsing, but trying to hold his mother as she fought him like he was facts. When Malakai spotted me, he silently took me by the hand and walked me away from them, almost as if he was sleepwalking, shaking his head. He couldn't stop shaking his head, on autopilot, heavy with denial. It was only when his mum and brother couldn't see or hear him that he fell so hard against me in an embrace that I tripped back into the wall, and when he wrapped his arms around me for anchorage it was so tight I could barely breathe. It was bone-crushing, desperate, his weight sagging against me as if he couldn't keep himself up.

I was ready to take it all, everything if I could, all of his heavy, all of his hurt. 'I got you. I got you, baby.' My voice shook and broke and we both slid to the floor right there in the hospital hallway.

I sobbed and rocked him as he whispered, 'How?', sobbed and rocked him as he whispered, 'I was supposed to see him today. He was gonna teach me golf. Said no son of his wouldn't know how to swing. I said, "Dad, that doesn't mean what you think it means."' He laughed, and it sounded sick and strangled and my blood curdled because this could not be, this couldn't be happening.

I sobbed and rocked him as he whispered, 'I want my dad, Keeks,' and this time a single sob came out from him too. 'I just want my dad,' he repeated, and then several jagged sobs tumbled out. 'I never said goodbye.'

With this came a howl, raw and primal, an animal dying. That sound imprinted itself on me, the sound of Malakai's heart breaking in real time in an irreparable way, in a way I wouldn't ever be able to fix, his pain lacerating through me.

Now

'He's late.' Aminah's voice is edged with irritation as she stretches, clad in pink leggings and a purple crop top, pink sweatband framing her ponytail like she's in a *Barbie* movie and *Step Up* crossover.

Shanti shrugs as she strolls in through the dance-studio doors in joggers and a sports bra. 'Weird. Maybe he thought that a mandatory pre-wedding dance class for the bridal party was overkill and chose to do literally anything else?'

Aminah snaps back up from her stretch and rolls her eyes at Shanti. 'Listen, I am not leaving anything to chance for the traditional wedding. Co-ed dance classes are mandatory so nobody can embarrass me on the day. Groomsmen *and* the bridesmaids need to be co-ordinated, like I would hate for the wedding to go viral on Bella Naija for the wrong reasons—'

Laide sips from her large mint-green Stanley cup, and drawls, 'Since when did *you* care about things like that?'

'Because! Kofi's mum said she doesn't want her son's heritage being drowned out and so this fusion dance to Nigerian Afrobeats and Ghanaian Afrobeats needs to be perfect—'

'And I told you,' Kofi says with practised equanimity, 'it doesn't matter, but I love you for the effort.' He raises his love's hand to his mouth and presses a kiss to her palm.

Laide rolls her eyes impatiently. 'OK, sure, but why do those of us who are not rhythm-impaired have to join?'

Aminah hitches her shoulder up, and raises her hands as if the answer is obvious. 'Equity, Laide! Some of us are good, kind people who care about supporting people with no rhythm!'

'I dunno,' Ty says, in his basketball shorts and loose vest. 'I think it will be kind of fun. Did you guys know that when I was twelve I took ballroom?' He takes Shanti by the hand, twirls and dips her and all of a sudden she seems to have no qualms.

'Also,' Kofi says, putting an arm round his fiancée's shoulder, 'it's just a fun, bonding activity with the wedding party. Get to know each other before the day. Now, respectfully,' he says, smile bright but eyes stern, 'will you people get it together? We've already paid for the studio time.'

Aminah tilts her chin with a small smile, patting his back.

'Thank you, baby.' She walks to the front of the class. 'Now, before we start, where the hell is Malakai? Everyone needs to be in pairs for this to work—'

Chioma, who has been sitting cross-legged on a plyometric box at the back of the studio flirting with *both* of Kofi's cousins, now gets up, purple harem pants falling around her gracefully as she chimes in. 'Sorry, *you're* leading the class?' Chi's usually chill demeanour is peppered with uncharacteristic annoyance. 'You dragged us here on a Saturday morning for a dance class that *you* are leading? When I'm the one with a Free Movement Level 1 accreditation?'

Aminah shrugs. 'Yeah, who else to set the tone of movement for my wedding? We want sexy, but classy – Kofi, has he picked up yet?'

Kofi shakes his head whilst frowning at his phone. 'Nah. I'm getting a little worried now – Keeks, have you heard from him today?'

I swallow. 'Um, no,' I say, trying to calm my own worry. I'd been in the corner of the studio surreptitiously texting him. Aminah is teetering on an edge and, frankly, I cannot deal with any tantrums that can be avoided. So far it's been:

- the bakery hasn't got the exact balance of pistachio and rose that she's needed,
- the renowned mixologist she wanted currently has a broken wrist (Kofi said a silent prayer of thanks for that due to his rate) and
- her mother has asked for her personal guest list to extend from 20 to 60 (legitimate outrage at this).

282

I'm already on slightly thin ice with her. She was pissed I missed her call the night before her venue viewing (it turned out to be a question about if I was super sure that lilac wasn't an 'overdone' bridesmaid dress colour) and only just about let go of me missing the viewing because I told her I'd been working late, ended up getting home at 2 a.m. and slept through my 7 a.m. alarm. It was fractionally true, if 'working late' included swimming in a stranger's pool with my ex-boyfriend.

Malakai and I have fallen into a frigid but polite rhythm since that night at the party, suppressing our conversations, ensuring we're in safe zones: 'Great idea!' 'Love that!' I think at one particular point, in front of Taré and in an effort to maintain appearances, we gave each other a high five, like we were children's-morning-show presenters, which wouldn't have been awkward if it wasn't so obvious we were trying to avoid prolonged physical contact with each other. Still, not so awkward that he would screen my texts.

Aminah rubs her temple. 'Man, this is eating into our time. Do you guys have some sort of work thing you've forgotten about or something? You know, like how you forgot about the venue viewing we had three weeks ago?'

The ice beneath my feet cracks a little. The room hushes at the pointed remark. Astonishingly, Aminah has been relatively relaxed about Malakai and I working together. When I told her as we were bridesmaids' dress shopping, rifling through samples, she'd nodded.

'Very retro. Uni era. Makes sense, though. You guys have some sort of creative synergy. That being said, historically, it's been a recipe for the kind of romantic angst only seen in an early 2000s CW show.'

I snorted. 'Yeah. It did give small *One Tulse Hill*.'

Aminah smirked. 'Dalston's Creek.'

I'd smiled, despite myself. 'Damn it. Well done.' Aminah had patted herself on the back. 'Thanks, but seriously, Keeks, just be careful. You were tore up when he left for America. I don't want that to happen again. You wore soft boots outside the house, if you left the house at all. I can't deal with that during wedding season.' She shuddered. 'Dark times.' And again I promised that it was all good; Malakai and I are professional. *Civil*. And even if I was prone to acquiring feelings again (which I'm not) Malakai has made it clear that he isn't (which is fantastic).

Now, I swallow my slight irritation at Aminah's shade. 'We have a recce for Taré's video shoot this afternoon, but nothing for now. Also, like I said, I didn't *forget* about the viewing. I just overslept—'

'Wait, oh my God—' Shanti has been absently scrolling on her phone, bored as we've been speaking, when she gasps and holds her phone up to me. 'Why are you and Malakai in the background of this photo of Daniel Kaluuya and Michael B. Jordan looking like the poster kids for Hashtag Black Love?'

'Um, I have no idea?' I frown as she comes over, zooming in on a picture on a Black celebrity Instagram page. Sure enough, it's from the night of the mansion party, with the two stars in the forefront. In the background, Malakai and I are standing close, looking into each other's eyes, which are squinted with glittering mirth, my hand on his wrist as we laugh. It looks like it was taken just after our conversation with Soraya. Shit. It disconcerts me for several reasons, including but not limited to the fact that it looks like it could have been taken when we were still together. It's mocking me: it's a lie. That isn't who we are any more, despite what this extremely beautiful photo is saying. Seriously, I look incredible. Shanti's skincare routine is working. Aside from that, though, the picture depresses me.

Aminah rushes over with Laide and Chioma and peers at the phone screen. I feel her ire build as soon as her gaze hits the screen. 'Why does it say the photo was taken the *day before* the venue viewing? I thought you said you overslept because you were working late? How does working late involve partying with the world's hottest men – Malakai exempt, of course. Were you just *hungover*?'

I baulk at her accusatory tone, and take her hand, pulling her to the corner of the room, because what we're not about to do is have a blowout in front of everyone. I lower my voice. 'I *was* working late. Taré –' I whisper her name, since our friends know that Malakai and I are working on a project, but not who the project is for – 'wanted us to go to the party with her and so we did. I mean she ended up not coming in the end, but it was *supposed* to be kind of a work social situation. And, yeah, I did oversleep because I've been exhausted with balancing working at the restaurant with working on *Phoenix*.'

'But why do you and Malakai look so cosy?' She narrows her

eyes in suspicion. 'Are you OK? You would tell me if you weren't, right?'

Theoretically, I would, but now, when my best friend seems to be perpetually on the precipice of a breakdown induced by whether she should serve bellinis or mimosas as a reception welcoming drink, perhaps not.

I force a shrug. 'What, did you want us to be fighting? Malakai and I are colleagues who get on. We're adults. Now, will you chill out?'

Suspicion still colours Aminah's face, but she nods in reluctant acceptance. 'Fine. Fine. And I guess if something actually were going on, you would know where he is right now. We'll just have to start without—'

The door to the studio swings open, and Malakai strides in, black hoodie, tracksuit and trainers on, his face uncharacteristically stormy. He looks like he hasn't slept, bags heavy under his eyes.

'Oh! Nice of you to finally make an appearance, diva!' Aminah's words are bulbous with sarcasm.

Malakai seems to barely register her voice as he makes a beeline for me. 'Kiki, we have to go. Yo, you all right, guys?' He barely waves to our friends as he walks towards me. 'I fucked up. I thought the recce was at three, but it's now. We're running late. T's already on her way. We have to go.'

I blink at him in confusion at his rudeness, at what he's saying. 'What are you talking about? I thought the location manager booked it—'

Malakai runs a hand across the back of his head in agitation.

'I sorted it because I know the guy who owns the club.' Malakai greets Kofi with a hand clap, and reaches out to squeeze Aminah's arm. 'Meenz, I'm sorry, but this is important. We have to lock in a location this week, and T—our artist has hated everything else—'

Barely contained irritation flitters over Aminah's pretty features. 'But how will you know the steps? How is this going to work without the best man and the maid of honour? You guys are supposed to *lead*—'

Kofi winds his arm round Aminah's waist, dropping a kiss on her forehead. 'Baby. It will be fine. This is just for *fun*, remember? Just to get us in the mood.'

'Um, sorry,' Laide interrupts, hands on her hips. 'If Kiki and Malakai don't have to do this, why do we? There's a really cute mezcal bar, like, *right* next door I've been meaning to check out. They do taco and margarita brunches. I know the manager – I'm sure we can walk in with no rezy—'

Shanti gasps with pleasure, completely forgetting the chaos she unleashed ten minutes ago. 'Oh yes, please! Can we bond over shots? It's my favourite way to bond.'

'You know what? Since I'm *actually* accredited in movement therapy through that online course, I actually know dances that could bond us as a group – *then* we can get mezcal margs,' Chioma offers.

Aminah's eyes widen, swivelling between Malakai and I. 'See! You guys are supposed to set the tone! You're messing up the tone!'

Kofi throws me a beseeching look, and I step closer to her, hands on her shoulders. 'The tone will be fine, OK? Malakai and I really need to settle on a location for this shoot otherwise we're screwed. The dancing will be fine on the day. I promise. Authenticity is key. You don't want it to feel over-rehearsed.'

I kiss her on her forehead, ignoring the fact she's fuming, and say goodbye to the rest of the group. Malakai is tapping on his phone impatiently, brow furrowed. It's a look I've seen on him before, just before we broke up. Distracted, annoyed, frantic. He looks up from his phone, face absent.

'We gotta go now, Kiki.'

I flinch at his tone, looking over my shoulder as I gather my things. 'Yeah, I know, you've said. What's your problem, actually? I don't like how you're talking.' I zip up my fitted workout jacket, and look up at him. 'Get it the fuck together, man.'

Malakai runs a hand across his face with a deep inhale. 'I'm sorry. I'm sorry. I'm just stressed.'

'OK, well, *unstress.*' I hitch my tote bag onto my shoulder, eyeing him as we walk towards the door, while in the background our friends are humouring Aminah's guidance to 'demure bum-flicks and wining'.

'It's thirty minutes away. We'll get there on time. You need to relax. Don't make your mistakes everyone else's problem.' I eye him warily. He looks exhausted, a little gaunt. I don't care. It's none of my business. I wet my lips, keep my voice light. 'Is there anything else bothering you? I'm asking as a colleague.'

He shakes his head. 'Nah, I'm cool. Let's just get there, yeah?' He shoots me an offensively brief, empty smile and walks through the doors. I roll my tongue in my mouth and nod to myself.

It's almost satisfying that I'm instantly thrown back to the time just before we broke up. At the end, he was closed off when it counted, unpredictable, flaky. In a way, I welcome it. It's a timely reminder.

Three years ago

Malakai wasn't here yet. I wonder how many free rolls I could eat before it became gauche. I tore a piece of granary bread and dipped it in some olive oil. I'd already finished a red wine, just asked for another, a merlot and then a cabernet just to mix it up, and I assumed they tasted different even though with every sip I could taste my own apprehension, this sick dread. I kept telling the waiter that the other half of my party was still coming because of course he was still coming – why wouldn't he still be coming? It was a dinner I'd planned for us, one of the last we'd have before he went away to America to work on Knight's next venture, and I'd come ready to make him lose his mind. I'd worn a strappy black mini freakum dress and heels. I'd got a wax, exfoliated, layered several scents on myself, just in case my pheromones weren't enough. I smelled good, and I knew I looked good and I was sat at the restaurant in the hotel with which I was planning to surprise him. I'd somehow got into doing 'Black Girl in Media' panels, as if I had any clue about what I was doing. One of them had been at a swanky five-star hotel in central London and, as a partial apology for the truly pitiful pay, I'd been offered a voucher for a night's stay, a night that ordinarily would have cost a smooth £650. I'd saved it for when I thought we really needed it, but there was no time for saving and we really needed it now. Nine months ago, Malakai would have answered my texts by now. Nine months ago, he probably wouldn't have had to reply to my texts because he would have texted me that he was going to be late, but nine months ago Malakai's life hadn't been ruptured. Nine months ago, Malakai was still talking to me like I was his partner, like he loved me, like I was his best friend. Nine months ago, Malakai hadn't spent nearly every night of the week away from me, drinking with his colleagues at industry parties, and when he was with me, wasn't saying, 'I'm cool, Kiki. Chill.' He was hurting, I knew that, but, bizarrely, refused to admit he was hurting and so we were stuck in this loop of him moving under a dark cloud and me charged with the responsibility of pretending that the cloud wasn't there, because if I pointed it out I was the villain – I was dragging him down. So I sucked it up, because this wasn't about me, couldn't be about me. My boyfriend had lost part of his world, had the whole world shift beneath his feet. In the space of a night, he became responsible for his little brother, for the well-being of his mother, had relatives pulling him in every which way. I couldn't bother him because what would I say? I wanted a movie night? For him to wake up and pull me to his body like he used to do? That I was never worried about him moving to America temporarily for work, but now I was terrified of what would happen when we had physical space between us because the emotional space we had was already killing me?

My heart spiked when I thought about it, my mouth went dry, my palms sweaty, my body going into something like shock, because I couldn't imagine a world where we didn't survive. It was unthinkable, inconceivable. I was beginning to feel like the ground that we had been standing on was beginning to tilt, and this dinner, this night, was a way to steady ourselves, get back to ourselves. We both lived with other people so this was an opportunity to be in our cocoon, be us. Fuck, I missed us. I sipped some more of my wine and felt my heart lurch because something already felt wrong, askew. I didn't know what I knew, but I knew.

He strode into the restaurant thirty minutes after we were supposed to meet, smelling like tequila, cologne and bullshit. He kissed me on the cheek before he sat down. 'Kiki, I'm so sorry I'm late. We got caught up—'

I controlled my rioting emotion, extracting grace from the reserves on which I'd been relying for almost a year. I feared I was beginning to run out.

I raised a brow. 'We?'

'Yeah. The team. It was after-work drinks—'

I laughed and rubbed my forehead, because, really, there's no way that Malakai kept me waiting for *half an hour* because he was drinking gin and tonics in some Soho pub with his colleagues. Malakai's expression stilled in the dim of the restaurant. He looked so different these days, the light in his eyes less buoyant, far away. It was like seeing a fairground without the lights, all the power out of the machines. Haunted. I used to look in his eyes and see love I could bite into, see him catching everything I would throw at him, ready, waiting for me and my spirit to come out, come play. Now irritation etched his face. I felt my heart crack.

'What is it?' he asked.

I shrugged. 'Nothing.'

Malakai shot a polite smile at the waiter as he came to take his drink order, then turned to me, brow furrowed, that storm cloud heavy above him. 'Kiki, I know you.'

'I don't wanna ruin tonight.'

'You think you holding your emotions in is gonna make it better?'

I stared at him for a moment as another arid smile slipped. The wine and my repressed irritation collaborated to say, 'You really wanna talk about holding your emotions in, Kai?'

Malakai nodded slowly and leaned on the table, rubbing the bridge of his nose. 'Cool. We're gonna do this again.'

'Do what, Kai? You may think you not talking about it is helping, you being a big strong man or whatever—'

'Don't take the piss, Kiki—'

'I'm *not*. I'm just saying that this macho shit serves no one and it doesn't suit you. It's not *helping* you. It all goes somewhere, baby. All the pain goes somewhere, and it's bleeding out, all over us—'

'Well, you know what, I'm sorry that my grief is an inconvenience for you.'

It winded me, knocked the breath out of me, pushed tears into my eyes immediately, my throat tightening. There was nothing to say to that.

Shame shadowed Malakai's face instantly, his hand reaching out for mine. 'Fuck. Scotch. That wasn't fair.'

'It's OK.' Again, pulling at the dwindling reserves of grace, because how would I know how I would be in his shoes? When my mum was sick, I damn near lost every ounce of my mind.

Malakai shook his head, reaching across to tip my chin up, and I saw a glimpse of my Malakai, my Kai, seeping back into his face, recognisable, soft. 'No. It's not. You've been by my side the whole time. Took days off work, checked on my mum and Muyiwa. I couldn't have got through these months without you.' I don't know how much I can believe this when it's like he's trying to do everything but spend time with me.

'But,' he said, releasing my hand and a breath through his nose, 'I just . . . I need to deal with it my way, OK? And my dad wants me to work hard. Climb ranks. He's always said that if I was going to do this, I have to be successful at it. And that's what I'm trying to do. This is how I keep his legacy. Making something of myself. And that involves extra-curricular shit. It means networking.'

I nod tightly, restricting movement, trying to minimise the amount of emotion the action might free up, expose. 'I get it.' I tucked in my hurt, my doubt, because what could I say to a man who thought he was doing everything he could to make his dad proud?

Malakai tilted his head to the side, his eyes scanning me. 'You look gorgeous, baby. Who you looking all bad for?' A thrill skipped through me, despite myself, warming me.

'Well, me and the waiter became well acquainted in your absence. And you seen him? It's very Paris Fashion Week.'

'Oh yeah. Handsome as hell.' Malakai laughed, the light returning to his eyes. I wanted to wrap myself in it, slather it on my skin, let it sink in. I'd missed it so much.

'Exactly. This is all for Adama. He's Senegalese by the way.'

'Yeah? Love to my Francophone brothers.'

'He's doing an MSc in Psychology too. Training to be a therapist.'

I briefly wondered if I should take the opportunity to bring up grief therapy to Malakai again – he claimed he hadn't been ready before – but I bit my tongue in order to preserve the moment.

It seemed like the right decision, because Malakai raised his glass, and looked me in the eye with a glimmer of his play back. 'Well, congrats to him and congrats to me. Tell Adama I'm the only one who's gonna ask you how anything feels tonight.'

I let our patter massage my nerves, smooth out their frays. I had nothing to worry about. We were good. We were so good.

Now

Malakai is pacing on the pavement in front of the locked-up South London bar, on his phone, hand running across the back of his head. His words are low, fast and furious and he keeps pausing to turn to the team to assure us that he's 'sorting it'. Something tells me that he isn't. Something feels off. His demeanour is jittery, skittish and Malakai is never disorganised when it comes to work. He may have been an inconsistent boyfriend towards the end, but he never played about his job. For the first time since working together, Taré looks vaguely annoyed, surfacing from her creative haze to come out of the sleek black van that carries our DOP, set designer and production assistant. They'd piled back into the van after it turned out that the venue we were supposed to be checking out has chains across its doors.

'Is everything OK? I really need to get back, so if we can just wrap this up quickly—' Taré is in huge sunglasses and workout gear, dressed for a quick survey of a potential video space and a return to the studio.

I turn to her from where I've been watching Malakai attempt to hide his panic, and paint on a smile. 'Everything's fine!' I say with absolutely zero certainty. 'Just a little mix-up! Why don't you chill in the van – it's cold! I'll tell you and the team when to come out!' I am vaguely aware that my voice sounds preternaturally cheery and a little deranged.

Taré nods, hesitant, before deciding to trust me, turning back to the sleek, tinted van. As soon as I hear the slam of the door, I casually approach Malakai and speak through gritted teeth. 'OK, what the hell is going on? Don't lie to me.'

Malakai is still on the phone, pacing, and he walks a little further away, into the narrow alley beside the building as he speaks. 'I think I know what day and time I booked this for – why would you play with me like this? . . . This is my job, man. Can you come and open it now? . . . Is this really how you're gonna do me? . . . Yeah. Calm. Cheers for fucking nothing.' Malakai hangs up the phone and tosses it onto the ground, putting both hands to his head, still pacing, eyes red. My skin pricks with panic – something feels desperately wrong. This isn't him. None of this is him. This is different from *flakiness*. I pick up the phone – thankfully not smashed – and approach him, reaching out for his arm.

'Malakai.' He isn't looking at me, his jaw tense as he stares into space. '*Kai*. Look at me.' He does now, eyes bleary, confusingly, heartbreakingly bleary. This can't just be about the job. 'What is happening? What's wrong?'

He shakes his head. 'I fucked up, Scotch. I've messed up the times and now the bar isn't available for when we wanna shoot. We're running out of options. *Shit*, man. How did I do this?' He looks furious with himself; I've never seen him so furious. My blood feels heavy in my veins, concern coursing through me.

'Hey – Kai – it's fine. Calm down—'

Malakai's voice comes out in frantic rasps, eyes shiny as he stares beyond my head. 'Nah, Keeks, you don't get it. I'm supposed to be good at this – this is what I'm supposed to do. Everything's supposed to be right today. It's supposed to be *right*. Everyone's relying on me for it to be right—'

His breathing has increased rapidly, and alarm sparks through me as I gently pull his hands from his head. 'All right, listen to me. *Look* at me.' He does, with hesitation, and what I see lances through me. I've seen the look before. It's this alone that makes reach up and hold his jaw. I slide his phone into my hoodie pocket, and place my other hand on his chest. 'Breathe with me, Kai. Can you do that?' He nods, numbly, and I nod with him, shooting him a reassuring smile, whispering, 'Thank you. OK.' I inhale and exhale deeply, and Malakai mirrors my actions, gaze clinging to me in the blur. 'Good. You're fine. You're fine, OK? We are a team. I get that this feels like a lot, but I'm right here with you. We will sort this out together. I got you. OK? I got you, Kai.' Malakai's breathing slows and his eyes clarify, homing in on me as if he's just come out of a trance. I drop my hands from his body and he stares at me nakedly.

'Please don't tell anyone.'

I swallow, trying to keep inexplicable tears from springing into my eyes. 'I-I won't.' I don't even know what I'm not supposed to tell anyone. 'Of course I won't. How are you feeling?'

He nods awkwardly. 'Better.'

'OK. So we probably have to come out now. If you want to go home, I can cover for you.'

Malakai shakes his head. 'Nah. I'm good now. I'm good—'

'Malakai, it's OK if you're not. What happened—'

'I told you,' he snaps, eyes flaring, not at me, I know, but anger at whatever he's clearly hiding from me. It's bitterly familiar, a refusal to let me in, shutting me out like I'm a casual guest in his space, not someone whose contours he knows. 'I'm just stressed. Like I said. There's a lot of pressure with this job, and we don't have a lot of time. Look, I'm sorry, I don't wanna put this on you. I'll just go out there and explain—'

I pull at the niggling thread in my mind, and watch it unravel into something that might possibly work. It's a risk, but it's the only choice we have right now. 'No. I have an idea.'

*　　*　　*

'Sákárà? Your parents' restaurant?' Taré is sceptical as she walks into the dining room, shades pulled from her face to nestle in her 'fro. 'Was this planned?'

Malakai and I exchange a look before I laugh in what I pray sounds like we have our shit together. 'Of course! We knew that other place was probably not going to work out, but we wanted to explore all our options before showing you our perfect choice. Right, Malakai?'

Malakai nods, slightly dazed, clearing his throat. 'Exactly.' He becomes more alert as Taré takes a turn around the premises, curious. 'It's cosy and authentic, has so much potential for creating a speakeasy vibe, and it's unique. Also, the space's history speaks to what you want to do. It represents community, culture—'

I nod, smiling at our part-time manager, Chidi, as we walk up to the front of the restaurant. 'We actually used to throw live shows here back in the day. There was an entire band, and people would come here on the weekend to relax, gist, dance. I really think with a little tweaking Sákárà can provide exactly what we need for the lead video. Any sale that happens won't be processed till after the date of the shoot, so we're good for time, and it would be a great way to send the space off. Also, it's a lot cheaper than the other options.'

Taré walks around the space, inspecting it shrewdly, casting her gaze across the room. Eventually, a smile slowly begins to grow on her face. 'Listen, I don't know what you guys pulled, but it's working. I like it. It's personal, has a story, has potential.'

She pauses and flicks her gaze between Malakai and I. 'Fine. Start figuring it out.'

Malakai's brows shoot up, throwing me a surprised glance. 'You're sure?'

Taré shrugs as she makes her way to the door. 'I'm sure that I trust that you both care enough about this project to not let this shoot flop. I'm heading back to the studio – are you guys coming with?'

'Uh, I think I'm going to hang back—'

'Same,' Malakai says. 'I think we're going to get a head start on locking down the direction now we know where it's going to be.'

Taré's gaze jumps between Malakai and I before she nods. 'OK. Cool. Good work, you guys. I'll see you Monday.'

As soon as she and the rest of the crew leaves, Malakai turns to me, body sagging with relief. 'Scotch . . . thank you.' He steps closer to me, eyes sincere, 'Seriously. I don't know how I would have pulled this off.'

The fact that we've now secured a location barely registers with me; I'm still rattled by whatever Malakai was going through. 'I told you. We're a team. Now, in the interests of us being a team, can you please tell me what happened earlier? Have you had panic attacks like that before?' I had a couple in school when my mum was sick, I recognise the patterns, the tells.

Discomfort shadows Malakai's gaze. 'It wasn't a panic attack. I'm fine. I'm just tired. Kiki, I'm grateful for everything you've done today. It means . . . it means a lot, but please . . . please, can we drop this?'

I shrug, my hands dropping to the side of my thighs with a slap. 'I wish I could, Kai, but unfortunately I find myself giving a shit about you – whatever that means in the context of this – I don't like what I saw in your face. The last time you looked like that was when—'

'Kiki.' My name shoots out sharp, like an arrow, stopping me in my tracks. He squeezes his forehead between his thumb and forefinger, massaging it slightly. 'I'm begging you. I can't do this today.' Malakai's gaze is torturous, almost fighting itself, reaching out to me and then smacking itself away. 'Leave it,' he says eventually, sinking an icicle into my chest. I don't know what this masochism is, needing to involve myself with someone who is doing everything to push me out. I say nothing, baring my palms and then bringing them together with a shrug of acceptance. Malakai nods, before he leans forward to kiss my cheek. It sends a rapier of yearning through me, cold and painful, as he whispers, 'Thank you, Scotch,' before he leaves the restaurant, in almost the exact same manner with which he left my life the first time. Turns out, we already have an answer to what would happen if we got to have a do-over.

Exactly the same thing.

CHAPTER 13

Live at Sákárà, Roses Really Smell Like Poo

'Guys, you *have* to stop staring. This is technically my job, and I would prefer it if she didn't hit my friends with a restraining order.'

'She's just so beautiful,' Aminah says as she looks on starry-eyed at Taré on the small low-level dais we've set up in Sákárà. 'That's custom Dye Lab she's wearing now, right? And she was wearing Ahluwalia earlier! That collection isn't even out yet! Do you think she can get me an in? I wanna get some bits for the bachelorette next week. Actually, could I just have what she's wearing? We look about the same size. Although she's done a lot for us already. I can't *believe* she offered up her South African house to us for the bachelorette.'

When I'd offhandedly mentioned to Taré that I was looking for locations for my friend's bachelorette do, she didn't blink or stop smoking her blunt as she husked, 'Oh, baby, why didn't you say earlier? I got invites to the Afrotopia Festival. I won't be going because I'll probably be working on finalising album stuff, but since it's after your job is mainly done you should for sure go. I got VIP, of course. I can hook you up.' And since all the girls had already saved, thinking that we were going to have to pay for accommodation, and with air miles, a well-timed online search and a mutual decision to use it as our annual girls trip, we'd managed to find reasonably priced flights to Cape Town. It's a relief to have something to look forward to after months of working on the documentary, planning this shoot and show at the same time, whilst engaging in an emotional tango with my ex-boyfriend, who happens to be jarringly excellent at scattering my senses before reverting into cool professional aloofness.

I watch him now as he bounces across the room, wired with game-day energy, sleeves of his flannel rolled up, talking to Taré as she gets her make-up fixed, instructing and bussin a quick joke with the sound guy, before dapping up a couple of his friends as they walk into the restaurant, a part of his personal guestlist. He's totally in his element, shining with it, easy in his skin and it's hard not to be mesmerised by the sight. Looking at him now, it would be easy to forget that a month ago he was walking around with shadows across his face. I haven't though. Despite his command for me to 'leave it', a week after what was definitely his panic attack, I texted him the details of a therapist that Chioma dated once. He was down-to-earth and funny and we all liked him – the only reason it didn't work out between Asani and Chioma was because he wanted to be exclusive and Chi had said she had a 'few more souls' she wanted to 'experience intimately'. Kai didn't respond to the link, but he did 'like' the message. I have no idea what that means materially. We haven't spoken about it, because that's what we do, allow the Unsaids to pile up, skate on superficial civility. Thankfully, my friends are too distracted by Taré to notice what I now realise is me actively thirsting and attempting to emotionally dissect the very same man they (Aminah) warned me to stay away from.

'Is her skin actually glittering? Look at that glow. I need to locate the body oil. Do you know where her MUA is?' Shanti continues on their collective sonnet on Taré's beauty, from where we're sat at our usual table.

'Please, Shanti.' Chioma looks like the humanoid manifestation of a heart-eye emoji. 'This is not a cosmetic thing. This is an inner thing. There's, like, an aura. I'm gonna ask her how she centres herself spiritually.'

Oh, this is a *merciful* abundance of kindle to roast them with later. I laugh as I lean a hand against the back of Aminah's chair. 'Yeah, maybe do it after the show?'

Malakai, Taré and I had come up with the concept together. She wanted something reminiscent of West African countries in the sixties, the air of freedom, liberation, women in short skirts, men still understanding the power of the woo, nations flexing their muscles. I'd thought of an old club my dad had told me about, one *his* dad had told him about, Kakadu in Yaba, Lagos, a bar and salon where people like Wole Soyinka and Chinua Achebe would come to gist, whose stage saw the likes of Fela and Sunny Ade. It'd been the heart of Lagos nightlife, the place to be, or to be seen at. It'd been destroyed in the civil war, and it had never re-opened. I felt that paying homage at Sákárà worked perfectly, a place where my parents had planted my hopes, found their freedom. It was a win–win–win – we'd found a location for the shoot, got to have a special send-off for the restaurant and I'd also secured a pre-bachelorette treat for the girls. The guest list was specifically curated to include writers, artists, activists, journalists, some tastemakers who went against the grain and our friends.

Taré had said, 'This ain't about who has the most followers. This isn't about influencers. This is about *culture*. People who wanna retain and maintain and innovate.'

So with that mission statement we didn't change Sákárà's interior too much, but rather amped the homey feel – Janet Jackson's 'Got Til It's Gone' featured heavily on Kai's mood board. We wanted it to feel like a living-room jam crossed with an intimate hang-out spot, and so rugs and mats were laid down, more lamps added, Ankara tablecloths, framed photos taken from our parents. It's early, about 10 a.m., but the lighting and window coverings makes it look like early evening. There's a bronzed, sensual look to everything, everyone, a warmth, congeniality, and we encouraged everyone to dress in earth-tones, with Shanti helping us source Black designers to provide the outfits.

The break has allowed me a moment to soak in all we've done, and a warm sensation begins to swell within me, something like pride, excitement, like I'm on the precipice of something big. The tingle starts in my fingers and works itself up to my brain. Granted, I did not sleep last night and I am on two coffees, but still. Something cements in my mind.

'Uh oh.' Aminah climbs out of the booth to sidle up to me. 'I know that look. Killa Keeks got a plan. What you thinking? We could just nab the clothes right? Like, she wouldn't notice.'

I grin. 'Well, as a producer on this project, I do have some jurisdiction. I'll chat to the stylist.'

'Ay! King Keeks! It's good to have a best friend in high places.' Aminah smacks my butt before throwing an arm round my neck. Things were momentarily tense between us after her mandated wedding dance class, but she seems to be in a better place now; we've relaxed back into our rhythm and it's a relief.

Laughing, I say, 'But, no, that's not what I was thinking. Doesn't this place look good like this?' I gesture to Taré, ethereal with her band, the people around the tables. 'What if,' I say, watching Shanti and Chioma pounce on Taré's MUA, who's just come out of the bathroom, 'what if this were real?'

Aminah frowns as she scans the room. 'How you mean? Is this a mass hallucination?' She gasps. 'Do you think the CBD oil Chi gave us all to relax earlier did this? I knew it was a bad idea, like even coffee makes me psycho.'

I turn to her, feeling my skin sing with a promise that Aminah's weak grasp on the efficacy of CBD cannot abate. 'Well, yes, also, you have an oat-milk flat white every day, but anyway, I was thinking, imagine a world where Sákárà did live music nights?

Every Thursday, a midweek pick-me-up. I could host. Established acts, newer acts, whatever. Everything is changing around this place, in life, but how about we restore it to how it used to be? But better. Updated.'

Aminah nods, her cute little flicked-bob wig shimmying with the movement. She looks like a Dreamgirl, effortlessly angelic in her russet mini smock dress. Her eyes, though, are narrowed with the shrewdness of a PR maven.

'Obsessed. You can call it Sákárà Sounds?' It's been a while since Aminah and I have been in sync like this, with her wedding schedule and my working on the project, so her no-questions-asked understanding feels like a high.

I smile and link my arm through hers. 'I love it. And – theoretically – how about we make it on a Sunday? That way we can broaden the audience. The young post-church crowd.'

'And the heathens,' says Aminah.

'Well, I was going to say non-churchgoers.'

'Well, you would say that. You're a heathen.'

'I go to church!'

Aminah stares at me. I cough.

'Online,' I clarify. 'Sometimes. Whatever. I'm spiritual, OK! You can't judge me. You haven't even picked a religion yet.'

Aminah shrugs. 'Being bi-religious is my Yoruba birthright. God knows my heart. You look beautiful, by the way. Mashallah.' Her face is completely straight.

I swallow my smile and shake my head. 'Anyway. My point is: we can expand our pool of patrons.' The excitement coursing through my blood slows a little to make space for reality. 'That being said, I don't know if I have the money for that. In fact, I'm pretty sure I don't. Like, it would up revenue, but to even start it off . . . and this job isn't even permanent. Also, my parents have already lined up buyers.' Panic slowly begins to set in, battling with the hope I've been feeling. 'Shit, how am I gonna do this?'

'Do what?' Malakai's affable, gravelly voice makes me choke on air.

'Oh, I got you the thing you call coffee, by the way. Hazelnut and vanilla syrup. Half hot milk. Completely disgusting.' He hands me the cup, branded from the coffee shop two doors down. Even when things are frosty between us – which is almost always – he always places my order with his. Our fingers brush as I take the coffee, and my body trills obnoxiously.

As a producer, most of my job happened before the shoot and I have a logistical manager running everything on set, but Malakai's job has really just begun, so despite both of us being here from 6 a.m. we've barely interacted. While this has been good, it's clear that it's heightened my sensitivity to his presence because the word 'thanks' comes out slightly choked, and I forget to make a jab about how his love of black coffee is a sign of masochism. He looks so unfairly fine, having removed his green overshirt to reveal a crumpled grey shirt that's the perfect balance between loose and fitted, and allowing me the full scope of his arms, exposing the taut bulk and the light smattering of hair on them. He has a slightly worn look on his face from being up since around 5 a.m. prepping, but his eyes are alive, bright. I know that being on set is his drug

307

and I get a second-hand high from it. It swirls within me, relaxes my spirit, but now those eyes are looking at me quizzically and I realise that I haven't answered his first question.

Shooting me a look that screams, *'The hell is wrong with you?'*, Aminah answers for me. 'Uh, well, Newbie,' she says, still shooting bemused looks at me while I attempt to compose myself, 'Kiki has had the genius idea of doing a sort of Soul Sunday here. Live music, every week. Sákárà Sounds.'

Malakai smiles, sparkling with enthusiasm, almost as if he never told me to stay out of his life. 'Yeah? That's sick. A great idea. With you hosting, right?'

Why is he acting like he gives a shit? Is this some weird extended performance? Technically, this is really none of his business, and the terms we're on are decidedly not good, but displaying that to Aminah would be an immediate tell that something happened between us. There's also the fact that his interest is warm, licking at my own excitement for the idea.

I shrug, pretending the idea sits lightly on my mind and isn't presenting itself more and more as a lifeline. 'Theoretically, yes, but it's not going to be an open mic night. It would be a lounge. Building culture from the music.'

Malakai's eyes glitter, and his smile broadens. 'That's amazing, Scotch.' He casts an eye out across the room. 'With a similar set-up to this, right? Intimate. Homely.'

He gets it, of course. He always gets it, and it makes me incandescent with rage at the injustice, because why must the (seemingly) only man who seamlessly slides into my psyche be an emotionally reticent headache?

His gaze glints, and I feel sweaty in my mini pink wide-necked 'iro and buba-inspired outfit, despite its ventilating wide sleeves, short wrapper and light lace. The heat between us flares again, undeniably, loud. It's the strangest thing. The air between us is sticky with the Unsaid, choked up with smoke from our crashing, our burning, and yet this pull between us always rises and floats above it, glowing.

I cough. 'Well, this is just kind of a pipe dream. My parents have three offers on this place. They'll probably be deciding within the next fortnight, and there's no way I'll be able to run Sákárà full time even if I still had the funds. So.'

'You don't have pipe dreams, Kiki. You have, like . . . various realities marinating. You have visions of your future and you know exactly the flavours you want.' He says it with a certainty that settles in me like it belongs there, fortifying my own surety, because he's right – I know he's right – but, still, the belief sends a tingle throughout my entire body. I need to get off this ride, but I don't even know when I climbed on again, have no idea how I got strapped in. I feel Aminah's eyes start to swivel between us suspiciously, and I'm grateful for the interruption of one of Taré's assistants Serenity.

'You got someone waiting outside for you. They're not on the guest list. I told them you were busy, but they insisted. They said there's an emergency with your daughter, Solange? Oh, and they said I should give you these.'

Serenity doesn't seem enthused as she dumps a bouquet of roses the size of my head in my arms before attending to her main charge.

'You hate red roses.' Malakai and Aminah's voices come out in inadvertent harmony, both with curiosity creased into their faces. 'You like ranunculuses,' Malakai adds.

They both glance at each other and my face heats in self-consciousness. It's been a while since I've experienced their doubled X-ray power specifically dialled in to my emotional nuances.

'I don't *hate* them, guys. Who hates red roses?'

'You do.' Flat bemusement flushes Aminah's features. 'You said they're basic. Now who bought you the Eden flowers? They're the most expensive florists in London. I know because I wanted them to do my wedding till Kofi saw the quote. He was, like, "Are they *actually* from the Garden of Eden? Is that why they cost that?" And why is this person saying you have a daughter with them called Solange? This bouquet is *hefty*.'

Someone's calling Malakai, but either he doesn't hear them or he pretends not to – his face has assumed a veneer of non-chalance, gently folded into mild interest. 'Yeah, Kiki, which snake got you a bouquet from Eden?' and he seems to regret it as soon as it comes out of his mouth. He holds rigid, eyes widening slightly in horror and Aminah looks at him as if he's grown two heads. 'That was a joke,' he adds with a cough. 'You know. Like a biblical one.'

Aminah rolls her eyes. 'Girl, anyway –' she gestures at me to read the note attached and I open it to have my knowledge confirmed.

Aminah's gasp is unnecessarily loud as she peers over my shoulder. '*Bakari?* I thought you guys haven't spoken in months?'

My skin prickles under the lace of my clothes and Malakai's eyes sear through me.

'Jeez, Minah,' I say. 'You could at least have pretended not to read the note.'

'That would have been a waste of everybody's time and you know it. How did he even know about today?'

I am extremely uncomfortable, and with all the lights and the post-sex tension with Malakai and the fact that I haven't told Aminah that I had sex with Malakai (including a very recent PPR session) and receiving flowers from my most recent ex in front of *the* ex, it's actually possible that I might die of heatstroke.

I cough and put down my coffee to sip from the large purple water bottle I'd put on the table next to us, in order to buy time, but it goes down the wrong pipe and I end up spluttering a little. Aminah pats my back and when I collect myself, unfazed by my near-death experience, they're still staring at me, awaiting an answer.

I sigh. 'It's not a big deal. He texted me a few weeks ago and asked me how I was and I told him. Obviously, this job and the shoot came up. That's all. He's just being friendly. We're, um, pals.'

Laughter falls out with Aminah's words as scepticism tugs a well-threaded brow upwards. '*Pals?* My dear, have you ever said that word earnestly in your life? Also, you can't be pals with your ex.' Aminah catches herself, eyes fluttering wider, and flitting between mine and Malakai's instantly stiffened faces, 'I mean you and Malakai can because it's been years, but you and Bakari? It's still fresh. I dunno. I think he wants back in. Which isn't totally a bad thing on the condition that the space has knocked some sense into him. Also do you think he has a contact who could get me a discount at Eden?'

'All right, you know what? I'm just going to see exactly what he wants,' I say, head spinning as I carefully place the roses on the table by me.

'Uh, we're turning over in fifteen minutes.' Malakai's voice is weirdly glacial as he gestures to the flowers. 'Also, we can't have these on set.' I roll my eyes at the fascinating simplicity of the male ego as I pick them back up. 'Fine. I'll be back in fourteen minutes.'

'Twelve, please. We're gonna need touch-ups.'

'Yeah true. Because of all the vigorous making out. No problem. Prep the make-up team.' I beam at Malakai's gratifyingly irritated expression, and head out of the restaurant, swinging my hips to the sound of Aminah's laughter.

'Kiki . . . you look great.'

He'd been leaning against the wall of the restaurant, scrolling on his phone, before standing straight at my appearance, his gaze flicking across me with a smile. He looks good too, in his navy knit beanie, white tee, leather bomber jacket and *leather trousers?* Bold. I immediately know that his assistant went and researched the best seasonal transition clothes for this year. It suits him, though; he carries it well, the look complementing his high cheekbones and lean frame. He kind of looks like a skinny Lenny Kravitz, if

Lenny Kravitz said he didn't really 'denote any sensory pleasure from music', but enjoys it as a 'technically enjoyable experience'.

'Thanks, Bakari. You're looking well too . . .' I dip my chin down at the roses in my arms. 'And thanks for these. They're beautiful.'

It's true that Bakari and I hadn't spoken since the night of the engagement party, but when he reached out to me a couple of weeks ago I thought it would be weird to ignore him. There wasn't any bad blood, there wasn't good blood, we were bloodless. Like a dead thing. It was polite, friendly, which is why the eight dozen roses have thrown me for a loop. Especially because Aminah and Malakai are right. I fucking hate red roses. I think they're unoriginal and that they *think* they're the bad bitch of the botanical world when really have you seen a deep purple ranunculus bloom? Fluffier, delicate, regal. Malakai always got me a bouquet of them on my birthday – a thought that has no business being in my mind right now when Bakari's smile is charmingly crooked.

'Well,' he says, 'I wanted to wish you luck with today. They're the best in the city, and that's what you deserve.' He casts his gaze to the bustling restaurant, with crew coming in and out, and the vans parked outside, doubling as green rooms, with hair and make-up spaces. 'So is this. This is such a cool thing you're doing here, Kiki. It's so amazing that you've found a transitional thing to do while you're finding your feet—'

How? How is he always able to do that? Use a compliment to cut hope you didn't know you had in two?

'Sure, thanks, um, Bakari, I actually have to get back to work, so is everything OK?'

'Yeah. Yeah, more than, actually.' He bounces on the balls of his feet, rubs his hands together. He looks *animated*. Bakari rarely does 'animated'. 'There's two things I want to tell you. The first is that our new parent company has acquired SoundSugar. Which means that if you want The Heartbeat back, all you need to do is say the word, and it's yours. I've already had a word with Amelie, and she's drawn up the contract—'

I choke on air. Is this possibly . . . a romantic gesture from a man who thinks a romantic gesture is letting me sleep on my usual side of his bed every other time I sleep at his, even though my usual side is his usual side?

'Wait – what? Bakari, this is so . . . I don't know what to say—' Which is not just true because of the shock. As much as I have thought about getting The Heartbeat back on principle, I've never really thought about what it would mean to have it back in practice.

Bakari looks uncharacteristically nervous. The spring sunlight dances across his face, brightening a latent vulnerability that reminds me of what I liked about him in the first place. 'Wait. Don't say anything yet.'

He takes a deep breath, and steps closer to me, 'The second thing, babe, is this. I've thought about the probability of meeting someone as great as you in the future, and it's extremely unlikely. You're intelligent, good-looking, kind with great morals. And though those morals may be . . . impractical sometimes, ultimately I'm glad you have them. Like, it's better that you have them than not have them. And I feel like we really needed this break to think and be certain that we're supposed to be together. I've missed your company, Kiki, and I really think we can build a long-lasting partnership together. Look, I know you were at M's party with Malakai. I was there. I saw you together.'

I frown, my mind sharpening around various points of his words, not bothering to elucidate the fact that though we were together, we weren't *together*. 'And why didn't you say anything?'

'Because it doesn't matter to me, Kiki.' His demeanour is odd, casual. And it's not that I needed any performative macho nonsense about the fact that he saw me with my ex, but I would at least expect *some* sort of emotional response that would put rest to the idea that he is, in fact, a robot. 'The past doesn't matter. Look, I wanted a break so we can both clarify our relationship, and this is what it's done—'

'Wait. Hold up.' I laugh blithely, holding up a hand in realisation. 'You didn't say anything, because you were with someone too, weren't you? At the party?' I tilt my head in gentle enquiry and a non-accusatory smile and Bakari looks uncomfortable.

'Look, Kiki, we're adults. We were both exploring our options—'

I snort, and my hand flies to my mouth, because, really, this is hilarious. My man has been going to *town*. Why haven't I been going to town? Instead, I've been wasting time doing an erotic emotional dance with one (1) man.

'Options? As in *plural*? Shit, you've been busy—'

'And I feel like we needed to do that to know for sure that we're right together. We work well together. Both determined Black professionals.' Ew, why is he talking about us like we're statistics? 'Also, I've actually nominated you for next year's 30 Under 30—'

Slowly, a picture is beginning to form in my mind, questions adding shade and colour to Bakari's Big Romantic Gesture. 'How generous of you. Is Kitty's podcast doing well?'

Bakari does an amazing job of looking confused. 'Well, no. They actually cancelled it. Obviously, I mean, she's not you—'

I nod with deep understanding. 'Obviously. So actually it would benefit SoundSugar to have me back, now they have that slot open in their roster. Also I've been getting quite a few messages on social media from listeners asking why the podcast isn't coming back. I'm sure it's leaked to SoundSugar's socials too. Having me back would be a PR blessing. Smooth over any whispers of nasty business. Right?'

'Well, sure, but I don't know how that's relevant—'

'. . . and if it benefits SoundSugar, it benefits you. Sweetens your deal with your new parent company if you can get me back, right?'

'I mean, of course, but that's nothing to do with—'

'And it would be so powerful if I had a big podcast in SoundSugar, and of course you have Oynx. We would be great. A Black power couple.'

Bakari smiles and picks up my hand. 'Exactly, babe. Think of how it would grow our personal brands?'

My eyes widen in delight, because, really, nothing is more euphoric than having complete and utter clarity on a decision. Here I have a man who wants to be with me, bringing up our *personal brands*. How could a girl say no?

'My personal brand was the first thing I thought of, actually. And, lowkey, you kind of love that I was at M's party, don't you?'

'Well, M's a major player in culture. Being at that party says something about who you are —' seriously, who the *hell* is M? — 'and the fact that we were both there shows that we're both at the same stage of life. We're *aligned*, Kiki.'

I shake my head. 'Oh man, Bakari, babes, I don't think we are.' I pull my hand from his. 'I think you're deceptively shallow and you hide it underneath bullshit tech-founder speak about *vision*, and *community* when actually all you give a shit about is yourself. How you appear. I'm not trying to be mean — I'm just . . . I feel like I need to tell you the complete truth for once. The worst of it all is that I don't think you're a bad guy. I just think you're a good guy who doesn't have the guts or the sense of self to live in his truth, and to me that's sadder. Because I know who you could be — that's who I liked and thought I loved. It's just . . . I don't know . . . you've kind of mutated as you've got more successful. And I don't even blame you for the end of us. I really don't. I just wanted adequate to be *enough* for me and it isn't.' I pause and squint into the air as I realise something. 'Which is actually kind of ironic considering how obsessed you are with being the best.'

Bakari looks like I've punched him in the face, and while I do feel marginally bad about that, I'm really having an epiphany and I can't stop now. I haven't really had time to think about mine and Bakari's relationship over the past few months and the opportunity releases a surge of realisation. I feel lighter, freer, during my pavement confessional. 'Anyway. I *am* sorry that I dragged us out for so long when, really, I was emotionally coasting. I wasn't challenged, and I liked that. I was so . . . terrified of feeling too much that I told myself that I was OK with not being known—'

Bakari finally speaks, frowning. 'Kiki. Come on. I know you—' Interestingly, he's only taking offence to the accusation that he isn't The Best At Relationships.

'Bakari, I don't really like roses. I think they're, like, the equivalent of a slogan T-shirt costing £60 that reads "divine feminine energy". I don't know how to explain that further. Anyway, I should have told you that. I'm sorry, but you also never asked. Also, I think it's sad that you read summaries of all the books on the Booker shortlist so you can have something to talk about at fundraisers instead of reading something you *actually* like. I mean one that isn't a self-help book called *How to Make Friends and Fire People*. I just want you to take some time to figure out who you really are and what you really like without thinking about who you're *supposed* to be, you know? I feel like you became this super-successful person super early, and then let that dictate who you are instead of the other way round. And I think who you really are is cool. Like I said, I liked you. I really liked you, Bakari. And I think you liked me too, in the beginning, but I think at some point you liked the idea of me better than me. Which I'm not taking personally, by the way. I mean, I know I'm fantastic. I just think you were too busy to like anyone other than yourself in any real way. I fit into your vision of a "good life", but I don't actually think you want to build one with me. Also, this job isn't something I'm doing while I "find my feet". I love being creative. I love that my heart steers my mind. It's who I am. And also, just by the way, it's like, *patently* obvious that you're fucking Amelie.'

Bakari blinks several times and pinches the front of his neck. He coughs and glances at the ground.

'It wasn't before we broke up.'

I smile cheerily. 'Ah yeah, but you were getting there, weren't you.'

Bakari says nothing. I should feel sad. There is a space in me where sadness should be and I'm waiting for it to fill up, but it's dry. Maybe there's some vague disappointment there, a touch of disillusionment, but overall I think I'm fine. Actually, I think I might be great. I feel unburdened, like even when we weren't together I was keeping a contorted version of myself alive, one that let herself call arid monochrome plains love, when I knew I was capable of a tropical rainforest, plush soil, plump fruit. Malakai and I didn't last, and maybe we weren't meant to, but what I felt was real, and not even he can take that away from me. That love is still mine to give.

'You know, in that whole speech – really gave *When Harry Met Sally* a run for its money there, by the way, especially the bit when you spoke about having a long-lasting partnership like you're a world leader of a global superpower looking to form a treaty with me – you never said you loved me once.'

Bakari's face softens. Not like he's sorry, but more like he feels sorry for me. 'Kiki, love is . . . whatever you make it out to be, as long as you have the same objectives as the other person, but . . . I get now that our objectives are different.'

'No, see, I disagree, Bakari. I mean I agree that our objectives are different, but I don't think love is "whatever". I think it's a definitive, persistent thing, that you can feel and touch and bite into, and it colours everything. *Everything.* You can't fold it away in a convenient place. You can't work around it. You choose it, and you keep choosing it and it becomes part of who you are and that's a good thing because, if it's right, it's built from who you are anyway – parts of your spirit and parts of the other person's spirit coming together to make this little world for you both. It helps to power you, navigating the world around you.'

Bakari looks at me like I'm a three-year-old talking about her imaginary friend. 'I don't actually believe we have spirits.'

'How were we ever together?'

'We were both extremely good-looking Black people at a party with sort of racist white people.' My laugh leaps out of me, propelled by a surprise flash of the guy I'd thought I'd fallen in love with. 'That was a joke by the way.' Bakari smiles and steps to me, pulling the roses from my arms, placing them carefully against the wall with impressively semi-wild abandon and pulling me into a hug. 'For what it's worth, Kiki, I do think I loved you. As far as I could.'

'I know. Same.' I pause. 'Sorry if I sounded harsh before. I think I got carried away—'

Bakari's chuckle is warm. 'Don't worry about that. I don't take it personally. I do think how I see things could be seen as shallow. The difference is I don't see anything wrong with that. We're just incompatible.' He releases me, but his hands stay on my waist. It feels comfortable, affectionate, like we're friends – actual friends, maybe for the first time that we've known each other.

'So.' His lips spike playfully. 'You're really not taking the job?'

'Bakari, come on.'

'Kiki, forget about us. I've cut you a great deal. I know you and SoundSugar don't have the best of relationships, but you can use it to your advantage. It's way more money. It's a consistent cheque.' He looks up and flicks his chin at Sákárà. 'And you could use it to buy this place. Hire someone to run it on the day to day. Think about it, OK?'

I waver. SoundSugar did me dirty, and now they're almost definitely using me to launder their reputation after a flopped deal, but there's a bigger picture here: Sákárà. My parents' legacy. Building something larger than me. And there's also the fact that I might have to go backwards to do it. The Heartbeat was such a huge part of my life, healing me when I needed it, but I feel like I've outgrown it, needing only to use the components that made it tick into a new configuration. Or maybe I'm just being an idiot, and I need to check out the second job that this very rich man is offering me.

Bakari kisses my forehead as I brace my hands on his arms. 'Think about it, Kiki.' He cups my face with a hand. 'Take care.' He grins, widely, genuinely. 'I love you.'

And I know how he means it, because when I say, 'I love you too, Chef,' I mean it in the same way, like I'm glad I met him, like we served our purposes in each other's lives, like if I see him out, I'll be happy to see him, like if we have anything, at least it's that very awkward time in bed where we tried to be kinky and it went horribly wrong.

A pointed clearing of a throat causes my hands to drop from Bakari's arms, and I turn to the door to see Malakai, face blank, headset round his neck, looking everywhere but our faces.

'We're about to start shooting.' He doesn't wait for a second longer before dipping back into the restaurant.

Amusement suffuses Bakari's face. 'I think he's pissed.'

I pick the bouquet of roses up off the ground. 'Good.'

CHAPTER 14

Live at Sákárà, No Letting Go

'It's not working.' Taré has called cut for the fifth time during the shoot and Malakai grits his teeth, manages to compose it into a smile and pulls down his headset. 'What's up, Taré? Reminder, we have limited time.'

Taré rolls her eyes. 'We have all the time in the world to get it right. This *has* to be right.' She points to a couple who are supposed to be taken over by lust, dancing to her music in the middle of the dance floor, a symbol of herself, lit in gold in a darkened atmosphere. 'That couple isn't doing it for me.'

The actors untangle awkwardly. I feel bad for them, but she isn't wrong. Whilst the small audience has a mix of regular people for authenticity, we picked professionals as the main couple in the video so it would be a little easier to direct, and they're gorgeous – both with smooth, dark skin, the girl with a close-cropped cut and the guy with locs – but they're stilted, relying solely on their

323

beauty, focusing on it, afraid to be free within their movements. I can see the strain in them trying to *be* in love.

Taré catches herself and throws them a quick smile. 'No offence. I mean they look *great*, *but* this has to be more than looking great. You have to be able to feel the *feeling*. I don't know. Maybe it's in the way they're holding each other? What do you think, Malakai?'

Malakai's hands are on his waist as he watches the footage back on his monitor and nods. 'Yeah. Yeah, I think you're right. It's a bit stiff. Might be a case of warming up to each other.' He raises a placating hand to the couple. 'You're doing great. It's just an ease thing. You're supposed to be a couple, consumed by each other. The only people in the room is you.'

'Maybe they need an example,' Taré offers. 'Malakai, let's show them, maybe.'

Malakai's brows quirk. 'Like, us – together?'

Taré rolls her eyes with impatience. 'Yes. Is that OK?'

'Sure. Yep.' Amazing. I'm about to watch my ex and my boss slow-dance in my family restaurant. No, seriously, *is* this an extremely sophisticated afterlife and is this because I never pay for a bag for life at self-checkout and once scanned an XL avocado as a regular avocado?

The music is cued, and Taré steps to Malakai, wrapping her arms round his neck, while his wind across her waist like they have undoubtedly done many times before. Her face nestles against his chest as they move, and the spotlight homes in on them. My stomach turns. There's no getting around this: I am violently jealous. They look like they fit; it's romantic. In a way, they're kind of a perfect love story in a 'we found love in a hopeless place' kind of way. Extremely pretty, extremely talented, they nurtured each other when they both felt broken. It's a narrative that works. It's sexy, it's gritty and it's realer than a university romance that turned sour. For the first time, I'm able to garner a physical image of what they're like together and it's even worse than I imagined, because they're *beautiful*. I know they both said nothing's going on, but anything can be reignited. I know that better than anyone. Malakai was able to be vulnerable with her, free in a way that maybe he wasn't able to be with me. Maybe he just got tired of wearing a mask around me. My skin pricks with heat, and I want to blame the lighting in this place, the room capacity, but really, I know, it's the sight of a man who I still have feelings for dancing with another woman. *Shit*. Why do I still have feelings for Malakai?

Just as I begin to fight the urge to flap at my underarms in panic, because really, I'm *sweating* now, Taré pulls away from Malakai and shakes her head. 'Wait, this isn't working. I need to, like, visualise it. Sweet Keeks.' She clicks at me. 'You. You know the music as well as I do, and you know the feeling he needs to capture. You guys are the best people to show what we need.'

I freeze, because surely I'm misunderstanding what she means, and I pipe up from where I'm sat in the role of what was supposed to be a nameless patron. 'I'm sorry, to clarify, to show them in terms of like . . . description? I can do that!'

A hint of impatience flits over Taré's normally genial face. 'The dance, Sweet Keeks. Obviously.' She clicks again at Malakai, who is looking slightly stricken. 'Come on. Yes, we can take all the time in the world, but let's not take the piss.'

Malakai's eyes dart to mine in question, asking if I'm OK with this. Everyone on set is watching us now, including Shanti, Chioma and Aminah. Aminah has a slight frown of concern on her face and Chioma and Shanti have looks of complete and utter glee on theirs. If I say no, it becomes a big deal, and it resolutely *is not* one. This is just two creative professionals coming together to help get the job done in the most effective manner.

I push out a bright smile. 'No problem. I'll try. I mean, I'm not a dancer.'

Aminah rolls her eyes. 'Are you joking? Your waist swirls like the sweetest cinnamon roll. And we don't do shyness in our family so I don't know why you're pretending.'

I pause. The flippant wave of her hand is more loose than normal. She's suspiciously lairy.

Chioma pipes up after her, 'Yeah, I second Meenz. Like, you are a boss on this set: stand in your power, you know, your alpha energy!' I narrow my eyes, and stare at the drinks – they're a sweet mocktail concocted to look like alcoholic drinks, but now I'm suspecting that at some point they spiked them to get things into a festive pre-bachelorette spirit.

I am sure of this when Shanti slaps my butt as I rise with, 'Get 'em, sis!'

I have no time to focus on this particular irritation because Malakai signals for the music to play as we position ourselves on the marks of the actors. We don't say anything to each other, can't say anything to each other – he simply nods at me, and I nod back as his arms slip round my waist, and mine round his neck. This is cool, so cool. I just have to dance with my ex-boyfriend with whom I've just realised I have more than non-lust feelings for, in front of everybody I am lying to about having any feelings for him. I try not to focus on the pressure of the breadth of his palm on my sides, nor on the fact that we are face to face, so close I could trace the shape of his lips with my tongue. Instead, I home in on the beat that feels safe to me. I know and love this song; it's called 'Solstice', one of my favourites on the album. This song is airy, feels like summertime, a mix of soul and modern Afrobeats, slowed down, sensual and soon awkwardness melts as my body falls into its rhythm and Malakai falls into mine. I close my eyes to feel it, let the melody sink into my skin, and Malakai pulls me in so I brush his chest.

'You see,' Malakai burrs, and his voice reverberates through my entire body, 'it's gotta be intimate. Sexy, but not lewd. The hands aren't trying to hold her down, but give her space to move, whilst letting her know that you've got her.'

My eyes flutter open and Malakai is looking directly at me and it makes my resolve to not fall stutter.

'There are boundaries,' Malakai says directly to the couple. 'This is the first date. It's tentative. We didn't choreo this, only gave light direction, because we wanted it to feel organic, but, still, focus on those feelings to direct you, like –' he raises a hand to hold my chin in a way that's respectful but intimate, light enough for me to want to lean into his grip, for me to feel his fingers press into my skin – 'how would he look at her? Like she's everything. Like her light makes you bloom.'

His eyes are back on me, dancing with their own light, and I remind myself that this is an exercise, that this is a performance, that I am at work, and also, crucially, this man knows exactly what he's doing. I remind myself that so do I. I know Malakai, know what tests his control, pushes him to the limit. I nod, and release a sunshine smile.

'Right, and in turn, you,' I say, talking to the young woman who plays one half of the lovers, 'need to remember your power. It's you that really controls this. You want to slowly unfurl, open up. Lean into your boldness because he makes you feel comfortable to do so, and you let him into your space because you decide that. You're tapping into your sensuality.'

Keeping Malakai's gaze, I drag my hands down his chest, letting my fingertips lightly, slightly explore the broad expanse. His mouth twitches before I slowly turn round and move his hands to my hips, keeping the rhythm, my butt very, very lightly grazing the front of his chinos. His hands shift on my hips, his fingers curving ever so slightly in a tightening of grip. I feel his smile in it.

'And you maybe do a little whisper, pretend to say something slick.' He bends so his lips are at my ear, the heat of his breath making every cell in my body alert in want despite the audience – shit, is there even an audience? 'Scotch, you're playing a very dangerous game.'

I lick my lips, making sure my voice hides within the music. 'You started it. I'm finishing it.'

'And there I was thinking that finishing is a team effort?'

My eyes immediately round, and I attempt to press an irrepressible dirty smile back into my scandalised mouth. Every single time I feel like I've lost the Malakai I thought I knew, a glimpse resurfaces, brighter than ever, more irresistible than ever – and I *have* to resist, because every time I feel like I can touch it, it slips away. It's a mirage.

Taré's squeal falls between Malakai and I, splitting us apart, and we both remember where we are, what we're here for, who we are – people who have no business looking at each other like this, touching each other like this.

'*Yes!* Yes! Exactly this! Push and pull. *Intimacy.*' Malakai coughs, and gestures to the couple. 'OK, so if you could just—'

Taré shakes her head. 'Oh no. No, no, no.' Her long, shimmering hooded cape drifts behind her as she comes up to us, holds both of our hands. 'It has to be *you* guys. Are you kidding me? You can't teach that!'

Malakai throws a panicked look to my widened eyes, and he says, 'Well, I mean, I have to direct.'

Taré waves a dismissive hand. 'Please. You can act and direct at the same time. You're pretty, but you can manage both. I'm sure we'll have an outfit that will fit you—'

I shake my head, feeling increasingly frantic, because I might not survive doing that again. 'Well, the thing is, Taré, I'm more of a behind-the-scenes kind of person.'

To this, Aminah pipes up furiously, 'Kikiola, no you are *not*! You're born to be centre stage!'

Oh, she's definitely drunk. Her voice sounds looser. What's going on with her? My annoyance and worry clash, but I have no time to interrogate either because Taré claps her hands in agreement.

'Exactly. Kiki, I have no time to argue. I want this project to be the best and you are the best choice in this moment. Get in costume, please.' Taré's voice has adopted an I'm Technically Your Boss tone she rarely employs. The only other time is when she insisted on us all having a 'replenishing nap' before continuing to discuss concepts. Malakai and I exchange a look, and I read him easily; he's down if I am. I sigh and rub the crease between my brows. How did we get here? This place where I am about to slow-dance with my ex-boyfriend in front of cameras for my job? How can I demolish that road so I never have to cross it again?

I smile sweetly. 'Of course. Anything to help!'

'Sorry – did you know that your dad can sing?' Aminah leans in to ask me as she watches my father take to the dais with Taré, singing 'Lifted' by the Lighthouse Family, one of his favourite bands primarily, I'm sure, because one half of the duo is a Yoruba man. My dad has a running database of all Yoruba people with a modicum of fame. Recently he informed me that the latest owner of Red Lobster was a man whose family hailed from a town next to the town where my family is from.

'We could be cousins. Looks like restaurant-running is in the family!' he'd said. My dad didn't actually know what Red Lobster was before the CNN Africa news item, but that didn't stop him from deploying it as a fun fact to anyone who would listen. I grin at the sight of my dad and his now best friend, Taré, who is struggling to get a hold of the mic, and cast my gaze to the rest of the restaurant. It hasn't felt like this in years; as a thank-you for using the restaurant, my mum and dad organised a wrap dinner for cast and crew, and Sákárà feels like it's come alive. There's raucous conversation and laughing, plates clattering, glasses full of my dad's Chapman clinking, my mum, for some reason, having an intense conversation with Malakai just by the bar (why is *that* happening?). Aside from that bizarre last part that demands further investigation, this is how it's supposed to look: vibrant, full-up, the set design breathing a new vitality to the space. My chest feels loose at the sight, and a pang immediately tightens it up again. It's a *set*. This is temporary. It's all going to be dismantled and this place will soon belong to people who have 'live, laugh, love, wine' in their social media bios.

I push a smile out and turn to where Aminah's sitting next to me on our table. 'I mean, don't tell him that. He already thinks he missed his chance at being the next Fela because his mum told him playing guitar was for vagrants. If that's the case I've got Beyoncé's breath-control because I can send voice notes while on minute five of the cross-trainer.'

'I mean you do. I'm ready for your world-class-performer era. Killa Keeks on tour. You're going to be in a *music* video. You killed it. Must have been awkward dancing with Malakai, though. You OK?'

Aminah dips her fork daintily in a bowl of abula in the only way she knows how, voice casual with enquiry.

Chioma laughs as she pours herself a glass of Chapman. 'Um, well, it definitely didn't *look* awkward. The erotic energy was crazy. I actually think I was turned on a little. I mean I've always said that I would watch—'

I narrow my eyes at her in slight perturbation. 'Yeah I know, and I've always said that was weird. Besides, I don't think I would perform well physically under pressure.'

Aminah stops chewing. 'Why are you acting like Chi watching you and Malakai having sex was ever a possibility?'

Shanti smirks slyly, sipping her drink. 'Well, anyway, you def *performed* well just then. You and Malakai were, like, *in* it.'

Aminah shakes her head. 'OK, can you give credit to Kiki's artistry? Because Malakai may have been in it, because, let's face it, Kiki's a spice. How can he not be? But Kiki's *evolved* and doesn't succumb to, like, emotional whims. Also, physical chemistry is a given. It's this, like, idea of the taboo. Forbidden. The fact that nothing's going on is what makes it hotter. It worked for the scene, but it doesn't mean anything. Now will you get off her back?'

I shrug and focus on carefully piling some plantain and fried rice onto my fork. 'Look, we were just doing our job. Taré wanted it, so we did it. It's all for the vision. Nothing more, nothing less.'

Shanti raises a brow, but says nothing at this. 'Uh, anyway, how was your talk with Bakari?' she asks instead. 'I heard he came around.'

I smile. 'OK, you know I saw you guys pretending to come in

332

and out of the wardrobe trailer during our conversation, right?
Doing up Chalé's Angels.'

Aminah nods unashamedly. 'Thank you for shouting out my
Ghanaian culture fusion, but yeah we did and we heard nothing.
You guys were speaking very quietly. I was just there for emotional
reinforcement, so I could, like, jump in if you looked distressed.
Which you didn't at all. Actually you seemed to be smiling a lot—'

'Well, for the record, I objected out of ethical reasons.' Chi
spears a plantain slice on her fork, 'but also I hate being the last
to know things, so . . .'

I adore my friends, however, the conversation with Bakari is
still too raw for me to unpack – not the break-up part, that was
actually a breeze and kind of therapeutic – but the part where
he offered me my job back. Was I really in a position to say no?
Phoenix is nearly over and I still don't know what I'm going to
do next. If I take the role, it would be a fixed salary and a way to
save the restaurant – it's a no brainer. So why am I beginning to
get a stress stomach ache about it?

My mum's soothing voice flows into our purview, as she places
her hand on my shoulder. 'Hi, ladies – can I borrow my daughter,
please?'

'Of course, Mama B,' Aminah says, 'and, please, when it's time
for her to come back, will you sit with us? I feel like this table
needs to be classed up.'

'I was going to do that whether you liked it or not. I've missed
my girls, and my husband keeps bragging about how he knows
all your gossip.'

'That's what we want him to think,' Shanti says. 'We save all the juicy stuff for you.'

'I knew it. We'll be back.' My mum winks at them before she shepherds me to our small reception room at the back of the bar.

My mum shuts the door behind us, and looks at me with eyes that are soft and knowing. The intermittent combination of relief-gratitude-love surges through me, like it has done these past few years. Relief that she's still here, gratitude that she's healthy, and love, so much love for the person who reads me like she's breathing.

'Nothing's wrong,' I say in response to her look.

My mum tilts her head to the side, folding her arms across her chest, and the sweetness of the image of her in her black jeans, sparkly T-shirt and Skechers combination counteracts the fierceness of her gaze. 'Kikiola, don't lie to me. You've had this look on your face for the past couple of hours. You've done an amazing job today. You should be proud. It's such a wonderful way to send off the restaurant – and, see, there's that look again. What's the problem?' She walks across the small living area, sneakers scuffing against the laminated flooring and lifts my chin so I'm looking at her. 'What is stressing you?'

I swallow, powerless under the loving steely stare. 'Uh, so I may have the chance to work for SoundSugar again –' I had eventually told my mum the specifics of what had happened with them – 'get my podcast back. It will be loads more money. Like *loads*.'

The expression on my mum's face, so much like mine, doesn't change. 'And isn't SoundSugar the place that disrespected you? That you walked away from?'

'Um, yes, but the money could help me buy Sákárà. Hire people to run it. And I have so many plans for it, Mama. It could really be great—'

My mum nods carefully, her classically red-painted lips pulled into a line. 'But you would have to work for SoundSugar. Is that what you want to do?'

'No, but—'

'Kikiola, is that what you want to do?'

'No.'

My mother shrugs. 'So there's your answer.'

'It's not that simple, Mum. The restaurant—'

'Kiki, you walked away from SoundSugar for a reason. Those reasons are valid. And if you wanted to still be working on the podcast, let's face it, you would. You created it from your *bedroom*. You don't want to do it any more and that's fine. Just think about yourself, OK? For once. I know what you sacrificed when I was in hospital. You looked after your sister, you pulled hours at the restaurant. Even now, you're balancing working with Taré with shifts here.' My mum gestures to the room we're in, virtually unchanged throughout the duration of my life. Framed pictures of parties at Sákárà are on the wall, family functions, staff socials, baby pictures. It's cosy, *home*. 'This place will always exist. What we did will always exist, because of you. The restaurant was important, but it's OK to let go.'

My eyes begin to fill, frustratingly, and my voice creaks. 'But everything's changing, Ma. And I don't know what I want to do next—'

My mum looks gently perplexed, and steps closer to me, wiping my tears with her thumb. 'Yes, you do, Kiki-pops, because you're doing it. You never choose the safe option, and it's what I admire most about you. You, my daughter, are a risk taker when you know it's the right thing. And that's how you grow. When Malakai got the job in LA, you didn't choose to break up because it would be easier. You said you would work through it.'

I blink. 'But we did break up.'

My mother tilts her head to the side. 'Are you being smart with me?'

'No, I'm just saying that that's truly an example of a risk that flopped, so I don't see how it's relev—'

My mum looks behind her, in wonderment, and back at me. 'Is there a ghost in this room? Because it can't be me you're speaking to like that.'

I clear my throat, catching myself. 'Sorry, Mummy. Um. You were saying?'

My mum continues. 'My point is, you tried it because you believed in your relationship. Whether it worked or not is irrelevant.'

I pause as this thought percolates. In the many, many hours within which I emotionally juiced the situation with Malakai, I never once entertained the idea that the relationship was a success because it happened. That I believed in us enough to want to jump in, soul as my skin, for five years. That I had enough to believe in for five years. That I believed in us till the very last second. 'Um,' I venture cautiously, 'I saw you talking to Malakai—'

My mother's smile is small, etched with an arcane knowledge. 'Yes. I was checking in, seeing how he is doing.'

This in itself doesn't surprise me. I never told my parents the exact details of our break-up, and I never spoke ill of Malakai to them. For some reason, I couldn't bear for them to think badly of him; it would have been almost as painful as the break-up itself. They loved him, and that was special to me. I couldn't handle going through another, separate heartbreak.

'It was nice to catch up,' my mum continues. 'He's a good boy. So interesting that he came back so long before the wedding.'

'Well, he had work to do here.'

'Hmm. Well.' My mum turns to fluff the cushions on the sofa. 'He told me he actually didn't get the job till he got here. You know, I've been talking to his mum—'

I sigh heavily. 'Mum—'

My mother rolls her eyes. 'Not everything is about you, Kikiola. We don't talk about you children as a couple. We're friends, I think of her as a dear sister, and I like to check in on her since . . . everything that's happened.' Her gaze flitters and she straightens. 'She said that Malakai's been a lot happier since he's been here. Lighter. She said he's been thinking of staying.'

I nod slowly, trying not to let this information settle within me, to scatter my belief that mine and Malakai's proximity is finite. I need it to be true, because I am using all my strength to stopper a deluge of useless feelings being poured towards someone who has no need for them.

'Well. Good for him.'

She stares at me for a moment, eyes twinkling, before she walks towards me. 'You know, you've always had a sharp tongue. Even when you were a child. You never really hesitated in telling people what you really thought, but it's the strangest thing. When it comes to your own hurt, you always used to keep quiet. I don't know why. It's like you don't want to . . . inconvenience people. Maybe it's our fault. You're the eldest and we put so much on you to be responsible. You grew up around us working and I think . . . I think you always tried to not be *in the way*. One time – I think you were about five? You were at a birthday party playing musical chairs, and a girl accidentally stepped on your foot – you were wearing sandals. You didn't say anything. You went into a corner. Your little lip was just shaking, face all scrunched up.' My mum mimics an approximation of my expression before her face melts into a laugh. She cups my cheek. 'The other girls at the party thought you were being stuck up, that you didn't want to play with them any more. I came to ask you what's wrong, and eventually you told me, breaking down in tears. Õ ké! I asked you why you didn't want to tell me before. You said you didn't want to spoil the party, but, my love, no one knew why you were upset because you didn't say anything. The girl didn't know she'd hurt you, and thought you just didn't like her. And really you could have enjoyed the party if you had spoken to the girl and given her a chance to say sorry. Which she did, after I brought you two together to talk it out, but it scared me, Kiki. It scared me because I realised you're someone who can hold on to your hurt and hurt yourself more in the process. And I'm sorry if you've felt that you couldn't *share* things with us because you didn't want to stress us, but I want you to know that your pain is never a burden.'

I can feel my eyes glimmering, my breath getting shallower. I'm wholly unprepared for this impromptu therapy session with my mother.

'Mummy, you guys were amazi—'

My mum shakes her head firmly, her expression as serene as ever. 'Let me finish. You don't have to console me. That is not your job. I know what I could have done better. Now, Kiki, you're so smart. And I know you're smart with who you choose to bless your love with. Aside from Bakari. That one I'm not so sure about. Did I hear that he was outside wearing *leather trousers*? Why? How can he withstand that much leg humidity? Anyway, my point is, you should be able to trust your instincts enough to trust whoever you love to understand your pain and not see it as a weight. Because you do that for other people. There is no virtue in tucking in your hurt. You don't get a medal for it, my darling. You just get more hurt. And after a while you will have to take accountability for that hurt. It isn't on anyone else.'

I bite my lip. 'Mum . . . mine and Malakai's issues were . . . complicated. So much happened—'

My mother is unmoved by this. 'I'm sure. So much happens in life. We grow, and that's OK. This isn't about you people getting back together. I just want you to be happy. My own thing is I don't want you to have any regrets. Just make sure you say everything you can say while you can say it. Respect yourself enough to do that. That's all *I'm* saying.' I'm pretty sure I'm making the same face I did when I was five at that birthday party. I press my lips together in attempt to keep the emotions in. Relief. Gratitude. *Love*. My dad may be the diva, but my mother will always be the astute queen, reserved, but never in the background, all-seeing, all-knowing. I nod. 'Noted. Thank you, Mama.'

She rubs my arms and gently tugs on my ear. 'Pẹlẹ, ọkọ mi. No more sad face, ṣo gbọ? Now let's go and remove that microphone from your father's possession. I think Taré is being polite.'

As we walk out into the din of the dining room, my mum makes a beeline for my father. I recognise a boom of a voice that immediately delights me; the tenor brings memories of university, simpler times, a home away from home. Just as my eyes skit across the room, I'm enveloped by a huge bear hug, a pair of arms lifting me up off the ground with an exclamation of, 'Ah, ah, Kikiola! Total wealth! Babygirl!'

I immediately hug back tighter, delighted, before Meji puts me back down on the ground and twirls me under his arms. 'Wow. Look at her! Glowing.'

I laugh as I do the royal wave, and prop my hand flat under my chin, batting my lashes. 'I've been up since 5 a.m., but I've always missed how you stay lying to me. When I used to come to Sweetest Ting looking like a feral cat during exam season you used to call me Nefertiti.'

Meji, looking ever the prince himself, handsome with high cheekbones, wise eyes that tilt heavy with knowledge and play, and a smart grey kaftan, bows to me. 'And that you were. I still don't know what juju this one used to bag you,' he says, turning to greet Malakai with a large hug, a dap and several pats on his back. He teases Malakai with a massive kiss on the cheek that Malakai playfully pushes off.

'The juju was your waffles,' I say, and I'm playing with a skipping rope made out of fire, I know, because I'm referring to mine and Malakai's first date at Sweetest Ting.

Malakai catches on immediately and his brow twitches, eyes glinting. 'And yet, it was me you couldn't get enough of.'

Shit. I find myself tucking filthy thoughts in as my gaze drifts back to Meji. Meji was our de-facto big brother in uni, owning the diner Malakai and I – and eventually all my friends – lived in. It was a safe space, a place for us to unwind, feel protected, feel at home, all whilst enjoying culinary innovations – suya burgers, plantain waffles and Supermalt floats, being some of many. The last time I saw him was around four years ago when Malakai and I went to his wedding. He'd winked at us then, told us that we were next.

I pack the mocking memory away and grin at my old friend. 'This is the best surprise ever.'

Meji presses his hand to his chest. 'I am honoured by the lie because I know Malakai once surprised you with tickets to that your babalowo book convention.'

'Um, let's sit somewhere!' I steer past Meji's reference to one of the many romantic things my ex has done for me, and look up at said ex himself. 'You joining us?'

Malakai runs a hand across the back of his head with some discomfort and shakes his head, barely meeting my eye. 'Uh, maybe later. I've got some work bits to do. Meji, bros.' He daps the older man up with affection. 'I'll catch you in a bit, yeah?'

'No worries, àbúrò, do your ting.' He claps Malakai on the back, as I try to figure out, yet again, why the hell Malakai is being so rude. Meji is not only one of his best friends, but a big brother, and he lives a good two hours away – it's not like he sees him often. Why is he being such a weirdo? And why am I always having to dissect what's going on in his head? And why can't I listen to him when he explicitly tells me to mind my own business? I push The Problem With Malakai to the back of my mind as Meji greets my parents before settling into an emptied booth in the back with me.

I beam at him. 'Meji, ẹ̀gbọ́n mi. To what do I owe the honour?'

'Well. The honour is always mine, but I linked with Malakai a few weeks ago and he told me about what you're doing here. I couldn't miss it.' He casts an eye around the room, his gaze lighting up. 'It looks like it went wonderfully. It's a beautiful space. And I'm sure, beautiful food.'

The acknowledgement cools my excitement as much as it warms me. 'Thank you. Your meal's coming, by the way. My dad's kind of like you – doesn't play about people going hungry – but, yeah, I really love how we've transformed the place. In an ideal world, I'd love to make it into a joint, you know? Kind of like what Sweetest Ting was for us kids back in the day. A spot to eat, hang out, commune, *be.*'

Meji dips his hand into a bowl of groundnuts on the table, tosses them into his mouth. 'OK. And what's the issue?'

I swallow the telling lump in my throat that always seems to appear when I talk about the restaurant. 'My parents are selling it. Too expensive to run – you know how it is. Looking to retire. And, realistically, it would be too much for me to do on my own.'

Meji nods thoughtfully, rubbing at his full beard. 'I hear that. Running a restaurant is not for the weak, but it's not impossible, with a vision and determination – ah, my friend, cheers.' A waiter places a plate of suya and a bottle of Supermalt on the table. Meji takes a swig. 'Did you know that Sweetest Ting has two branches in the southern-eastern region now? Of course, the one at Whitewell will always remain the best because that's the one you blessed us at, but Alhamdulillah, it's doing well. And I was actually looking to expand in London. It's been hard to find a location that *fits*.'

My knees and elbows feel like they have heating pads wrapped around them, spindles of sharp warmth rising through me and making tensions relax, and for some reason tears are tickling my eyes. I don't let them out, not yet. He can't be saying what I think he's saying. 'And I don't want to start over, not at my big age. I'm getting old!'

'Please, Meji. You're a baby boy.'

'Ehn, so my wife says,' he replies with a twinkle, 'but, still, I have to be practical. I've been looking for somewhere that has history, where building footfall wouldn't be so tough. That wouldn't be a transition culturally. You know, somewhere that already speaks to *us*. You know what I mean by 'us', ehn? And if say, theoretically, I was taking on an existing restaurant like Sákárà it's likely that it would be a merge rather than a takeover. I would want to work *with* someone. Perhaps even create something new. Keep the name, update the menu with Sweetest Ting staples – you know, the plantain waffles, the suya burgers, with Sákárà's traditional ones.'

Meji slides a thin piece of grilled spiced beef off a skewer with his teeth. A short hum of approval is thrown from the back of his throat as he chews. 'Although, your dad's suya really is in tight competition with mine.' He releases a cragged laugh. 'And your plans for this place really fit into the evolution I want for my eateries. Live music. Interactive atmosphere.'

'Meji.' I lean forward and reach for his hand, barely breathing, scared to believe what's happening could be happening. 'Meji, please don't play with me.'

Meji's smile widens. He was about thirty-five when we were in uni, and now, eight years older, he looks pretty much the same, eyes only slightly wrinkled at the corners, but still handsome, probably even more, looking like a Naija Mahershala Ali with locs. To me, though, he's always going to be the guy who looked after us when we struggled to look after ourselves, and it's a wonder he was able to expand with all the ridiculously discounted meals he gave us when we were studying, with extra freebies thrown in. He's my big brother in all the ways that count.

'Now, why would I play with you? I take you very seriously. You're a big madame, now. A potential partner. Of course, I will bring an offer formally to your parents, but only with your permission. I can buy this place, and run the day to day so you can do your thing, but you can set the tone, use it to run your nights. The name Sweetest Ting don't matter – it's the culture. What it represents. Community. And that's what this place is.'

344

I get up from my chair and slide to his side of his booth, throwing my arms round him, the heavy spiced scent of oud winding around me with his own arms, tears filling my eyes. 'Ah, ẹ̀gbọ́n mi. Ẹ ṣé gan ni. This means everything.'

'Ah. Why are you thanking me? We're about to make money together. I should be thanking you. I need your brains.'

I release him, body fizzing with relief, possibility. 'You don't understand, Mej. The timing is crazy. If this had been, like, *one* week later . . .' I hold still. The timing *is* perfect. My smile fades. 'Wait – you mentioned live music earlier. I never mentioned live music nights to you—'

Meji's smile freezes on his face as he forces a shrug. 'Ahn ahn. Do you need to mention it? You're Kiki Banjo. All you know is music. It wouldn't be you without trying to do a music thing.'

He waves his hand, laughter stilted. I narrow my eyes with suspicion. 'Meji. Am I supposed to believe that you just happened to show up a couple of weeks before my parents sell their restaurant with a ready-made pitch by accident?'

Meji relinquishes some of the tension in his shoulders and leans forward, eyes sparkling. 'Well, it depends. Do you really believe in accidents? Because I really am looking for a location. And I just so happened to mention it to a mutual friend of ours last month.'

My breath leaps with realisation, and I feel warmth gush through me, everything I'd been repressing, dampening down, rushing forward, calling forth feelings to bloom, rivers to flow, suns to shine. I search the restaurant and see Malakai studying something on his tablet with Taré, face focused on his work.

'Oh my God.'

'Kiki.' Meji follows my gaze. 'Our mutual friend made me promise not to mention his name to you. He was very adamant about it. And I want you to know that I wouldn't have considered this if it wasn't a smart business decision. I love you – you know that – but I also don't play about my money. This is not a handout. This is work. I know you, and what you're capable of. So does he. He believes in you, so much. He didn't say that everything you touch turns to gold. He said you *are* gold.'

I angrily blink away my tears. 'Shit. *Shit*. Why would he do something so kind? Why would he do that for me whilst pushing me away? Like this is probably the best thing anyone has ever done for me. It's fucked! Excuse my language, Mej.'

My old friend is looking at me with a smirk. 'What?' I demand.

Meji chuckles warmly, shaking his head, the twinkle in his eyes dancing, 'You both are funny. Just walking around with that sweet heat. You know when something is peppery and hot and makes you sweat, but it's also delicious? Addictive? And then the fire cools down, down, and it somehow tastes even better in your mouth? Still hot, but less hectic. The flavour deeper. Something that lasts. Has different lives.'

My laugh comes out stiff, stilted. 'Meji. Malakai and I are over. *Been* over.'

'Yes. A phase you had was over. The first version of you is over, but let the second round come and you will see it might taste even better.'

My mouth parts to refute this, expecting my logic, my sense, to slip against the absurdity of the notion, but instead it wraps around it, holds it.

I suddenly have something very urgent to do. 'Sorry, will you excuse me for a second?'

Meji grins as a waiter brings his pounded yam and égúsí plate. 'Please, go ahead. I'm very fine over here.' He shoos me away. 'Go and do what you need to do.'

I plant a kiss on his cheek, before winding my way through the tables to where Malakai and Taré are stood by the bar. 'Sorry to interrupt – Malakai, can I have a word with you? It's, um, a work thing, really boring, logistical stuff,' I say to Taré quickly, ignoring Malakai's quizzical face at my franticness.

'Oh, Malakai and I were just talking about work. My friend's looking for someone to direct a thing here in December, but our pretty friend here has just let me know that he's going back to LA. Why, I will never know. Can you tell him to stay, please? He won't listen to me. We need the presence of fine men in this country to boost national morale. This is, like, treasonous to Black Britain.'

I turn to him, dizzy from drastic emotional lurches, desperately trying to keep my feelings from my voice, transfer the dryness of my throat to my eyes. 'Why would you leave?'

Malakai swipes at his jaw, and glances at me in a way that has time-slowing effects. I'm sure it's a brief moment, but it feels like both now and forever, hurtling into an unnameable emotion that wraps around my heart. Then, his eyes drop to my neck, bare of the chilli pepper pendant. It's been lying on my dresser ever since that night at the pool. When his gaze meets mine again, they're cooler.

'I feel like I've done what I needed to do here.'

I shake my head, baffled. 'I don't understand why you're sounding like a superhero on the way to his home planet. What does that even *mean*?'

Malakai's gaze flares into mine. 'I feel like it's clear. There's nothing really for me here—'

'Um, your *mum*? Your brother?'

'They'll visit, and mum's planning to move back to Lagos anyway.'

I feel like I'm living on a different planet. Perhaps Malakai's home one. I have no idea what he's talking about, and I'm feeling frenetic, panicked, because what does he mean he's leaving? He just got here. He just came back (to me). He's supposed to be here (with me). Parentheses are flying around my mind, intrusively, obnoxiously. I remember that I'm still in front of Taré, still have a mask to uphold, still have to pretend that I'm not sluicing parts of my heart away in order to be around him, them.

'So –' I manage to keep my voice even, throwing a shaky smile at Taré – 'you're just going to give up?' I pause. 'On, um, London?' (On me, me, me.) Malakai's neck tilts by a fraction, and I see the shutters lift. Like a tide rising, I see a glimpse of what he's been hiding, a wave of heartbreak mingled with the swell of something sweet and hot that surges through me, reaching out for me, looking for something to hook into, to believe and hope for.

'You can't give up on something that isn't yours, Kiki. London's grown, you know? Moved on. I don't know where I fit in here any more. And that's OK. It's good, even. You have to know when to let things go, and I think I do now.' I feel like I'm choking. Like everything I'm supposed to say has become a lump in my throat and I'm supposed to act like I'm OK, because I told everyone that this was OK. We're trapped in this pretence. And why is he acting like he's doing this incredibly noble thing while ignoring the feelings that I haven't told him about yet?

Taré laughs into our quiet, unaware of the barely contained explosive intensity before her, her eyes bouncing between us. 'See, *this* is why your dance sequence was hot. It was my favourite part of the shoot, you know? You have a synergy. It's been so cool watching you guys create something incredible. After this, you two should get back together and—'

Aminah, who is walking by, sipping her Chapman through her straw, splutters slightly. 'Oh no. No, no, no. Kiki cried for *months*. I once went in her room and she was crying into his *hoodie*. And then she wore that hoodie to brunch. To *brunch*. My best friend is absolutely not going through that again, not on my watch.'

It's possible my body has turned to stone, because I'm suddenly finding it extremely hard to move, and actually breathe. Malakai seems to be very still too. He looks at me, eyes almost numb with horror, if possible and questioning. I almost laugh. He thinks *I* know what's going on? I don't know the answer, because I don't know what I should even be asking. I didn't tell her that Taré didn't know about Malakai and I because I didn't think I had to. Somehow, I didn't think my best friend would bring up my break-up to my boss, and now I'm feeling something that I never thought my best friend would catalyse: humiliation.

Her eyes immediately widen upon seeing my reaction. 'Oh no. Oh *no*.'

'What I actually meant to say,' Taré says, voice chillingly calm, 'is that I think that after this project they should get back together and work on something again, but I don't think that matters any more. Team, shall we have a quick meeting?'

'Do I look like a prick? I have eyes. About three weeks in I knew you were the ex that Malakai had been cut up about that month we hung out.'

She sits herself down on my ocean-blue velvet sofa, tucking her legs beneath her, looking more hurt than angry. It's kind of awkward that the 'production office' also doubles as my flat. Malakai and I position ourselves gingerly opposite her like school kids in the headteacher's office. I cannot believe I'm about to get told off in my living room. My cheeks flame and Malakai holds rigid.

'Taré,' I say, leaning forward, 'nothing's going on between us right now. And we're sorry we hid it from you. And we get that you're feeling disrespected. And, honestly, it was my idea – Malakai would have told you—'

'*Kiki.*' Malakai tries to jump in, but I put a hand on his knee, quietening him.

'He would have told you, but the truth is this job meant a lot to me and I was worried that your previous, um, history with him would interfere with your thoughts on us working together. Which

I know is *so* insulting, but I really didn't want to jeopardise what I knew would be an amazing thing—'

Taré's fury abates, but the hurt doesn't. It stays glimmering in her orange and blue shadowed eyes.

'*We* don't have a history,' says Taré. 'History is five years of dating, which, by the way, is very easily accessed on the internet once you know what you're looking for. And the only reason I even snooped is that, I swear, even if you guys were discussing what to have for lunch it felt like I was watching a very specific porn category. And don't look at me like that – again, I don't care as long as you get the job done, but what I *do* care about is trust. You don't owe me anything, but you basically lied to me and by the time I figured it out, it was proven that you're both excellent at your jobs. I'm crazy about lying. You know how many people I've worked closely with to find out I couldn't trust?'

I nod. 'I do. Which is weirdly why I didn't tell you. I didn't want you to think you couldn't trust us. Which is fucked up, I know—'

The annoyance on Taré's face relaxes into a grudging softening. 'Look. I also know how it feels to care about something enough not to risk it, and I want to believe you care about the project.'

'We do,' Malakai adds, 'and it was also a joint decision. It's our business and we didn't want it to be a distraction from our work, but we're sorry that it felt like we were playing you. We weren't trying to do that, Taré. The thing is, though, Kiki's vision along-side yours helps form the soul of it, and if you really think that this is inappropriate I don't mind coming off the project.'

I whip round and stare at him. 'Malakai, what are you talking about? You can't—'

Malakai's eyes drift easily to me, his voice calm, low, a rippling lake. 'You can't tell me what to do, Kiki.'

My blood spikes. His tone is gentle but firm, and I know he's serious. While this is enraging on its own, what's even more frustrating is the immediate fizz it sends through my veins, the challenge that's piqued. 'Um, I can when what you want to do doesn't make sense. You do realise that by leaving you'd be making a decision for both of us? We work together. We're a team. My work works because you get it. You're not being some kind of knight in shining armour by doing this. You're being arrogant. Why don't you consider the fact that I actually *want* to work with you?'

Malakai's gaze softens and Taré scoffs loudly, shaking her head, her lips twisted in bemusement. 'Are you guys serious with this shit? *No one* is leaving. I have spent too much money already, I don't have time to replace you and you guys are doing a great job. It's not a big deal, I just want to make sure it doesn't interfere with my shit.' She rises, elegantly, a sprite on a cloud, her skirt shimmering with the movement. 'OK, I'm bored with this. We're going to continue and from now on we're going to be straight up with each other. No bullshit.'

'Of course.'

'Absolutely.'

But before she reaches the door she throws one last thing at us. 'I just hope you know that hiding it makes it a bigger deal than it is? Because if there was truly nothing going on between you then telling me wouldn't be a thing. So maybe think about what you're running away from.'

When she leaves, Malakai and I are sat in a silence that's as loud as my crashing thoughts. I hate running. Malakai clears his throat as he casts his eye across my flat; the rug of pink, blue and yellow geometric shapes over the pale slate laminated flooring, my pink arm chair, the Kerry James Marshall and Deborah Segun prints, framed pictures of me and the girls. My favourite thing about this place are the wide windows my parents put in that show peeks of the east London skyline, and they pour sleepy sunlight in from the satiated early summer day, illuminating the room. 'This is a really cool place you've carved for yourself, Scotch—'

I shrug. 'Thanks. It's small but—'

'Nah. You've made it big. It's you. Colourful. Full of life. Bright. Bold.'

I look at him, and his eyes are an earnest beam. 'Thanks. I'm proud of it,' and I want to say thank you for helping me keep it, but I remember what Meji said, so I keep my gratitude tucked in my throat. Instead I say, breath hitched, 'What are you going to do when you go back?'

He shrugs as he picks up a coffee table book, *Called To The Camera: Black American Studio Photographers* and flicks through, absently. 'More of the same. I'll figure it out.'

I swallow. It isn't till this moment that I realise that I bought it because it reminded me of him; or more accurately, because of the interests he piqued in me by his passion. 'You were miserable at work.'

'Maybe I didn't try hard enough to not be.'

'I don't think that's how it works. And Kai, you were going to quit this job? What's that about?'

'If it meant you would stay on. It's not a big deal, Kiki.'

'Nah. Don't do that. It's a big deal. This gig could help you make your film.' I clear my throat, venture in carefully, picking through my words, 'It's . . . it's about your dad, isn't it? Kai, you have to make that film.'

Malakai puts the book down and glances across the room, his gaze snagging on my record collection next to my player. His face breaks open in a small smile before releasing a low whistle. 'Of course she has her own collection going. Do you mind if I—'

I shake my head, distinctly aware of the fact that he's avoiding my question. He bends over the black metal stand, flicking through, and I try not to marvel at the fact that Malakai is here in the space I created after we were no more, and he's moving through it with ease, as if he belongs, as if he were always here, his warm, spicy-amber scent filling up the space and making itself at home.

He clears his throat, not looking at me as he sorts through the vinyl, speaking casually, 'I think it's good what we've done together. This time in London, working on this, with you, has been good. Despite our shit. I'm glad I got to do it with you. Made me remember what it's like to make something I love. That I'm proud of. Like I feel like your voice has clarified my eye. And that's made me feel more like myself again. Whether I make the film or not, I'm grateful for that.'

Why does it feel like he's saying goodbye again? My chest

twists as he pulls out a record – D'Angelo's *Voodoo*. He looks at me now, quirks a brow, 'Can I?'

I nod, a leaden ball in my throat, my eyes inexplicably stinging. He carefully slides the vinyl out of its sleeve as I say, 'I'm still on the hunt for the original *Brown Sugar* vinyl. Someone outbid me.'

He kisses his teeth. 'Fools. Don't they know that *Brown Sugar* belongs to two people? D'Angelo and Kikiola Banjo.'

He gingerly places the record on the player, and then, almost tenderly, lifts the tonearm before gently lowering it back down. I know the song immediately. I get up and walk into my open-plan kitchen and pour us two glasses of water as 'Send It On' flows through the room, mingling with the sunlight, softening and sweetening the air scented with my unlit tuberose candle and him. It's intoxicating. I've forgotten the context of this. Forgotten that there are people downstairs. Forgotten that we are who we are now. Malakai meets me in the kitchen, leaning against my cabinet, opposite where I'm stood after I pass him his glass. The look on his face picks up my pulse like he did the tonearm, seeking, warm and honeyed and reaching.

He looks into his glass of water before meeting my gaze again. 'You happy, Scotch?'

I swallow. My pulse stutters. 'You're going to have to be specific if you're gonna ask messed-up questions like that, Kai.'

Malakai's eyes blaze into mine and steal an exhalation from me. He looks like he's about to speak when a knock splits through the air, the music, the Unsaids, the possibility of grace. 'Kiki? It's me! Can I come in?'

* * *

Aminah's been distraught. Malakai's left to give us privacy, and now she sits on the sofa next to me, squeezing my hands with eyes that glisten. 'Oh my God, Keeks, I'm so sorry! I didn't know she didn't know!' I hate seeing Aminah upset, so the sight of her takes the edge off my irritation – and for her to risk ruining professionally applied make-up is true proof of her devastation.

I shake my head. 'No, you couldn't have – maybe I should have mentioned it to you. It was dumb of me to lie about it anyway.'

'No, no, I totally get why you would! You didn't want her to think you were doing a nepotism or whatever, I get it! Even though Malakai is no Tracee Ellis Ross. Was she pissed?'

I shake my head. 'Nah. She got it. I just . . .' I pick my words carefully, venturing into new ground with watchful steps. 'Meenz, why would you say all of that shit? About how down bad I was after the break-up? In *front* of him?'

Aminah groans, a hand flying to her face. 'Honestly, it's the worst thing I've ever done. I'm so, so sorry, Kiki. I just said the first thing that came to my mind. I wasn't thinking, and I've been drinking—'

'Yeah, and you got an early start with that, I noticed. Why?'

Aminah blinks in confusion. 'I'm sorry, I didn't think it was a big deal. I just thought it would be a fun pre-bachelorette thing—'

'Sure, but, Aminah, this is my *job*, you know?'

Aminah bristles a little, saying slowly, '*Yeees*, and it's important to me too. Obviously.' I mean, is it obvious? 'But, if Taré had known about you and Malakai, what I said wouldn't have been a big deal. That doesn't have anything to do with my drinking. Literally nobody but you could tell—'

I'm unsettled now by how little Aminah is seeing my point, by how jarringly out of sync we are, unable to hear me over her defences. 'Aminah, isn't that enough, though?'

Aminah's stung, blinking in a flurry like I've slapped her. 'Well, I would hope that you knew that a little of your dad's Chapman isn't enough to make me move mad, especially in a professional setting. Why don't you act like you know me? I've been stressed, OK. And if you haven't missed hanging out for the last couple of weeks you would know why—'

'Um.' I can barely believe I'm having this conversation. 'I've been missing it because I've been working, Aminah—'

'Right, right. Like the time you and Malakai went to a sexy celebrity party and you hadn't missed the venue viewing.' I stare at her, trying to detect when and how my best friend had morphed into a Bridezilla. I had been toying with the idea of telling her about Malakai and I sleeping together, but now it's reified the idea that this would, in fact, be the worst idea possible at this moment. If she's already blaming my job, my situation with Malakai is fair game.

'I have been to all the things I needed to be at, Aminah. Fittings, even tastings that Kofi couldn't make it for! I have *tried*, but I'm so sorry I can't be there physically to smell flowers with you – pictures will be fine—'

'Pictures don't convey texture!'

I pause. There is something crazed in her eye. We are prepped to go on a holiday together in a week, so I don't ask her if she needs help locating her mind. I just about manage to refrain from saying that I don't understand what she means by *texture* since as far as I know all petals feel the same.

'All right. You know what, Aminah? I'm sorry for snapping. Of course I know you wouldn't be messy on purpose. I'm just . . . I'm embarrassed.'

Aminah's eyes are drained of annoyance, and my best friend seems to kick out the bitchy spirit that was using her body as a host. 'I'm sorry too, Keeks. For exposing you out there, like that. Honestly, I feel so shitty about it, but only two people should be embarrassed and you're not one of them. The first is me, for letting the proximity of couture excite me to the point that it messed with my ability to eat, which then affected my usually impressive capacity to handle liquor.' Her eyes are serious as she recounts her sin, and I can't help the smile that kicks up on my face. Damn it, I love her.

She picks up my hand. 'And the second is Malakai Korede, for fumbling you.'

'Well, that's sweet, Meenz, but a fumble kind of hints at clumsiness. I think Malakai deliberately wanted to let me go. And that's OK.'

THE END

(Three and a half years ago)

After our argument, dinner happened without further hitch; we were ourselves, laughing, flirting, undressing each other with our eyes, sometimes with our words. Malakai asked if we should get a cab, and when I surprised him with the hotel room he had picked me up and spun me, kissed me so soft and deep my mind went missing. We were good, so good, as we played music in the room, as we had a very serious unserious dancing competition, popping and locking like we were in a straight to video *Step Up* sequel, as Malakai playacted Magic Mike and stripped for me, as he skimmed his hand across the smooth material of my dress, a teasing ghost touch, as he whispered, 'You're so fucking sexy, Scotch.' He kissed my neck as he said, 'Beautiful,' and then my mouth as he said, 'Everything. You're everything,' as his hand slipped down my back to cup my cheeks, to squeeze, growling as he slapped, and he reawakened a sleeping hunger in me because this, this was what I had been waiting for, him wanting me, voraciously, like before. His thumb stroked my mouth and it opened for him. Closing my eyes, my tongue met his touch, tasting his tenderness. I sucked lightly, instinctively, and my eyes fluttered open to see an electrical storm of both pain and hunger on Malakai's face, gaze a black crystal flame.

'I love you, Kiki.'

My eyes sprang with water, because he was still in there; he was just fighting to get out under all the hurt, all the grief. He was doing what he could. The first few months were hard, harder than anything I've experienced – when my mum was ill I could self-soothe, console myself, hope. What's to hope for when the person is no longer here? Everything felt futile. Still, I tried. Malakai focused everything on funeral planning and then being there for his mum and brother, and then sorting out will and estate issues, going to Lagos once to sort out land disputes, feeling guilty at his own inheritance, recognising the cost. I was there in every way I could be, going with him to every meeting that was appropriate, my parents supplying them with meals from the restaurant every day for as long as they needed, and giving him space when he asked for it. Still, he never talked about his own loss. The only thing he spoke about was logistics, planning, his mum, Muyiwa. Then when everything had settled he poured himself into work, doing late nights, weekends, anything to avoid being alone with himself, and by extension me. I used to feel guilty whenever I'd feel lonely, isolated, like I was making his grief about me. So I pushed it to the back of my mind, to the back of us. Who was I to tell him what I wanted when he was dealing with the world as he knew it ending?

But this 'I love you' fell on me like rain in a drought, and my spirit lapped it up, greedily. I smiled, cupped his face.

'I love you too, baby.'

And then his phone buzzed. He'd thrown it on the bed, and it flashed. *Jade.* I'm so sorry about tonight, it said. I'm so embarrassed, it said. I hope this doesn't make things awkward, it said.

My blood cooled immediately, the heat fleeing from my body with a swiftness, because I could sense it, smell it, an unnatural disaster. I stepped back, pulled his hand from my face. My voice was eerily cool. 'What is that, Kai?'

He swallowed, all the burn in his eyes becoming frantic, spitting sparks. 'It's . . . Scotch, it's not a big deal.'

'Yeah, that's for me to decide, I think. What the fuck is Jade from your job embarrassed about?'

I'd had the pleasure of meeting Jade before. I was Malakai's date for a swanky, self-aggrandising event his boss was throwing at his Mayfair penthouse, and I'd left him to mingle. I was halfway chewing through a sixth mini-burger by the bar, texting the group-chat with one hand to say I'd just seen a forty-something white American ex teen drama star with *another* dark-skinned Black actress, and asking how many counts as a fetish, when a woman approached me, looking at me as if she knew me, which was terrifying. She had large hazel eyes and expensively coloured bronde curly hair. She was beautiful, and she shot me a bright smile that immediately informed me that she had a crush on my boyfriend, even before she said, 'Hey! You're Malakai's girlfriend, right? Man, I love a girl brave enough to eat at these things. Woman after my own heart.'

This. Bitch.

I chewed deliberately slowly before dusting my hands off and put a hand out to shake. 'Kiki.'

She waved a hand and said, 'Don't be silly,' and pulled me into the most awkward hug I have experienced in my life. She patted my back. I gritted my teeth.

'I'm Jade, one of Matthew's assistants. Me and Malakai have been working closely over the past year.'

I shot her an equally saccharine smile. 'Oh? Lovely to meet you, finally.'

I didn't say that I'd heard so much about her, even though I had. I'd heard about how her dad basically ran the BBC and that she'd once said 'no offence' with a *wink* to Malakai straight after she'd talked about how much she loved the BBC. This had led us to believe that the only reason she'd really talked about loving the BBC is so she could say 'no offence' to Malakai, because, really, no one randomly talks about how much they love the BBC apropos of nothing unless they are a government official or part of the royal family. Although, in fairness to Jade, she had family members who belonged to both things. I did think it odd for a woman who ostensibly had some Black heritage to say this, though, so really I think she wanted to talk about my boyfriend's dick and gauge his reaction. I couldn't necessarily blame her. I'm sure it worked for her at some point. I did blame her for trying to play in my face, though.

'Yeah, he's basically my work husband,' she giggled.

I stifled my eye-roll. I was bored. If she was waiting on jealousy, she would be disappointed. Malakai told me everything, and trusting him was the easiest thing to do. I knew this was an exercise in delusion, some strange power-trip; she fancied him and was trying to sow seeds of discontent. I felt kind of sad for her. What was the point of this? Why would you want to work *this* hard for a man? Yes, Malakai was beautiful, great, but, even so, surely Raya was easier than this.

I kept my face pleasant, not reacting to what she thought was a revelation and sipped from the glass of water I'd asked for. 'Yeah. He did say you insist on calling him that. I think it's cute.'

It was subtle, but she caught on to it. I'm not new to this – I'm true to this. Jade's smile went frigid on her face. She didn't know about me, that as a Yoruba woman, my knives were made from iron gilded in sugar. Most times I keep them sheathed, but, unfortunately, she'd pushed me.

'You must be *so* proud of him.'

'Sure am.' I wondered what her play here was.

'You know, the America opportunity is so exciting, and Matthew's only asked me and Malakai to join him. Isn't it sick? Will you be coming with? I can imagine long distance will be such a *chore.*' And there it was. I held very still as the first tremors of major change hit my world as I knew it, delivered from Jade of all people, a woman who was wearing nude glitter nail polish. Though there's nothing inherently wrong with nude glitter nail polish, on her it jarred me, a lazy attempt to seem fun. My insides roiled with confusion – how could he not have told me? Was he thinking of taking it? To Jade, though, I kept my demeanour placid. 'Nothing's a chore when you're in love. Have a great night, Jayda.'

'It's Jade—'

I quickly excused myself to go to the bathroom, but Malakai intercepted me, apparently tracking my movements from the other side of the room. He gently held my elbows, ducked his head to keep a gaze that kept darting everywhere to avoid him, because if I looked him in the eye I was very sure I would cry, and I wasn't about to cry in front of *Jade*. It wasn't America itself, it was the fact that he hadn't told me, and if it was true that Malakai didn't tell me everything that was going on in his life, then what else was he hiding? What the hell even were we?

'Hey.' His voice was all at once tender and protective. 'What's wrong, baby? What did she say to you? Did she call me a work husband again? I swear—'

I inhaled deeply. 'Let's talk at home.'

'Kiki—'

'This is a work event. Do what you gotta do. We'll talk at *home*.'

'I won't be able to focus. Please, Scotch. Tell me what's up.'

I sighed and dragged him through the corridor into a nearby bathroom, arousing no suspicion because there was apparently a lot of group trips to bathrooms going on.

'When were you going to tell me about America?'

Malakai was stricken, stepping back, rocking back on the ball of his foot. 'Fuck. *Fuck*.' He rubbed his brow. 'She *told* you that?'

'Yes, because she has obviously moved to you very recently

and is desperately thirsty, but it's not even about that. It's the fact that you made me look stupid by not telling me. I mean I could never look stupid, but you *risked* me looking stupid.' I paced the bathroom. There was an old-school bathtub in it, gold clawed feet and everything, and as my non-Louboutin heels clicked against the tile I marvelled at how grand the backdrop was for a domestic. There was a BAFTA on the shelf behind the toilet. 'Seriously, Kai, I'm supposed to learn that you're going halfway around the world from *her*?' I noticed a stack of Penhaligon perfumes on a recessed shelf against the emerald green tiled wall. I angrily sprayed myself with a cocktail of scents. Malakai coughed, which made me spray harder, more chaotically.

'We don't keep things from each other. That's not who we are. What's going on? I don't like looking like a prick, Kai, especially by girls with manicures that look like they're from 2006!'

Malakai approached me, gently removed Empressa and Halfeti from my hands, so he could replace them with his own. 'Kiki, I am so sorry. You could never look stupid.'

'I know. I just said that.'

'This is entirely my fault.'

'I know that too.'

'OK.' Malakai nodded, a tiny smile on his face, even though this shit wasn't funny. I could feel my anger receding despite myself, the irrevocable truth cooling it down. Malakai wouldn't willingly keep things from me. 'So, last month Matthew came to us with the opportunity to go for six months. He would pay for accommodation for two months, money would be more and . . . and there would be a chance to carve a career out there. He wants us to help out with his next project, but then someone just tried to scout me in front of him, like, just now. One of his frenemy director friends wanted me to work under him. Then he offered to pay my rent for six months. I mean it's mainly just ego, but, still, it's a huge shift. Anyway, even before now, I just wanted to think on it. At a work lunch – a group lunch, by the way – I'd mentioned, casually that I hadn't even told you yet. Jade was there. She just wants to stir—'

I was still confused. 'Malakai, it's objectively good news. Matthew believes in you; he wants to *invest* in you. It's a once in a lifetime opportunity. And now he's basically paying your way? Why didn't you tell me?'

Malakai's face was casual, his eyes darting to something beyond my head. 'Because there's nothing to tell. I'm not going.'

I snatched my wrists from his hands in shock. '*Why?*'

Malakai shrugged. 'I'm not doing anything that's going to take me away from you.'

My heart lurched. I got it. I was terrified too. I already felt our paths diverging slightly, our worlds overlapping less and less and a whole new country would add a whole new dimension to it. Still, my hand flew to his face, forcing him to look at me. 'OK, but you do know nothing could, right? Remember how I went to New York after uni for my internship that summer? You encouraged me, even though it was going to be our first summer together, and I'm so grateful for tha—'

Malakai's thumb swept across my cheek. 'That was six weeks, Scotch. This is six months—'

366

The perspective made me momentarily dizzy, but I was still held down by the conviction of what we had. 'We'll figure it out. I can get some time off, visit you for a few days? If anything changes at the end of the six months, we'll reassess. Maybe I can look for something out there.' I swallowed as the reality of it dawned. Since that first summer, Malakai and I hadn't been apart for longer than three weeks. 'The idea of you leaving makes me sick, only because I'll miss you, but, Malakai –' I took his hand from my face, squeezed it, needing to impress how much I meant what I was saying – 'You have so much to do and I'll never forgive myself for getting in your way. I'm *excited* for you. And you don't get to make decisions on my behalf. You don't have that right. Now, do you want to go?'

Malakai's eyes shone. 'Yeah. I do.' I nodded and kissed him lightly on the lips. 'So you go. And we're not just gonna survive, we'll thrive. You'll see. I'll hold it down, building over here, and you'll be over there chopping it up at some Rich Black Guy brunch or some shit.' Malakai chuckled and I lifted his knuckles to my lips. 'It will be good for both of us. I promise.'

That was five months ago. That was Before. Before his dad died, before Malakai started retreating from me. Now, he had the audacity to step closer to me calmly despite the clear nerves jouncing in his eyes.

His voice was even as he recounted the evening. 'OK, we were all out for after-work drinks. All six of us, including Jade. Someone introduced shots. I lost track of time, realised it was time to go so I went outside, decided to get an Uber to get here, thought it would be quicker. I'm waiting outside for it, and she joins me. She's making conversation, just chatting shit really. She starts talking about how gassed she is that we're going to LA. That we'd be living in the same building. I don't really respond. I'm barely listening. I swear, Scotch, I don't say shit. My car comes, she moves to hug me goodbye, which she's never done before, but I think nothing of it.' His eyes squared with mine, and his jaw tensed. 'Then she tried to kiss me. I put an end to it quick. She apologised. I said I had to go.'

I sat down on the bed, the weight of my heart in my stomach disrupting every gut feeling I thought I had. I felt sick. I stared ahead. 'Cool.'

'Kiki. Kiki look at me.' He bent in front of me, on his knees. 'I didn't kiss her back. I would never disrespect you like that. Come on, you know me—'

I swivelled my heavy eyes to him. 'Do I?'

Malakai stilled, audacious hurt skittering across his face. 'Kiki, *nothing* happened—'

'Nah, Malakai, something happened. You lied to me. You fucking *lied*,' and I hated my voice for cracking, hated the hefty tear that slipped down my cheek. 'Something you were never supposed to do. You were never supposed to be that guy. When did you become that guy?'

Malakai shook his head, his eyes flaming. 'Kiki, I'm sorry I hid it from you, but I didn't lie to you. I would never lie to you. I just didn't tell you because I didn't want you to get upset over someone who is so fucking irrelevant to me. It's not important. She's not important to me. She's a non-factor—'

Was he *serious* with acting like it wasn't something worth saying? As if she was a random girl who made a pass at him at a bar? I was beginning to rage, my voice hardening, the aloofness evaporating and forming a steam coming from my ears.

'Yeah, she's a non-factor you're gonna be living in the same building with for six months, Malakai. *Ooh*, Malakai Korede.' I smiled about absolutely nothing. 'Do not act like I'm stupid. I beg you do not. It will not end well for you. Why did she even feel comfortable to move to you—'

'Really, Kiki? You're gonna ask me what I did to encourage her? You can't just trust there's never a situation where I would actively let a girl know that was OK to do—'

'How am I supposed to trust you in that situation when you couldn't even tell me?'

'You're supposed to trust me because I'm me, Kiki!' He pounded his chest with a flat palm. 'You're supposed to trust me because that's what we do.'

I shook my head with disbelief that he wasn't understanding. I got up and spun round, as he rose to meet me, putting my hands together in prayer and pointing them in his direction. 'Malakai, it's so crazy that you're talking about trust and how I'm supposed to know you when I have to *beg* to see you these days. Do you know how *humiliating* that is? It's like you're running away from me—'

'Kiki, this shit ain't about you—'

'Yeah, I've gathered.'

'I've told you why I'm busy. You *know* why. Scotch.' He stepped closer to me, controlling his breathing, his eyes pleading, 'Please. *Please* let's not fight over this random girl trying it. Let's not insult what we have by doing that—'

I released a little screech of frustration, an unleashing of months of pent-up feeling, 'Oh my God, you don't get it, Malakai! It's not about her. I don't give a shit about her and her ugly nude glitter nails. She could try and give you a handy in Leicester Square for all I care – hitting on an openly loyal person with a girlfriend is a kind of humiliation kink I can't fathom – but it's about *you*. If I felt secure about where we were, this wouldn't even be a thing! It's about the fact that you're pulling away from me when you're moving away in a month. It's the fact that, a year ago, you would have come in laughing about how that girl tried it on with you, made a joke about how you still got it, not hid it from me—'

Malakai gesticulated, his own annoyance simmering to the top, and I felt it, the ground beginning to quake beneath us. I began to smell the smoke in the air. 'Scotch, I didn't tell you because you already suspected the girl and precisely *because* I'm moving to LA at the same time as her. I knew how you would react—'

I released a pastiche of a smile. 'OK! And how am I reacting, Malakai? Please enlighten me.'

Malakai straightened, his words as deliberate as a bullet from a sniper. 'Like someone who isn't mature enough for a long-distance relationship.'

My heart and stomach dived to my bare feet, and my tears began to chase each other, joining each other for company. I nodded, turning my lips down as if impressed. In a way, I was. Finally, some feeling from him. I kept all emotion out of my voice. I kept calm despite the fact that I could feel the sky falling heavy on my skin, weighing me down. I could have fallen down.

Instead, I said, 'Oh. There it is. Is that what you've been doing, then, Kai? A slow-fade break-up? What, are you too cowardly to actually do it? Do you want me to make it easier for you?'

Malakai held still, his eyes glinting. 'You're talking reckless and I don't like it, Kiki. In what world are we going to break up—'

'In a world where you rock up to dinner half an hour late smelling like another woman's cheap perfume and calling *me* immature, guy.' I could feel it, all the repressed hurt from the past few months reaching boiling point.

Regret flitted across Malakai's face, but it mingled with anger, so it stayed stolid. 'Kiki, I said I'm sorry.'

'Yeah, but you're not, though.' I rose a finger and rocked back onto the ball of my foot as the tears streamed down my face. 'And I don't need you to lie to me again.' I shook my head. 'Because the truth is you have been running from me for the past few months and you're talking about how I need to trust you.'

Malakai scratched his jaw, his eyes dark and weighty with a war of emotion. 'Well, Scotch, this isn't gonna work if you don't. And maybe because we're in different career stages that you don't relate to—'

I choked out an empty husk of a laugh. 'Fuck you, Malakai. How dare you? What, I don't relate to drinking in bars with sleazebag directors?'

'Is that what you think I do, yeah?'

'How would I know? It's not like you let me in any more. And, yeah, you're working hard to please your dad, I know, but just be careful you're not making the same mistakes as him on the way. Make sure you still have a home to come back to.' I gasped as soon as the words were in the air between us, serrated blades that I could see cut through him immediately. My hand flew to my mouth as Malakai's eyes became shiny, and all emotion drained from his face, hurt so acute that his body instantly packed it away.

'Shit. Shit, I didn't mean that, Kai.' I moved closer, but he stood back, shook his head.

'Nah, you're right, Kiki.' His voice sounded alien, like it was coming from a different body, a different person, 'Maybe I'm just like him. Maybe I rushed into something too serious in life. Maybe it's not that you're immature, it's that we both are.'

'Malakai.' I rushed towards him, held his face in my hands and the fragments of our world that were falling around us. 'No. No. I was just pissed.'

He pulled away from me. Fuck, he was pulling away from me.

'Kiki, look at what we're doing to each other? I'm going to LA in a month and look at where we *are*?' He bent at the knees, hands outstretched, eyes shiny. 'We're *killing* each other.'

It was then that the panic set in. Because now there was no question. We were teetering on the brink. It's like I could see the bright, light pieces of what we were falling around us, scraping against the jagged edges of what we are now.

'So what are you saying, Kai?'

The look that Malakai threw almost made my knees buckle. I'd never seen it in him before. Defeat. His own eyes were full and gleaming. 'I'm tired, Kiki. I can't do this and deal with everything else right now.'

'Malakai, *what* are you saying to me right now?' My voice was ragged, frayed and barely coming out in a whisper, so scared of what was happening – this could not be happening. We were inevitable, a sure thing. We were the sun itself. We were us, forever us. What was happening?

Malakai crumpled and his hand came to his face, to hide within it, to run against it. 'I don't know. I don't know, Scotch. It's just . . . it's too much.'

It wrapped around my heart, squeezed till I couldn't breathe, and without realising what I was doing I went to him, and wrapped my arms round him, and he wound his right back, holding tight as if he was trying to anchor himself to me, tether himself to us. He pulled slightly away to look at me, and his eyes were so bright with our old love, and instead of giving me hope it killed it, because they were bright like a supernova, our love flaring like a star on its dying breath. And even then every part of my body was reaching towards him. My fractured heart pounded with all its diminishing might with need, desperation, the rhythm pulsing right through to the junction between my legs. Malakai, reading the look on my face like he'd written it, because he had, silently laid me down carefully on the bed, like I was built from gossamer and glass. We stripped each other of our clothes. We weren't going to talk any more – we couldn't, shouldn't. What was there to say? Time was slipping, the sun was sinking, the ocean dying. When we kissed it was with ferocious sweetness, our bodies tangled, needing as much skin touching as possible, our tongues licking into each other's mouths as if to capture all the words that refused to be released, that were too heavy, too light, too useless; hands roaming, squeezing, caressing, surrendering to the alchemy of us as I turned to river under his touch and he turned to rock under mine. He leaned over me, a hand cradling my face as my hands pressed against his back. We paused, as if trying to suspend time, knowing this would be the last time. My eyes were already filling, but Malakai's eyes were focused, leaden with intensity and concentration, like he was anchoring himself to this moment, as if we only existed inside it, as if we had to be, otherwise we would turn to dust. I followed his lead, not wanting to waste this time and this world where the only air I was inhaling was his breath made rapid by my touch, this space where the only thing I could see was him seeing me, our Pangea where my skin and his skin knew no borders. I spread my legs wider round him in welcome, and Malakai brought his face to my neck, his lips hot on my throat as he sank into me deep, so deliciously deep, boundless-ocean deep, that I cried out with both pleasure and pain as he filled me with all his pleasure and pain, slowly rocking me with it, his fingertips pressing hard into the flesh of my thigh, and I wanted him to press into me harder, like maybe if he did he would leave indents of his body, of his love, that I could trace when I missed him, which would be always.

My arm moved to slip down his back till it slid over a firm, smooth curve and pushed him closer, and he growled and somehow went deeper. This time he pushed tears down my face, bringing his face to mine, and he kissed me slow as we passed our hearts back and forth to each other. It felt like hours, saying goodbye over and over, till it was no longer just about feeling, but being, in the moment, staying suspended, not wanting to detangle, delaying reality. I didn't know when we fell asleep, but we did, in each other's arms, sweaty, all our energy given to each other as tribute. When I opened my eyes, it was around 5 a.m. and peachy-pink dawn was stretching through the windows, mocking us with its freshness, its hope. He was sat in the armchair in the corner of the bedroom, dressed. When he turned to me, his eyes were reddened, tired. I was tired too. Bone tired.

'Scotch.' I knew from the sound of his voice. It sounded exactly like the crack of a heart.

'Don't say it.'

'If we stay together, if I go when we're like this, we won't make it. You don't trust me. After everything we've been through, you don't trust me, and that shit hurts, Scotch. And I need to focus on this job when I'm away.'

What was I supposed to do? Argue? Beg? I didn't beg. Malakai had been silently screaming for his space and who was I to deny him that? We were supposed to be in this together, that was the agreement, that we got each other through whatever, and if he wanted out I wasn't going to stop him. I could have said that I wanted him to stay, to fight for us, with me, but how worthy is the fight if you have to ask? So I swallowed it, alongside everything I'd been feeling for the past few months.

'You're right.'

How did five years become this? One fight. One goodbye fuck. One heart being shredded in a hotel room. Because, surely, he was just fine. I mean breaking up is unpleasant, but there is no way he would have chosen this if his heart was on the line. Because this felt like hellfire. I felt like I was burning from the inside. He got up, made some kind of gesture, like he wanted to hug me, which couldn't have been right. I stayed where I was in the bed, in the huge T-shirt I'd pulled on – ironically one of his that I'd stolen from him.

He nodded to himself. 'Kiki. I hope you know I love—'

'You don't need to do that, Malakai. Don't tell me that. I don't want to hear it. If being apart from me will make you happy, then go be happy, but please don't insult me by telling me you love me.'

Malakai's expression was shadowed, and I knew he was bounding up everything he felt, ensuring he showed nothing, avoiding agitating the volatile atmosphere.

I sniffed. 'I'm, um, I'm gonna have a shower. If you're gonna go, go while I'm in there, please. That's the only thing I'm gonna ask.'

I wasn't about to break down in front of him. I couldn't let him have that.

He was looking at me with his fists balled, trembling, as if he wanted to touch me, hold me. That couldn't have been right. He wanted this. Nobody who wanted this could have an inclination to comfort me, stop the hurt. He was the cause. He came to the bed and bent over to press a kiss to my forehead. A tear pushed itself from my eyes, but nothing else moved. I was numb, still, everything in my body slowed to inertia. It was only when scalding water was pummelling my skin, when steam was rising up around me, mingling with the smoke of our destruction, it was only when I heard the thud of the door closing, that I sobbed. Big, gulping, racking sobs. I slid to the floor and rocked myself, wrapped my arms around on myself, hyperventilating, gasping for breath, trying to fight a reality that was aggressively, necessarily, clawing its way into my consciousness. Malakai and I were no longer together.

CHAPTER 15

How Does It Feel?

A few days after the video shoot, I come home from holiday-shopping with the girls to a slim package that reads 'Fragile'. Dumping my bags on the floor by the door, I open it carefully to see an original *Brown Sugar* vinyl. My heart stutters. I know it's original by the gentle creases, the fading of the sleeve, and when I delicately pull the vinyl out, the small scratches tell me more. They're like kisses. It's one of the most beautiful things I've ever seen. It was listened to, loved on. Not worn, *lived* in. Fulfilling purpose. I peer into the package for a note, and there is one, folded in half, and I know who it's from even before I see the curving scrawl that's as familiar to me as my own handwriting, seen in birthday cards and anniversary cards and Post-it notes stuck on the back of my uni room door that read 'Gone to get my coffee and your ice cream, Sleepy Head'; a message from an early riser to someone violently allergic to mornings. The note before me now reads, 'To the rightful owner x'.

My eyes blur. I swear under my breath as warmth surges through, because *fuck* him, bless him. I put it on immediately. I light my candles, pour myself a glass of red wine, strip down to my underwear, fold myself on my bed and watch the sunset through my wide windows, physically still but my mind moving through music, through time. I close my eyes and my hand slips under my panties, between my legs and feel him feeling me; I barely think about it, it's obeying the call of memory, and like the ocean holds both past and present, so does my waters, history repeating itself, waves washing up facts of want, my body shuddering complicated truths, then aching at the absence of a hard truth. I cry out and I cry. I fall asleep and dream of a memory so exquisitely vivid that I'm shocked to open my eyes to an empty bed at 2 a.m. I'm suddenly frantic, and acting on impulse, without acknowledging knowledge, I grab my phone from my side table and send a text.

Keeks
D'Angelo came to my house yesterday.

He replies immediately.

Kai
Oh yeah? Did you ask him when the next album's coming?

Keeks
Thank you, Kai. You didn't have to.

Kai
I did. Civic duty. Can't have Voodoo without Brown Sugar x

I stare at the 'x', glowing in the dark of my room. Malakai may have affection for me, but that doesn't mean he wants me. He's being kind because he's kind, I know, but I stare at the 'x' like it's marking the spot that the dream version of him hit inside me, making me come in my *sleep*. I swallow and note the time, the immediacy with which he replied, and it's this that informs my boldness.

Keeks
Why you up?

Kai
*Couldn't sleep. Editing. You look great in these by the way. It's
    shaping up so sweet. Mapping out the new film too.*

I can't help the smile that licks at my mouth. I slide down under the smooth of my covers, of possibility.

Keeks
I'm glad.

Kai
I think you should keep doing this. I mean, after this is over

Keeks
What?

Kai
*This work you do. It's needed. The places you have pulled Taré
to with you . . . only you could have done it. And I'm looking
at the footage and you're like, fucking glowing. I think the
SoundSugar thing was a blessing. And you were right to walk
away from that shit. It takes balls to do that. Always been brave.*

There's a pause while I gather my emotion, try to corral the
rush of convicting heat, to garner some control of whatever it is
that threatens to spill out of me, then he continues.

Kai
So why are you up?

Keeks
Practising Renaissance World Tour choreo

Kai
*Say swear? I just perfected Usher's U Don't Have To Call floor
choreo to get the blood going*

Keeks
Retro

Kai
You know me. I'm a classic man

I laugh, then bite my lip and decide to test the truth.

Keeks
I couldn't sleep either.

Kai
Bad dream?

Keeks
Not sure. Depends.

Kai
On?

Keeks
Whether you've had it too.

There's a pause. I see 'typing . . .' and then it disappears again. After a few more maddening seconds, a message appears.

Kai
How did it make you feel?

I swallow. Free. Honest.

Keeks
Good. Confused.

Kai
I've had it too.

There's a break within which my breath is suspended, my heart hammers, then:

Kai
Goodnight, Scotch. Sleep well, yeah?

Hope lands on reality with a thud.

I hear him loud and clear: sometimes dreams are just dreams. Not a hope making itself known or a desire telling you that it's in your grasp. Just a silly, insolent, naïve want to keep, a plaything that would crumble once it hits reality, buckling under the weight of history.

CHAPTER 16

Winking, Smiling and Wanna Attack Man

'OK, I know I said bachelorette merch was tacky, but, can't lie, baby tees that say "Aminah's Angels"? *Actually* incredible. I feel like I'm on my own world tour.' Aminah gestures to my chest, emblazoned with her name in lilac like it's a superhero crest, while perching herself on the wide marble island of Taré's glorious sprawling villa.

I snort as I measure out some crème de violette, lime juice and tequila into an ice-filled jug for the special-edition margaritas I'm making for the group – purple for Aminah's favourite colour. They promise to be suitably vile.

'Yeah?' I say. 'What would your tour be called?'

Without missing a beat, my best friend replies with, 'Minah Money Moves.' She reclines on the ball of her palm, kicking her legs in her white mini bandeau dress and sipping a violet drink from the previous jug I made. The light pours in from the tall, wide bifold doors that lead to the back garden. A bright azure pool reflects the sun back to the sky, and early noughties female R&B pumps through the speakers as sunlight streams in, the combination of everything recharging us, and prepping us for Day 2 of the beach festival.

Taré looked appalled when I double-checked that she was still OK with us staying in one of the villas she rented out, saying with some disgust, 'Must you *keep* disrespecting. Of course you have to still go. Don't be annoying.'

For my part, I'm extremely grateful for the opportunity to switch off from everything work and ex-man related and Aminah was over the moon to find that her bachelorette wasn't compromised. Due to her only direction to me being 'Soft life, hard liquor', she seems satisfied with the result. The house really is stunning, and with ocean views and a modern luxe décor of cream and pastels, it's finely tuned to Aminah's specific tastes. Her eyes survey the location with awe, and she sighs, sipping the pastel-hued liquid out of a metal straw.

'This is heaven. You've outdone yourself, Keeks.'

I do a little bow. 'Well, the best for the best, innit.'

Shanti eyes us knowingly, watching us carefully for discord. Although Chioma, with her peace, love, kombucha and hemp vibe, might be the best person on paper to detect and mediate drama, Shanti is truly the one equipped to be on Beef Watch. She doesn't mince words, has a sharp eye and is the one who comes into my room, later on, while I'm unpacking, to lean against the doorframe and enquire, with folded arms and a raised brow: 'So are you and Aminah gonna be weird this entire trip? Because I truly don't have time for this shit. I paid to spend time with my best friends, and you guys being overly nice to each other is basically wasting my money.'

I fold a T-shirt into the wardrobe, managing to look confused. 'First of all, you paid to come to one of your oldest friends' bachelorettes.'

'I mean I guess.' She flips her wavy ombre hair over her shoulders before walking in and sitting on the bed, cute in the lilac minidress she's already changed into for tonight.

'Secondly –' I bring out a pair of heels from my suitcase – 'Aminah and I are always nice to each other. What are you talking about?'

Shanti blinks. 'Really, Kiki? It's so boring when you do this. Aminah might have the time for this, but I don't. I'm talking about what happened last week. I'm talking about Aminah blasting your business in front of your boss. I'm talking about the fact that you guys have been acting like a couple on the brink trying to make things work for the kids for the past fortnight and it's driving me and Chioma mad. You know I'll choose Aminah in the divorce because she has more work perks. Fuck am I gonna do with tickets to an intimate acoustic show of some obscure soul artist? No offence, love you, mean it.'

Ignoring the fact that we were currently *in* a work perk of mine,

I sigh and shut the door to my room, sitting next to her on the king-sized bed. I'd been repressing what happened at the video shoot because I had to, in order to not lose my mind. Not only have I been finalising the plans of the bachelorette we're currently on, I've been in talks with Meji and my parents, exploring the buyout, working on the last parts of *Phoenix* and avoiding Malakai whilst working on *Phoenix*. Meji had told me that Malakai hadn't wanted me to know that I told him about the plans for the restaurant, and while I wanted to respect that, it was also torturous. It's definitely the best thing anyone has ever done for me, and also the most jarring, because it's by someone who doesn't want me close. How do you thank someone who wants you to leave them alone? Who would rather leave a country a second time than talk to you? With all these easy, breezy situations, I didn't have time to go through the fact that Aminah had very nearly jeopardised my job, and very much did embarrass me in front of Taré.

'Look, am I still kind of annoyed about what happened at the shoot? A little, but it's not worth bringing it up. I should have told Taré in the first place. Plus Aminah's stressed about the wedding and there's just too much going on to not let it go. We'll be fine.'

Shanti crosses her legs and lays down flat on my bed with a soft thud. 'Well, you better be. Because when she finds out you and Malakai have been sneaky linking and you didn't tell her, she's gonna lose her mind, and I don't have time for that.'

I hold still. 'What did you just say to me?'

Shanti sits back up and eyes me incredulously. 'Are you

joking, Keeks? Please. In fact, the only reason Aminah hasn't seen you guys be all googly eyes and giggly with each other is because she's got an insane case of Nigerian Bride Brain. Just, you know, a general extra dollop of self-involvement. Which is understandable considering her mother has invited approximately five hundred people, but yeah, come on. The picture from that party? How you were acting with each other at the shoot? The real question is, why do you think we're dumb? You and Malakai are notoriously bad at hiding your feelings from each other, like, historically so.'

'Um,' I say, when I manage to collect my thoughts, and recover from the shock of information, 'it isn't about *feelings*.' I'm oddly shy, having been stripped bare so easily like this. Gone goes the illusion that I'm a sexy enigma. 'We just like, *you know* . . .'

Shanti is incredulous and slightly disgusted, a sharply brushed brow tugged upwards, her mouth in a half-snarl. '*You know?* Don't piss me off. I'm sorry, are we twelve? Tell me more about the *you know*, please. And make it fast. Aminah's having a shower and Chioma is on an international call with her married boyfriend and girlfriend. As in the boyfriend and girlfriend are married to each other. She's so hellbent on this throuple thing, when she knows she doesn't have the bandwidth to manage that many people's erotic energies. She's quite a sensitive soul. Anyway, speaking of erotic energies, let's get back to you and Malakai.'

Taking a deep fortifying breath, I unleash all the angst, all the tension, all the back and forth that has happened over the past six months. The liberation that comes with sharing with Shanti is surprising, but welcome, and a layer of anxiety lifts from my skin with it. Shanti immediately shakes my hand after.

'You know what, friend? I'm impressed. This is some good, organic, homegrown sweet tea. Also I really didn't think you had this in you. A secret affair—'

'Hardly an affair.'

'He fucked you against the London skyline.'

'Well, technically that's not where the main fucking occurred. It was actually—'

'Anyway, has all of this made you catch feelings again?'

I pause to think about it, because how do I describe it? The fear isn't that I'm catching feelings *again*, but that I'm being forced to confront feelings that never went away. And that those feelings may not even matter, because their existence does not mean Malakai and I are meant to be together, and they definitely don't mean that Malakai feels the same way. I settle with a 'No.'

Shanti's sceptical. Her mouth twists into a dry smile. 'Sure. Whatever you say. Look, I'm no Aminah, but I'm here if you need me, OK? Because I don't know how you carried all this tea on your own. The need to gist would kill me.'

'I mean it truly almost did. It's juicy shit even for me. I'd be into it if it wasn't giving me stress sweats.'

Shanti snorts and a smile tugs at my lips despite the direness of the situation. All of us are close as a foursome, but we're naturally divided into closer pairs – me with Aminah and Chioma with

Shanti – it works, feeds into our balance and functionality, but I'm warmed by the reminder that I really am held by my girls on all fronts.

Shanti stares at me incredulously. 'Why are you smiling like that?'

To her horror, I launch at her, flopping onto where she is on the bed and kissing her cheek.

'Thank you, Shanti. I needed this.' I say it mostly to get on her nerves, cloying and sweet, and she mimics a retching sound.

'Oh my God. Yeah, see, this is why I can't be an Aminah replacement. You guys are too Sisterhood of the Travelling Pants.'

'Nah. All of us, together, are Sisterhood of the Travelling Bants.'

'All right. If you don't let me go now, though, I'm gonna have to believe you hate me.'

'No, Mummy.' Aminah is resplendent in a heavily sequined white minidress, silver heels clicking against the tile as she paces. 'We can't add any more people to the list! It's enough! Also, what do I care if your friend's first daughter's wedding colours were rose and mint like me, that was ten years ago – and no we can't skip kente! What? Have you missed everything I have said for the last six months? If Kofi is wearing an agbada at the trad, how can I skip kente? We're doing two outfits!'

Laide creeps up to her sister and does what none of us can do, which is take the phone from Aminah, and say, 'Mummy, we love you, but Aminah is on her bachelorette right now and you are killing her vibe. Leave her alone for the next twenty-four hours, please. She will talk about inviting your old school-sister who you haven't seen in thirty years when she's back in London,' and hangs up.

Relief washes through me. I'm glad to have one big sister on deck. (Aminah's eldest sister was too pregnant to fly the twelve hours, and, besides this, very obviously didn't want to come.) A blood sister can control the Mother Pressure without the threat of the mother thinking you're a disrespectful badly brought-up influence on her daughter who should be banished from her life. Besides, the harshest thing I have said to Aminah's mother is, 'No thank you, Auntie, I just ate,' and even then I ended up eating five puff puffs. I mouth a 'thank you' and Aminah tries to compose herself, picking up her glass again and glugging it down. The girls and I exchange a look. Things have been going relatively well; we'd gone on a pre-sunset boat tour while drinking some of South Africa's best wines, and Aminah and I were relaxing more, leaning into the moment, laughing with each other. She'd sighed on the boat as she looked out onto the majestic, towering Table Mountain, set back against orange and lilac hues, looking as if it held all the mysteries in the universe.

'Kiki, thanks for planning this,' she said. 'I know you've been busy.'

I threw an arm round her, drew her to me. 'Are you joking? Wrangling three women with various dietary requirements who all wanted the second-biggest room was a piece of cake.' I bumped my hip with hers, but she barely cracked a smile as she stared out into the water. There wasn't even an attempt to shade. This gave me slight cause for concern. 'Hey, is everything OK? With Kofi and stuff?'

Aminah nodded quickly. 'Oh, Kofi is amazing. Like, a dream. You know he booked a spa weekend for me for next week because he just wants me to chill out? I just . . . I don't know.' She paused, and made sure the rest of the crew were at the back of the boat, still talking to the Calvin Klein-model-looking tour-guide, asking him where the best spots to go out in the area are, whether he can come, and whether he has friends.

I shifted closer to her. She was wearing shades and a floppy hat with her white sundress, so I could barely see her face, but, still, I felt that something was off in my bones. Aminah doesn't get *down*. She has moments of despondency that she feels and then shakes off. This felt like something deeper than I've seen before.

'Aminah.'

'You ever just wanna run away and open a bakery?'

OK, seriously, *who* had taken my sister's brain?! 'I'm . . . Aminah, what?'

'Like, theoretically. When we were walking through town earlier and we went into that bakery called Lesedi's and I noticed that the lady who worked there looked way too hot and young to own a bakery. Not that you can't be hot to own a bakery, but, you know, normally, I imagine them to be owned by either grandmas or posh white men from Fulham who got burnout from working in tech with easy access to seed money. *Anyway*, while you were taking that phone call from Taré, I got talking to Lesedi and she

392

said she had this high-powered job at some legal firm and she had made her parents very happy, but she loved baking. Always has done since she was a kid. Collected all the baking books, and people loved her stuff. Anyway, one day she stopped and questioned why she was doing law. You know what she realised? Not one of the reasons was because of her. Anyway, she quit and used the money she'd been saving for a house for the bakery. Isn't that wild?'

I nodded slowly, trying my hardest to follow. 'Yes. Aminah . . . do you want to quit PR?'

Aminah huffed out a laugh. 'My job is literally to control how people think. No, it's my dream job.' She paused and sipped at the wine she was holding. 'It's just a lot sometimes, you know. It's a lot, balancing it all. Being good at my job, being a good daughter, daughter-in-law, wife. And it's not about Kofi either – I love him.' Her voice was convinced, unshakeable as she leaned over the white bars and looked out at the crisp, rippling blue, lined up against the mountain. 'But I just sometimes feel like getting married is part of a long list of things I've done because I have to—'

'Aminah, you are not someone who does things because you *have* to. Didn't you cause anarchy in your boarding school because as head girl you called out the slave-owning links of the school's founder?'

'Yeah, and I only became head girl because my older sister was head girl, and if she was head girl I couldn't *not* be head girl. She set the standard, and I had to follow.'

'Well. You went to Whitewell and studied Marketing and Public Relations, instead of engineering, medicine or law, two of which your sisters chose to study. That wasn't easy, Meenz. You carved your own path—'

Aminah released a strange, empty imitation of a laugh. My concern sharpened.

'You know I wanted to go travelling? Before uni? I wanted to explore the world, and find myself. My parents told me that was a complete waste of time. I got into Cambridge – I told you that, right? – but Whitewell seemed like a better fit, more flexible, less stuffy, less . . . *insular*. So that was the compromise. I'd go to uni right away as long as it was Whitewell. And I loved it, and it was the best time and I would meet the most important people in my life.'

She looked at me then and smiled, a real one. 'And I truly think I was meant to meet you then. And Kofi. And Chi and Shanti. You guys opened up my world, but, still, I kind of feel like I haven't really been able to do anything on my own terms, you know?'

I tried to configure the information in my mind, matching it against her behaviour recently. Something was definitely askew and, just as I was about to interrogate it further, Aminah lifted her sunglasses, pushing out a bright smile.

'I'm sorry, I didn't mean anything . . . I'm sorry. Shit, I don't know what's wrong with me. This,' she gestured to the expanse before us, 'is bliss. It's bliss. I just sometimes feel the urge to run away. That's normal, right?'

I froze. The worry spiked. I managed to school my face to calm as I tried to formulate an answer that wouldn't freak her out.

'Uh. I think . . . yeah, it's normal to feel pressure. It's a huge life change. I just think that maybe we should talk about the source of that urge—'

'Smallie,' Laide called out, from where she stood by our tour guide, one hand round his neck, the other round the neck of a tequila bottle she'd somehow smuggled onto the boat. 'Kiki, can you guys stop snogging, please! Lubanzi has said he'll do shots with us.'

Aminah's face smoothed over and broke open in a laugh. 'Coming!' She turned to me, smile bright, and eyes not quite getting the memo. 'Forget it. I'm just in my head. Watching my sister flirt with someone who I am very sure is gay will fix it. Did you know her first boyfriend was gay? I don't know why she has a thing for unavailable men.'

'Aminah, wait—' She turned to me, teeth fixed in a grin.

'I'm fine. I'm fine! Let's drop it.'

So I dropped it, but now the look on her face has me wondering whether that was a good idea. We were pre-gaming when her mum called, ready to hit the evening leg of the festival, and I could feel Aminah's mood slipping through her fingers. I rise from the cushy bouclé armchair I'm in, holding my flute of champagne, and pulling down my dress-code-adhering lilac crop top and miniskirt.

'You know what I think we need before we go out? An old school noughties and nineties sing-a-long. Who can sing an Ashanti song word for word? Do Lisa Left Eye's verse on "U Know What's Up" without blinking?' I slip off my heels and clamber up on a cream pouf in the middle of the living space. 'All of us, right? But who can sing the lyrics without tripping on a word? And I mean not even a stutter? Slightly more difficult, isn't it?'

Shanti raises a brow. 'Not really.'

I smile broadly. 'Oh, I am so happy you said that, friend, because I think this poses a challenge. I'mma pick a song that you *think* you know, and you gotta do it all, ad libs and everything. Or you have to pay penance with a shot. *Or* streaking in the garden. The very same one with a low fence that faces the beach.'

For the first time since speaking to her mother, Aminah grins, eyes lighting up. Nothing like a little bit of schadenfreude to cheer my sister up.

'Oh my gosh. I love that. I will not be partaking, but this is excellent entertainment. Like, I know I expressed my wish for no strippers – as well as penis straws, penis cakes and sashes that say "bride" – but I *do* appreciate a little bit of nudity on my bachelorette. Be the stripper you want to see in the world!'

'Nuh uh!' Laide cries, holding a bowl of crisps up in protest. 'Um, no fair. Both Aminah and Kiki can't be allowed to sit out.'

I laugh in what I think is a gracious manner, involving lightly touching my chest, like a princess being asked why she doesn't go to Costco. 'Oh, friend, me being involved in the game is unfair. I have an encyclopaedic knowledge of this era—'

Aminah sips her champagne and shoots me a delicate smile. 'I love you, sis, I do, but don't you think that maybe this is a wonderful opportunity to prove it?'

I raise a brow and smirk. 'You know what?' I hop off the pouf. 'Sure. In fact, I will *enjoy* putting you all to shame.'

*　　*　　*

'That bikini wax is *clean*, sis. Who is your lady?' Shanti asks, smiling entirely too widely. Truly, I can see all her professionally whitened teeth. She looks like a very gorgeous witch.

'Oh, we share the same one. I'll give you her number,' Aminah says as she opens the bi-folding doors that lead to the lawn. I managed six whole rounds. *Six*. Chioma streaked once, easily, strolling into the garden and doing an interpretive dance to the sounds of the ocean. She asked us to record her doing it. Laide had just done it anyway, without participating in the game. I think she forgot what we were supposed to be doing. She was pounding back the champagne. Shanti hadn't gone yet, which I found particularly annoying. I don't know how this is happening to me, but I am standing here, in a full face of make-up, completely stark naked as my friends chant, 'Don't be scared! Just go bare! Have some fun and show your bum! Come on, Kiki! Get fucking litty and show your titties!' and I'm both impressed and disturbed by how fast they were able to come up with a series of rhymes to encourage my nudity.

It was the 'I Wanna Be Down' remix that tripped me up. It had been going so well till I got halfway into Yo-Yo's verse, which is such a shame because Queen Latifah's verse is where I really shine. Still, I'm a good sport and Aminah seems light, free, and that's all I ever want her to be so I remove my hand from where it's covering the full extent of mine and Aminah's waxer's merciless and exact technique, and say, 'You know what? Sometimes it's good to show my imperfections. Gotta keep relatable somehow.' And I sashay onto the lawn, hips swaying as I walk around the pool, twirl, a hand on my hip, while the girls blow wolf whistles, screech and I, for the first time in a long time, feel weightless. Free of tension, stress, doubt. I let the sounds of the ocean, the breeze wash over me, like an elemental purification. This is me in my finest form.

Then I hear the back door of the neighbouring villa open, and out tumble male voices, falling over each other, and I hightail it back to the house, laughing till I'm breathless, making it inside – I think – just before they see me.

The girls struggle to breathe, and Aminah's eyes are watering with mirth. 'Oh-oh my God, Keeks, that was amazing! Incredible!'

I bow deeply. 'Thank you. I would like to thank my maternal grandmother for my fat ass, Don Julio for the confidence and my girls for the morale boost.' I pull on my underwear and slip back into my outfit. 'OK, now we have crossed several platonic boundaries,' I say in between pants, 'we have fifteen minutes before we have to call a cab so—' As I'm speaking, the walls of the villa thunder with the sound of Giggs, 'Talking The Hardest'. The girls and I look at each other, intrigued.

'Black Brits,' I say.

'Millennials,' Chioma adds.

'Men,' Laide finishes. 'I say we peek.'

'*Why?*' I turn to my girls in grave disappointment. 'I have to say, guys, this whole situation is not passing the Bechdel test.'

Chioma shrugs. 'I mean it's a bachelorette for a marriage between two cishet people. I just feel like this whole situation innately doesn't pass the Bechdel test so why not just lean into it. And by lean in I mean check if the guys next door are fine. Let's introduce ourselves.'

Shanti pumps a fist. 'Yes! I love it when Chi Chi Baby is dragged to my level!' I can't believe I've lost my usually dependable ally.

I turn to the main girl herself for salvation. 'OK, well, I don't think Aminah wants to hang out with a bunch of strange men—'

'Actually . . .' Aminah's voice surprises me, and I turn to her incredulously. 'Why not? I mean *hang out* is a stretch. We can just go look and see before going out. It'll be fun for the girls, and, also, it's a story.'

'A *story*,' I repeat, dumbfounded. This is maybe the third time in the trip I've been convinced that my best friend has been body swapped.

Aminah's shoulder twitches. 'Yeah. Like an adventure.' Before I have time to question what she means by that Laide squeals and jumps on her sister, hugging her tight. 'Ugh, I *knew* my fun genes would jump out in my baby sis at some point. I've waited my whole life for this! Shotgun the finest one!'

CHAPTER 17

Dummies Guide to Catching Clouds: Must Use Salt

'I just want it on record –' I hesitate in pressing the bell for the third time – 'that I think this is a terrible idea— wait, are they playing "Int'l Players Anthem"?'

'See! They have taste!' Shanti says as the ocean breeze picks up. 'Can you hurry? My buzz is wearing off! It's getting chilly.' She stamps on the ground theatrically and wraps arms round her torso, covered by tight slashes of fabric.

Aminah nudges me. 'Come on! It'll be fun, Keeks!'

Well, far be it from me to be the party pooper, even though we don't know exactly how many men are in this house and I have *grave* concerns about them knowing that there is a group of women in the house next to them.

'Aminah, do you still remember our moves from our Get 'Em Bodied MMA class?'

Aminah punches the air. 'Hit 'em in the neck with some *Diva* choreo!'

'Also,' Laide says, 'I have pepper spray in my clutch. It's legal here. I know a guy.'

I frown, confused by the implications of her statement. 'Well, which one is it? Is it legal or do you "know" a guy?'

'We won't need it,' Chioma chirps reassuringly. 'I did a blessing of protection for us on this trip.'

'Ugh, I thought I smelled sage coming from your room, Chioma,' Shanti says, whipping out a perfume tester from her silver clutch and spraying it on both her and Chi. 'Could you refrain? Gonna have my hair stinking of one of your spells.'

'Anyway,' I say to put an end to the squabbling, 'I know the number of the local police and I told my little sister to text me in thirty minutes. I told her if I don't respond she needs to call Taré, but now that I think about it maybe I shouldn't have given my little sister the number of a celebrity—'

'One of the things I love most about you is how chill you are,' Shanti offers wryly.

'OK, well, excuse me for not wanting to be true-crime podcast fodder.'

'Don't worry, we won't. You know they only make them about white women.'

'Thanks, Shanti, super comforting as always.' I roll my eyes, press the bell and the girls squeal like we're twelve. A strange thrill skips through me. I have to admit there's a sense of freedom that comes with throwing caution to the Capetonian winds. Also, technically, I'm single. I mean I *am* single. I'm single, and I look great, and I got the African sun-glow on me and on the other side of the door there may be a headache of men from which I can take my pick. Well, everyone but the hottest one that Laide has laid claim to. The promise tickles at me. For the first time in months, I am Malakai Korede-free, and stress free, with a sexy night of promise potentially about to unfurl before me. A tall figure approaches the hazy panel in the door, and my belly trills. Is it possible for a silhouette to be hot? The silhouette is hot. Aminah was right, this is *exciting*. I could be Stella, about to get her groove back. The door swings open, and the Hot Silhouette becomes flesh . . . and taut muscle and a beautiful face that becomes slack in shock at the sight of me. *No.*

'You know what's mad?' Malakai says when he recovers, with a sloping smile. 'I swore I recognised you.'

'You *saw* me?'

'Well. Not your face.'

'Come on, Scotch,' Malakai whispers to me as he joins me behind the counter in the open-plan kitchen of the boys' villa as I pour myself a tequila lemonade. 'Lighten up.'

'I'm light. I'm a fucking featherweight even though my carefully configured schedule has been drowned out by Moët, Casamigos and the inherent horniness of our friends,' I say as I pour liquor into a tumbler, watching both the bridal party and the groom's party enjoy an impromptu karaoke session, each with a beverage in hand. Aminah and Kofi, so sickeningly in love, were surprised but delighted to see each other and assumed that Malakai and I had planned it this way, so we were beholden to pretend it was a stroke of genius, an ode to love and friendship, and not the fact that Taré owns two neighbouring properties in Cape Town and a heart so big that all the generosity doesn't seem to leave much room for logic. She offered the house next to us to the groom's party, supposedly not thinking anything of it, and not mentioning that *I* had staked a claim first. Malakai and I, still on stilted speaking terms, and overwhelmed with *Phoenix* work, hadn't communicated where we were planning our respective pre-wedding parties, leading to this: my worst nightmare.

We were supposed to leave for the beach club where the festival is happening an hour ago, but after the initial shock, the boys invited us to join them for pre-drinks and pre-drinks became drinks and drinks became karaoke and karaoke is soon going to morph into an orgy if the way Laide is looking Kofi's cousin in the eye as she sings along to 'Goodies' – whilst mimicking Ciara's exact choreography – is anything to go by.

Malakai releases a low chuckle, brushing behind me to go to the fridge for a bottle of mixer. I ignore the frisson that fizzes through my form as he moved, his chest against my back. 'Kiki, it's a South African house festival. It's only 11 p.m. We're good. And, anyways, you were definitely in free-spirit mode earlier.' He leans against the counter next to me as I mix my drink. 'Is that you, yeah? *Streaking?* Can't lie, I'm impressed.'

403

I sidle a look at him, tilt my head to the side. 'Why, you think you're the only one who can get me naked? Conceited.'

'I meant in public.' His eyes darken, and because I know the kaleidoscope of his orbs, I see the grit of delightful dirt glitter like gold in them. 'I know what you're capable of in private.' He brings a beer to his lips, and looks at me from above the rim, lids falling heavy like black-out blinds, trying to conceal the glare of his thoughts. My mum's favourite movie of all time is *Sound of Music*. We watch it at every Christmas without fail. Now, a refrain whirls in my mind. *How do you solve a problem like Malakai? How do you catch a cloud and pin it down?* Because there are several facts that, together, form a conundrum:

Fact 1: Malakai is attracted to me.

Fact 2: Malakai is so drastically hot and cold that right-wing nutters might deny he exists.

Fact 3: Neither of us have actually confronted our break-up fully.

Bonus fact: he looks vexingly sexy tonight.

He's wearing an ecru Cuban-collared shirt with navy bògòlan-fini stitching on it, paired with black jeans that fit him so right I'm jealous of them. His gold chain glints on his neck, lazy, assured of its place, nestled amongst a slight smattering of chest hair. I want to lie where it lies. He smells good too, his oaky amber scent wafting towards me as he brings the bottle down next to where I'm making my drink.

'But anyway.' A milder mischief twinkles in his eye. 'What were you even doing knocking on the door of a villa of strange men?'

I shrug, stir my drink with the straw in my cup, sip. 'Thought we'd introduce ourselves. Be neighbourly.'

'Neighbourly,' Malakai repeats with dry scepticism.

'You know. Borrow a cup of sugar. Lend a cup of sugar.' I cast an eye out to the party unfolding before us. Aminah has clambered on Kofi's back like a marmoset to a branch, and they are now singing 'My Boo', booming like they have a Vegas residency. They're suitably distracted so I venture recklessly, irresponsibly, 'Be the cup of sugar.'

A cloud floats over Malakai's face. 'Are you joking, Kiki?' The atmosphere between us gets confusingly chillier. We're not on good terms, but, still, I thought we had a tacit agreement to not make things weird for our best friends' respective pre-wedding parties.

I angle a brow. 'What does it matter if I am or not?'

'You can do whatever you want. I just didn't have you pegged as a cheater.'

'Wait, *what*? What are you on about?'

Malakai pauses, his eyes flicking across my face and lighting a streak of fire through my body. It's hurt and want all bound up in one, and I know the look way too well. It's etched into the back of my mind so clearly that I know all its contours.

'Kiki, I saw you. At Sákárà. With your ex. If I can even still call him that. Telling each other you loved each other. You're really gonna lie to my face?' His words are low, coming out like blunt bullets before they can backfire.

Jagged jigsaw pieces cascade in my mind, slotting into place.

Was this why he was being so colossally strange at the shoot? And why he was so stilted over text that night? I throw a casual glance to our friends. They're egging Aminah on, and I join them with a well-timed, 'You better sing it, Meenz!' I look back up at Malakai, who's blinking bewilderment at me. 'Malakai, Bakari and I were saying goodbye to each other. We're over. Like, for good. And we do love each other. In a way. Just not in the way that a relationship needs in order to function.'

Malakai looks like a thunderbolt struck him. 'Are you serious?'

'Why would I lie about that? And if you actually bothered to –' I lower my voice, hoping that our friends think this increasingly heated discussion is because we're getting intense over which one of us will give a speech first at the wedding – '*talk* to me, you might know that.'

Malakai stares at me in confusion. 'Kiki, ever since we slept together, you basically told me to leave you alone. I was respecting your wishes.'

Chioma, doing an extended bit, is singing 'Call Tyrone' by Erykah Badu, which the crowd – namely Shanti – adores, loudly, and it provides the perfect cover for our conversation and my incredulous, 'Are you *joking*, Kai? Why wouldn't I want to get out of there when you basically said I was a *welcome bang* for you in London? You know how people go to Hawaii and get a lei when they arrive at their resorts? You basically called me a lay lei!'

Malakai looks like he's about to speak, face indignant, before he catches himself, picks up a jumbo pack of tortilla chips and pours it on the floor.

I frown at him. 'What are you doing? Are you throwing a *tantrum?*'

Malakai squints his eyes at me. 'No, Kiki. I'm providing us with an alibi,' he says quietly, before projecting loudly, rigidly, 'Ah, shit. Dropped the crisps. Kiki, can you help me pick them up? They're everywhere. I can't find the broom.'

I have to hand it to him, it's kind of genius. I'm impressed. We both dip to the floor, behind the cabinets, as I proceed to not hand it to him. 'Porno acting.'

'They're too drunk to notice. Which is a shame, because it's Emmy-worthy, actually. Anyway, Kiki, you hopped off me after we had sex like you were ashamed. Like I was the biggest regret of your life. Or a sentient vibrator.'

My heart staggers as I replay the events of that night from his perspective. The way he looked at me, just after we'd had sex, the way his tenderness threatened to break me open.

'I was scared,' I whisper, voicing a truth I've barely been able to think.

Malakai's eyes glint, and cross my face, my lips, my nose, like he's given himself permission, and he says, 'Well, what do you think I was, Scotch? I was terrified. This shit is terrifying.'

'It wasn't supposed to feel like that. Like, it wasn't supposed to feel so . . .'

'Right.'

'Good. *So* good.'

'Best.' Malakai's eyes hold my breath ransom.

'Intense.'

407

'Us.'

I can feel the wet building in my eyes, because, yes, it's us – that's the issue. *Us* will always feel right and good and intensely best, and what if we're just rain in a desert? Real, but fleeting, transient and yearned for?

I shake my head, my voice a ragged whisper: 'What do we do with that? I don't know what we do with that, Kai.'

'Hey, guys.' Laide's voice interrupts Shanti's ear-splitting rendition of 'Love' by Keisha Cole. Malakai and I glance at each other, before we both pop up like meerkats to see Laide standing on a chair and waving her phone in the air. 'So my DJ friend is on in, like, thirty minutes and I promised him I'd be around for his set. Can we go now? Kiki and Malakai, can you guys call cabs? Honestly, you guys are running a pretty loose ship. Fix up.'

'I'm ready! Piano, piano!' Aminah screeches from where she is on Kofi's back.

'Piano, pia!' the group calls in reply. Mine and Malakai's chant lags a bit, due to the fact that we're looking at each other, eyes bold and bright, new light and ancient mingling, forming something mystic, curious.

This is what we do with the beat. Possess it, flirt with it, bow to it, make love to it, throw it out and catch it, tease, toss, play, lose ourselves in it, find ourselves in it, see God, fight the devil, let it teach us. It's like a cloud formed of vibe vapour. It's like some of it has raised to form a cloth around Table Mountain, like she wants to groove too as she looks on against a tapestry of stars as my friends and I dance, in the middle of others dancing with their friends, limbs both loose and controlled, body abandoned to the custody of the music. Aminah's silk press is curled at her edges, hair encouraged to tap into its roots, be free in sync with her, as she moves, smile wide, eyes wild.

She looks to me, throws her arms round me, screams, 'I fucking love you,' and she turns round and kisses Kofi and says, 'Will you marry me?'

He says, 'Only if you marry me first,' and then they begin slow-dancing to a syncopated beat, carving their own world, their own rhythm. Laide is on stage, of course, with her DJ beau, at one point grabbing a mic and saying, 'Shoutout to Aminah's Angels! My baby girl's getting married, everyone scream CONGRATULATIONS!' to her sister's current delight and future mortification. Shanti, Chi and I form a little circle, shades on, and have all the spirits of girl groups past possess us, falling into sync, head flicks symmetrical, hip juts precise, attitude sharp. And then our queen Aminah arrives, I shout, 'MinahMoney with the vibes right now!' and she slips into our middle as we continue to hail our bride, wooing and commanding her to get it, because we've arrived at the Afrobeat section, and this hits on the intricacy of our language. We are organised and wise, but not over-wise, not arrogant, always deferring to the rhythm, but holding our own, carving our pockets. The boys are here, elsewhere, maybe getting us drinks, maybe not, but their problem if they're definitely not. It's winter here now, but it's not cold. Chi Chi is in her lilac bralet and black cargo bants, Shanti in her lilac body-con mini with sneakers, me in my white mini babydoll skirt and lilac tee; we are balmy, comfy in our sweet heat. The circle loosens as the boys call us back to our table with shots. One Boy hands me mine, says the word 'mango', his eyes locking with me before we back them and the world stops. The others leave, and I say I want to rest my feet, and he says he needs a beat. Our friends ask us if we're sure and we assure them that we are, which is ironic, because the only thing I'm sure of right now is how unsure we are. Our friends throw themselves back to the throng, at the mercy of the rhythm.

Malakai's eyes are hazy, and mine are too, hazy with the night, with exhaustion of what this is, hazy with that mystic light. We say nothing. His tongue darts out to his lips, and I track it like a hunting, hungry thing. I look back into the crowd, and I'm sure they can't see us, so I take the salt-shaker from the table, sprinkle some between my thumb and forefinger. I step closer to Malakai and he watches me like he's a hunter being hunted, his eyes avaricious and aware, panther eyes, like gold panned from the richest soil. I want to be planted. I want to bloom. I swipe my thumb across his bottom lip, leaving a trail of salt. He watches me, eyes heavy. I lift on tiptoe in my canvas sneakers, press myself against the length of his body, swipe my tongue across his mouth and then suck and then savour. He never needed any salt to taste good. I feel him begin to mould into hot rock against me. I pick up an extra shot from the table, and pour it down my throat. With the way Malakai's staring at me, it might as well be water, because it's nothing on the wave from his gaze. Sharp, strong, it could kickstart ovulation.

'Cheers,' I say.

Malakai's mouth lopes and then splits, like the ribbon for an opening ceremony. 'It's like that, yeah?'

Let the games begin.

Our table is VIP so it's semi-private, hidden behind trees, and branches form a curtain, so the night only slips in shy whispers, the music present, but not obtrusive. Malakai backs his own tequila shot before he picks up a lime slice. He steps closer to me, curving his hand round the back of my neck, warm and smooth.

Looking down at me, gaze calm, steady, he says, 'Open your mouth for me, Scotch.'

An incessant, persistent pulse pushes an immediate rush between my legs, and my lips part because I want them to. Malakai drains the lime slice into my mouth and tosses it, before he captures my chin. His eyes flicker a question, and I answer by grabbing his T-shirt. He kisses me filthily, tongue licking me in firm strokes and pulling tides from my pulsing hunger.

'What do you want from me, Scotch? Because if you want me to tell you how badly I still want to fuck you –' his hand slips underneath my skirt and he runs his finger across the dampening material pressing against it – 'I can do that. I can tell you how much I've thought about tasting you.' He cradles the back of my head, his words landing in my mouth, hot and slick and decadent as he kneads into my need. 'How I can't get the sound of you coming in my hand that night out of my head.' His voice is a burr, shaking feelings and facts and mixing them up, making them interchange-able as he increases the pressure of his touch, loosening a moan from me. 'How I missed that sound. The feel of you gripping me. How there's nothing in this world that feels as amazing as being inside you.' His lips gently bump mine and it feels like a flame. 'How it feels like that's where I'm supposed to be. How making you feel good makes me feel holy, ordained. I can do that for you, Scotch. And it would be easy.' Malakai releases me, and cool air rushes against me mercilessly. The smouldering want is still in his gaze, but it recedes, making way for a satiny steel. 'Because it's all true, Kiki. And it's only true for you, but I don't want to, because that's not all I want to be to you.' He's stepped back from me now, raising his arm to run a hand across the back of his head. I blink at him, bewildered.

'Kai . . . that's not . . . that's not who you are to me. Why would you think—'

'Scotch, that night at the pool, you said that I was only capable of being casual with you. You said that's what I do—' I pause as I spot something on his inner bicep that I've never seen before. It has to be new: a tattoo. Numbers. A date. A date that I know. It's in the recesses of my mind, but I know I know it. I still remember my high school best friend's house phone number, so I know that I'm right in remembering this. Malakai drops his arm as he follows the direction of my gaze, but I move closer to him. I round my palm against the hefty breadth of his arm and stroke my thumb across the dark imprint on his skin. This was the date of the recce. The recce where he snapped at me, shut me out, where he had a panic attack, where he seemed angry at the world. It also was the date of his dad's birthday. My hand flies to my mouth, my heart pumping rapidly.

'Oh my God. Oh my God, Kai. I am so sorry – I should have—'

Malakai shakes his head, and I can see the battle begin within him again, emotions unsettled, rubbing his tattoo as if he's erasing the fact that I saw it. 'Don't, Kiki. It's not a big deal.'

'It is, actually. It is. And I'm sorry. I should have known.' I pick up his hand, and his gaze glazes over. I pull him towards me, wrap his arms round me as I wind mine round his back. For a beat, his arms hang loose as if resisting submission to a nameless enemy. Then they tighten, tighten so hard it's as if he's using me for gravity. His hands press firmly into my skin, as if he's been looking for somewhere to lean for some time, as if he's exhausted. He buries his head in my neck and I smooth my hand across his back.

'Let's sit,' I say.

Malakai releases me, his eyes cloudy, jaw pulled taut. 'The others will be wondering where we are.'

'So let them wonder. I don't give a fuck. Let's sit down, Malakai. Talk to me.'

Malakai maintains my stare for a beat, before deciding obedience is best. He settles down on the wicker lounge chair, and he leans forward, elbows on his knees, staring at the slithers of night through the branches. He slowly worries at the knuckles of his left hand with the thumb of his right. 'It was his birthday the day I first met Taré. I just wanted to forget. It was a cumulation of things. Losing you. Losing him. Being angry at myself because leaving you was voluntary. Knowing I had to didn't make it easier. With my dad, it's got easier every year in the same way it's got harder. I learn to manage my emotions better, but it's harder because it's, like . . . it's weird. The longer it is the more it's, like, cemented into fact. Life. That he's not here. And every time I'm reminded it knocks the wind out of me.' He glances sideways at me, as if he's not sure if he can trust himself to show too much. 'His birthday is a massive reminder. This year would have been his sixtieth.'

He's speaking in sharp, stark sentences, stripped of as much emotion as he can, as if he's avoiding words so heavy that they may break him. 'And, Scotch, I'm mad. So, so angry that he left. That he left just as we were getting good. He was trying. Nothing could ever erase how badly he fucked up with us, but he was putting in the work with mum. She forgave him, and wanted me to, so I tried. They were figuring it out, planning to move to Lagos together. He was putting in effort with Muyiwa, taking an interest in me. He told me he was *proud* of me, Scotch. Proud of what I was creating for myself.' He laughs and rubs his chin. 'He was even proud of me for being with you. Called you my "Giant Tiny Warrior". Big mouth, small frame. Said you were smarter than me, and that he was shook of you, that you were good for me. Said to make sure I don't make the same mistakes he did; to not let you go, not break your heart.' His voice cracks and slices into me, just as pieces come together, building a picture I never imagined I would see. 'And finally,' Malakai's eyes blaze with anguished fury, 'he decides to be dad, be a better husband, be a better man, and then he just fucking

414

leaves, Scotch. It's messed up. It's typical. Cliché. How is that fair? How is it fair that I get him just to lose him again?'

I curve my arm round him and rock him against me, kissing his head, his neck, his back. 'It's not.'

My voice is thick, but I try to keep the tears out, because they are his, but I miss Mr Korede too. He and I had built up a rapport in the couple of years before he passed. I went from being the mouthy girl who told him off in his son's uni room for being a shitty father, to his sparring and debate partner at family gatherings, where he'd be affectionately lamenting, 'OK, so what is Kikiola going to bully me about today? Why my goal to own a private jet is "problematic"?'

He'd tried. He'd put in the work for redemption. I'd welcomed it if only for Malakai's sake.

Malakai looks at me, his lip tucked into his teeth as his knees jounce. 'I uh, started going to that therapist you sent me. Thank you. For ignoring me and not leaving that alone. He's cool. It's tough as fuck though . . . he's so inner.' He breaks off in a ragged laugh, 'but I think it's helping. It's loosening some stuff for me.' A jolt of surprise blossoms into a ferocious warmth, 'I'm glad, Kai. It takes a lot to go there. I'm proud of you.' His smile is faint, and it disappears as he clears his throat, and rubs his jaw. 'I uh, wasn't late to the engagement party because my flight was delayed. I had a panic attack before I left for the airport and missed my flight.' My heart immediately twists. 'I think the idea of coming back . . . it put me into the same headspace I was in just before I left. Kiki, I didn't let you in because I wanted to protect you from this. From me. You were so good to me after my dad died. You deserved more than a mess. I didn't ever want you to see me like this.'

It's a relief to know that he was purposely shutting me out, but it's also infuriating, and I battle with my rage.

'Malakai, who do you think I am? *Look* at me.' I straighten, and so does he. I grab his chin. 'I wanted *all* of your mess. What about me, *us*, told you that I didn't want to carry it with you?' Something hot and molten pumps through me furiously. 'Malakai, you broke up with *me*. You remember that? And I know I said some mad things. You did too, but it was *you* that ended our relationship—'

'Kiki, you didn't trust me. We weren't gonna survive.'

'And how the hell do you know that?' My voice cracks. 'You never *tried*, Malakai. You never even looked back. You were waiting for me to give you permission to leave and am I an idiot to try and hold a man who don't want to stay? And all of this now . . . how am I supposed to believe that you want more when you were able to let go so easily? How do I know this isn't just nostalgia? Maybe you just want something familiar, because it's comforting. I just want you to be honest with yourself, Kai. Did you ever really want to be with me for real? Because you said it yourself, you're not *built* for a long-term relationship. So what does that make me, then? A glitch? A blip in your life? A gap-year relationship? And what does that make *this* here, this thing between us right now?' I gesture to the tiny space between us, 'How can I trust it? Look, if you wanted to stay you could have. Don't give me bullshit about protecting me. This was about you. Which is fine, but please don't act like breaking my heart was an act of benevolence. I will never accept that.'

Malakai pauses, eyes glistening before he speaks, voice raspy. 'Fine, Kiki. And I will never accept that you couldn't have trusted me more. That you can't trust me more. '

'So maybe we just leave this where we left it in the first place, then.'

Malakai nods tersely. 'Right. A mistake.'

Shanti bustles into our section, sunglasses askew, and a random spray of glitter on her right cheek. 'Yo! Mum and Dad! The crew are waiting by the gates. Villa afterparty neowwwwwwwww!'

Exactly what I need after a meticulous emotional evisceration.

CHAPTER 18

Dancing in the Moonlight

I'm in a bed that isn't my own. At 4 a.m. in the boys' villa, in the midst of pizza and a dancehall and bashment session as DJ'd by Shanti, someone (Laide) yelled, 'Pool party!' We ended up dripping, laughing, splashing, tossing each other in the water, under the moon, as speakers proclaimed that we were so special, so special, so special. Even Aminah seemed to be brighter, lighter. Her previous doubts – wherever they had come from – had vanished.

'I'm sorry about this.' We were floating next to each other in a pool, after a very vigorous race between her and Shanti (I'm pretty sure Shanti had let Aminah win – she used to run in school). 'I know it was meant to be a girl's trip—'

Aminah laughed, her ponytail piled on top of her head in a bun. Further proof of her carefree state is further negligence of her silk press. 'Are you joking? Babes, we're in the boujiest place with our best friends,' she said, looking out at the squawking and the splashing of both parties. 'This is special to me. How often are we all together like this these days? The Blackwell crew, my sister, Kofi's guys. The love here . . .' Her eyes were sparkling with joy. 'This is perfect. The wedding itself is going to be so hectic and I don't know when the next time is that this can happen. Everything's changing so fast, you know? It's good to have moments like this. And also this is a result of your new job! I'm so proud of you, Keeks. You're progressing, evolving – Shit, *Shanti*! I'm going to have your ass for that!' she shouted as our friend splashed us, saying, 'Oh my God, guys, get a room.'

Aminah floundered after her, while my mind replayed Aminah's declaration. *Evolving.* I wondered if there's any definition of emotional evolution that involves a tense situationship with the man who broke your heart. I don't think I ever spoke about that on the podcast. The party raged on while Malakai and I raged on inside, remaining on opposite sides of a pool, a room, a conversation until Kofi threw Aminah over his shoulder and announced the end of the gathering. It wasn't till I'd finished collecting the girls' discarded bags and shoes from the boys' villa to take over to our own that I'd realised that I was locked out, and everyone was either knocked out, having sex, or with a dead battery. I called every single one of the girls and pleaded in the group chat, but everyone appeared to be preoccupied and unable to save me from the now custom humiliation of crying in front of my ex. I whispered a string of swearwords that magicked the word 'Scotch?' behind me, like some kind of curse.

I was forced to slowly turn round. 'So it seems –' I cleared my throat – 'that my friends have locked me out of the villa because

419

they're too busy sleeping or having sex, but it's fine. I think we left a downstairs window open. I can shimmy through. I've always wanted to do that. I was a good kid and never got to sneak out of the house, so.'

The corner of Malakai's mouth twitched slightly at this, which was quite irritating because I was being serious. 'Nerd. Well, to avoid injury,' he said, 'I just wanna put it out there that we have a spare room. One of the guys couldn't make it in the end.'

'That's OK. I'll, uh, throw rocks at Chioma's window.'

'Kiki.'

Why?

'Fine, but only if you promise not to say anything to me on the way there. And I mean not a word. I don't want to talk about . . . us any more.'

'Gladly.'

In silence, he walked me to the spare bedroom next door to his, in a villa that's almost identical to ours, escorting me gallantly like a knight to a lady. The corridor was dark and the only light within was coming from the large windows casting columns of moon on the terracotta tile. When we got to the door, he held a hand up, signalling for me to wait, before holding up a single finger – one minute. In a quarter of that time, he returned with a large clean black T-shirt for me to wear to bed. Malakai can't help it. He has to frustrate all decisions to be angry at him.

'Thank you.'

Malakai didn't say anything. He just inclined his head and turned to return to his room.

This should have been fine. It is fine. Except I can't sleep. Every stem of argument Malakai and I have ever had is whirring in my head alongside every single vignette of Malakai and I laughing together, having sex, crying together, till they all tangle. I can't see where the good times end and the 'hard times' start any more because they all feed into each other. They're all us. *Us.* Us, living life, going *through* life together. I've never fought with anyone like I have with Malakai, because I've never felt like this about anyone else. My heart stutters a new knowledge; I'm not fighting with him. I'm fighting this living thing between us and it is futile.

I don't know how to reconcile that with my fear, the stinging, sore spots that are still hurting. The problem is he's my favourite kind of trouble and I've never known how to resist. I've said so much, but still so much of our conversation is unfinished – we are unfinished – and I need to stop running from it, stop letting the Unsaids fester and become dank in our minds because I'm scared of what will come when the Unsaid is no longer Unsaid, when they are left to grow outside the confines of our complications and cowardice.

How will I know if they'll blossom or gnarl if I don't let them out? So I get up, feet landing in a light slap on the cool tile, make my way to the door, barely giving myself time to think and frankly I am quite over thinking, chewing my thoughts till they become distorted, distended versions of what they're supposed to be. I open my door to step out just as Malakai has opened his door to step out, shirtless, in boxers, momentarily disoriented and deliciously disorienting and perennially glorious, and we both look at each other in the corridor, moonlight shining between us, a column between our feet, and isn't the moon a reflection of the sun anyway? So we meet in the middle, stand in it.

'Scotch.' It's a low, burning burr. 'I need you to know that you could never be a mistake, a glitch, or a blip. You're the only thing that makes sense to me. You're everything. Every fucking thing to me, and leaving you broke something inside me, but you have to understand that I thought I was already broken. I felt like I didn't have anything to give you. The thing is, Keeks, you see me. You always have. It's always made me feel safe, but I've always been shook of it, if I'm honest. Which I think I haven't been, not enough, not with you.' He steps closer to me. 'You're right – I did leave. I ran away, but it wasn't from you. God, Scotch,' he shakes his head, releases a huff of surrender, 'you're the only thing on earth I want to run to. I can't run from you – you're part of me. The best part of me. The only person I'm sure I'll find in the dark. And I did. In my darkest moments, I still saw you. Still knew I was capable of feeling something because of you. You're the only person I've ever chosen, but it never felt like a choice, it felt like instinct. Loving you was like muscle memory from a time before . . . shit, I even knew I existed.' He pauses, fortifying himself, 'But back then . . . when everything went down, I was running from myself, Scotch. I'm not proud of it, but I didn't want to look at my pain. I was scared of it. It felt weak to me. I was scared to feel weak. And I knew you would give me a safe place to feel. I didn't want to feel. I felt like feeling would like . . . incapacitate me. And it's impossible to be numb with you. All my senses, all my cells, are wired to feel you. Like they're at . . . optimum capacity around you. So I hid from you.'

Malakai's eyes meet mine, overfull, heavy with a reflection of the sun, of our sun, the one I thought had died with us. 'And I didn't tell you about the situation with Jade because I was so used to hiding. I should have told you and I'm sorry. No excuses. And I know I didn't give you a reason to trust me. I should have fought for you, but the truth was I didn't want to fight for you and let you down. Scotch, I really did think I was doing right by you by letting you go. I couldn't think straight. My mind didn't feel right. I felt heavy. And I even told myself that ultimately you were relieved. When Aminah let slip – at the shoot – how cut up about it you were, it fucked me up. Really, really bad, Kiki. I never wanted to hurt you. I'm so fucking sorry. It would have destroyed me if I'd thought I was. I told myself that I was ripping a plaster off for you. I thought you deserved a version of me that was fixed. I thought I could bury myself and emerge like a new version of myself, but I didn't realise that I was isolating you. And then when I thought a new version would never come, I left. Told myself fucked up lies about how you never really wanted this, that only your ego was bruised.' He swallows, 'I was a coward, Keeks. I didn't want to believe that I'd broken your heart. Didn't want to believe I was capable of that. Look, I love my dad, but you were right. I was making the same mistakes he did. He shut himself out. When he finally stopped, there was already . . .' Malakai's voice falters, pain lacing through, '. . . so much time wasted. I don't want to do that. Scotch, I will never forgive myself for making you feel lonely within us. This –' he steps closer to me, points to the space between us – 'here, is the one place you should never feel lonely. And I'm so ashamed of it. Because the truth is there were three things that got me through the darkest months. It was the thought of you, my mum and Muyiwa. And I never properly thanked you. You were there for me even when I couldn't be there for myself. You were brave when I couldn't be. You were brave enough for the both of us.'

Malakai pauses, takes a breath that I forgot to take.

It rocks me, loosens something in me that causes tears to stream. When I speak, my words are so soft they feel like they will fall apart once they touch the *us* bound up in energy between us, hot, taut.

'Malakai, I never wanted anything more from you than *you*. I need you to know that you were always more than enough. Kai, you're the most. You're *most* to me. And you are strong. You were there for your mum and brother whilst dealing with your own pain. Feeling that pain doesn't make you weak, Kai. It's real. And one of the best things about you is how much you feel. That's your strength. Don't run from it. If you can't feel the bad, then you can't feel the good. Everything you are is most and enough and *right* and you make me feel most and enough and right. And, yeah, it sucks that you locked me out, but I never told you that. I probably made the issue worse for myself by not telling you that on time. And I should have trusted you enough to know that if I told you that you would have listened. I'm sorry I didn't. Because you've never once stopped having my back. I get it now. Even when we

broke up, I . . . I realise that in your grief-haze you thought you
were having my back.'

'But it came out so fucked, Scotch. I just . . . I didn't know what
to do . . . how to tell you . . . I could barely keep myself together—'

'We both messed up at some point, Kai. Neither of us trusted
each other enough. I'm not saying I would have done it perfectly,
but I think I could have tried to leave some grace, some space for
that for what was going on in your head. You must have been so
lonely. I locked you out in a way too. And if I had let you in maybe
you would have let me in. I was just so scared. You had so much
on and I didn't want to add to it—' I stop and catch myself. I'm
terrified, again, of being turned inside out, flesh hitting the air,
heart exposed to the atmosphere.

'Scotch,' Malakai says as he brushes his thumb across my lips
and sends a jolt through my entire body, 'I never want you to feel
like that again. Who you are is an abundance, not a burden.' His
gaze blazes into me. 'You're *my* abundance.'

It breaks something open inside of me, lets all the light in. I
bite my lip to control my emotions. 'I want all of you always, Kai.
Give me all of it always.'

The look Malakai directs my way sears through the fear and
heats all the coldest corners in me. Now that I feel us coming
together again, I see that these bit parts, broken pieces of what
we were, were making me famished. All they did was remind me
of how hungry I am for more of him, for more of us. I pull back
and stare at him. Truth pumps through my body, making my ears
pound, the warmth that barely bubbled under the heavy surface

of fear, of hurt, bursts through, blooming. It affirms what I've been trying to run away from: there was never any falling out of this. I never stopped loving Malakai, being *in* love with Malakai, there was just a repression, a pretension that I had what it took to stop loving a man that looked at me like I was the universe poured into form, who reminded me to feel the power I have at my fingertips. Who was smart, and sensitive, and did things like secretly help me save the thing that was most important to me in the world. Even if it were possible to stop loving him, I wouldn't want to.

This feeling of being known so deeply that every part of you seems to sink deeper into its place around that person, the feeling of stubborn ease that overrides animosity, of feeling capable, powerful, *enjoyed*, of enjoying *them*, that feeling is euphoric. Fuck physics – we're transcendental. Our sun is generated from our heat and can't burn out, can't be destroyed. It just rests, even in the face of the terror that you might lose it all again, waiting to rise again, to create something anew, shining light on the debris and revealing precious stone, metals, minerals, things to rebuild. We could do this together, I think, maybe we can work this ruin, because how disastrous could our ruin really be when the nature of what we had was wondrous?

'Everything that's me is yours, Scotch.'

My hands have found their way to his chest and then his own hands spread on my waist, spanning everything it takes to hold me, to grip me tight. Our lips bump and the kiss isn't so much an explosion as a delicious sweet-slow burn that's even better, exquisite, heavy and confident in knowledge, our tongues taking time to lave and relish. I want more, and Kai will give me more, I believe that.

He pulls away only to ask a question: 'What else did you want when you came to knock on my door, Kiki?' His eyes are quartz, and the question hooks into my stomach. My body answers for me, because I lift a leg and wrap it round his waist and Malakai picks it up, and then the other, as my mouth replies as well, in tautological emphasis: 'You, you, you,' in between deep, ravenous kisses that make my eyes blur. All I can think is *Kai, Kai, Kai*, the sound of my heartbeat thrumming between my legs, which have tightened around him, hips bucking against his growing need, hard and hot and pulsing, and he moans into my mouth. He pushes his door open and carries me inside, wisely shutting the door, because I have a lot to say, to sigh, to scream. He lays me in the bed like I'm delicate, long-sought-after treasure. Slowly, he lifts my shirt up and discards it on the floor, before tugging my underwear down my legs, looking at my bared self like I am the first sunrise.

'Look at you,' he says, his voice a low hum of wonder. 'Thank God for you,' and it makes me feel like a soulful note, suspended in the air, the kind that makes you want to close your eyes and sit in the sweet of your spirit, the kind that raises goosebumps on the skin.

I have goosebumps all over mine as he runs his hands over my body lightly, skimming just under my breasts, dancing and brushing and taking their time, chasing his touches with feathery kisses. His mouth is on my stomach and it lingers, in tropical suction, nipping, like he's ensuring he's relished every part of me, and I wonder how an innocuous area can feel so charged? The kiss on my belly fans a flame, and I moan, and the kiss rises to my breasts where he rolls my nipples in his mouth, in maddening circles that spiral down to my pussy. At my sigh, he lightly grazes it with his teeth, then sucking, flicking, teasing me with his tongue, before moving to do the same on the other bud. Might Kai be the death of me? No, he's part of the life of me.

Everything feels too good to bear, and I need to get my revenge, so I say, 'Get over here,' and then he's licking at my neck as I slip my hand into his boxers and curve it around the impressive heft of him, enjoying the power of him getting improbably firmer in my hand, before I stroke the velvety heat slowly at first, the way I remember he likes, and Malakai swears, asks me what I'm trying to do to him, and I reply, 'Exactly what you do to me.'

My kiss is messy, swiping at his lip before biting, opposing the deliberate touch, the contrast amping up the static between us. I crave him. I push his boxers down and increase the pace of my strokes, stoking my own thirst as Malakai bucks his hard length into my hand to meet my touch and begs me, calls me a 'very –' a bite on the base of my throat – 'wicked woman'.

I nip his shoulder back, show my fangs as I whisper, 'Kai . . . just so you know, I'm good. Still got my IUD and got tested before I came out here. Just to be sure.'

Malakai's eyes flash. 'Me too. I'm all clear. Got tested before I came to London. I haven't been with anyone but you, since that night.'

This sends an entirely ego-driven thrill through me and I try and fail to curb a cocky smile. 'You knew no one would compare, huh?'

'Something like that,' Malakai's eyes dance across my face like he's cataloguing every cell and his thumb sweeps my lips before tugging my mouth open. 'Exactly like that,' he says before he kisses me again, licking into my mouth ferociously, which has the immediate effect of pushing my legs further apart, grinding shamelessly against his arousal as my own tongue meets his hunger.

It's filthy and exquisite, and I pant, 'I want to feel you.'

His eyes brand me, blue-flame bright. 'I told you, Scotch. It's yours.'

And my craving reaches a critical point, but so does my need to drive him crazy. I suckle at his neck as I lightly drag my wetness against him, and Malakai groans and raises a hand to press against my neck firmly but gently. 'Be easy.'

'Where's the fun in that?'

Malakai tilts his head to the side in response, the slant of his mouth wicked, before he nestles himself against me and rubs his smooth tip on my sleek opening. I gasp and writhe at the searing sensation, the curve of his lips a dangerous place for me to slip and slide.

'If you wanna play dirty, we can,' he says. 'Just don't forget that I'm better at this game than you. Behave yourself.' It's my favourite thing to be bested at, but what's there to gain with early admission? Better to wait, gather more knowledge, joy, graduate cum laude. His hand rises to lazily tug a nipple.

I say, stubbornly, biting in my mew, 'You can't make me do shit.'

Malakai's eyes glint, jagged sugar glass, and his tongue dives into my mouth, fucking it greedily, deliciously, mercilessly, whilst he slides his hand down between my legs and runs two fingers down my slit, coating it with all the desire he conjured, and hauls out a moan into his mouth that he swallows.

He pulls away, slightly, his words brushing my bruised mouth. 'You sure? Because I can think of at least one thing I can make you do, Scotch.' His voice is a hoarse grit of want. He keeps my misty gaze captive as his tongue darts out to taste me on the pads of his fingers. I've never seen a prettier pink than that of his tongue dipped in me. The illicit sight drives me singularly wild, almost makes my eyes blur.

'*Nasty.*' My gasp is rough with awe-drenched lust, and I kiss him, tasting my sweetness on him. 'Please keep being nasty.'

'I solemnly swear,' Malakai says, pushing himself gently between my legs and making my hips jerk in greed, 'to continue being thoroughly disgusting with you.'

'Good to know. Start with getting inside me. Now.'

'Always so demanding.' His voice is strained, gruff, as he positions the thick, smooth domed head snugly against me and I draw a tight breath, feeling myself soaking him, desire pooling between us. 'Don't you have manners?'

I lift my hips to graze him politely in response, welcome him in, and Malakai's eyes roll back, a man on the brink.

I smirk. '*Please.*'

'Nah.' His whisper is rough, broken, barely holding it together.

'Been so long you've forgotten the rules. What's my name, Scotch? Say my name.'

He pushes into me a little further, and I'm desperate; the pleading would have happened anyway, gladly, hungrily. 'Please, Kai. Please, I need you inside me. Now, *now*, baby—' I mean every word, and now all play has fled his face, and intense primal need replaces it; it's the first time I've called him 'baby' since he's come back, and all restraint that Malakai has disintegrates in an instant. He slowly plunges into me, working through the taut, silken entry, the stretch piercing and perfect, till I'm delectably full. I gasp sharply at the total pleasure, our groans harmonising as we find our rhythm.

'You're so beautiful, Scotch.' The tender sincerity sets in my bones, sets my bones, and I remember his *'You're my abundance.'*

This feels so right that I can't remember how I survived without precisely this, with him. My legs are wanton and widen as far as possible to welcome him in; it feels like nothing that I've felt before with him, a cumulation of everything we've been, everything we are and everything we could be, and we rock with the waves of the pleasure of the past, the possibility of the present, the promise of the future.

'Is this what you wanted, Scotch?' Malakai pushes my bent knees back and asks in between exquisitely paced strokes that have me seeing the cosmos behind my eyelids, and I say yes, sigh yes, scream yes, it's a rain dance that has made me slick enough for him to go deeper and I beg for him to give me more, more, more, and he does, and it feels good-good-good. I feel as if my body can't contain all the good, but somehow every time I feel like I've reached the capacity for pleasure, I survive and Malakai bends to kiss me, slow and sweet.

He bends and whispers, cradling my face, 'You look so fucking sexy taking me, my love. You feel so good. Hold on for me, baby. We're not done yet,' and it turns me inside out, my body just sensation.

I tell Kai to flip me because I want to harness all of this; I don't want to lose it so soon. He does and then I'm on top and riding our rhythm, holding it. His hands slide up to my breasts and squeeze in frustration, in barely constrained pleasure, bringing me closer to the brink, before they lower to grip my hips firmly as his own hips jerk to buttress my movements, intensifying the delectable depth as obscene commands scrape out of his mouth, rough and sexy and driving me deranged, pushing my legs further apart, making me move wilder.

'Just like that, Scotch. Take what's yours. It's all you. Everything is you.'

At the sound of his voice, gruff with raw need, the pleasure compounds, builds, rises, I can't stop, don't want to stop. He says my name like an incantation, 'scotchscotchscotch', then, simply, 'It's only you,' like a benediction, and though I try not to cling to it – his tongue is lust-loose – it changes the tenor of this. He makes the ocean bloom in me, we shame the stars and make the sky turn pink and purple and red; we're the sun, bright enough to make fire sweat – this is a story of a new creation.

Kai sits up and his arms brace me to his chest, our skin sticking to each other as he thrusts into me in sharp, decisive, delicious bursts that have me biting his shoulder, clawing at his back as I squeeze around him, making him growl, 'All you,' and he gives me all his feeling, generous with it, fierce with it, and I give it back and then he gives it back, and forth and circular and there is an abundance of it – *love* – and even when some of it spills out of me through a loud cry, through his groan and gasp, and inside me, there's still an overflow left between us, ready for the giving, ready for the taking.

CHAPTER 19

Walk of Shame

When I wake up the next morning, my body tangled in white sheets and feel Malakai's arm scoop me to his naked body, back against the wide, hot expanse of his chest, I think it's a dream. The room is too warm, too bright from the morning sun, and I don't even recognise where I am; everything is a sweet pastel yellow, wardrobe an Atlantic azure, and curtains ecru linen. It's all too *heavenly*. I turn round and see his softened sleeping face, criminally adorable, and then I remember all of last night, how it felt like home.

This isn't a fantasy. This is the man I can't seem to stop loving sleeping next to me. His eyes flick open and his smile is sure – not a hint of regret or hesitation in his face – looking like he won something.

'Good mornin', Scotch.' It rolls out slow like hot caramel.

My smile spills out sloppily, broadly; it can't help itself. I'm so *happy* (it turns out that's what this feeling is), with a bright blossom inside me, a buoyancy, a sensation of supposed-to-be.

'Good morning, Kai.'

'Did you have a good night?'

'Nothing much to report. Though I had the maddest dream.'

'Same. I made you come three times.'

'Two and a half.'

Malakai bites at my arm and I squeal, laughing before throwing my leg over his hip. He immediately wraps a hand round my thigh, then cups a butt cheek and kisses me, slow and deep and dizzying, biting my bottom lip, and causing me to grind against his erection, like a feral thing. I'm wide awake. He pulls away with an inky, heavy-lidded gaze. 'OK. My bad. I can take constructive criticism. Let me fix that.'

And he does, slipping out of the king-sized bed and dragging me by my legs to its edge. He's standing, naked, new sunlight skimming his skin and he's so glorious looking at me like I'm glorious, in a way that gets my breath tangled, my thoughts twisted. Still cradling my gaze, he falls to his knees in front of me, as if in prayer, seeking absolution. Mine fall apart, make space for him, as if giving grace. 'Never stopped thinking about this pussy. Let me taste you, Scotch.' My teeth dig hard into my bottom lip and as I tilt my hips towards his mouth greedily, he places wide hands on my knees and pushes them further apart as he nestles between them. I feel myself get wetter in anticipation, as Malakai says, his nose grazing against the lips, his breath warm and teasing, 'Mine.' He lightly traces a feather-soft finger between, gently skimming my clit, and my breath catches, the sight of his tight coils on his head between my legs, the lithe muscles on his shoulders and back, going blurry. Then, his tongue is on me, in me, dragging and diving, starved and sucking like I'm the answer to a drought, the belief to all doubt. I'm cursing and then I'm blessing and then my hand reaches down to splay across his head, and Kai grabs me firmly by the hips to haul me further into his mouth, as if there is anywhere else I would rather be. He groans inside me, in delight, in *relief*, and he calls a wave forth, so when his finger joins his tongue and teeth, dipping, dripping, curving inside me, conjuring a storm, I hear how wet I am. I'm trembling, calling his name, climbing towards ecstasy and when his hand slides up to press at the base of my belly, as his tongue flicks at the most sensitive spot, I buck, writhe, coming undone as he feasts, and I say jaggedly, 'Yes, just, like, that,' just like this, forever like this, please, please, please, in hope, in prayer, in belief.

By the time I come to, I feel boundless, despite the fact that all my bones feel like jelly. I'm lying across his chest and I smile against his lips. 'I've missed you.'

Kai raises a brow, 'Missed me or missed that?'

'Do I have to choose?'

Malakai smirks in self-satisfaction. 'No. You can have both for as long as you want, whenever you want.' He briefly lifts my wrist to kiss the image of the sunrise inked on my forearm. 'I've missed you too. Missed you so bad I couldn't think straight.'

I grin and trail my hand across his chest. 'Hey. Should we put on a sex playlist? Maybe play a bit of Taré? I've heard her new stuff is great.'

Malakai groans and splays a hand across his face. 'I take it back. Haven't missed you at all. It's too soon to joke about that.'

I peel his hand back. 'No. We gotta joke about it to get through how fucked up your meta sex was. I mean you had sex with someone whose voice we listened to while having sex. That's mad, you know.'

'OK, we never *listened* to her purposely while having sex. She was, like, sandwiched in between Usher, Marsha Ambrosius and Jodeci while they were on in the background.'

'So did you ever put my podcast on in the background with her? Just to even the score?' Malakai doesn't laugh. His brows furrow as he stiffens. In a different way to how he woke up. 'Kai, I was kidding—'

'Nah, it's not that. Because the answer to that is yes, of course we did. We actually listened to your podcast episode about her music to make it extra meta –' he ignores my little kick to his shin – 'but, no, I was thinking – do you think Taré booked us in these villas on purpose? To fuck with us?'

My mouth drops open. '*Shit*. Shit! Of *course* she did.'

'I mean, it's well played. Diabolical, but well played.'

'This might be the weirdest job I've ever had in my life. And I once had a bad date show up to one of my Heartbeat live shows. This is a guy who told me he didn't "believe in fiction". Anyway, he put his hand up. Asked me how I could ever find love if I was so stush.' I laugh. 'You know my audience, right? Dude was basically *carried* out. Booed right the fuck out.'

Malakai chuckles. It's low and rolling and eases into the new, unfurling space between us. Shaking his head, he says, 'Man. I think if I had asked a question when I came to one of them, you might have found a way to kill me dead.'

Confusion stiffens my smile. 'What? Don't you mean *if* you came?'

At my questioning look, Malakai runs a hand over the back of his head, apparently immediately regretting the confession. 'I've been trying to find a smooth way to drop that, but I guess I fucked up. Uh, a year ago? I came over to visit my mum and brother for a week. I was on Instagram and saw people posting about the event. I was so proud. Like, you *did* it, Scotch. You carved out something from your passion. Anyway, I wasn't gonna go, but somehow I bought a ticket just in case. Somehow, I ended up in the area. Walked in and there was your face on this big screen.'

He smiles at the memory, his eyes gleaming with genuine pride that shortens my breath. 'Surreal. Coolest thing I've ever seen. A room full of people just for you. You deserve a room full of people listening to you. One of the best parts was sitting in the audience, waiting, hearing people talk about you.' He laughs and shakes his head. 'Man, Keeks, did you know that you have *stans*? I wanted to go, "I know her. She's mine." Felt like an intrusive thought, but then you got up on stage, Scotch, and you spoke and you looked so . . . alive. Happy in your purpose. And again it happened. I wanted to go, "I know her. She's mine." And then at the end there was a Q&A, and someone asked a question. "What inspired the podcast?" And you said it was always in front of your face – doing that sort of work. It's just a reiteration of what you did in uni. And then you said . . .'

I remember what I'd said. I'd said, 'But really . . . I got my heart broken and I realised that I could just sit there and feel like the world was ending or I could get up and rebuild. So I did that. Found the beauty in other things I loved and used that.'

And I remember being on that stage, and the lights blinding me and thinking I saw a glimpse of him at the back, and then thinking that I was delusional and, besides, somebody would have told me if he was in the country and, besides, why would he be there? Why would he want to be?

'You . . . were in London? I had no idea.'

Malakai shrugs. 'I kept it on the low. I didn't want to see many people. Went to my mum's and went to Kofi's—'

I freeze. Kofi and Aminah were living together by then.

'So . . . you saw Aminah?'

Malakai shakes his head. 'Briefly. As she was leaving the flat. She told me not to bother you if I didn't plan on staying, if I wasn't going to be serious. Said she didn't want me to "disturb your peace". I mean I fully planned on airing her, but I thought about what she was saying and realised she was half right. The thing is, I was so serious, the most serious, but then I thought about how I would be disturbing your peace, and for what? To say I made a mistake and then go back to America? Stress this whole life you'd built for yourself on a whim? It felt selfish. It killed me, but I left it.'

I try to keep a hold of the conflicting emotions careening through my mind: Malakai being in the same city as me and

Aminah knowing; Malakai coming to see me and Aminah telling him not to see me. Why would she do that?

Malakai misinterprets the look on my face, panic skittering across his own. 'Maybe I shouldn't have gone to see you. I thought it would be OK if you didn't see me. Like, maybe I wasn't encroaching on your boundaries—'

I shake my head. 'It's not that. I just wonder how different things might have been if I'd have seen you. Where we could have been by now.'

Malakai cradles me to him, and kisses my forehead. 'It don't matter. We're here and we're here.'

I smile against his chest, kissing it. 'We're here and we're here and I'm glad, but I have to go now before everyone wakes up.'

Malakai tilts his head to the side. 'Why?'

'Aminah doesn't know. And I want to be able to tell her properly. Plus, I don't want to make this trip about us.'

Malakai looks at me oddly. 'But what does it matter if people know about this? This isn't some dumb holiday fling like what Laide has going on with Kofi's first cousin. Which is really fucking weird by the way.'

'*So* weird, innit? Their kids would be almost double cousins. Some weird *Game of Thrones* shit, but, no, I know this is a big deal.' There's a slight tightness in my stomach. It isn't from us but from something external. I want to protect us for as long as possible, build our foundation so we don't crumble again. It's probably why I haven't said 'I love you' yet. Wait – why hasn't *he* said 'I love you' yet?

'This is huge. Heavy. Can we take it slow? I'm in this,' I say. 'Please know I am so in this. I'm in this *so* hard.'

Malakai releases a slow grin. 'So am I.'

I snort and I lift a fist for Malakai to spud me. 'Congrats, but seriously. I just . . . I want to do it right this time. We were together since uni before, and we went straight into something intense, so quickly. Maybe that's why we got overwhelmed. We never really dated as adults. I just want to give us our best shot.'

The shadow leaves his face, and he pushes his lips against my shoulder, pushes a smile out. 'Of course. Whatever you want. On your time.'

I kiss him, drawing him in deep, and it feels like home; it feels like being known.

'Thanks, Kai. I'll see you later.'

I peek my head out of the door, swivelling left and right like a bad movie spy, causing Malakai to push out a wry, 'OK, James Banjo.'

I hiss a hush at him as I step out, careful that my rubber slippers don't make a noise on the tile. I mentally rehearse my disgusted, '*Well, if you didn't lock me out, I wouldn't have had to stay in the spare room of the boys' house!*' trying to sift through which inflections would be the most convincing. It's when I think I've got away with it that Aminah comes out of Kofi's room, practically skipping, hair tied up in a similar messy bun to mine, wearing a large T-shirt and basketball shorts. I almost smash right into her. Her smile is wide and satisfied until she clocks me. Then the smile dissolves and her mouth drops open in shock.

I swallow, unsure of what to say. Am I supposed to apologise?

For being a grown woman who had mind-blowing sex with someone I'm attracted to? I approach her slowly. 'Um. Yeah. Malakai and I slept together last night, and I'm really happy about it so don't freak out because—'

Aminah baulks at this, shock filtering through her features. 'Why would I freak out? I mean I'm happy if you're happy, I guess. Even though you did say you weren't going to, but whatever. You're grown.'

I'm not sure I like her tone, but I skip past it, push out a breezy smile, like this is normal, like this is like when were in uni and we used to bump into each other in Kofi and Malakai's flat, like we were in some awkward polycule.

'I am. And I don't have any regrets. Don't worry. Malakai and I won't let anything between us mess up your day—'

Aminah blinks several times. 'What is *that* supposed to mean? Like I'm some freaky tyrant who wants to control your sex life and not a friend who cares that you do not get your heart broken again.' She folds her arms across her chest, her passive pretence steadily melting with annoyance. 'I mean I'm just confused. Like, what's different this time? Have you guys talked it out?' Her reaction dampens the remaining fizz in my blood from the multiple orgasms.

'Aminah, it's like seven in the morning. Can we talk about this later, please?'

Aminah's brows pop up. 'Since when do we not talk about a thing like this immediately? I'm sorry, you just slept with *Malakai Korede*. Why are you so chill about it?'

I roll my tongue in my mouth, because I see that we're really about to do this now. 'I dunno. Maybe because my best friend acted like any stress that ensued from me sleeping with him would ruin her wedding—'

'Oh, so now it's my fault for not wanting you to get hurt? Well, ring the alarm – shitty friend alert! No, really, Kiki. That's my bad.'

Our voices echo along the hallway and both Kofi and Malakai appear from their rooms, and make the grave mistake of attempting to interject.

'Kofi, stay out of this—'

I whip around to Malakai, who is still shirtless, his cute morning face creased in confusion. 'This is none of your business.'

'I just heard my name, though.'

'*So?*' Mine and Aminah's simultaneous screech echoes along the hall, and both men do the needful and shut the fuck up.

'Oh, please, Aminah.' I turn my attention back to her. 'This was never about me. This is about you not having anything in your head, but *wedding*, *wedding*, *wedding*. And I am so happy for you babe, I really am, but you have left *no* space for me to talk about anything. Which is why I never told you about the first time I slept with Malakai—'

Aminah holds still and my heart seizes. 'What? When was the first time?'

My throat suddenly feels extremely tight. I hear Kofi say, 'Oh shit,' and, even though it's a deeply unhelpful addition, I have to say I echo his sentiment. I wasn't supposed to tell her like this, but it came on a train of pent-up frustration and now it's too late to pull it back in.

I inhale deeply. 'The night of the engagement party.'

Aminah's mouth drops open, and she's silent for a few seconds, which is actually innately disturbing considering the fact that Aminah always has something to say.

'Oh,' is all she says. Aminah pauses and starts blinking rapidly. Shit. This is a surefire sign that she's about to blow. She steps back, her hands on her hips. '*Oh*. Um. Does anyone else know?'

'Aminah, what does it matter—'

'It matters to me, Kiki. So I can know what an idiot I've been.'

I swallow. 'You haven't been an idiot, Aminah, but Shanti guessed.'

Aminah releases a heavy exhale through her mouth and she laughs mirthlessly. '*Oh*. Cool. So you just lied to me. Lied to my face like I'm a prick. I mean it's your business, but *really*?'

Aminah very, very rarely swears, not in English anyway. Daily curses are in Yoruba; special-edition furious curses are in English. Hurt fractures through her angry face, and I realise how badly I've messed up, because now I know it's never about the thing itself, just the act of lying. I walk up to her, frantic now, unease crawling up my body. Aminah and I don't fight, not like this.

'I didn't intend to, Meenz. I didn't know what it was then and part of me thought it was going to be a one-off and then . . . and then we started working together and . . . it got complicated. I didn't want to pull you into my confusion—'

Aminah shakes her head, eyes sharp and shiny, and I can't remember the last time I saw her this hurt. It scares me.

'You made it a big deal by keeping it a secret, and now look – we're talking about you and Malakai on my *bachelorette*. This is so selfish of you—'

This digs at me, because this is *rich*, but I bite my tongue because now is not the time and she is right, this is her bachelorette party, and I will not ruin this for her, and the deposit on wine tasting is non-refundable.

'OK. I understand you're angry, and I'm really sorry I kept it from you. Can we talk about this later? We have wine tasting booked for this afternoon, and I also got all these spa treatments you can do to prep and recover from last ni—'

Aminah rolls her eyes. 'No, we can't, Kiki. You running away from things is the reason why we're here. You ran away from telling me, and you ran away from your feelings for Malakai, which is why you ran away from telling me – and is it a friends-with-benefits situation? Because I really don't think you can handle that—'

'OK, Aminah,' I snap, reeling from the offence, 'you know what, it's actually none of your business, and maybe I didn't tell you because I thought you would tell me I was making a mistake and I didn't want to hear that. And, truly, who are you to tell me about keeping secrets when you didn't even tell me when Malakai came to London? You didn't even tell me when he was coming to London *this* time! Not in time! You wonder why I didn't tell you when you didn't exactly make me feel like I had a safe space to—'

Aminah blinks, startled, thrown off her high horse for a second before she recovers. 'Well, maybe I was right! Look at how you're acting. Running around in secret with him like you're a *child* instead of facing up to your shit—'

Hurt tears spring to my eyes. 'How am I *acting*, Aminah? If we want to talk about behaviour, can we talk about how I have been trying to balance my job, and being your slave-for-hire for *months and* being around my ex, and you never *once* asked me how I was doing with it? Malakai was the love of my *life*, Aminah! The truth is you did not want to know, so don't come at me for not telling you. Oh, and thanks again for humiliating me in front of my boss, super classy. Shit, I feel like I don't know who you are any more.'

Aminah's eyes are glistening, and guilt floods through me, immediate regret weighing me down and I want to eat every single word I said, both the truth and defensive jabs.

'Aminah, I didn't mean it. I'm sor—'

Aminah shakes her head. 'No, you're right, actually. Thank you for that.' She plasters a smile on her face, and straightens, scary and plastic, a pageant queen. 'Totally right. Let's go back to the villa. I need to nap properly and get ready for wine tasting. We need it right?'

I'm seriously freaked out now, and panic stabs at me. 'Aminah, wait, let's talk about—'

'Nothing else to talk about,' she snaps, and I become cold. 'We are good. Let's go back to the house. I can only wear menswear outside of the confines of a bedroom for fifteen minutes before my sense of self starts to depreciate.'

The boys interject again – we both say we're fine, that they should go back to their rooms. The truth is we both want to be alone, away from each other. We are so not fine. We walk back to the house in the first bout of silence Aminah and I have had between us in our entire lives, and I attempt to stave off the guilt, and anger and the sick feeling that threatens to swallow me whole.

'Aminah, please. Can you open up? I'm about to call the taxi to get to the vineyard. Also you haven't eaten so I've made a sandwich for you to have on the way!' I knock on my best friend's door for the fifth time, getting increasingly frantic. I've called multiple times and it's gone to voicemail. She's been in her room since we got back to the villa, making a crack about how she didn't get any sleep last night, the same rigid smile on her face.

'Seriously, how bad was your fight? She hasn't answered any messages in the group chat since last night,' says Shanti as she approaches the bedroom, holding a bowl of yoghurt and fruit.

I swallow. 'It was bad. Really bad.'

'What was it about?' Chioma has shown up, rubbing lotion on her arms, somehow missing her many bangles. 'Also it's really not like her to not be out already—'

'A lot of things, but mainly about how I kept what had happened – well, what's *been* happening – between Malakai and I quiet.'

Chioma nods. 'Ah. Yeah, I was wondering why you didn't tell us about that, but wanted to respect your process.'

I stop banging on Aminah's door. 'What, seriously? You *knew*?'

Chioma looks at me like I am a baby bird with a broken wing.

'Sweet, Kiki. I knew the second Malakai stepped into London. Let's be serious. Now, have you tried opening the door?'

'I think she locked it from the inside—'

Chioma pushes past me and takes what looks like a razor blade out of the bra she's wearing underneath a crop top that says 'Eat Me, I'm Vegan' and fiddles with the lock till the door clicks open.

Shanti smiles, impressed, and holds up a hand that Chioma immediately high-fives. I open the door. Her bed is empty. I check the bathroom and there's nothing there but a whole Sephora worth of skincare products. I don't know if it's better or worse that her phone isn't here either.

'So she locked it from the outside,' I say, my heart rate increasingly rapidly. 'OK, OK.'

'I'm sure it's fine,' Shanti says, although I see her tamp down the alarm on her face for my benefit. 'She's so dickmatised by that fiancé of hers she probably went in for an afternoon quickie. Give him a call.'

'Right,' Chioma says, coming back from where she was on the balcony. 'She probably snuck out to the other villa. I remembered that Laide is out shopping at the mall, saying she'd meet us at the vineyard. I opened our Aminah's Angels group chat to check if Aminah went with her, to get some space maybe, but Laide has sent a picture of a scarf to the group chat and has asked Aminah if she should buy it for her since she noticed the "huge Kofi marking on your neck when you were coming in this morning". So I'm guessing that she hasn't.'

I nod. 'Right.' I attempt to calm my breathing. 'You're right. She's probably over there.'

Kofi picks up on the first ring, and when I ask, 'Hey, Aminah's with you, right?' he pauses.

'Kiki, I was just about to ask you that. All my texts are going undelivered . . .'

The panic in his voice has also settled into my stomach and I'm beginning to feel sick. So she's got her phone but it's *off*? Aminah's phone is never off. I try to keep it together for Kofi's sake, 'Uh, well, her door was locked from the outside, but I'm sure that there's a reasonable explana—'

'I'm coming over.'

There's an extensive team search of both villas by both the guys and the women before I start to hyperventilate. Kofi paces our living room, talking about the police, sweating, and Malakai attempts to calm him down, puts his hands on his shoulders.

'Bro, let's think first. What was your latest conversation about?'

Kofi shakes his head. 'I . . . I don't know.' He stops, and the look on his face makes me feel queasy – he's terrified, abject fear in his eyes, and it makes me want to cry. 'She – she said she loves me, but asked if I was marrying her because I felt like I *had* to, but it was early in the morning and I thought she was just playing and—' Kofi turns to me. 'Kiki, what do you think it is?'

My eyes begin to water. 'This is all my fault. It's our fight. I really shouldn't have said what I said.' I'm crying now, shaking, and Malakai leaves Kofi to put his arm round me.

'Kiki. I got you—'

449

I squeeze his hand briefly in appreciation but shake my head, approaching Kofi. 'I am so sorry, Kof—'

Understandable annoyance shadows Kofi's face and I see him battle it, swallow it when he registers what I presume is the acutely distraught look on my face. 'You and Aminah fight like sisters. She loves you, and the argument can't have been the thing to make her disappear like this. It has to be something else. Honestly, she's been acting a little . . . *carefree* lately. Yesterday I asked her which shirt to wear out tomorrow and she said it was "up to me".'

Shanti gasps from where she's sat on the burnt-orange sofa behind us, which really does nothing to alleviate the gravity of this situation, but I get it: this is cause for serious concern.

'Keeks, I'm scared she's having doubts—' Kofi breaks off and rubs his chin. 'That's not even it. I'm scared she's having doubts and that she's not telling me. I . . . I don't know what I'd do if . . .'

Kofi is breaking and I realise that I can't break too. Aminah is fine – she will be totally fine.

'There is no *if*, Kofi. She's fine. We will all figure it out together. What were our last –' I pause, amend – 'What were our latest conversations with Aminah?'

'Well,' Chioma says, from where she's sitting on the kitchen counter, 'yesterday when we were by the pool she said something super weird about how she wishes she could do what I did – you know, the Bali thing. And remember I was dating that couple out there? You think she wants to open up her relationship, Kof, and doesn't know how to tell you?'

Kofi stares at Chioma for a few seconds before shaking his

head. 'Nah. No, I don't. No offence, but she once said she found polyamory an "unnecessary energetic depletion".'

Chioma shrugs. 'OK, well, some would say that it's just having an abundance of love—'

'Chi Chi, I have to say,' Shanti says, inevitably about to say something that she absolutely does not have to say, 'I think all of this is actually evidence of your intimacy issues. I think you're an avoidant—'

'I think,' I say, cutting in before we veer too far from the subject at hand, 'Aminah was talking about travelling.'

'I checked for her passport. It's still in her room,' Shanti says, swerving back to topic, worry shadowing her face.

'Where could she even have gone? It's not like she knows this place,' Ty asks as he picks up a cupcake from the counter in the open-plan kitchen. 'Sorry, I eat when I'm stressed.'

I stare at the *fourth* (seriously fourth? A man can stop being a rugby player, but the rugby player never leaves him) cupcake Ty is chewing and something occurs to me. 'I think I know somewhere we can check. Kofi, let's go in your guys' rental car—'

'I'll drive,' Malakai offers, and I nod at him in gratitude.

'Shanti, Chioma, could you please stay here in case she comes back? Ty, tell the boys to keep watch in your villa.' The crew affirm and take their positions whilst Kofi, Malakai and I rush out to the car, and I try to slow the rapid beating of my heart. Aminah is OK. She has to be OK because she *can't* not be OK, and I shouldn't have shouted at her on her bachelorette and what kind of friend am I anyway?

Malakai squeezes my hand on the way to the car on the driveway, letting Kofi overtake us slightly, whispering, 'She'll be all right, Scotch. It's not your fault.' And I desperately try to believe that's true.

CHAPTER 20

Sisterhood and Closures

'She'll be fine, right? Kiki, she is fine,' Kofi says from the front seat, talking to himself as much as me.

I reach in front to squeeze his shoulder, trying to keep my own anxiety at bay. 'Come on. It's Aminah. Of course she will be. She loves herself too much to not be fine right now. Even if she's not fine she's fine, you know what I mean?'

Malakai nods, his eyes straight on the road. 'Exactly. She's one of the toughest people I know.'

'I just,' Kofi says, 'I love her so much. Like fuck all this marriage shit if she doesn't want to do it. I just want to live my life with her. Not waste any more time. I'm never not *me* around her – I just wish she could have talked to me—'

'Hey,' Malakai says, 'her not talking to you isn't about you, man, I promise. She's probably in her head about something and doesn't want you to stress. One thing I know for sure is that woman loves you. It isn't about how she feels about you. I can almost guarantee that.' He catches my eyes in the rear-view mirror for the briefest of moments before his gaze returns to the road. 'Sometimes it ain't about love – it's someone just trying to figure out their head.'

I nod. 'Right. We want to believe we can fix everything someone we love is going through, but sometimes it's . . . beyond us. And we have to give them the space to figure it out. And it can be really . . . really hard, but we kind of have to let go a little. You fall in love and you live your lives together and parts will merge and you're on a journey together, but, you know, we still have our own paths to figure out. That doesn't mean she'll leave—'

Kofi shakes his head, and he's barely holding it together when he speaks. 'Guys . . . I dunno what I would do without her. Like, I know they say you can have loads of people be your soulmates or whatever, and maybe that's true, but, the thing is, what's the point of that when you meet one person and you can't even imagine another person being right for you? You being right for another person? Like, I've known from the moment I met that girl. And I know I was supposed to date around and play the field, and look at me – it was def poss – and I get why that works for other people, but it ain't me. I've never seen the point of that shit. The soul-mate thing is almost irrelevant because the point is that Aminah is everything I could want. I just wanna be able to help her continue to do her. Whatever that takes. And she does the same for me. She makes me better at doing me.'

My heart cracks, breaks and soars and, not for the first time, I'm so happy that Aminah and Kofi found each other, that I can look to them and know for certain that world-shaping, galvanising love can exist for people our age, can survive.

'For what it's worth, Kof, she said the same thing to me about you,' I say, through a tight throat. Malakai lifts a hand off the steering wheel to hold Kofi's shoulder, and I look in the mirror to see that his eyes, trained on the road, are hard and shiny.

'Just here, on the left,' I say, pointing to a bakery as we pull up to the street I found when I googled. I look through the window of the front of the bakery, Lesedi's, my heart bundled up in my throat in fear, and I immediately see the side profile of a Black woman with a sleek top bun. She's wearing a white sun dress, sipping what looks like an iced coffee with a small plate containing a cupcake. She sits outside, on a little circular table on the pavement, under the veranda, shades on, looking like the cover of a travel guide.

'Oh thank God.' Kofi's voice is laden with a physical relief. 'Thank God.'

It floods through me too, and I almost cry from it. It's heady and I don't realise how severe my fear that I was wrong was until I realise that I'm not.

'Malakai and I will find somewhere to park and you go in,' I say.

Kofi shakes his head. 'You go first. I want to give her space. Maybe she can tell you what she can't tell me.'

'You sure?'

Kofi nods. 'Yeah, Keeks. You're the only other person who

knows her as well as I do. And if it's a me thing, I just want her to feel safe to open up.'

This makes me want to cry again. 'Of course.'

Aminah is sat mindlessly scrolling through The Outnet, her comfort site ('so many beautiful things at a discount!' – while Aminah loves luxury, she also loves a good bargain), when I walk in front of her. 'Hi. Is there space for an extremely apologetic best friend to sit down?'

Aminah lifts her chin and her sunglasses, placing them on her head. Her eyes are void of make-up, and it's obvious she's been crying. 'I'm surprised you can recognise me, considering I'm not the same person any more.'

Ah. There's my petty bestie. I sit down and reach out for her hand.

'Aminah, I'm so, so sorry. I shouldn't have said that—'

Aminah presses her lips together in an attempt to keep emotion in, pausing before speaking. 'No, you definitely should have. You were right. I haven't been myself. I haven't even felt like myself, recently.'

'Meenz . . . is that why you left without telling anyone? Ignoring our texts? We've been worried sick. Kofi is beside himself. He was about to call the police—'

'What? Why? I haven't got any texts! Also, I sent a message to the group chat before I left saying I just needed some space! I only left because I needed time to think and my mum was stressing me out about party favours . . .' She slides her phone from her rose-pink Gucci bag, and when she checks it her face collapses. 'Oh crap. I never sent it. Plus I muted my messages because I was trying to do this whole "disconnect from the world; be attuned with yourself" thing. Yet another example of me being a flop. Stressing my friends and my man out for no reason.'

I shake my head in alarm and squeeze her hand. Aminah never, ever speaks badly about herself. It scares me.

'Aminah, stop. What are you talking about? You're anything but a flop, and you know that. What's going on?'

Aminah presses her hands to her lips, and squeezes her eyes shut, trembling. I immediately move my chair so I'm next to her, holding her. 'Kiki . . . I am so, so sorry. About what I said. Not seeing what you must have been going through these past few months with the restaurant, and Malakai and Bakari and all of it, actually. To be honest, I'm just sorry for my behaviour generally the past six months. I've just been . . . This wedding has been so much pressure.'

'It's OK. I should have asked more questions – I saw something was off, but I was so wrapped up in my shit. I should have pushed—'

Aminah laughs humourlessly. 'One thing about me? I will pretend everything is fine so well. So well that even my *twin* –' she squeezes my hand back – 'who knows me better than anyone, can only get a little whiff. And even that's a lot considering how well I think I hide it. Thing is, Keeks, I'm good at project management. That's my thing. So I treated this wedding as a project I needed to manage. Even when I felt like the wedding wasn't mine any more, even when my mum and Kofi's mum were throwing all these . . . *expectations* on me, I just focused on everything being right. And I never thought about who it was right *for?* And I love them, I do, but it just felt like nothing belonged to me any more. And then I started thinking – how many things have I done in my life that I've done my own way? I mean I love my job, but even that – I'm still working for an agency because my parents said it was safer and they said I'm not ready for the risk of being a freelance consultant, when really – I feel like I am. Can you imagine? *Minah Management.* I got it registered and everything. And – Keeks, I think I was projecting all of that on you. Not telling you when Malakai was around, trying to protect you and manage the risk . . . First of all, it's your life and you're grown and you deserved to have known. And also, selfishly, at the back of my mind, I was thinking that if *I* wasn't ready for a risk, then surely you also weren't ready for a risk. It's stupid and I'm sorry and I swear I never thought about it that way at the time . . . I just thought I was protecting you.'

'You were, Minah. In your own, over-involved, boundary-less way. Let's be honest, around that time, I'd just got my life together. The podcast was doing well and I'd just started seeing Bakari and . . . seeing Malakai then might have derailed everything. I think I was supposed to be with Bakari to get to where I am now. I'm not saying I'm glad you kept it from me. I definitely would have wanted the choice. Because, sis, that was wild, even for you—'

'I *know.* I can't even blame it on bride brain. I'm sorry again—'

'I know you are. And I'm just saying that . . . I know it was out of love. Like everything you do. Look, I do think what we're having here is a regular quarter-life crisis, which is totally normal. Remember when Shanti switched from Gel X extensions with detailed nail art to plain red shellac because she thought she had to be a "serious woman"? Doing up "quiet luxury"?'

Aminah nods gravely. 'Serious quarter-life crisis.'

'Right. Anyway, my question to you is, do you still want to marry Kofi? If you don't, that's OK, but we will have to tell him.'

'That's the thing. That's the only thing I'm sure of in this whole wedding. I want to marry Kofi. I wanna be with him. He's the best thing in the world. I know I can be a lot to people, but Kofi never makes me feel that . . . the same way you never do. He makes me feel like I am just a lot of Enough. Like, so much of Enough. A sexy surplus! Doesn't matter how extra or dramatic I am. He makes me feel like I can do anything.'

She straightens suddenly, eyes frantic and wide. 'Oh God, he thought something must have happened to me. Is he OK?'

'He's fine. He was beside himself, but he's OK now that he knows you're OK. He's waiting down the road in the car with Malakai.'

A groan ekes out of her. 'Oh no. I've ruined everyone's trip—'

I smile and peel off the hand she's splayed over her face. 'Get over yourself. We're in Cape Town, bitch, and we still have two days left. We love you. I love you. And I'm so sorry I wasn't there for you—'

'I love you too, Keeks. So much. And I'm so sorry I didn't give you space to talk about Malakai. I never even stopped to think about how you're handling him being back properly. How's it going? And most importantly how was last night?' I can't help the idiotic smile that crops up on my face, the flutters in my belly. 'It was . . . incredible. Like the same as it was before, but somehow *better*.'

She smirks. 'Like absence makes the pussy grow fonder?'

'Something like that. Uh. Yeah. I think . . . I just wanna try not to get too deep too quickly, you know?'

Understanding warms my best friend's eyes. 'I know. You're strong and smart and capable and will make a decision that's true to your heart *and* smart. Whatever you do, I dey your back. And if you do wanna pursue things with Malakai, it's not you going *back*. I'm sorry I said that. It's part of your evolution. Both of yours. And, Kiki, Malakai has grown too. I'm sure he has. And let me tell you, my dear, he *never* left the deep with you. It's impossible to.'

The idea of it forms a lump in my throat. 'I'm super scared.'

Aminah laughs. 'Sis. So am I, but we gotta see the difference between self-preservation and cowardice. I think getting the good things in life are always a risk. There's more at stake, you know? But only you can decide if it's worth it. I think maybe you have to ask if your *whole* self feels safe with him. All your precious parts. And if you can trust him with them. If you're free within that space. Love is never not a risk. But if the answers to those questions is "yes" then, to quote something that someone moderately wise with a sexy bum once told me, "You have to try. You have to take that risk."'

'She sounds annoying as fuck.'

460

'Sometimes. But mostly she's the best.'

My gaze mists. 'One quarter-life crisis and you're a life coach?'

Aminah nodes sagely. 'Turns out my stressing was my blessing. My crisis was my catharsis.'

My heart overflows with pure, undistilled love for my fiercely protective, sensitive, strong best friend and I squeeze her hand. 'Thanks, Meenz. And *you* know that Kofi is worth it. And . . . he's walking towards us. Do you want to say what you said to me to him? Minah, he loves you so much. He only wants to be there for you, and you really don't have to carry all of this on your own. You don't have to act like you feel together when you don't. Let him help you.'

Aminah nods, her big doe eyes gleaming, and throws her arms around me. 'Thank you, sister. Also thank you for knowing where to find me.'

'It wasn't too hard. How are the cupcakes?'

'Honestly? Kind of dry. Can't lie. Maybe Lesedi should have stuck to her day job.'

Regardless of anything, it's comforting to know that I remain utterly obsessed with Aminah Bakare.

Aminah throws herself into Kofi's arms when he reaches the table, and I slip inside the café where Malakai joins me. We watch them as they talk intently outside, their hands gripping each other's for dear life.

'They're OK, right?' Malakai asks, sipping his coffee. 'Because I don't think I could handle it if Kofi and Aminah broke up. Aminah would give up all her visitation rights for me immediately.'

I cackle. 'Oh, come on. She may send you a "HBD" once a year.'

'She already did that for the entirety of the time you and I were together. No emojis or anything.'

I snort and Malakai tilts his head at me, his eyes glittering with something that makes hope sing in my veins. 'Last night was . . .'

'Amazing.'

He grins a slow, sexy smile. 'You were amazing. I was just doing what you inspire. And I don't want to put any pressure on us. I get that you're coming out of a . . . serious relationship.' I can tell that saying it is uncomfortable for him, but he reaches for my hand across the table, and when I place it in his palm he grips tight. 'But I want you to know when I said I wasn't built for something long-term, what I really meant was that I'm not built for something long-term with someone that ain't you, Scotch. So I'm ready to go at your pace. We can date again. Go with the flow. Whatever you want. All I know is that you're all I want, Kiki.'

I didn't think it was possible to feel this particular flavour of joy again. It's sweet and hot and I want to dive head first into it, which is the very thing that makes me hesitate. I can't play with this. I need to make sure I have what it takes to carry the new weight of an evolved relationship with Malakai. Man, being a responsible adult is so boring, but I don't know what baggage I'm carrying from my relationship with Bakari, the same way I didn't know the baggage I was carrying over from my relationship with Malakai to the one with Bakari. I owe this new iteration of us all of me.

I squeeze his hand in response. 'You know what I haven't done in ages?'

'It's only been, like, four hours, Kiki. Chill. I'm not a piece of meat.'

'Oh. My bad. You're right. I mean I was gonna say *kissed you in public*, but . . .'

Malakai grins and it's wide. His joy is a reflection of my own, I know. 'I'm sirloin. Ribeye. Wagyu. Suya. Saki. A whole fucking barbecue. Get over here, Kiki Banjo.'

I walk over to him so I can sit myself on his lap in the middle of a café, because this is the sort of thing I do when I'm with Kai. My arms wind around his neck, and he cradles my face delicately, smiling tenderly as he pulls my lips into his mouth, his tongue gentle, sweet, joint melting. Just as we tear apart from a dizzying kiss that is just shy of probably getting us thrown out, Kofi and Aminah come in, hand in hand, pulling up a chair to our table. I get extreme déjà vu – or is it nostalgia? – and the memory washes over me, warming me: all of us at a table at the campus coffee shop, or Sweetest Ting, eating plantain waffles and suya burgers and taking the piss out of each other and *happy*, no worries and pressures other than maybe an assignment and an ACS event and how we're going to spend more time with each other after spending all our time with each other.

Aminah grins brightly, and it's now that it's gone that I see the shadow that was cast over her before. Her spark is back and thriving, and I'm affirmed of this when she says, 'Aww. I've missed you guys being a threat to public decency!'

I baulk at this, because, really, the nerve. 'Need I remind you about the photobooth during Afro Winter Ball?' Aminah stares at me incredulously. 'Exactly. *Photobooth*. Privacy.'

'So I'm guessing you guys are good?' Malakai asks, expertly derailing our conversation, years of knowing my and Aminah's patter patterns paying off. Aminah and Kòfi smile at each other, their hands clasped.

'Yes,' Aminah says, 'we're really good. Talked everything through.'

Kofi continues: 'So it turns out that we're both feeling the pressure from the wedding.'

'Right. So it isn't that I don't want to get married. Other people's voices were the issue, but I think that now that we've recognised the issue it'll probably be a lot easier.'

I nod slowly. 'How?'

Aminah shrugs. 'The thing is the traditional wedding is most important to both of us, anyway, and it isn't that we don't want to share it with our family. It's just that we need to make our voices louder.'

I'm still not hearing any practical steps. 'Aminah, in a dream world, what would your ideal wedding be? I mean right now.'

'It used to be the huge fairytale wedding. The whole works. And I don't know . . . some of that is important to me, but also . . . something small could be cute too. A beautiful backdrop. My friends. Ew, who am I?! I sound like someone who gets married in a refashioned barn and serves champagne in mason jars. Next thing you know, I'm gonna say I want a bouquet of wildflowers. I'm just saying maybe I'm realising it doesn't have to be crazy elaborate to be special, just . . . *elegant*, intimate—'

My brain is whirring as a wild idea begins to fall into place. Malakai adjusts himself so he's able to look at my face and at the same time he and Aminah say, 'What's your plan?'

They both look at each other and Aminah smirks. 'I've kind of missed you, Newbie. Nice to have my junior sibling-spouse back.'

'Missed you too, Meenz. I am still older than you, though.'

'Not spiritually.'

'Fine. Does she still have that look on her face – the one that looks like That's So Raven having a premonition? I can't see properly from this angle.'

'Yup.' Kofi squints at me. 'Sometimes, it looks like she's holding in a fart.'

I narrow my eyes at him. 'I feel like it looks more like a genius having genius ideas. Which is what is happening right now. So, stay with me. Kofi and Aminah, you have all your best friends here – Kofi, your cousins are here and, Aminah, your sister's here. We're in a beautiful country . . .' Malakai squeezes my waist. 'And didn't you say you had that private sunset wine tasting at the Black-owned winery? I bet they do weddings all the time. There'll definitely be someone to officiate.'

Amazingly, Aminah doesn't immediately reject this idea. That's already a good sign.

'This sounds completely insane, but –' she looks at Kofi – 'is it?'

He kisses her shoulder. 'No. Not if you want to do it.' Kofi is so blissed out from Aminah being absolutely fine and obviously still besotted with him I think he would agree to get married in a

Slug & Lettuce in Monument at this point. Which is objectively hell on earth. 'We're going to need a registrar, though,' Kofi says, 'and getting one on short notice would be impossible—'

'Not impossible when you're connected to a global popstar. I once heard an unreleased Rihanna track when I was with her.'

Aminah gasps. 'Sorcery.'

I nod solemnly. 'So you see what we're dealing with. Look, this way you'll have something small and intimate just for you. And so when you get stressed about the wedding you'll be able to relax because you've already had something your way. We have this wedding, you cancel your white—'

It's at this moment that I think Aminah might pass out. I almost see the blood drain from her face. She's been doing pretty well so far, so I guess it's about time for a freakout. 'My mother might actually claim I'm trying to kill her—'

'Right, which is why we still go through with the traditional. Have a faith leader of your choice do a short blessing of the marriage there. You might lose a few deposits, but you'll get enough money back to maybe extend your honeymoon and do a little travelling. I'll help you call vendors as soon as we're back? Don't worry – it's the best of both worlds. Also, you can wear your white dress at the traditional. What's one more costume change? It'll be like a Beyoncé tour. Minah Money Moves on tour.'

Aminah stares at me as a smile begins to grow on her face, her eyes lighting up. 'Killa Keeks, this is why you are my maid of honour, wife, best friend and emergency contact. OK.' She claps her hands. '*OK*. Text the group chat. We need all hands on deck.

I packed four different white dresses for this trip, and all of them are beautiful, I gotta say. I love a theme. I just need non-ugly flowers – you think I can trust Laide for that?'

'I'll take Kofi shopping and tell the others what's happening,' Malakai offers, 'and I'll call the vineyard.'

'Whoa,' Kofi says, offended, 'Why do you need to take me shopping?'

'Because I've seen what you packed.'

'Coming from a man who leaves three buttons unbuttoned.'

'If you got it, flaunt it, man. You should join me. I'm proud of my tiddies.' I grin and reach over the table to hold Aminah's hands, ignoring the lovebirds. 'All right. Let's get you married.'

'I already am,' she says, 'to you, but I get your point.'

CHAPTER 21

Never Too Much

Aminah looks like the feeling you get when you first see a blossom on a tree after a frigid winter. She's radiant, the love and joy singing from her skin as she stands opposite Kofi, whose entire face is taken over by his smile; his eyes, concentrated bliss, directed at his bride, who reflects it all back to him.

Table Mountain presides over the vineyard majestically, and makes for a ridiculously stunning vista, the green sloping expanse of the vineyard unfurling beyond us like a carpet, the air sweet and soft and warm to the nose. The sky seems to have got the dress code too and winks lilac among the pink of the sunset. Aminah breathes the best sort of life to bridal clichés. She looks like a fairytale queen, ethereal, so stunning it makes my breath catch, and it isn't just her clothes, it's the look on her face — total contentment, surety in her choices, fealty to the sanctity of this moment. And she really does have the perfect dress: a cream strapless floral-embroidered floor-length tulle over a bandeau mini dress.

She's holding a tumble of lilies that her sister, overjoyed at the idea of a small rebellion against their parents, ran to get. Aminah looks both delicate and daring, like her, splendidly her. Kofi looks so handsome too, wearing an impressively fitted suit that Malakai managed to find at an outlet store. His dark skin gleams with a deep-seated triumph, all his white teeth on show in a confident joy boosted by the fact that his dreams have become material. He is currently breathing in his biggest wish and his wish has given life back to him.

Malakai and I barely got to talk to each other whilst we were running around prepping, doing our duties diligently, gladly, so it's the first time we've seen each other properly since the bakery, standing here opposite each other at our best friends' sides.

He catches my eye and my stomach somersaults. He mouths, 'You're beautiful,' and my joints feel incapacitated. My dress is a backless purple, orange and fuscia floral chiffon maxi that skims my curves. I'd wondered if it was a little casual, didn't rise to the occasion of my best friend's wedding, but Malakai's looking at me like I am all the gold in the world, and now I have to use all the love I have for Aminah and Kofi to keep myself upright.

I mouth back, 'You too,' because he does, in his simple white button-down shirt and navy trousers, the unbridled love for his friends glittering over his face.

The wedding party sits on white fold-out chairs behind us, all in their bachelor/bachelorette party best, which, it turns out, is very impressive. No one questioned the plan; it made sense, felt right. Taré informed us that she called M, who apparently had heard about the two rogue guests who had taken a dip in her pool and was so impressed by their 'audacity' that she pulled strings. Soon, the owner of the vineyard was delighted to extend our time there and expand our tasting feast to a full braai banquet.

Laide had got the famed global superstar DJ she was juggling with Kofi's cousin to come and preside at the reception. Shanti did Aminah's hair and make-up, and Chi, with limited resources from a florist and craft store, had transformed what had been a simple set-up into a mini-wonderland.

Aminah had gasped, her eyes shining, when she saw it. 'Oh my God, this is . . . this is perfect,' and Kofi had lifted her hand to his lips, because that is what she is to him – he didn't even have to say it – and it was just about enough to set me off, the first of a million times throughout today.

The ceremony is gorgeous, sun dousing the couple with blessings as they say the most precious words I've ever heard to each other. Kofi calls her 'evidence of the divine', Aminah calls him 'the only man who reached my preternaturally high standards'. She thanks him 'for being the softest part of me' and I think I might have let out an audible sob at this point. Chioma is swaying, as if literally entranced by the display of love, Malakai's eyes glisten and Shanti bites her lip, desperately attempting to keep her make-up intact. Tears stream down Ty's face and I really should take a picture to send to the legions of female fans he has online to show the capacity of the prototypical beefcake, breaking down

470

in emotion in witnessing the marriage of his friends. The gentle breeze blows reverently, in consecration of the moment, and it's clear we're in an enclave of unfiltered love of each other, of their love. This is real-life magic. And then they kiss and we're cheering and I'm crying again and Aminah comes and throws her arms round me in pure delight and says, 'Thank you. I love you. I'll never forget this,' and I say, 'I love you. Thank you for letting me be part of this. You deserve this,' and she says, 'So do you, friend.'

She winks and passes me her lilies.

Laide yells out, 'Hey! That's cheating!' and so I pass the bouquet back to Aminah, who in turn grudgingly tosses it, and Laide catches it and falls into Ty and Shanti in the process.

She smirks at them. 'I'm so sorry, sis. Today, he's mine.'

Ty turns to her and says, 'Oh?'

With a roll of her eyes, Shanti informs Laide that, 'This is the greed they warned us about in the Bible.'

Before the DJ arrives, I add to the music of our friendships' flow and put on my playlist and then we're floating to eighties soul, Luther Vandross flowing through the breeze, through laughter, through a-thousand-kisses, Kofi and Aminah's song, and they test the theory over and over again, insatiable with it.

I'm dancing, swaying, floating on joy, when there's a hand on my waist and Malakai pulling me to him. My body crashes and then melts into the contours of him, his heat finding nooks to nestle into in me.

I smile up at him, the beautiful man who is my favourite kind of

471

trouble. 'Hi. I want to tell you something. I'm tired of not telling you something.'

'OK, but me too. Can I go first? Because I'm trying this new thing of not brooding and just telling you exactly how I feel when I feel it.'

'Oh! Exciting. OK, show me, show me.'

Malakai holds my face with one hand and wraps the other round the curve of my hip. It fits there, I fit here. 'Here is the thing, Scotch. There was never any reason for me to come to London six months before my best friend's wedding. Let's be real.'

I grin as his thumb strokes my lip, and his eyes brand me with love, love, love, 'I did wonder what it was about cake-tasting—'

He surreptitiously pats my right butt cheek. 'The same way there's no reason for me to go back to America later this year either. The fact of the matter is, Scotch, I just want to exist near you. The fact that you let me in is a blessed bonus. I just want to be next to you. Talk to you. Touch you. Every time I see you, I'm thinking, *God, how? How are you possible?* I'm thinking about how I can't believe I had you, that I let you go. I think about how I've never had a friend like you and never will. Because, really, you're my best friend. Don't tell Kofi. I'm thinking I want to build with you. I want to sweat for this, work on this. I'm thinking that taking it slow is the last thing I want to do with you. Baby, I'll do it if you want me to, but I want to dive in all the way with you. I don't know how to scale back my knowledge of you. Mitigate my love for you. Because that's the other thing: I'm so in love with you, Kiki. Never fell out of it. Never tried, because getting to love you is what makes my life extraordinary, and maybe that's selfish, but so be it. I'm never going to stop loving you. So. Yeah. You just have to deal with that. What were you going to say?'

My smile is so broad my bottom lashes could brush the top of my cheeks, and my heart is so full I can taste it; *joy*. 'Oh, I was just going to say kind of exactly that, and also that I was full of shit earlier today. I was scared, but I'm not any more. I mean, the very fact that this exists makes me feel brave . . . I trust this. I trust us. I was going to say fuck the flow. Fuck going slow. That rhymed. I didn't even realise that. See, my love for you is like poetry? I love you. Deeply, for so many reasons, but with no reason.'

Malakai grins so wide, and my soul sings so loud. 'But with rhyme.'

'I'm so talented. And baby, I know what you did for me. With Sákárà. And I'm so grateful—'

Kai shakes his head in dismissal. 'Scotch, I wouldn't be where I am in my career without those years with you beside me. I know that for a fact. You don't have to thank me. It's you. It was already going to happen. I didn't do—'

'Maybe it was already going to happen, but you helped nudge it along. You did something. A really wonderful something, and it means so much to me.'

Kai's eyes glisten. 'I would do anything for you, Scotch. I got you.'

'I know. And I got you. Also, when we were having sex earlier today, you said something. Something about saying "when". I put it down to, like, being in the throes of passion—'

'*Throes of passion*, Scotch?'

'But did you mean that? Because that's a big thing.'

Malakai shrugs. 'We're a big thing. Some may argue the biggest thing.' The breeze whips around us and at my braids, as if trying to push us together, as if we could be closer together, and the sun, in its generosity, decides to share some of the light it's given to Kofi and Aminah with us. Malakai's face glows in it, matches its intensity, and his lips curve in sincerity and mischief. He wraps his hand round the back of my neck, and lowers his face to mine, his mouth hot next to my ear, his low voice vibrating through my anatomy at the exact frequency of my rising desire. 'Plus, you should know, Scotch, I never lie when I'm inside you.'

And it's so stupid and it goes right between my eyes, right between my thighs, sinks into the sinews of soul and skin, and I laugh because the truth is he's always inside me, always within, so what now? We're here and we're here and we try and we try and we dance to the joy of our friends, in joy of our friends, in pursuit of our own joy, in joy of the pursuit of love.

EPILOGUE

Sákárà Sounds

Two years later

This is what we do with our love. We are dancing, we're all dancing, in the dining area of Sákárà, on the anniversary of our reopening, as a band plays, as someone sings a cover of a classic Afrobeat song, as talking drums yell even though the lyrics sing of a love that's tender. The air is fluffy like puff-puff straight from the air fryer and thick with good feeling. Sweet perfume hits against muskier colognes, the air a little greener in some areas of the room where some people have snuck out to the garden to partake in some heavy lifting, if you know what I mean.

I told that joke to Malakai and he said, 'Everybody knows what you mean, Scotch. Nerd.' And then a kiss.

As I sway, as I swing to the beat, I have a gurgling child on my hip, a little girl with curls that reach for the sky and eyes like her mum and a smile like her dad's, face always ready to compete with the sun. Aminah of Minah's Management comes up to me and tickles the baby in my arms.

'She needs nappy changing,' she says, and coos at the child: 'Don't you know your auntie won a Grammy for Best Music Film—'

'Grammy nominated as a producer—'

'Same difference,' she says. 'You're Taré Souza's creative consultant and a famed cultural producer with your own docu-series. My point is she can't be pooing in your arms anyhow.' She plucks Adeyinka Aurora Akua Kikiola Bakare-Adjei from me and promptly places her in Kofi's arms as he's passing by, dropping a kiss on his cheek. 'My darling, your princess needs a nappy change,' and Kofi acquiesces, immediately making silly faces at his cherubic daughter – my goddaughter – whilst she gurgles in delight. Aminah beams at them both before telling me she'll be right back. She wants to get more of Meji's suya chicken-pops that he's added to our menu, a joint venture in which me, my parents and Meji have shares, a sweet amalgamation of old school and new school.

Our whole family is here, Malakai's mum and brother gisting with my parents and sister, Chioma and her new girlfriend are in our booth, Laide with Ty, giggling at something he said, which is so interesting because I've never heard her giggle like that before. In a corner, Shanti is smirking flirtatiously up at the handsome lead of Malakai's film, *Apple* – an indie darling and a stunning meditation on fatherhood and love that received standing ovations at festivals.

The first time I saw Malakai's name in the credits of a cinema screen I cried with pride. And also the second, and the third.

Then, Malakai himself looks my way, and a light in his eyes bounds, sharp and dark. If music suspends time, then we are suspended even further within that moment. I feel a disorientating floating feeling that could just be the Champagne mixing with my dad's Chapman, but I've done that before and this feels different.

They say there are certain dramatic, life-changing occurrences that a person can recognise are about happen, immediately before they happen. A hope fulfilled, for instance. Malakai approaches me and bundles me into his arms, his hand lightly brushing the slit in my yellow sun dress and sending desire and goosebumps through my body.

'Again, Kiki, here you go trying to kill me in front of all our friends and family.'

'Ten years and I still haven't succeeded. I need to change tack.'

Kai grins, and pulls me to the corner by the bar, just behind the photobooth, and kisses me, tongue slowly caressing, deeply, sensually, with precise abandon, and I lose my mind and find it again, twice. How has the hunger not abated? How have I never felt more satisfied? He drops a cushiony peck on my lips tenderly, making me blurry eyed, fall off my bone. 'I love you a freaky amount, Kikiola Banjo. Are you aware of that? You cool with that?'

I compose myself after my customary melting. Every time I do, I find myself more fortified – not against him; I don't need to be against him. Against the world, against doubt. We've learned to unpick the tangles of the heart and loosen the Unsaids, no matter how painful, how exposing, to trust one another to hold each other's jagged edges. We've worked to protect what is so easy for us. I'm so secure in this; even the hard parts have been a revelation of how far our love can go, how fathomless its depth is.

'So cool with it,' I say, 'that I've decided to see your freaky amount of love and raise it a *wild* amount.'

'Freaky beats wild, but that's fine, I guess.' I pinch his arm and he smiles. 'I'm so proud of you, Scotch. Look what you've done.'

'Proud of us. Look at what we've done.' I look around, at our home full of joy, and us, still here despite, still here because.

I look up, meet his sparkling gaze. 'When.'

Kai freezes. 'What?'

My smile broadens. '*When.*'

Malakai's face is the sun itself and it nourishes me, his smile radiating hope and promise and safety to me, adoration to me.

'Thank God. About time. Been carrying this around in my pocket for two years. And I've been waiting for this moment for ten.'

I thought I was just giving him permission for a near future but it shouldn't surprise me that Malakai, a Sundance Award-winning director, has thoroughly prepared for this moment. He calls out to the house band, says, 'Now!'

Then the love of my life, twice over, drops to his knee and brings a small box from his pocket as an amazingly bizarre Fuji version of 'Thong Song' begins to flood the aural atmosphere of the room. I hear Aminah exclaim, 'Oh my God, finally. It's happening!' but, actually, it's right on time. We are always right on time. Malakai beams love up at me, eyes shining, takes my hand. Yes to what we've been, yes to where we are, yes to where we're going. We've grown, we are growing, we will grow and we've always been *this*, always had this, and we will choose, commit to, sweat for, what our hearts already know. That's what makes it sacred. Glory. The sun in me rises further in my new-ancient world, more entrenched, more present, just when I thought it couldn't get any higher.

The End (The Beginning)

Acknowledgements

I firmly believe that your next book should always demand more from you than your last one. That you should grow, evolve, and challenge your craft and skill with each new creation. With that being said, with *Sweet Heat* I was like, 'Okay, I get it, it's enough. I'm growing, *damn!*'. I mean, I really don't think the book needed to beat my ass the way that it did. I tore my hair out a few times. Booked emergency therapist sessions more than a few times. There are a couple of reasons why it stressed me out so much I think. The first was the subject matter: how do you write two people who are still madly in love and are aggressively denying it, whilst maintaining a righteous anger at each other? An anger masking deep heartbreak? How do you write the emotional push and pull of that journey, the tension, the yearning? The history, the trepidation; the fictive hate battling the love? *'No seriously, how do you*???' I asked into the void. It took several attempts for me to be satisfied; it needed to feel right, to be exhaustive, to address as many emotional angles as possible.

Love – especially post university love – is complicated, and I wanted to deal with it with the reverence it deserves. The pressure also came from knowing the characters inside and out, not wanting to fail them, making sure I wasn't forcing them to do what I wanted them to do, to allow them to lead me. It took meticulous work to ensure that their complex emotions were done justice in my eyes. My chaotic sweeties. It meant breaking down their individual trauma and pain, understanding how their love would mature and grow as they matured and grew. That took time. I resented myself for needing the time, but when I realised I needed it and stopped punishing myself for it, it became easier. The second reason I found myself weeping into a lukewarm cup of tea, was because it is a sequel. I wanted to do right by Kiki and Malakai and the people who loved them as individuals and as a couple. So much so that I felt stagnated. Then I realised – or rather remembered – that the only focus I should have is writing a story that feels true – true to Kiki and Malakai, and true to the kind of story I want to tell. Then, I felt freedom. I felt like I was flying. I fell in love again with my craft, rediscovered it. What a joy it was! It was *my* second chance romance of sorts. Reconciling who I was with who I am, and approaching my craft with a reverence for both. God, I love writing. How blessed am I that I get to do it over, and over. I've grown a little more with each book, but this one really compelled me to look at myself, remember who I am and learn how I have evolved. This story means so much to me - Kiki and Malakai mean so much to me, their world, means so much to me. I am so, so pleased that it is out there now, that Kiki and Malakai have their ending (or rather, beginning). I love those crazy kids, and I love their love – heartbreak and all – and I wanted to really excavate how layered it is, and in doing so, I believe I grew up with them. Regardless of what happens with this book, I feel proud that I did that. However, I didn't do it on my own; I was empowered by community, by my team, by the people who help my world make sense.

Mummy and Daddy! My rocks. You have never doubted me, my cheerleaders, my biggest fans. Even though you are absolutely not allowed to read this book, you are the reason it exists. My confidence as an author absolutely comes from being a kid whose parents bolstered her dreams. Thankfully, not to the point of delusion, because I actually did it, thank God. Mummy, thank you for your no-nonsense love, the food dropped to my house, the timely, 'Bolu, get over yourself' missives that sure, sometimes I need, and the belief that I have something to give, and I will surely give it. I know you brag about me to your students, ha. Thank you for always picking up the phone, whenever, wherever, to listen to me about whatever, for helping me be an adult. For help forming my spine (I guess, both figuratively and literally), for being directly responsible for my inability to take rubbish (I self-censored here). Daddy, thank you for loudly believing I'm a genius and that I should win a Pulitzer, and for having me on Google alerts. I've reduced my tweeting because it's quite humbling when you post a viral tweet I've made about *Love Is Blind* onto the family group chat like I've done something magnificent. Thank you for being my Yoruba verification portal. I can speak but I cannot always spell, so you help me breathe life into the words. Thank you both for your pride. I stand on your pride. Thank you for the name you bestowed on me. God is indeed great, especially for making me your daughter. You're both the best. Thank you for teaching me love. For exemplifying love.

The siblings and cousins! Bomi, Demi, Ibukun, Ore, everyone in Gang Gang. Bomi especially, honestly, thank you so much for helping me run around and do stuff when I was in the bowels of my writing cave! Much sweeter than I could ever be.

My wonderful agent Juliet Pickering! What a journey it's been so far. Thank you for your belief, for being my warrior, my cheerleader, and believing in me all those years ago. I will never forget that email saying you wanted to rep me just from my little short story *Netflix & Chill*! Thank you for answering the erratic late-night emails with such calm (at a decent hour), thank you for reading the random scraps I send you and taking them very seriously! I feel such comfort with you, and my words feel safe in your hands. Thank you for always advocating for me, and for my time and for my mind and for the stories I can tell. I'm so happy to be on this journey with you, with the knowledge that we're still really, at the beginning.

Jennifer Doyle at Headline, thank you so much for your work as an editor on this book, and taking it in so seamlessly! Thank you so much for answering my wild and erratic questions so swiftly, for holding this story with so much care and consideration and patience and love and for understanding how precious it is to me! You allowed me the time to sink into this story, to shape it, and trusted that when I was rewriting the entire second half of the story (HA!) or adding a random extra chapter (HAHA!) it was for good reason. Your encouragement honestly was so important at really pivotal moments. You alleviated so much anxiety.

Katie Ogunsakin. Thank you for being my ride or die editor from the very beginning, for knowing me, knowing the worlds I built so intimately, for being so committed to this journey – even when you literally got a new job! *Honey & Spice*, and indeed *Sweet Heat* is being brought into the world because you believed in the stories I had to tell. We're truly locked in, officially and unofficially lol. Your insight and knowledge of my characters was truly crucial. The questions you asked caused me to ask myself questions that helped form a direction for this story and I was so bolstered by your love for it. Thank you!

Julia Elliott at William Morrow, thank you so much for being my Stateside editor! Thank you for understanding and loving the book, for your gentle guidance questions and knowledge of the story that helped me broaden out what I thought this book could be. My US readers are so important to me and it's such a relief knowing that I am in safe hands.

My PR baddies!! Alara (UK) & Eliza (US), your hype for the book made me more hype, and your belief in what it is and your care in making sure it is communicated is so important! You handle it with such care and understanding of the people it needs to reach, the people who need to see it. You help manage how it reaches the world, and to do that effectively you need to understand the book and the author – and you do! Your enthusiasm truly means a lot to me, and I appreciate you so, so much. Thank you for riding for Kiki and Malakai as hard as I do!

Kashmini – thank you for your patience in neatly adding in my *numerous* amendments to what was supposed to be a finished copy! You're a star.

The entire team at Headline and William Morrow, everybody who works so hard on making sure the book lives the life we want it to live, thank you! It means so much to me.

Thank you to Jessi Stewart and Jenny Maryasis, my UK and US TV & Film agents for letting me write this book (lol) and take an extended break from um, many projects. Thank you for knowing it is for the greater good! And knowing how important my stories are to me.

My friends and family! Charlet, my bestie, my sister, my beta reader, the literal kindest person on earth, thank you for your ardent belief in me, your encouragement, your timely 'Ummm Bolu remember who you are!!', for just being by my side, and helping to balance me. The world would be a better place if people had your heart. Danielle Scott-Haughton, first of her name! My big sister. Thank you for your prayer warrior mode, the fact that you don't PLAY about me, your encouragement, your belief. Thank you for the chance to be a little sister! For the safe space that I have with you, the fact that I can call you whenever about one tiny thing and you will pick up and simply be there. Invaluable. Bernita, I love you down girl. I don't think you even know how much your consistent encouragement means to me. Thank you for inspiring me to double-down on not taking any rubbish lol. Thank you for being the perfect example of having a massive, tender heart whilst also being strict! Sasé, my bougie princess, thank you for the laughter that propels me through the writing process. You have permission to tell people you're my muse if you want. Amna, thank you for your sweet spirit, for knowing me, for being somewhere for me rest around. Ivié thank you for heading up my Lagos delegations of readers! Folarin, thank you still, for reading *Netflix & Chill* all those years ago. To the Candice Carty-Williams for starting the competition that I submitted my short story to, all those years ago before we were both published! Look at what it started! There are so many of you; Tayo, Gabs, Asha! The group chats; Twisty Bobcat Pretzels, and the one with Zara and Cam titled with emojis; again, lifeforces.

To Uncle Ferdinand. I still have the many encouraging, loving texts you sent me. 'I also take satisfaction in your. . . literary success. I look forward, with much eagerness to what I am sure, will be your incredible evolution as a writer and thinker.' Your loss – right in the middle of writing this book – rocked me in a way that I am still feeling, and yet your words propelled me in the depth of grief. You were the great writer. I can still scarcely believe you are not here. We had so many more things to talk about! If anything I now know the urgency of having conversations with those you love immediately. Thank you for being the very best friend my father could have, a brother in the ways that matter, and thank you for loving me like your own daughter. I hope I make you proud. I will forever work to channel the belief you had in me, to give it life. How blessed was I, to have your light shine on me? Rest in peace and power, with God, sweet Uncle.

My Nigerian readers – you are so special to me – thank you for stopping me in the middle of a dance to tell me how much you feel Kiki and Kai, ha! Very in keeping with the book.

My wonderful readers – all of you. Honestly, your support renders me speechless – and you guys might guess; I love a good yap. I am so grateful that my books have had life all over the world, and they take me all over the world; it's given me the privilege of meeting so many of you, and I am never not awed by how much you engage with these little worlds of mine, and in effect, me. How you're right there with me in believing in the power of real love, unapologetic with it, bold with it. Love is global!! Universal! And our community is strong! I am so blessed to be among you all. Thank you for your messages of support, being patient with me, and knowing that when I'm taking a long time to cook, it's for a reason! So glad you're with me on this journey.

Thank you to my therapist, who reads me so gently and very necessarily.

My fiancé, T, who proposed right after I handed this book in, and in doing so, made this book inadvertently meta. Thank you for listening to every editorial knot that barely made sense when said out loud and letting me talk it out with you, thank you for the cuddles, thank you for living this writing process with me, thank you for the dance breaks, thank you for the pep talks, thank you for all the cooking, thank you for the space to be, thank you for telling me to go to sleep, thank you for answering every 'Okay does this make sense?', thank you for saying 'No you're not acting crazy' even though I was probably definitely acting crazy, thank you for making all the clichés about love very true, thank you for the space to breathe, thank you for asking me 'Are they in the pool yet?' thank you for being my survival pack whilst writing this, thank you for slow dancing with me in the living room, thank you for the belief, the unwavering belief even when I barely believed myself, thank you for you, for you, for you. Man, I'm into you. Let's get married.

Thank you God for this life of mine, for the privilege of doing what I love, for the spirit that compels me to write and for all of the above.